The Rest of My Life

The Rest of My Life

Sheryl Browne

Published 2016 by Choc Lit Limited
Penrose House, Crawley Drive, Camberley, Surrey GU15 2AB, UK
www.choc-lit.com

A CIP catalogue record for this book is available
from the British Library

ISBN 978-1-78189-280-0

MIX
Paper from
responsible sources
FSC® C018072

Printed and bound by Clays Ltd

*To all those readers and reviewers who have supported
me every step of the way – THANK YOU.*

Acknowledgements

I'd like to say a huge thank you to Matt Bates,
Head Fiction Buyer at WH Smith Travel for
bringing my work to the attention of Choc Lit.

To all at Choc Lit for making sure my
novel is the best it can be.

And to my family, in particular my dogs,
who warm my feet and my heart and wait
patiently for walkies while I write.

Chapter One

He'd seen her again. He'd slept fitfully, woken with a start, and she was there, yet not quite there: ethereal, indistinct. He could never make out her features, but it was her: Emily, her sadness so intense he could feel it. Adam was glad he hadn't been alone last night.

Shaking off the haunting remnants of his dreams, he hitched his legs over the berth and ran his hands vigorously through his hair. 'Are you sure you don't need me to give you a lift?' he called, looking up as the bathroom door opened and a shapely female leg appeared.

'No need,' the reassuring flesh and blood owner of the leg replied. 'It's only a short walk into town. You stay and catch up on your beauty sleep.'

Adam smiled as she squeezed past him in the small confines of his cabin. 'You're a stunning woman, Lisa, do you know that?' he said, catching hold of her hand to pull her towards him.

'And you're a flatterer.' Lisa laughed, twisting out of his grasp to tug on her jeans and top. 'I have to go. I'll be late for work,' she said, plucking up her bag. 'We'll have another night out again soon, yes?'

Adam's smile widened. 'I prefer the night in bit,' he said, his eyes roving over her. He was glad she'd rung him. He'd really needed the company. Since Emily, he preferred a solo existence – life was less complicated that way, but there were times when he craved a warm body up close, someone to talk to. Not about the dreams. He never talked about those or the remorse that came with them. He couldn't, not to anyone, male or female. But then, thanks to the reputation he'd earned, deservedly, over the two years he'd been moored at Severn Valley Marina, there weren't that many local blokes who cared to pass the time of day with him anyway, which suited Adam. With Lisa though, at least he *could* talk, act naturally. Lisa was intuitive, understanding – and married, ergo wasn't looking for complications. As friendships went, theirs was a mutually satisfying one. At least Adam hoped it was.

Grazing a hand across his chin, Lisa turned for the door. 'I'll ring you,' she promised.

'Anytime,' Adam assured her, reaching past her to push the boat doors open and check the coast was clear. His own dubious reputation he wasn't much bothered about. Lisa, though, would probably prefer the village drums didn't convey she'd been associating with him. Noting there were no early risers on the other live-aboard boats, in particular the guy moored on the pontoon next door who wasn't keen to have him as a neighbour, he turned back to her, his eyes coming to rest on her soft, infinitely kissable lips.

Far too tempting, he decided, quashing a pang of guilt and leaning in to close his mouth gently over hers. 'Thanks, Lisa,' he murmured huskily. 'I, er ...' He trailed off. *Appreciate it*, he fancied, might sound contemptuous.

'My pleasure.' Lisa snaked a hand around him to clutch a handful of his backside. 'Speak soon,' she said, waggling her eyebrows then nipping deftly up the steps to the deck.

Watching her slip off the boat and head quickly towards the marina exit, Adam smiled to himself and then turned in search of caffeine to kick-start his brain. Lisa was nice, a good friend, his only friend, apart from Nathaniel. He'd hate her to think he might be using her, though he supposed he actually was.

'Yes, Dad, the plumbing's fine now, honestly.' Sienna reassured her father all was well at the cottage she was renting as she headed from the lounge to the kitchen, wondering where on earth Tobias was. A great lolloping black Labrador was hardly difficult to miss, after all. 'No, honestly, it's all in working order, everything flushing and clunking as it should be. Nathaniel, the marina manager, recommended a plumber.'

'You're sure you don't need me to check it over?' her father asked her, hinting at coming visiting with his toolbox.

'Dad, honestly, it's fine. I'm not going to get flooded out or freeze to death, I promise.' Sienna tried to reassure him again, and then mentally tuned out as her overprotective father took up the opportunity to warn her about the dangers of carbon monoxide poisoning, again. She'd already told him she'd got an alarm. Granted, when she and her best friend Lauren had moved into the renovated property it had been a typical spring bank holiday, wet and blustery, and the central heating boiler had been suspect, to say the least. However, as it was now mid-June and twenty-four degrees plus outside, she doubted they'd be putting the heating on anytime soon.

'Yes, Dad,' she said dutifully, in all the right places, nodding her head accordingly and trying to concentrate on the conversation. Her attention, however, kept straying to the marina fronting her kitchen window, from where the view had been rather spectacular yesterday.

She and Lauren had caught a glimpse of the well-sculpted torso of the owner of the little white river cruiser moored at the quayside directly opposite – the man they'd christened Lothario, having noted certain nocturnal activities on board. Due to his late comings and goings, Sienna hadn't really spoken to him, other than a passing hello – and then he barely acknowledged her, but she could see what his obvious attraction to women was, on the surface anyway. Tall, toned, tousled dark hair, bronzed skin the colour of caramel mocha latte, the man was definitely eye candy. They'd spotted him again last night. Living up to his reputation, he'd been sneaking a woman onto his boat, amidst much shushing from him and giggling from her. They'd both been tipsy and, judging by the need for secrecy, they were obviously having an affair.

'Yes, Dad, I am eating properly. Stop worrying. I'm a big girl now.' Disappointed that Lothario hadn't made an appearance yet – fancying himself as a super-stud the man was clearly shallow, but he was fascinating in terms of fodder for her flagging screenplay – Sienna turned her attention back to her father. She loved her dad to bits and she understood why he worried about her. It had been so hard for him after her mum died, wondering what he could have done differently. He couldn't have done anything, in reality. Sienna had watched over the years. Even through her confused child's eyes, she'd known. Hyper-mummy was a happy, fun mummy, but in her down times there'd been no way to reach her.

Her dad's mission since had been ensuring Sienna was happy, and she was, largely, though, she wasn't as confident as she pretended to be. Her self-esteem sloshing about somewhere near shoe-level after her last horribly humiliating relationship, what she needed, she'd decided, was space to just be herself, unencumbered emotionally. So here she was, in a picturesque little honey-coloured cottage with its own al fresco dining area, offering breathtaking views over the River Severn.

Her eyes strayed hopefully towards the boat opposite once again. On a needs must basis she'd secured a part-time job in the local pub, where Lothario made an occasional appearance to flirt with women, notably not her, and she had bags of space and time to herself to concentrate on her scriptwriting. She still couldn't believe she'd been shortlisted in the TV Romance Script competition. After struggling with her degree it was a dream come true. The only snag being: she now had re-writes to do and no clue how to do them. The editor she'd hired had suggested she needed to include an actual sex scene, rather than the 'closed bedroom door' scene she had; and to make her ending more upbeat, as in boy-meets-girl, boy-gets-girl, despite all obstacles. But how do you write about sex and romance when your experience of it has been unfulfilling, to say the least? She couldn't. Unlike Lothario, who obviously had sexual magnetism in abundance, Sienna's characters were about as alluring as copulating camels. If she was going to write about some steely-eyed Adonis bringing his heroine to the roller coaster heights of orgasmic passion; about love conquering all, she needed to believe in the fairy tale. Sienna wasn't sure she did anymore.

I bet Lothario could supply a steamy 'open door' bedroom scene, she thought, her cheeks heating up and her gaze straying to the window, yet again, as her dad got onto the subject of the security of the property.

'Yes, Dad, we do make sure the cottage is well secured at night,' Sienna assured him, dragging her unmanageable strawberry-frizz tresses from her face and glancing around again for her only male admirer, Tobias. 'No, Dad, I haven't "met" anyone yet.' She smiled wryly, wondering at the irony of her thoughts around the 'man' subject and her father's concerns clashing.

'No, not even a prospective someone,' she answered the next question with a roll of her eyes. It wasn't likely she'd be meeting anyone even remotely prospective in the tiny Worcestershire village of Little Crookley anyway. And nor did she want to. Sienna swallowed back a fresh wave of humiliation as she recalled the last awful 'date' with her ex-boyfriend, the dreadful names he'd called her as she'd scrambled from his car.

And still he kept texting her. He'd even rung her, intimating again that it was her who had a problem, which was obviously his way of denying his own. Attempting to consign that cold night to history, Sienna blew out a shuddery sigh and with her phone still clamped to her ear, she headed upstairs to check out the beds. Despite his dodgy hips, Tobias was very likely to have snuck up there and tucked himself under a duvet. Lauren's possibly, which would have Lauren plucking dog hairs from her face for a week.

'Well, don't take any nonsense when you do. Any man who messes you around will have me to answer to. Make sure to tell them that, Sienna,' her dad said as, seeing no suspicious dog-shaped lumps under duvets, Sienna started to panic.

'I will,' she dutifully replied. She wouldn't, though, nor had she. A psychiatrist by day and a marathon runner and keen keep fit fanatic in his spare time, Sienna had no doubt her father might be driven to flex his muscles and try to fight her battles for her. She didn't want him to do that. 'Got to go, Dad,' she said over him as he veered the conversation back to his paying her a visit. 'Running late. Speak soon. Love you. Byee!'

Ending the call on a cheery note, lest her father decide to drive from Gloucestershire to Worcestershire to check on her welfare anyway, Sienna dashed to the front door which was slightly ajar, and which opened directly onto the quayside. Oh, no … 'Tobias!' she yelled, skidding out and shielding her eyes against the morning sun to scan the marina. 'Tobias!'

Coffee made, Adam had barely taken a sip when the boat dipped heavily to one side. *Damn.* He squeezed his eyes closed, guessing it was Nathaniel, who'd obviously seen Lisa slip ashore and was about to give him one of his lectures, attempting to steer him away from his 'self-destructive behaviour' as was Nathaniel's tendency lately. But then Nathaniel – his best friend and who was supposed to have been best man at his wedding – had always tried to look out for him, even in their schooldays, Adam reminded himself and tried not to mind.

Nathaniel didn't disappoint. 'So, it's Lisa who's getting the dubious pleasure now, is it?' he asked, rapping on the doors and clumping down the cabin steps.

Realising there wasn't much point in denying it, Adam smiled sheepishly and wandered back towards the berth to get dressed in something other than his boxers.

'How long has that being going on, then?' Nathaniel followed him.

'A while,' Adam said evasively, and then, lack of sleep catching up with him, he yawned and parked his coffee on the bedside table.

'You're unbelievable, do you know that?' Nathaniel imparted, obviously not impressed with his behaviour, again.

Glancing back, Adam caught the despairing look. 'What?' he asked. 'Can I help it if she's lonely? If he cared a damn about her, her old man would stop slinking off on his so-called business trips, wouldn't he? Stay at home instead, and give her a—'

'Pack it in, Adam.' Nathaniel's already overripe cheeks flushed furiously.

'I was going to say, a bit of attention, Nate.' Aware of his friend's propensity to embarrassment on the subject of, and around, women, Adam went on less flippantly. Nathaniel was okay, one of the good guys as far as women were concerned. He'd often said he wished he could be more

7

like Adam, confident in female company. In truth, Adam sometimes wished he could be more like Nathaniel, living in hope that one day he'd meet his soulmate, every day thereafter bathed in a rosy glow of perpetual sunsets. Adam tugged on his cut-offs. She didn't exist. He knew it. He'd been there, done it; nurtured the hope. And then viewed the world from the bottom of a very dark pit he'd had to claw his way out of. Still felt as if he was trying to sometimes, when the dreams came to haunt him.

Picking up his mobile, Adam checked his messages. Despondently noting no new ones, he scrolled to his photos, finding the one he wanted: Lily-Grace, aged three months. How would she look now, he wondered, just turned two years old? She'd be talking, walking ... Why the hell hadn't he found the courage to just go and see her?

'And that's where you come in, is it?' Nathaniel's tone was scathing. 'You can't run away from commitment forever, you know, Adam.'

Here we go. Adam steeled himself for another one of Nate's save-Adam-from-himself pep-talks. 'I'm not running.' He shrugged a denial, dearly wishing Nathaniel wouldn't insist on dragging him back down bad-memory lane. A familiar feeling of panic knotting his stomach, Adam closed his eyes against the inevitable flashback of Emily's shocked face, Darren's *c'est la vie* shrug. Two years his senior, Adam had looked up to his brother, wanted to be just like him. That day he'd wanted to kill him. Might have done, if not for his so-called father's intervention. Trailing his fingers over the deep scar he wore on his cheek as a constant reminder, Adam wasted no energy dwelling on that.

As for Emily ... Adam's supposedly hardened heart cracked all over again as he recalled the last time he saw her. She'd looked so fragile, her face so pale against the stark sterile white of the bathroom. She must have felt so lonely. He had loved her, utterly. Why had he back-pedalled then? But Adam knew the answer: because he'd felt trapped, not by the prospect of marriage, but by the prospect of being financially controlled by his old man, working in the business owned by his father, living in a property ditto, being indebted to a man he simply didn't like, becoming him. Instead of finding the courage to talk to her, suggest they ditch the whole white wedding thing and just take off somewhere, he'd pulled away. Driven Emily away. Clamping his eyes closed, Adam swallowed hard. Why hadn't he tried to contact her sooner? When he'd found her ... that had been his defining moment, when he'd decided to relinquish love over sex.

'In any case, her husband's not about to find out,' Adam finally replied, pulling in a calming breath, and seating himself on the bed to pull on his trainers. 'Is he?' he asked, glancing worriedly up.

Nathaniel paused before answering, disconcertingly. 'Not from me, no,' he said finally, saving Adam from imminent minor apoplexy. 'Look, Adam, I don't like what you're doing, but—'

'Odd jobbing, that's what I'm doing, Nate.' Adam went back to flippant, in hopes of cutting the conversation short. 'Can I help it if women are so impressed with my gardening skills they throw in a bonus? Got to go.' He grabbed up a vest from the permanent pile of clothes on the floor, which was crumpled but at least clean, and headed for the door. 'I have three lawns to mow, six Leylandii to prune and the fence up at Hawthorn Farm Stables to mend. The more money I make, the sooner I can get my boat fixed and then sail off into the sunset.' A not-so-perfect sunset maybe, he'd be lonely sometimes, bound to be, but Adam could live without the romance.

'And shag a girl in every port,' Nathaniel muttered behind him.

Adam turned back. 'Hopefully,' he said, eyeing Nathaniel curiously. 'And your problem is?'

Nathaniel did it again, that awkward pause that meant he was going to go all holier-than-thou on him. 'I drink with her husband, Adam,' he said, blowing out a disgruntled breath.

'Whose? Sally's? Rebekah's?' Adam couldn't resist, though he'd never actually met anyone called Sally.

'Lisa's,' Nathaniel clarified tightly. 'I socialise with the man. I like him. He's buying one of my boats. They've just commissioned the fit of the interior, him and Lisa, together. I like her!'

'You do? Well, why didn't you say something? I would have backed off if I'd thought you—'

'Not like that. And you very well know it.' Nathaniel scowled, his fair-skinned cheeks flushing again.

Better not provoke him further, Adam decided, their friendship and the two months' mooring fee he owed him in mind.

'You're a good looking bastard,' Nathaniel went on grudgingly, 'even if you do insist on dressing like a bloody hobo.' He eyed Adam's thrown-on choice of attire with a shake of his head.

'All the better to show off my finely-honed physique, Nate,' Adam joked, tugging his vest over another noticeable scar on his torso.

Nathaniel ignored him. 'I just don't want you hurting anyone or sailing off into the sunset with regrets. You'll have some someday, you know. There will be a girl sometime whose feelings you wish you'd been more caring of. Why don't you think about staying put, Adam? You're a good boat mechanic, skilled. You don't need to odd job.

You could put your skills to use here, rent a property, put down some sort of roots, if only you'd—'

'I don't *want* to, Nate,' Adam said firmly, probably too firmly. Nathaniel's face fell. 'I prefer to be a free agent, you know I do. And I don't hurt anyone,' he pointed out, less vehemently. Yes, he'd been involved with married women, women whose husbands basically didn't give a damn about them. Lisa's, for instance, who made no effort whatsoever to appreciate her. It didn't make Adam a saint, but making her life a little less lonely didn't make him a complete bastard either, did it?

'Yes, right.' Nathaniel didn't look any more impressed. 'Whatever.' He sighed. 'Just be careful, that's all.'

'I always am,' Adam assured him. He did actually care about women, but he couldn't allow himself to care too much *for* them, not again.

'Particularly at the farm,' Nathaniel's voice now definitely held a warning. 'Sherry's husband is not the forgiving sort. He has a shotgun and a licence to use it.'

Oh. That gave Adam pause for thought.

'Just don't go making a move on her while you're odd jobbing there,' Nathaniel went on, heading past Adam up to the deck. 'If you've got any sense, you'll—'

'Nathaniel, I have no intention of "making a move" on Sherry.' Adam pulled his door shut and then leapt the handrail to land on the quayside. Given Nathaniel's revelation about the shotgun he decided not to mention the fact that Sherry had already made the move.

'Right.' Nathaniel rolled his eyes and followed him down onto the quay, though rather more carefully. 'They all chase you, I suppose.'

'I'm obviously irresistible.' Adam tried a little levity.

Nathaniel sighed and shook his head. 'Just practise a bit of restraint, that's all I ask. There are only so many married women you can bed without causing serious grief somewhere along the line.' He paused, wiping a bead of sweat from his brow as he sweltered in a long-sleeved shirt and unforgiving temperatures.

'I don't bed married women,' Adam said with a sigh, wishing Nathaniel would drop it. 'Not regularly. I just—'

'Willingly oblige, because it comes with no strings?' Nathaniel finished shrewdly.

Adam shrugged evasively.

'It won't do my business any good, having your body bits splattered all over the marina, you know,' Nathaniel said, walking on.

'No,' Adam conceded. 'Wouldn't do my body bits a lot of good eith—'

'Tobias!' Both men looked up as a girl called loudly from the bank.

Bloody hell. Adam did a double take. It was the girl from the cottage. Innocent-looking and fresh-faced, a radiant smile as she chatted to the punters she served at the pub, seemingly unaware of most of them eyeing her up, Adam had tried hard not to notice her. He couldn't help but notice her now. She was wearing the shortest of shorts and the skimpiest of bra-affair tops he'd ever seen in his life. It was her hair, though, which she was now wearing loose, that really caught his attention. Red hair flecked gold, tumbling carelessly down her back, it was stunning. She was stunning. Barefoot, with tanned long legs, she was undeniably attractive. Definitely his type, he might once have confided to Nate – as he had when he'd first met Emily. She'd been barefoot too, he recalled the image vividly, fishing from the side of a boat with her father. Pretty hopelessly it turned out. She hadn't had a hook on her line, because she hadn't wanted to hurt the fish. She'd caught him that day, the day he'd learned to smile again after his mother had gone. Emily had been his first love. His last love, too, as far as Adam was concerned.

'Tobias, here boy!' the girl called tearfully again, now peering out over the water.

She was precariously close to the edge of the bank, Adam realised. 'Dog, do you reckon?' he asked Nathaniel.

'Well, she has got one.' Nathaniel furrowed his brow and glanced around. 'It's such an ancient old thing, though, I can't imagine it's gone—'

Nathaniel's speculations were cut short by a suspicious heavy splosh, followed by an ear-piercing scream that had Adam's heart racing. '*Shit*,' he muttered, glancing quickly from the water to the girl, who looked about ready to jump in.

'Tobias! Help! He can't swim!' she screamed, now hanging onto one of the boats and dangling a foot towards the water.

Hell, she was going in. 'Stay there!' Adam shouted. 'That water's twenty feet deep!' And ice cold, he thought grimly, setting off at a sprint.

Clambering onto the deck of a moored boat, he dived from the starboard side, giving himself enough clearance not to get crushed between bows and sterns as boats bobbed together on the surface. He was braced when he hit the water, but still the freezing temperature paralysed him. *Move*, he instructed himself, his whole body juddering from the inside out. Surfacing, he trod water, blinked the rank stuff out of his eyes and spat it out of his mouth. Where was the dog? Scanning the water, he saw no sign of anything moving. He turned full circle. *There!* Adam spotted it three boats along, not much more than its head visible and hazardously close to two large vessels. If the dog drifted in between them it would stand no chance. Kicking back hard, Adam swam towards the dog and made a lunge for the animal which was now very close to going under, and frantic, judging by the whites of its eyes. Adam was feeling pretty frantic himself, with trainers like deadweights on his feet.

'Come on. Good boy,' he coaxed, swallowing another lungful of foul tasting water, and then, seizing the dog's collar and somehow managing to keep its snout and himself above water, he waited while Nathaniel used his bodyweight to hold two boats off.

'Now!' Nathaniel shouted, gesturing him forwards.

Adam took a breath and went for it, manoeuvring himself, plus dog, precariously through the gap between the boats and back to the bank.

The dog safe on the quay with one of the boat owners' assistance – no doubt he was an animal lover, because he certainly didn't waste any energy helping Adam – Adam heaved himself out, shook his dripping hands, for what good that could do, and then watched as the girl dropped to her knees. Careless of the shower of freezing cold water it shook all over her, and its manically lapping tongue, she embraced the bedraggled animal heartily, planting a kiss on its sopping wet head, before getting to her feet to take Adam by surprise and squeeze him into an enthusiastic hug. An extremely enthusiastic hug, which was way too close, given what she was barely wearing.

'Our hero,' Nathaniel said, giving him a look somewhere between 'well done' and 'that was close', as the girl finally pulled wetly away from him.

'He is a hero,' she agreed wholeheartedly. 'He absolutely is. Thank you.' She smiled, blinking innocently at him, leaving Adam feeling definitely off kilter. 'I can't tell you how grateful I am. Tobias is my whole life. I would have just died if—'

'So you let him run loose in a marina and he can't *swim*?'

He dragged a hand through his dripping hair, his expression incredulous.

'No, I ... He got out.' Sienna felt her cheeks flush under his gaze. His eyes were brown, dark decadent chocolate-brown, framed by unfairly long eyelashes, little droplets of water dripping from them like tears from a frond. 'I was on the phone and I—'

'And you didn't think to put a life jacket on him?'

Shame made Sienna want to drop her gaze, but somehow she couldn't. 'I, um ... No, I—'

'He could have drowned!' Lothario's eyes were now lasering into hers right down to her toes. '*I* could have drowned!' he pointed out, now seeming definitely angry.

Sienna swallowed. 'I'm sorry,' she croaked, her throat feeling parched. He was right. Of course he was, and had every reason to be annoyed. But why did his palpable anger seem to be doing strange things to her pulse rate? Confused by his definite assault on her senses, Sienna inhaled a steadying breath. 'I'm really sorry,' she repeated firmly. 'I didn't think.'

'Obviously not,' he grated, now glaring at her as though she had half a brain. 'Honestly, I do wonder about some people,' he muttered, then sweeping now despairing eyes over her, he shook his head and turned away.

Unbelievable! God, he was rude. But God, he was hot. Holding firmly onto a panting Tobias' collar, Sienna watched him go. The wet, white cotton vest clinging to him, accentuating his torso, did nothing to dampen her curious arousal. But why was she aroused? If he hadn't gone gallantly to the rescue of Tobias, she'd have been tempted to spit in his contemptuous eyes. *Some people?* What was that supposed to mean? She hadn't asked him to help. Yes, she had. Screaming help at the top of her lungs probably counted as a subtle request.

His wet cut-offs were clinging to his thighs, she noticed. Muscular thighs. Did he work out? Well, obviously he did, regularly, she thought, cynically. Even sloshing water as he walked, he looked steamily sexy. Yes, and obviously also arrogant and ill-mannered. Peeved, Sienna continued to watch, as he climbed onto his boat. The boat he'd snuck the woman onto and had subsequently been rocking and swaying half the night, the same boat woman-in-the-throes-of-ecstasy sounds had emerged from half the night. With an early team meeting to attend, Lauren had been far from amused this morning.

'You'd think they'd give him his own segregated shagging area,' she'd grumbled, bemoaning the bags under her eyes as she'd applied her concealer.

'You all right, Miss Meadows?' Nathaniel's voice pierced through her meanderings.

Shoot! Sienna had almost forgotten he was there. 'Yes. Thanks.' She smiled wanly, attempting to oust an image of what her reluctant hero had been doing exactly to bring a woman to such obvious heights of pleasure. 'Would you tell him … Pass on my, um, thanks to, um …' She nodded towards the boat.

'Adam,' Nathaniel supplied. 'I will.' He paused, then added, 'Can I offer you a little word of advice?'

'Hmm?' Sienna tried to focus her mind away from the soggy sex God, realising she must appear as rude as he was.

'He's bad news,' Nathaniel imparted, rather awkwardly. 'Adam. I wasn't sure whether you realised, but he's a bit of a womaniser. I thought I should warn you, just in case … you know.'

Well, that much Sienna had gathered. And if she'd been imagining there might be anything remotely attractive in *that* kind of man, she really must have half a brain.

Chapter Two

Adam had agonised over making the call. Receiving the frosty response he'd expected, he was now beginning to wish he hadn't. He could hear a toddler snuffling tearfully in the background. It could only be Lily-Grace.

Waiting for his would-have-been sister-in-law to come back to the phone, he noted Sherry's car pulling up at the farmhouse and hoped she didn't come directly over to him. It had taken him almost two years to make this call. He should have done it somewhere more private. He should have done it sooner.

'Is she okay?' he asked when Nicole came back on.

'Just tetchy,' Nicole assured him. 'She's a bit over-tired, that's all.'

Adam nodded, not sure what to say next. He had a million questions, but no clue how to ask them.

'So, why the call?' Nicole broke the awkward silence.

Adam had no idea what to say there either. That he'd wanted to call before? Every day since the day he'd last seen Lily-Grace, he'd wanted to call, but could never find the courage? Sounded pretty lame, didn't it? In Nicole's eyes, if he'd cared at all, he would have made sure to call more than the one and only time he had. He did care, though, despite his attempts to convince himself he didn't. There wasn't a day that passed when he didn't think about Lily-Grace, wonder whether she was healthy, happy. Not a night when Emily haunting him, more and more lately, didn't remind him he should know how she was.

'You're a bit late if you want to wish her happy birthday, Adam,' Nicole went on, her tone tinged with sarcasm. 'Her birthday was last week, you might recall.'

'I know.' Adam sucked in a breath. Of course he bloody well knew. 'Can I see her?' He blurted out the question he'd steeled himself to ask and braced himself for the answer. He fully expected her to tell him to do what he'd done up until now and stay out of her life.

'Why?' Nicole eventually asked.

'Because I want to,' Adam said simply. Sharing the fact that he felt Emily also wanted him to, he fancied, would probably make him sound certifiable.

'Yes, but why now, Adam?' Nicole forced her point home.

'To see how she's doing,' Adam gave her the only answer he could. 'How she is.'

'But *why*, Adam?' Nicole repeated. 'Don't tell me your guilt gene has kicked in and you've finally realised you give a damn.'

Adam swallowed. 'The guilt is always there, Nicole,' he said quietly. 'I know it might not seem like it, but I do actually give a damn. I always have.'

'Right.' Adam heard the cynicism still in her voice. 'Enough to want to be a part of her life?' she asked the crucial question, the answer to which they both knew would impact on all their lives.

'Yes,' Adam answered immediately, 'providing it's okay with you and it doesn't upset her.'

Nicole paused again, and then, 'Without a paternity test?' she asked, cutting to the chase.

Adam sighed inwardly. Barbed that comment might be, but the fact was it was the truth. As far as Nicole was concerned, he really hadn't given a damn when Emily had gone through the pregnancy on her own; the birth; or when Lily-Grace was tiny, vulnerable, parentless. Too wrapped up in his own grief he hadn't visited since, hadn't even enquired how she was, his overriding concern being *whose* she was.

'She's okay, Adam,' Nicole said, a determined edge now to her voice. 'She's doing fine without your input. She's a healthy, happy little girl. I'm not sure it's a good idea, particularly if you're imagining she might be better off with you suddenly. The psychological consequences would be—'

'I'm not imagining she would be better off with me, Nicole. I don't doubt she's happy with you,' Adam interrupted, before she said an out-an-out no. Without the paternity test, he had no rights. He knew it. Nicole had taken responsibility for Lily-Grace when he'd been so messed up he'd been incapable of doing anything but drinking himself into oblivion, when his brother refused to even acknowledge the child existed.

'But even you seeing her would be disruptive, Adam,' Nicole said, after another heavy pause. 'Surely you must realise that? As far as Lily is aware I'm Mummy and Phil's Daddy. It might confuse her.'

'I know,' Adam said quickly. 'That's why I'm asking, Nicole, not insisting. I'd like to see her. I'm happy for it to be on your terms. I know you've been there for her, all that she needed you to be. I would never do anything to upset her world, I promise. If she does seem upset, in any way, I'll back off. I give you my word.'

Adam held his breath as Nicole went quiet again. 'All right,' she eventually relented. 'A short visit, though, initially, Adam. We'll see how things pan out.'

He blew out a sigh of relief. 'Thanks.'

'I'll let you know when and where, but Adam ...' Nicole hesitated again, obviously about to add a caveat, '... if you're planning to see her regularly you're going to have to prove yourself, you know that, right?'

As in make sure he could be relied on not to make a complete mess of this, as he had everything else. Adam got the message. 'I know,' he said, wondering if he could ever live up to that task. 'I'll wait to hear from you. Thanks again, Nicole. It means a lot to me.'

'Don't thank me yet,' Nicole warned him. 'Let's get the first meeting over with. We'll take it from there.'

Pocketing his mobile, Adam went back to work on the fence Sherry had hired him to erect. It was almost finished. After that, he had another few jobs lined up around the town, and then ... He'd cross that bridge when he got to it. He'd see Lily-Grace. Long-term plans though, he wouldn't make, not yet. It might not work out. Nicole might decide he wasn't fit to be any kind of a father figure to her. Momentarily poleaxed by that thought, Adam mulled it over in his head. Could he be? Did he really want to be, given he didn't actually know he was the father? He honestly didn't know. What he did know was there seemed to be an empty space inside him where that child should be. He needed to do this. It made no sense; in fact, the more he thought about it, the more absurd it seemed, but he also felt Emily needed him to. He'd tried to tell himself it was his conscience conjuring her up, but he could *feel* her, her loneliness, her longing, growing stronger each and every time he saw her.

Nicole was right, though. He did need to be reliable if he intended to barge into Lily-Grace's life. If he wanted to be involved in her future, he'd need to contribute financially, too. Despite Nathaniel glibly saying he had skills and should use them, it wasn't going to be that easy. His reputation as a womaniser meant that he wasn't exactly loved by the blokes in the area. He got the cold shoulder most places he went, particularly in the pub, either that or killer looks. He couldn't blame some of the husbands, he supposed, albeit they probably cared more about their own reputation than their wives. That was okay. Adam could live with it, though he wasn't quite sure why a gang of Neanderthal thugs had jumped on the bandwagon, tossing snide remarks after him, slashing his car tyres once, he suspected, which was worrying. Also worrying, now he'd decided to try to do something about his finances, or lack thereof, was that his card had been marked by at least two local car workshops. Mechanics being the only thing he was any good at, it didn't leave him many options employment wise. Short of a paper-round, Adam couldn't see how he was going to get a regular job.

But then – he reached for the final plinth to finish the section of fence he was working on – wasn't he getting a little ahead of himself here? Nicole might even change her mind and not get back to him. In which case, his boat needed to be ready to go. He needed to be ready to do what he'd done since his world fell apart – move on. There was nothing else to keep him in the area, no commitments, and that was the way Adam preferred it. Other than Lily-Grace, he couldn't envisage surrounding himself with family, only to lose them all over again. It was almost inconceivable now that he'd actually been making wedding plans once. He'd wanted to marry Emily, she must have known that. It wasn't commitment to her that had been the problem. Emily had his heart, all of it, he couldn't have been more committed than that. But then, maybe he hadn't had hers.

History. Don't dwell on it. Preferring not to disassemble it all over again, try to work out when it was exactly that she'd decided to sleep with his brother, Adam poured his energies into his physical endeavours instead.

Turning for his drill, he noted Sherry walking across from the house. 'Hi, Adam,' she called, pausing behind him. 'I thought you could use a drink.'

Dragging an arm over his forehead, Adam straightened up and turned to face her. 'I'd love one.' He smiled.

'In the kitchen,' she said, nodding towards the house. 'A

21

beer, so cold the glass is perspiring. I thought you might like to cool down while you drink it.'

'Sounds like a plan.' Adam's smile broadened. The heat was relentless, unusually for mid-June. He squinted up at the cloudless blue sky. It didn't look as if there was going to be a break in the weather anytime soon either.

'Fabulous, isn't it?' Sherry followed his gaze.

'Definitely.' Adam grabbed his vest from the post where he'd hitched it and used it to wipe the sweat from his torso, before tugging it back on. 'Though not so great when you're working in it.'

Sherry trailed her eyes over him. Adam could read the look. 'You could take a shower,' she offered.

'Erm.' Adam glanced sideways to where her husband was leading a horse to the stable blocks. 'Probably not a good idea.'

'I wasn't proposing to join you, Adam.' Sherry gave him an enigmatic smile and turned back towards the house.

Adam watched her as she led the way, her hips swinging in that provocative way women's hips did as she went, but her demeanour all business. Pity. She was an attractive woman. She had nice eyes: cornflower blue, he'd describe them. Adam recalled how she'd reeled him in with those eyes, locking them unflinchingly on his and asking him outright whether he thought she was attractive. What was he going to say? No? When she'd leaned in to brush his lips with hers, trailed a fingernail suggestively from his chest to his abdomen, was he supposed to pretend he wasn't interested? Uh-uh. He'd defy Nathaniel not to have done what he'd done and taken up the invitation, particularly as it was obvious her husband was giving yet another new stable girl so-called riding lessons.

She had nice lips, too. He returned Sherry's smile as she turned to beckon him in through the back door. Soft, full lips. He'd like to taste them right now, but Adam wasn't about to try. It didn't look as if she'd been so thrilled by the action the first time she wanted a replay. Plus, there was the matter of the shotgun; possibly a bloody big shotgun, of which he'd prefer to steer clear. Accepting the beer Sherry offered him from the fridge, Adam concentrated on satiating his thirst.

'Good?' Sherry asked, once he'd glugged half in one mouthful.

'Very,' he assured her, wiping his forearm across his mouth.

'Come and sit down,' she said, helping herself to a beer. 'Take the weight off your feet for five minutes.'

Adam nodded and followed her to the table.

'I have a proposition for you, Adam,' Sherry said, removing the cotton shirt she wore loosely over her strappy top, as he sat.

'Oh?' Adam eyed her over his beer and his eyes lingered. He couldn't help it. Her breasts were fabulous. She had a fantastic figure. He had no idea what the husband was thinking, playing around. Clearly, he wasn't. Sometime, probably soon, the guy was going to lose her. With no children to consider – her husband apparently didn't want kids – Adam figured it was only the business keeping them together.

'How's the boat coming along?' Sherry asked, flicking back her auburn hair as she seated herself opposite him.

She had nice hair, too. Coloured possibly, not natural like the girl's on the quayside this morning, but still sexy. He'd felt bad about losing his temper with the girl the way he had. Even if he had almost come to a watery demise, along with her dog, he'd been well out of order. He wasn't even sure why he'd been so angry, other than there was something about her that had reminded him of Emily, evoking feelings he'd worked hard to forget. He was going to have to swallow his pride and apologise, he supposed.

'Good,' he answered Sherry, pulling his thoughts away from a girl whose name he didn't even know, and who would probably tell him where to stuff his apology. 'Still a fair amount of work to do, interior mostly, electrics and upholstery.'

Sherry arched a curious eyebrow. 'Leather upholstery, I assume?'

'If funds allow.' Adam tried not to read any innuendo into the statement. 'It's probably the most serviceable.'

'You can't beat the smell of leather.' Sherry sighed, taking a sip of her beer.

'No.' Adam watched mesmerised as she wiped the froth from her lips with the pink tip of her tongue, and then, mindful of the husband out in the yard, he glanced down and busied himself with his own beer. 'The hull's sound now, though,' he went on. 'The engine needs an overhaul and I've yet to finish paying for it, but a few more decent jobs and I should be almost there.'

'You're good with your hands, aren't you?' Sherry commented.

Adam glanced sharply back up. 'Some people say so, yes.' He nodded, now definitely confused as to where this was leading.

'So why do odd jobs, then, Adam? Didn't you ever think of maybe setting up a business?'

'Putting down roots? No, not really.' Preferring not to talk about his past, the shared business with his brother, the boatyard they were due to take over from the father he no longer saw and had flatly refused any further financial help from, even when he'd been at his lowest ebb, he ran a finger contemplatively over the rim of his glass. Boats had always been part of his life. As a kid he couldn't keep away from them. He recalled how, attracted by the still of the water, the boats under renovation in the dry dock, he'd spend hours sitting on the lock gates at Diglis in Worcester, a vantage point to the River Severn. He used to think about his mother a lot then: why she'd left him behind, where she'd gone, why she hadn't been in touch. He knew why, though, in his heart. He'd watched his father's bullying day after day.

With no wish to be stuck behind a desk when he'd left school, he'd initially relished every minute working at the boatyard. He'd enjoyed working with his brother, too, though they'd always been competitive; trying to outrun each other on the track at school, on the rugby field. Darren had also taken huge pleasure in proving who was better at martial arts, to Adam's physical discomfort. He hadn't realised how competitive his older brother was though, until he'd moved in on ... *History*, he reminded himself. *Forget it.*

'Maybe, one day,' he said, coming back to the present. 'For now I prefer to travel light, though, so ...'

Sherry nodded thoughtfully. 'About that proposition,' she said.

Adam eyed her quizzically, wondering if she might be about to offer him something more permanent. He wouldn't say no to short-term employment, particularly now.

'I'm afraid I'm running out of jobs around the farm, Adam.'

'Ah.' Adam nodded. He guessed she might be. Once the fence was finished, he'd fixed pretty much everything that needed fixing.

'I wondered whether you fancied continuing to see me anyway, though,' Sherry went on, outwardly confident, but her eyes were clouded with uncertainty, Adam noted. 'You know, continue seeing each other, I mean. Not as a couple, obviously, as, um …' she trailed off, clearly flustered.

Adam looked her over curiously. 'Friends?'

Sherry nodded, her eyes flicking down and back.

'With benefits?' Adam added cautiously.

'Yes,' Sherry said, looking relieved. 'I know time is money, so I'd make sure you weren't out of pocket, and we wouldn't have to meet here. I have the holiday cottage, we could, you know …'

Adam searched her face, bemused. Did she have any idea how many men would think they'd won the lottery if offered a proposition like that?

'Well, what do you say?' Sherry wet her lips with her tongue and swallowed nervously.

Adam smiled. Their previous liaison hadn't been a complete disaster then. 'Did you honestly think I'd say no?'

'I hoped not.' Sherry laughed and exhaled a long breath, her shoulders visibly relaxing. 'I'd better let you get on.' She nodded towards the yard and got to her feet. 'We'll liaise on the phone as to timings, yes?'

'Anytime,' Adam assured her. 'I'll, er, go and finish that fence then.'

Standing, he debated, and then walked around the table and took a step towards her. 'You don't need to make sure I'm not out of pocket, incidentally,' he said softly. 'Trust me, Sherry, seeing you is plenty incentive enough. You're a very desirable woman.'

'Pity my husband doesn't think so. I can't remember the last time we …' Sherry trailed off again, humiliation hot on the heels of the uncertainty he'd seen in her eyes.

The man really was a prat. Adam despaired inwardly. 'He must be blind.' He smiled and reached to brush a stray tendril of hair behind her ear.

'You're a hopeless flatterer, Adam Hamilton-Shaw, but lovely with it.' Sherry sighed and turned her face to his touch, her eyes now closed, her lips slightly parted.

Irresistible. Adam trailed his thumb downwards, tracing their outline. Risky though it was with the husband outside, he was sorely tempted. One kiss couldn't hurt, could it? Leaning in to find her mouth with his, he probed softly with his tongue, hopefully leaving her with no doubt that he really didn't need any inducement. Seeing her vulnerability, he wanted to kiss away her insecurities.

He wanted her. Breathing heavily, he eased back and steered her away from the window. He couldn't go too far, not here, it would be completely insane, but … Adam scanned her face and then, finding what he needed there, he pushed his tongue back into her mouth, kissing her hungrily, before grazing his lips across her chin to kiss his way down the length of her neck. Tentatively, his pulse racing – his antennae on red alert for sounds from outside – he trailed his mouth along her shoulder, peeling one flimsy strap of her top down as he went.

'Extremely desirable,' he whispered, pulling her towards him. His hips hard against hers, he held her gaze, one hand pressed to the small of her back, the other peeling her remaining cami-top strap back.

'And you're doing terrible things to me,' he grated, pressing his mouth back to hers. Time of the essence, he didn't linger, kissing his way once again downwards, he paused at the soft hollow at the base of her neck, between her breasts, easing the top down as he did. 'You should never doubt yourself, Sherry,' he murmured, venturing to take one inviting breast into his mouth, sucking gently, circling with his tongue, until a low moan escaped her.

Now feeling distinctly frustrated and most definitely turned on, Adam found his way back to her ear. 'When and where?' he whispered throatily.

'I'll call you, as soon as—' Sherry stopped, her eyes

27

pinging wide. '*Hell!* It's James.' She paled as the male voice right outside the window forced them apart like a thunderclap.

'*Crap.*' Adam gulped, stepping back, then forwards again to help her with her straps. 'You're an attractive woman, Sherry.' He caressed her lips briefly again with his. 'Definitely desirable, trust me. I'd pay you. I mean ...'

'Go,' Sherry said, laughing, urging him onwards. 'Use the front door. I'll ring you.'

'Do.' Adam winked over his shoulder, quashing a fleeting feeling of guilt as he left. Why he should feel guilty when the husband ... husbands ... were usually cheating without compunction, he wasn't sure, but he always did.

Chapter Three

Sienna was coming back from her early morning walk with Tobias the next day when she heard him. 'Morning,' he shouted across the marina.

Looking up from her phone and yet another intimidating text from her ex, a man whose feelings regarding women were definitely, frighteningly skewed, she glanced back across the marina to see Lothario standing on the back of his boat.

'Nice day for it,' he said.

'Depends on what you have in mind.' Sienna couldn't resist a sarcastic retort. In his case, flaunting himself to every passing female, it seemed. She looked him over, noting he was wearing his staple wardrobe, cut-offs and vest, revealing an awful lot of toned caramel mocha latte, which was undeniably tasty. Pity his attractiveness was only skin deep.

'Not a lot.' He cocked his head to one side, appraising her, appraising him. 'Staying around the marina today mostly. I thought I might give taking a dip in it a miss though. Bit cold.'

Sienna flushed, not sure what to say to that. She'd already apologised, hadn't she, or at least tried to.

'I meant it's a nice day for sunning yourself,' he said, looking her leisurely up and down now, causing Sienna to blush, right down to her not exactly demurely dressed décolleté. She was wearing a bikini top, she realised, and cut-offs. Oh God. *Let she who casts the first stone …*

'Did you get him one?' he asked confusingly, as her cheeks radiated enough heat to give them both a suntan on their own.

'Sorry?' she asked, feeling a disturbing tingle of sexual tension shoot right through her, as his eyes came to rest on her breasts.

'Your dog.' He looked back to her face, the expression on his own intense, dark, thoughtful. Sienna swallowed. 'I wondered whether you'd managed to get him a life jacket,' he went on, running a hand through his hair.

Tousled, touchable, clutchable hair, Sienna thought a little breathlessly, and wondered whether she'd taken complete leave of her senses. 'No. I mean … not yet.' She blew out a heated breath. 'Right, well, I'd better, um …' She indicated the cottage behind her, intimating she should go, whilst resisting an urge to cross her arms over herself as his eyes flicked over her, yet again.

The furrow in his brow deepening, he smiled a short inscrutable smile, and turned towards his cabin. And then turned back. 'Look, about yesterday, I er …' he hesitated, now looking nervous. 'I owe you an apology. I was completely out of order and I—'

'Sienna!' Lauren called from the cottage window at the crucial moment. 'Your dad's on the phone.'

Sienna made sure he wasn't around before setting off back across the marina again. In light of his attempt at an apology she'd debated whether she might have been judging a book by its cover. But even if her judgement was right, she owed him a proper apology too, she'd decided. It wasn't a little thing he'd done. He'd actually been extremely brave. He had saved Tobias, at huge risk to himself, and he'd done it instinctively, which had to count for something. Also, she had to concede, whatever his lifestyle, however promiscuous he was, he quite clearly didn't try to take what wasn't offered freely by women.

Sienna's breath caught in her chest, her mind shooting

immediately again to her texting ex, who simply refused to go away and let her forget. Trying hard to dismiss him, even as her phone pinged in her pocket, she swallowed and focussed her thoughts back on her mission. Whatever Lothario ... Adam ... did, it was none of her business. There was obviously more to the man than met the eye. She might be wrong, of course. He might well be exactly what he appeared to be, an attractive man with no particular ambition in life other than to have regular sex. Unless appearances really did deceive, though, he was obviously caring of women's needs, particularly in the bedroom.

Stop it. Pulling herself up, before her errant mind ran away with her, she went into the chandlery. Seeing no signs of Nathaniel at the counter, or behind it, where he could often be found mooching for spare boat parts, she went around it and tapped on his office door. She'd made up her mind to get Adam a bottle of something by way of a thank you. Clearly being his friend, as well as his landlord, Nathaniel would know what his preference was, she'd assumed. Perchance, while she was here, she might just find out a little bit more about Adam. Her curiosity was definitely piqued, and Sienna wasn't sure it was purely in the interests of research.

'Nathaniel?' she called, tapping again when Nathaniel didn't answer. She was sure he was in. The chandlery had been open and she thought she could hear a radio playing inside his office. Knocking again, she waited and then tried the handle. Finding the door opened, she went on in – and stopped in her tracks.

Oh, dear. Nathaniel was in it seemed, shaving with an electric razor, gyrating his hips to Robbie Williams' latest, and wearing only his boxers. Very baggy boxers, adorned with a kissy lip motif. '*Oops.*' Sienna hid a smile as he caught her reflection through the mirror he had perched on his filing cabinet.

'Bloody hell!' Nathaniel whirled around, his face beetroot red. 'Crap,' he mumbled, scrambling for his shirt hanging on the back of his office chair.

'Sorry.' Sienna turned away, unfortunately too late to save his blushes.

'No, no, I am,' Nathaniel said behind her. 'Hold on, give me a tick.'

Sienna waited, hearing the sound of other garments being tugged hurriedly on, trousers – thankfully – judging by the sound of the zipper.

'Right, I'm decent,' Nathaniel assured her after an awkward pause, 'ish,' he added as she turned back around.

'Sorry, Nathaniel. I know it's early but the chandlery was open and I, um …' Sienna trailed off, noticing the sleeping bag on the floor in front of his desk, the alarm clock parked on the desk; general signs of living.

'Paperwork,' Nathaniel supplied, shrugging with embarrassment. 'I had some to catch up on, so …'

'Oh, right.' Sienna nodded and offered him an understanding smile.

'Actually, that's bullshi— Er, not quite true. I'm living here and I'm rubbish at lying.' Nathaniel sighed and turned to put the kettle on.

'But wouldn't you be better off on one of your boats?' Sienna asked, puzzled.

'Definitely. Unfortunately, someone's just bought the one I was kipping on and the only other one available is due for a refit, so …' He shrugged apologetically again. 'Come on in, Sienna. Would you like some toast?'

'No. Thanks, Nathaniel, I've already eaten. And you don't have to explain, you know. It is your office, after all.'

'Nate. Call me Nate. It's less of a mouthful,' he said, ambling over to what was obviously his kitchen area, a toaster and kettle on top of his fridge. 'There's nothing much to explain really.' He turned, waggling a mug in her direction.

Sienna shook her head. 'I've just had a coffee, thanks, Nate.'

'My girlfriend decided she wanted to do her own thing,' he went on, turning back to pour water into his own mug, 'with another bloke, unfortunately, so here I am, for a while at least.'

'Oh, Nate ...' Sienna felt for him. She didn't know him that well, but from what she did know he seemed to be a genuinely nice guy. The sort that would easily get taken advantage of, she imagined. 'I'm really sorry. It's just awful when that happens.'

'Oh? Same thing happened to you, did it?' Nathaniel enquired, casually.

'No. To a friend.' To Lauren, more specifically, but Sienna doubted she'd thank her for sharing that bit of news. 'I, um, don't have a boyfriend, right now.'

'You don't?' Nathaniel looked surprised. 'I'd have thought you'd have had them queuing at your door, a beautiful girl like you.'

'They obviously have the wrong address,' Sienna joked. 'Actually, with my writing and my job, I'm not really looking for a relationship at the moment,' she added, wanting to deflect discussion on that topic.

'So, what can I help you with?' Nathaniel clapped his hands together. 'A boat trip, is it? We've got the *Queen of the River* going out later, if you fancy it.'

'Adam,' Sienna supplied.

'Adam?'

'I wanted to thank him properly for saving Tobias. I thought I might give him a bottle of something. Unless you can think of anything else he might like?'

Nathaniel's smile slipped. 'I could think of plenty he'd like,' he muttered, drawing in a tight breath.

Such as? Sienna waited, while Nathaniel seemed intent on studying his feet.

'Red wine,' he suggested, sighing as he turned back to his fridge. 'Merlot is his tipple of choice. I usually grab him a couple when I do the supermarket shop. Here,' he pulled the fridge door open and produced a bottle, 'take one.'

Sienna eyed him curiously. He did his *shopping* for him?

'We look out for each other,' Nathaniel offered by way of explanation. 'I've known Adam since we were kids. He'd do the same for me if I was a bit strapped for cash. He's a good bloke. Where women are concerned, though ...' He held her gaze as he passed her the wine.

'He's bad news. Yes, I know. You said.' Someone she should absolutely avoid, then, Sienna suspected. Still, though, she couldn't reconcile his 'bad news' image and his selfless rescue of Tobias. He'd seemed so instinctively caring, yet, conversely, so angry.

A conundrum, definitely. Sienna had no idea why she was bothered what he was. The man was already in a relationship – several, possibly – and, even if he wasn't, he *quite* obviously wasn't relationship material.

Offering Nathaniel a smile of gratitude and taking her leave as he headed for his ringing telephone, she reminded herself she wouldn't know how to be in a relationship anyway. She'd never had a proper relationship, always out of synch at school, reluctant to invite friends home for fear of her mum's ups and downs. When her mum died, she'd seemed even less able to fit in, people seeming awkward around her, even her friends. Sienna recalled how some of the girls had avoided being alone with her because they hadn't known what to say. With the one or two boyfriends she'd had she'd always felt inept, somehow, at intimacy.

And then she'd met Joe, her possessive texting-ex. A trainee solicitor at the office where she'd worked part-time to fund her degree, he'd seemed nice at first, seeming to understand that she'd prefer to take things slowly. Clearly he hadn't understood. Sienna pulled in a shuddery breath. And clearly he hadn't cared about her. He'd been vile that night in the car.

Closing the chandlery door behind her, Sienna blinked back a tear as she recalled the contempt in his eyes, the accusation, as if it were her at fault. His swearing and shouting. He'd called her immature, a little daddy's girl. She wasn't completely naïve but, in Sienna's mind, lovemaking was supposed to be a caring experience that happened between two people who mutually desired each other, not something you did under threat of being labelled frigid or immature. Maybe she was naïve. It was only a shag, after all. He was her boyfriend, wasn't he? He was 'fucking entitled'.

Yes, and *she* was entitled, Sienna decided, with a determined nod of her head, to choose to have sex when she wanted and *with* who she wanted, preferably someone who would ignite her desire enough *to* want to.

'I have no idea why you're bothering,' Lauren said, giving her perfectly spiralled blonde hair a final spritz of hairspray. How did she do that, Sienna wondered bypassing her in the hall. Lauren could curl her hair in the morning and come home with it still stylishly curled at night. Sienna could give her hair an industrial spray of superglue and it would inevitably be limp frizz five minutes later. But then Lauren had always been stylish and coordinated, whereas Sienna's look was more boho. 'Happy Hippy Chic,' Lauren had once kindly referred to it, but even she tended to look her casual dress preference over dubiously.

'Because he rescued Tobias,' Sienna reminded her, heading to the kitchen to flick on the kettle. Swilling a mug, she watched Adam's boat through the kitchen window. She couldn't decide whether its tilt and sway meant he was just going about his morning business – or whether he might be going about other business.

'So he's a hero by all accounts?' Apparently satisfied with her titivations, Lauren came into the kitchen to peer out of the window alongside her. 'From what else you tell me he also has "women issues", Sienna. The man is obviously bad news.'

So everyone keeps telling me. Sienna sighed.

'He should raise a shagging flag, for a start.' Lauren nodded out of the window as the boat dipped stern end. 'Course, it would be permanently raised, no doubt,' she added, po-faced.

'Um, beg pardon?' Sienna's mouth curved into a smirk.

So did Lauren's. 'You know what I mean. He's a heartbreaker, Sienna, isn't he, Tobias?' She glanced over at Tobias, who snoring contentedly in his basket obviously had no opinion one way or the other. 'Someone you should definitely avoid, given past experiences.'

'Lauren …' Sienna felt her cheeks flush. Would she ever be free of her ex, she wondered, a constant reminder of her inadequacy in choosing and handling men?

Lauren wrapped an arm around her and gave her shoulders a reassuring squeeze. 'It was his problem, Sienna,' she said forcefully, 'not yours. I'm just saying don't go courting trouble, that's all. Not that I imagine he's much into court—' Lauren stopped, and gawked, as the bad-news-man himself appeared up on deck. 'Oh, my God!' she gasped. 'A serious heartbreaker.'

Shoot! Sienna smartly sidestepped. He wasn't wearing anything! Well, he was, but not much that left anything

36 .

to the imagination. He was dressed in just his cut-offs, the button undone at the front – she shuffled sideways for another surreptitious peek – and, '*Oh, my...!*' echoed Lauren's sentiments. He was, like, wow! He had the perfect physique, in Sienna's mind anyhow, lean but beautifully sculptured.

Was that a scar on his tummy? She squinted, recalling the one on his face, which perversely only added to the man's attraction. Was she? Attracted? Sexually? Obviously he wasn't perfect, inside or out, but was that precisely why she *was* attracted?

He had chest hair, just the right amount to be sexy; a thin line trailing from his chest temptingly down to ... she swallowed ... below open button level. His shoulders were broad. Not over-muscular, but he most definitely worked out: loads of press-ups, obviously. She quickly tried to dispel that image, but couldn't quite. His hips were slim. His abdominal muscles were phenomenal. Sienna closed her eyes, her own pelvic muscles contracting in delicious ... *anticipation*?

'God, it's hot.' She flapped a hand in front of her face.

'*Ye-es.*' Lauren folded her arms and looked her suspiciously over. 'He is, very. Steer clear, m'dear. Take my advice and give the man a very wide berth.'

'I wasn't intending to steer anywhere near him,' Sienna insisted, wondering herself whether she actually was. Whether, in fact, she really was attracted to heartbreakers, in which case she probably needed relationship counselling before she'd even got started. 'I was going to give him a bottle of wine by way of a thank you, Lauren, not my body.'

'Oh, yes?' Lauren looked her over again, as she collected up her briefcase and bag, taking in Sienna's cami top and shortest of shorts.

Sienna tugged the hem of them down a bit. 'It's hot.'

'You said. Just be careful, Sienna, okay? Men like him are dangerous.'

Sienna opened her mouth, ready to defend him, but then realised she didn't actually have much to offer in his defence. 'I will,' she promised instead, smiling reassuringly. 'Say bye-bye, Tobias.'

'Bye, Tobias.' Lauren rolled her eyes and headed to the hall, then poked her head back through the door. 'Concentrate on your script,' she suggested. 'Do some research or something. That should take your mind off other things.'

I'm trying to. It's not working. Sienna sighed and trailed across to the kitchen table whereupon was her under-used laptop, as Lauren left for work. Then she flew back to the window as she heard Adam say brightly, 'Morning. Looks like it's going to be another beautiful day.'

'Depending on whether one's managed to get any sleep the night before, of course.' Sweeping derisory eyes over him, Lauren blew out a sigh and marched on.

'Ah, sorry about that,' Adam called after her. 'I'll try to, erm ...' Clearly not sure what to say next, he ran his hand through his hair, watching her go. Having a good look too, judging by the curious tilt of his head, which most definitely didn't help Sienna's confused mood at all.

'It's now or never, Tobias,' Sienna said determinedly an hour later, during which time Adam's boat had remained relatively still. She hoped he hadn't gone out while she'd been in the bathroom trying to do something with her own hair, only to give up and end up tying it up in its usual bedraggled topknot. She'd tried a few of Lauren's lipsticks on, too. The lust-red gloss she'd thought looked quite nice, applying it and arranging her mouth into a provocative pout. Yes, that had worked. She looked like one of the undead after a blood fest. She had no idea why she was worrying about how she looked anyway. Tugging in a breath, she grabbed up the wine from the table and headed for the door. Yes, okay, she did fancy him, she conceded, but that was just a fantasy. He obviously was a heartbreaker. Nathaniel certainly seemed to think so. He was definitely chauvinistic, as already demonstrated. He also had a girlfriend. A girlfriend he was obviously extremely satisfied by. With!

'Come on, boy,' Sienna beckoned a waggy-tailed Tobias and fastened his lead securely. Adam had been right, of course, about the life jacket, her carelessness. She reminded herself why she was bothering to take the wine. Complicated feelings aside, she was truly grateful. He *had* saved Tobias, who with his dodgy hips and arthritic limbs would surely have sunk like a stone.

Closing the cottage door before her courage failed her, she walked Tobias the short distance across the marina, noting again how tranquil everything seemed, resplendent white yachts and multicoloured narrowboats bobbing lazily on the sun-dappled water. A backdrop of woodland and greenery as far as the eye could see. Ducks dipping and splashing, long-necked swans gliding majestically by, blue skies. It really was the perfect setting to fuel creativity, if only her mind would stop wandering in one particular direction.

Pausing at Adam's boat, she gave the father of two wayward teenage sons a smile as she went. The man, looking nosily over from the deck of his boat moored on one of the pontoons adjacent to Adam's, didn't smile back. Misery guts, Sienna thought. If he was that miserable it was no wonder there didn't appear to be a wife in evidence.

So where was Adam? Gone down below, she supposed. Standing on tiptoe she peered over the handrail at the back.

The cabin door was open. Ah, he was obviously still at home. Sienna deposited the wine on deck and was about to climb on board to knock on his door, when a female voice from within froze her to the spot.

'I'd better go,' the woman said. 'I have to get you a key cut for the cottage.'

'Key?' Adam's voice. Sienna ducked swiftly back down.

'Well, it's standing empty at the moment,' the woman said. 'No happy holidaymakers booked in for the next month, so you might as well have a key.' A pause then, interspersed by an, '*mmmm*'. Were they kissing? Sienna strained her ears. They were! Oh God, what should she do? Make a dash for it back to her cottage, or wait it out in case she attracted their attention? Wait it out, she decided, sidestepping, and then freezing again as the boat swayed.

'Sherry, I thought we'd already settled this payment for services rendered thing.' Adam sighed exasperatedly from inside. 'You don't—'

'You're amazing,' the woman cut him short. 'A frustrated woman's fantasy come true.'

Unable to resist, Sienna took another quiet sidestep and had a furtive glance through a gap in the curtains at the window.

'Keep it,' the woman said, placing several crisp twenties on his bedside locker. 'Put it towards your leather upholstery.'

What? Sienna's eyes shot wide. *Un-believ-able*. She was paying him! Blushing up to her topknot, Sienna dropped out of sight.

The woman – most definitely not the same woman Sienna had previously seen emerging from his shag-pad – was actually paying him for sex! Sienna blinked bewildered at Tobias. She hadn't been mistaken. She'd seen it with her very own disbelieving eyes.

The man was an absolute trollop!

Sienna up-periscoped again, and then ... '*Shoot!*' ... almost swallowed her tonsils.

'Nothing like the smell of leather,' Adam said, smiling a slow satiated smile from where he lay on his berth, and then rolling lazily over onto his stomach. At which the woman pulled back the duvet and gave his extremely firm buttocks a good thwack.

Ooh, hell! Sienna ducked, as Adam flew off the bed to catch the woman by the hand. 'If there's any spanking to be done,' she heard him growl, '*I'll* be the one doing it.'

Ye Gods! He was a complete perv! Sienna took several slow breaths, and then ever-so-carefully raised her head again, just in time to see Adam spin the woman around to face him. 'You're a very sexy woman, Sherry,' he said huskily. 'Your husband must be insane.'

Husband? Sienna closed her eyes. He was, wasn't he? She'd wondered what he did for a living. And now she knew. He really was pimping himself out, offering services to frustrated women.

'Oh, Adam ...' The woman practically melted in his arms.

Sexual satisfaction guaranteed, obviously. Disgusting. Sienna felt an electrifying jolt of excitement run right through her.

He wove a hand through her hair, pulled her head back and ... Sienna's pelvis flipped right over ... pushed his tongue into her mouth. She was clawing his back! Sienna watched on mesmerised as, unperturbed by the woman's fingernails assaulting his flesh, he trailed his tongue across her jaw, down her neck, licking and nipping. She shouldn't be watching. It was voyeuristic. It was wrong. It was ... Sienna gulped ... a total turn on.

'I have to go,' the woman said breathlessly as he worked

his way along her shoulders.

'Not yet,' Adam murmured. 'I want to taste you … all over.'

What? Sienna's eyeballs almost shot out. *Oh, no. They weren't going to… Help.* Sienna dropped down as he pressed his mouth back to the woman's and led her towards the berth.

Stunned, Sienna slid further down – to her haunches, trying unsuccessfully to look inconspicuous as a woman emerged from the chandlery to cross the marina. She couldn't breathe. Physically unable to inhale past the tight knot in her chest, in her tummy, she panted out instead, short shallow breaths. She had to go. Now! Crawl, if necessary. Get out of … Damn! Sienna's deliberations for tactical retreat were cut short as Tobias' lead twanged tight. 'Tobias,' she whispered. 'Tobias!'

The cat that sprang from the top of Adam's boat hissed. With no intention of obeying, Tobias lunged forwards, his tail slashing manically, his lead stretching dangerously, then, '*Woof! Woof! Woooof!*'

The cat, a huge white furball of a cat, spat. Tobias strained. The cat turned tail, and … Splat. Sienna was face down on the quayside. 'Tobias!' she screamed, realising she'd lost hold of his lead. 'Tobias!' Panic-struck as she sensed movement behind her, Sienna scrambled quickly up to all fours.

Don't turn around. She told herself firmly. Do *not* turn around, she willed herself, as an angry male voice shouted, 'I don't bloody believe this! Can't you keep that dog on a leash?'

Her? Keep her *dog* on a leash? 'Well, that's rich!' Shakily getting up on her feet, Sienna turned to face him, her cheeks flushing furiously. 'Really rich, from someone who quite obviously needs to keep his penis on a leash!'

Sienna looked Adam over disparagingly, and then reaching up to tighten her lopsided topknot, she turned to flounce off.

'Sienna! Are you all right?' Panting and obviously out of breath, having bolted from the chandlery on hearing the commotion, Nathaniel stopped her outside her cottage.

'Yes!' Sienna said shortly, her eyes welling up, her knee smarting, her pride badly bruised. 'No thanks to *him*.' Holding Tobias firmly by his collar, she glanced over her shoulder to where Adam was helping the woman from his boat. Proper little Sir Galahad, wasn't he?

'Oh, no, not again ... I bloody well warned him,' Nathaniel growled as Sienna dragged a hand under her nose and limped on. 'I'll have a word,' he called behind her.

'You might have to shout,' Sienna suggested huffily. 'He probably won't hear otherwise, above all the bumping and grinding! Come on, Tobias.'

Feeling very close to tears, Sienna closed her front door and unhooked her disobedient, but loyal, best friend's lead. 'Good boy,' she said, bending to plant a kiss on the dog's snout. 'Not like *him*.' She sniffed. '*He's* very bad, Tobias. Very bad indeed.'

God, she was *so* angry. Hobbling to the kitchen, she topped up the panting dog's dish with water, and then reached for some paper towelling, wetting it to press to her grit-pitted knee. But why was she angry? Because she'd wanted him to have some redeeming features? Despite her denials, had she truly been harbouring a hope that he might metamorphose from angry-man into Mr Perfect? That his eyes might be opened to his heart's desire, his every fantasy fulfilled standing before him to the exclusion of all others, making her the only woman he brought to the heights of orgasmic pleasure at night? She really had, hadn't she, gone quite barking mad? The man was a male prostitute, for goodness sake. Someone women *paid* to pleasure them. Yes, and he was obviously worth it.

Sienna gulped back an uncomfortable lump in her throat. She had been hoping to see another side to him, she realised, though preferably not his backside. And therein was the basis of her anger. He'd burst her bubble. Ruined her silly fantasy that his anger might only have been about the situation he'd found himself in, sopping wet and feeling foolish. That he might even fancy her. *Hah!* He'd been nothing but obnoxious to her.

She didn't care. He wasn't worth wasting a single second's emotion on. Sienna swiped at a tear on her cheek. He could sell tickets for all she cared. He probably could too. He'd make a fortune. Ignoring her beeping mobile, which was obviously the ex with more frighteningly persistent, '*Why are you doing this?*' texts, Sienna sat gingerly on a kitchen chair, then cocked an ear as she heard Nathaniel shout, '*You are a complete prat, Adam, do you know that?*'

'Nate, I said I'm sorry.' Adam sounded contrite.

'Not good enough, mate!' Nathaniel didn't sound any less angry. 'Just bloody well pack it in, Adam, or you can find somewhere else to moor up.'

'Nate, for Pete's sake—'

'And if you're thinking of going near either one of those girls in that cottage, just don't, okay!'

Chapter Four

That hair was truly amazing, wild and fiery. *Sienna*. Adam mentally rolled her name around on his tongue. It was a beautiful name. It suited her. She blushed as he watched her, clearly flustered and not meeting his gaze as she struggled to pull him a pint that wasn't all head. 'Thank you,' he said, as mission finally accomplished, she banged the glass on the bar in front of him.

'My pleasure,' she said shortly.

He tried a smile. 'Obviously.'

Ignoring him, she held out her hand for payment, po-faced still, as she had been from the minute he'd come in, seating himself at the bar, rather than a table further back, where he usually sat attempting to avoid any trouble, particularly from the tyre slashing thugs, who were in tonight, he'd noted. No doubt they were watching him from across the lounge. Adam could almost feel their scorn burning into him. He had no idea what their problem was, unless … Was it possible one of them was related to someone he'd had an affair with? Could be. Adam dearly hoped not.

The landlord, who didn't exactly welcome him with open arms, didn't look too ecstatic to see him here either. Adam wasn't worried about any of that though. If looks could kill, he'd have been six feet under long ago. His concern was for Sienna, who'd avoided him since the boat incident. Three times he'd seen her over the last two days. He'd almost bumped into her coming out of the chandlery. She hadn't said hello as she usually did, hadn't smiled. She'd just dropped her gaze and hurried on, and that concerned him. She'd obviously seen or heard something. She was way too close to his boat not to have done. How much he wasn't sure. 'Keep the change,' he said, trying for some kind of dialogue as he handed her a five pound note.

She looked at him at last. Her eyes were green, forest green, and shining with an angry luminosity, not surprisingly. 'That's very generous of you.' She glanced at the landlord and then quickly back to him. 'Especially as you're obviously so desperate for money!'

Oh, crap! Adam almost missed his mouth with his pint. She'd seen Sherry leaving the money! He looked after her disbelieving as she flounced off to serve another customer. Now he felt really bad for her, and not very proud of himself. Nate was right. He was a prat. She must have been shocked, to the core probably, and then he'd gone and humiliated her, again, yelling at her, like some kind of Neanderthal. In his own defence, he'd been pretty shocked, too, and he really hadn't realised she'd fallen over as he'd stormed up on deck. He'd been too busy being annoyed because she'd been in the vicinity of his boat; because he'd guessed that she might have seen what had been going on inside, and it had bothered him. She bothered him. He'd felt something. Seeing her, looking at her properly for the first time the day he'd rescued her dog, he'd felt something more than sexual attraction, felt emotions similar to those he'd had when he'd first met Emily, and it had scared him.

Adam ran his hand through his hair, feeling thoroughly ashamed. She obviously thought he was pathetic. She was probably right. He should go, he decided, his eyes straying again to Sienna as she served someone else. Not sit here as if he was revelling in her humiliation.

'Another?' she asked, coming back as he finished up his beer.

'No, thanks. I, er …' Adam glanced at the landlord, who shot him a look of pure contempt. Adam supposed he'd every right to, having caught him red-handed in the car park with one of the female clientele, '... should probably go.'

She shrugged indifferently. Good riddance, Adam got the message. 'Does it hurt?' he asked, awkwardly, attempting to redeem himself in some small way. 'Your knee,' he added, when she looked at him, puzzled. 'You grazed it when you fell.'

She shook her head vigorously, causing a spiral of her glorious hair to fall free. Adam badly wanted to reach out and run his fingers through it. 'Tobias saw a cat. It sprang from the top of your boat ...' she started.

'Look, I'm sorry,' he said quickly, wanting to get his apology out there, whatever her reaction.

She looked at him, her lips slightly parted in surprise. Fabulous, full, gorged pink: they were infinitely kissable and wouldn't need any enhancing with make-up. She was naturally pretty. Very pretty. 'About what happened on my boat,' he tacked on, clumsily. 'I've been a bit of an idiot, haven't I?'

Sienna folded her arms. 'A lot of one,' she assured him.

'And that.' Adam smiled, embarrassed. 'Anyway, I just wanted to say I'm sorry. I know you don't think much of me. I don't blame you. I wouldn't think much of me either.' He paused and considered. 'Actually, I don't think much of me, but that aside, I'm truly sorry.'

Sienna eyed him sceptically. 'Truly sorry?' she repeated, after a second.

'Truly.' Adam dipped his head apologetically. 'I've acted abysmally. Upsetting beautiful young women isn't something I'm proud of.'

She searched his face and then nodded, blushing again as she did, exquisitely in Adam's eyes. This was one girl he really would like to get more intimate with. *Damn!* He needed to stop thinking like that. There was no way on God's green earth a girl like her would come near someone like him anyway. 'I'd, er, better go.' He glanced again at the landlord, who was eyeballing him with open hostility now over the glass he was polishing.

'Right.' She continued to study him, her head tilted to one side, as if trying to work him out. She'd succeed where his psychiatrist had failed, if she could.

'Can I ask you something?' she said as he made to leave.

'Ask away,' he replied, hoping it wasn't going to be anything too personal in public.

She beckoned him closer. 'Do you really charge for sex?'

What? Adam glanced quickly around. That was definitely too personal in public. 'Erm ...' he laughed self-consciously. 'No, not always.'

She studied him. Curiously? Suspiciously? Adam wasn't sure. 'I need to talk to you,' she said.

Adam scanned her face. Her expression, aloof now, didn't bode well. 'About?' he asked, apprehensively.

She held his gaze. 'Your activities.'

'Ah, right.' Adam dropped his. Obviously she was about to ask him to move his boat to somewhere his 'activities' would be a little less troublesome. That wouldn't surprise him. He'd been asked to move on before. 'I, er ... Fine, but do you think we could maybe not do it here?'

Sienna followed his gaze to where the landlord was still staring at him. 'I'll come to your boat tomorrow.' She nodded determinedly.

Definitely about to tell him to sling his hook, Adam decided, which might just give Nate the perfect opportunity to claim he hadn't got another mooring spot and tell him to do the same. Served him right, he supposed.

'No problem,' he said despondently, pushing himself away from the bar. 'I have an appointment around noon.'

'Oh.' Her gaze went back to curious.

Obviously she was wondering what kind of appointment. 'A lawn to mow,' Adam elaborated, with none of his usual blasé amusement. 'Any time before then is good.'

'Fine.' She nodded. 'How about nine-ish?'

'I'll make sure I'm out of bed and fully dressed,' Adam joked half-heartedly, and then, noticing her gaze hit the floor, dearly wished he hadn't.

Sienna watched him head for the door, not making eye contact with anyone, as was his tendency. Well, he was definitely an enigma, wasn't he? She pondered his apology as she pulled a pint for a waiting customer, the spark of vulnerability she'd seen in his eyes. He didn't like himself. He'd said as much, meaning his Lothario image, she assumed. The fact that he had apologised, come in especially to apologise, seated himself right at the bar, which couldn't have been easy – the landlord seemed to hate him – meant that he did have feelings beyond his sexual urges. Sienna felt her face heating up at the thoughts that conjured up. But then she'd known there was more to him under the lady-killer façade, despite his best efforts to convince the world there wasn't. Would a man who had no feelings dive spontaneously into a freezing cold river to rescue a dog? Sienna still thought not.

'Oi, Sienna, watch what you're doing,' the landlord called, jolting her out of her Adam contemplation.

Sienna followed his gaze down to the pint, which was now spilling spectacularly over. 'Whoops, sorry,' she said, hastily retracting the glass.

The landlord eyed the ceiling and walked over to her, with a sigh. 'He's a bad lot, you know, that one.' He nodded towards the door through which Adam had just left.

'I gathered.' Sienna glanced down and then quickly back as the door swung open again and Adam reappeared, a carrier bag in his hand.

Nodding at the landlord, who folded his arms across his chest and eyed him beadily, Adam walked back to the bar. 'I didn't bring it in earlier because I wasn't sure you'd want to talk to me, but ...' he shrugged with embarrassment and placed the bag on the bar '... I got you this. And no, I'm not trying to buy your affections, in case you're wondering.' With which, he gave the landlord another short nod and sauntered back out.

But possibly not all bad, Sienna decided, smiling delightedly as she peered in the bag to find a dog-sized life jacket.

'Are you decent?' Sienna called through his cabin door, bright and early next morning.

'As I'll ever be,' Adam assured her, hastily stuffing motor magazines and papers under one cushion on the seating area and straightening another, and then deciding it looked too straight and squashing it down again.

He was decent, too. Clean T-shirt and jeans. He'd shaved, tidied up. He had no idea why. Yes he did, because he was hoping he could dissuade her from suggesting he move his boat. He'd made a spectacularly bad impression. He really did feel bad about that. He wanted her to know he was genuinely sorry, for what it was worth. He liked her, he conceded, which was crazy when he didn't even know her, but there it was. He'd never be someone she'd entertain going out with ... Adam paused to ponder that. He hadn't considered 'going out' with anyone in the proper sense since Emily, nor had he thought he ever would. Whatever the outcome of this meeting, though, he'd like to be able to talk to her, if only over the bar at the pub. Apart from Nate and the odd woman who felt safe to be seen with him, he generally sat on his own. His own fault, he guessed.

'Is it all right if Tobias comes in?' Sienna poked her head around the door. Her hair was loose again, Adam noticed immediately. Reflecting a thousand iridescent flecks of gold and red, tumbling over her shoulders to her creamy full breasts, it completely took his breath away.

'Er, yep.' He smiled and shook his head, feeling definitely disorientated. And then shook it again, as she bent to lift the dog into her arms. She was *carrying* it in?

'He's got bad hips,' Sienna explained, puffing her hair from her face as she struggled through the door, dog in her arms.

Adam rolled his eyes. He was all for kindness to animals. He loved dogs. He'd been considering getting one himself since Snowball, the fluffy white Chinchilla cat, who'd actually been Emily's, had died. Wasn't carrying the dog down the steps taking it a bit far, though?

'He doesn't do steps very well,' Sienna enlightened him, negotiating the first step into the boat, 'so I …'

'Be careful,' Adam warned her, moving to lend her a hand. 'Those steps are slip—*Crap!*' Adam got an armful of dog, a face full of dog-tongue, but was unfortunately too late to save the lady.

'Oo-*ouch*!' Sienna sat with a splat, cracking her head on the steps behind her as she landed.

Dammit, he just knew she was going to do that. Setting the dog down, Adam turned quickly back and eased an arm around her to help her to her feet. 'You okay?' he asked, worriedly, helping her walk the short distance into the cabin area.

'Nothing bruised but my pride.' She smiled, a bit of a wobbly smile, Adam noted. 'The boat's swaying,' she said.

'It's not, it's you. You gave your head an almighty crack on the way down.' He scanned her face and then looked intently into her eyes, searching for contracted pupils.

Beautiful, he thought, even when slightly crossed.

Instinctively, his hand went to the back of her head to check for damage, the other he threaded around her waist, holding her up, holding her to him. Adam breathed in the sweet scent of her as she looked up at him. Her pretty green eyes locked on his, she seemed to be looking right into the depths of his soul. Too close. Adam's breath hitched in his chest. 'I, er ...' He swallowed hard, his gaze now on her full, pillow soft lips, which were only inches from his. 'You need to sit.'

Adam stepped quickly back, putting a safe distance between them, and steered her towards the seating area. 'Can I get you anything? Tea? Coffee?' he asked, shoving his straightened, squashed cushion aside to give her some room.

'Aspirin,' she suggested, sitting gratefully.

He looked back at her, concerned. 'Really?'

'No, I'm fine, honestly,' she assured him, offering him another smile. She had a nice smile, natural. God, those lips were tempting. 'Tea would be lovely. Thanks.'

Cautioning himself to concentrate on something else, Adam mentally dismantled his engine as he headed towards the galley to put the kettle on. 'So, how do you like it? The, er, tea, I mean.' He really wasn't doing himself any favours on the distraction front here.

'Milk, no sugar. I'm trying to be good.'

Adam glanced over his shoulder, thinking she already looked pretty good from where he was standing. 'So how did you know he couldn't swim? Your dog?'

'Tobias,' she supplied, as he filled a dish with water and offered the waggy-tailed Labrador a drink. 'He has hip dysplasia. I took him to a hydrotherapy centre, thinking it might help.'

'I take it it didn't?' Adam helped himself to a Coke from

the fridge, fished the teabag out of the mug, added milk and passed it to her. Then, realising it might look a bit pointed if he remained standing, he seated himself in the only other available space: on the seating area alongside her.

'No.' Sienna took a sip of her tea. 'He couldn't breathe very well from the bottom of the pool.'

'Ah.' Adam nodded and tried, yet again, to focus on something other than her lips. Nope wasn't happening, not when she ran the tip of her tongue over them like that. 'You really shouldn't have let him run around a marina without a life jacket, you know?'

'Of course I know. I didn't deliberately throw him in. And I did try to thank you for saving him, but you were too busy shouting at me to notice.'

'I wasn't shouting,' Adam protested.

She gave him an arch look.

'Okay, I was,' he admitted, his mouth curving into a contrite smile. 'I apologise, again. In my defence, I was bloody cold.'

'And wet,' Sienna reminded him.

'Sodden.' Adam nodded soberly. 'Right down to my socks.'

'You weren't wearing any,' Sienna pointed out, and then blushed. 'Just trainers.'

Adam really wished she'd stop doing that. It made her look about sixteen, which would make the thoughts going straight from his brain to certain other parts of his anatomy, despite his best efforts, wholly inappropriate. 'You noticed what I wasn't wearing, then?' He couldn't resist.

She blushed again. Those two bright spots on her cheeks really did make her look very pretty. Extremely. Adam had a glug of his Coke.

'I noticed what you weren't wearing on your feet,' she said primly. 'Mostly because you were so determined to glower at me, I didn't know where else to look.'

'Sorry.' Adam took another slow sip of Coke.

'Thank you for getting him one,' Sienna filled the following brief silence.

'My pleasure.' Adam smiled. She didn't need to know it had cost him his last meagre funds. 'I thought it might save me from getting sodden all over again.'

She dropped her gaze, leaving Adam wondering whether he hadn't just ramped up her guilt. He really did despair of his glib sense of humour sometimes.

'I bought you some wine, some Merlot,' she said, after another pause. 'To thank you for rescuing him, but you were, um, busy when I, um, so I left it behind the lifebelt.'

'Ah, I, erm … Sorry,' he said again. He really did mean it. She was young, twenty-two or three, maybe? Okay, so age didn't necessarily dictate how sexually naïve, or not, she might be. But the way she looked, blushed so easily, she seemed so innocent, susceptible somehow. He really wished he'd been a little more caring of her feelings.

'So, why live riverside with a dog with dodgy hips?' he asked, attempting to move the conversation away from the 'paid for sex' incident.

'I never imagined he'd fall in. I wouldn't dream of walking him off lead around the marina.' Sienna gave him another look, an attempt at a scowl. It wasn't a very convincing scowl, though. Even when she wasn't smiling, her mouth curved up ever so slightly at the corners. He really would love to prise those lips open and press his tongue into her mouth.

'No, of course you wouldn't.' He coughed, and steered his mind towards his battery top-up fluid.

'I'd got my heart set on the cottage and I couldn't bear to leave him, so …'

'Girl's best friend?' Adam suggested.

'Absolutely.' Sienna nodded, her mouth forming into its more usual smile. 'I love the water.' She answered his question about why she moved into that cottage in particular. 'The sun rising resplendently over it, the blaze of orange, purples and pearly-pinks as the sun sets, the scribbles of gold it reflects when the moon hangs above it. The peace and quiet ...' She stopped to give him a pointed look that had Adam wanting to blush, and then laughed when he obviously did.

'I love boats, the way they bob lazily on the water, as if beckoning you to climb aboard and slow down,' she continued, an infectious enthusiasm in her voice that had Adam now looking at her in wonder. He couldn't stop looking at her. He wanted to drink in every little detail, from her sexily messy hair to the freckles on her nose, to the tiny dimple in her chin; leisurely peruse every inch of her, right down to her coral-painted toes.

'I'd love to own one, one day; live a freer way of life.' Sienna fixed him with her mesmerising green eyes, a definite sparkle dancing therein. 'Not free, free, but free, you know ...' She pushed her hair back from her face, wayward wispy tendrils brushing the soft curve of her breasts, as she did.

Battery connections, Adam attempted a distraction. *Need to get those checked out.* 'I do,' he agreed, wholeheartedly. 'I love it, the smell of the diesel when the engine's ticking over, the open air. Plus the freedom, of course, to do what you want when you want. Suits my lifestyle.'

Sienna nodded and looked away. Maybe mentioning his lifestyle wasn't such a good idea. Again, Adam despaired of himself. 'So are you from around here? Worcestershire, I mean. You don't have a local accent.'

'Suffolk, originally. Gloucestershire now,' Sienna attempted the Gloucester accent, rolling her *rr*s. Adam smiled. He was sure he could sit here watching and listening to her talk all day, whatever her accent. 'My parents moved when my dad's mum got sick. I suppose they must have liked it because they stayed. So, here I am.'

'Don't they worry about you being here, though, renting a cottage right on the river?' Adam was fishing, trying to get to know a little more about her. He couldn't help thinking he might worry if she was his daughter, though, and not necessarily about the possibility of floods.

'Incessantly.' Sienna rolled her eyes. 'My dad, that is. My mum died when I was in my teens. He's had to bring me up alone since and he tends to be … Well, let's just say a little over-protective.'

'Oh.' That blindsided him. Adam looked her over, feeling for her. Losing someone you love at any time was hard, he could attest to that. He'd missed his mother so much sometimes, the pain inside was like a physical thing. For a girl to lose her mother in her teens, that must have been devastating. 'Do you miss her? Your mother?' he asked softly, wishing he could say more, but not sure what.

'All the time.' She glanced at him and the look on her face smashed through the fortress Adam had erected around his emotions in an instant, forcing hard-suppressed memories to the surface: the expression on Emily's face that last time they'd argued at a family function in front of everyone, sadness etched so deep into her eyes it cut him to the core. He'd tried to explain; to tell her that he did want to marry her. It was his father's involvement he didn't want, on the wedding day, in their lives thereafter. Emily hadn't been listening. After all her planning, why would she? She'd fled to the toilets, away from the flapping ears, and hushed whispers. He'd gone out for some air. Adam recalled the night vividly, the wettest, most miserable of nights. When he'd come back, determined to talk to her, even if he had to do it through the toilet door, Emily had left. She'd wanted the fairy tale. He'd shattered her dream. Why had he done it? Why in God's name had he chosen that moment …

Adam's thoughts ebbed away, like sea clutching at sand. It was happening again. His heart rate quickened as his eyes flicked to a space beyond Sienna. The figure was smoky, intangible, like mist would be to the touch. But it was there. No visible features, he couldn't possibly tell who it was, yet he knew. He could feel her. Emily, she was here, and this time he was stone-cold sober.

Panic gripping him, Adam snatched his gaze away, back to Sienna. She was unaware; real, beautiful, tangible. Adam mentally shook himself.

'Are you all right?' Sienna asked him as he squeezed his eyes closed, willing the apparition away.

'Yes,' Adam assured her quickly, relief flooding through him as he risked another glance past her to find Emily had gone. 'Sorry, I was just thinking how devastated you must have been.'

'I was.' Sienna's gaze drifted briefly down again, and then back. 'My dad was there for me though. He's a psychiatrist,' she went on, changing the subject, one she obviously felt uncomfortable with. Adam could relate to that. 'Always trying to analyse people, you know?'

He'd have a field day with me, then. Adam smiled wryly.

'What about your dad?' Sienna asked. 'What does he do?'

Adam tugged in a breath. I don't have one, was his stock answer, which generally steered the conversation away from a subject he wasn't comfortable with, but … 'I don't see him.' He opted for the truth instead. Why, he didn't know. Apart from Nate, who'd always been there, getting him out of scrapes even in their schooldays, the one person who'd been there for him when he'd hit rock bottom, making sure he attended his psychiatrist's appointments, Adam hadn't talked to anyone about personal stuff. 'We, er, don't see eye to eye,' he elaborated, intending to leave it at that.

'About what? Your love life?' Sienna's look this time was teasing.

Adam frowned and swilled his Coke around. 'More about my brother's.' He smiled, hopefully indicating subject closed.

'Oh.' Sienna scanned his face, a question in her eyes. She didn't pursue it, thankfully. 'So, what about your mum?' she asked instead.

'I don't see her either,' Adam said quickly, knowing she'd probably wonder why, given her own circumstances. 'It's a long story, probably better saved for another day.' He forced another smile. 'Fancy some more tea?'

He went to fetch himself a fresh Coke anyway when she declined. He was struggling, he realised. Talking to someone meant you had to have something to talk about: Who you were. Future plans. History. The history was a no go, and beyond the hope that he could meet Lily-Grace, he didn't have any future plans. As for who he was, a depressive struggling with post-traumatic stress disorder, a paid-for-sex womaniser …? Adam really wasn't sure he liked who he was right at this moment.

'Living here's actually cheaper than living in the city.' Sienna saved him, returning to their original topic as he came back from the kitchen area. She was sitting on her hands, swinging her long, shapely legs. Adam really wished she wouldn't. 'And the cottage has all mod cons, including Internet connection, thank God. I'd be hard-pushed to write my script without my PC.'

'You're a writer?' Adam asked, impressed.

Sienna sighed. 'Trying to be. I have my degree in Creative Writing. I entered one of my assignments in a script writing contest and, well, they like it, but it needs some work.'

'That explains why you're so poetic.' Adam sat down again, where the view wasn't quite so distracting.

'Poetic?' Sienna eyed him questioningly.

'Blaze of orange, purples and pearly-pinks as the sun sets? Sounds poetic to me.'

'Ah.' Sienna smiled modestly. 'I do tend to get a bit verbose sometimes. Sorry.'

'Don't be. I like listening to you talk,' Adam assured her. 'So what's the script about?'

'Well, it's a love story, but I need to include a bit more sex, according to my editor. You know, as in show rather than tell, steamy erotica type stuff,' Sienna said blithely as Adam was attempting chaste thoughts around fan belts.

Adam spat out his Coke. 'Erotica?'

'That's what I wanted to talk to you about,' Sienna went on. 'I thought I might, you know, hire you.'

What? Adam wiped his arm over his mouth and stared at her, dumbstruck.

'To help with my research.' She shrugged casually, as if she'd just passed a comment about the weather.

'Help with your ...?' Adam shook his head, bemused. 'Okay, Sienna.' He smiled embarrassedly, after a second. 'I've got the message. Joke over. I'll make sure to be on my best behaviour from now on.'

'I wasn't joking.' Sienna looked at him, deadly serious, much to Adam's bewilderment. 'I know it's not usually the done thing, even in this day and age, for a woman to proposition a man, but as you no doubt get loads of propositions, I thought you ... um ...'

She stopped, searching his face uncertainly, as he continued to stare at her, utterly shocked, even though he had no right to be, because she did have every right to ... Just as much right as he had to ... *Jesus.*

Dragging a hand over his neck Adam looked her over. She *was* kidding, wasn't she? She smelled of strawberry body wash, for Pete's sake. She looked about as likely to hop into bed with someone she hardly knew, someone like him, as sprout wings. And she wanted to *hire* him? For what?

Sex with no bloody strings. Adam gulped back a bitter taste in his mouth, reminding himself angrily what *he* did, the way he liked things.

Well, that put paid to any hopes he might have had that she'd consider going out with him. She didn't consider him boyfriend material, and who could blame her? Nothing quite like a taste of your own medicine, was there? God, he really was a spectacular failure.

'You didn't answer me,' she said, scanning his face, her green eyes huge, wide …

'No!' Adam stood abruptly. 'No way, Sienna. You've got it wrong. Sherry … The woman you saw … She didn't pay me, she—'

'She did. I saw her.'

Adam raked his hand through his hair, frustrated. 'You *thought* you saw. It wasn't how it looked, Sienna. She's a friend. We …' He trailed off, no clue how to explain.

'A girlfriend?' Sienna eyed him questioningly.

'Yes. No. I …'

'Just someone you fancied, then.' Sienna summed it neatly up for him.

Adam blew out a sigh. He didn't answer. He really didn't know what to say.

'Right, well, as I obviously don't float your boat, I'd better go, before I make a complete fool of myself.' Sienna jumped to her feet.

'No, wait.' Adam took a step towards her as she turned to the door. 'You do. I just don't—' What? Don't want to *not* care about you?

'Fancy me?'

'Of course I do. Any man would. It's just—'

'But not enough to want to sleep with me?' Sienna fixed her questioning gaze unflinchingly on his.

Dammit, what the hell was he supposed to say now? That he did, absolutely, but that he wanted it to mean something. To her? That he couldn't bear the fact that it wouldn't. Adam closed his eyes.

'God, how embarrassing.' Sienna emitted a strangulated laugh. 'My seduction technique is obviously on a par with the rest of me, isn't it, pathetic.'

Great. Adam tugged in a breath. He was really going for it, wasn't he, humiliating her not once, not twice, but three times over. 'No, you are *not*, Sienna,' he said firmly. 'You're a gorgeous, utterly desirable woman.'

'But you don't want to make love to me.'

Adam held her gaze. If only she knew how much he did. 'Make love?' He smiled sardonically.

Sienna pulled in a breath. 'It's a figure of speech, that's all,' she said, notching up her chin. Her tone was challenging, but the look in her eye ... self-doubt. He'd put that there. Adam cursed himself angrily.

'I'm sorry you're so obviously appalled by the idea,' Sienna said, now looking anywhere but at him. 'I think I'd better go. Come on, Tobias.'

'Sienna, wait.' Adam caught her arm as she turned back to the door. 'It's nothing to do with you.' He stepped around her, willed her to look at him, to believe him. 'Everything to do with me. I ...' He trailed off, his heart flipping in his chest, as she looked cautiously back at him. Her beautiful eyes were clouded with confusion and brimming with tears.

He'd done that. This was the only thing he was any good at where women were concerned. He'd hurt her, he knew it, and he had no idea how to undo it. 'Don't, Sienna,' he said hoarsely, tentatively reaching out to cup her face in his hands. 'Please don't cry,' he implored her, wiping a slow tear from her cheek with his thumb.

She swallowed, her wide, vulnerable eyes holding his.

'Don't go. Please, Sienna,' Adam said quietly. 'Not like this. I—'

Her lips brushing his, like the soft brush of a butterfly's wings, stopped him mid-sentence. Adam caught a breath in his throat, willing himself not to reciprocate. How could she not end up getting hurt? He wasn't capable of being anything but what he was, messed up, broken. Never in his wildest dreams could he be good enough for this girl.

A whisper away from him, Sienna scanned his eyes, and then, hesitantly, she leaned back into him, and Adam was lost. Closing his mouth over hers, he kissed her back, gently at first, easing her lips apart, and then more boldly as her tongue found his, inviting him into her mouth. He wanted her. His pulse kicked up. His blood thrummed through his veins. His kiss grew more urgent. Whatever it was this girl wanted, sex with no strings, whatever, he wanted her. Winding her gloriously messy hair around his hand, he eased her head back and crushed his mouth against hers.

Chapter Five

'Not here.' Adam pulled suddenly away, having kissed her more thoroughly than she'd ever imagined possible, his tongue probing and plunging the depths of her mouth, sending spasms of pleasure right through her.

'Where then?' Sienna asked, reeling from the impact of his assault on her senses. Her skin was tingling all over, and her heart was fluttering so manically against her ribcage it was in danger of bursting right out of her chest. Her tummy muscles had all but turned to goo when he'd sought her breasts under her top, grazing his thumb so gently over her nipples, it was sheer, sweet agony. She'd had no idea.

'I have a place we can use,' Adam said, turning away to collect up his keys.

'Is it yours?'

'No.' He looked back at her, his eyes now devoid of the burning passion she'd seen there, guarded almost. 'Coming?'

'I need to take Tobias home,' Sienna pointed out, as he walked past her to the steps.

Adam sighed and turned back. 'Come on, boy.' He lifted the dog into his arms, climbed the steps and planted Tobias firmly on all fours on the quayside.

'Thanks.' Sienna smiled, joining him.

Adam nodded tightly and pushed his boat doors closed. 'I'll wait in the car. It's in the car park. The old PT Cruiser. Blue,' he said, and turned to walk away.

Right, well … Thanks for your patience. Sienna nipped her bottom lip, then winced from the bruises he'd left there.

He didn't speak as she climbed in the car, offering her

nothing but a short smile as he started the engine.

'Where is this place?' she asked him.

'Not far.' He glanced at her. 'Okay?'

Sienna wasn't sure whether he meant 'is *that* okay', or 'are *you* okay', so she just nodded.

'You'll need to fasten your seatbelt.' He indicated the belt and then turned his attention to the windscreen.

'Are you okay?' she asked him as they pulled onto the road.

'Never better,' Adam assured her, smiling briefly again in her direction. It didn't reach his eyes, though.

'Are you sure?' Sienna pressed him. Had she upset him? Did he think she was a rubbish kisser? Had he changed his mind?

'Positive.' He shrugged. 'Just thinking, that's all.'

'Oh, right.' Now Sienna really didn't have a clue what to say.

Silence ensued, Adam seeming to drive in quiet contemplation, Sienna wondering at the sudden chill that had replaced the definite charge between them. Had she imagined it? Had it been just part of his technique?

'What kind of place is it?' she asked, after another silent minute ticked by.

'A cottage. A friend's. Mine for the temporary use of.' Adam glanced at her again, his look unreadable.

Sienna debated this and then asked hesitantly, 'Your girlfriend's?'

Adam shook his head. 'I don't have a girlfriend, Sienna.' He smiled wryly. 'Not in the sense you mean.'

'Oh,' Sienna said again. 'I thought the woman on the boat might be—'

'Nope,' Adam said over her. 'Like I said, she's just a friend. That's the way I like things. I won't be stalking you or anything, Sienna, don't … *Damn!*' He cursed suddenly, banging his hand against the steering wheel.

'What?' Sienna asked, alarmed. He'd seemed so amiable back on the boat, so easy to talk to, and now he seemed distant, tense; different.

Adam blew out a sigh. 'Nathaniel.' He nodded through his rear-view mirror. 'He just passed us.'

Sienna twizzled her neck, but the car was long gone. 'Is that a problem?'

'I, er … No, no problem.' He shrugged. 'Sorry, did I scare you?'

'A bit,' Sienna admitted.

'Sorry,' he said again, reaching for her hand and squeezing it, but only briefly. Sienna wished he'd held on.

'We're here,' he said a short drive later as he turned onto a pretty hedgerow-lined track, presumably leading to the cottage.

It was beautiful, Sienna thought, as she caught sight of it. A proper white-walled, roses around the door cottage. She turned to comment to Adam as he parked in front of it, but he was already half out of his door.

Sienna's tummy flipped over. He hadn't said anything. She wasn't sure what she'd expected him to say or do once they'd arrived, but she hadn't expected him to walk to the front door and let himself in with hardly a word.

He assumed she'd follow, she supposed. Sienna hesitated. She'd seen him angry, for good reason, when she stopped to think about it. She'd also seen him apologetic and courteous. He was caring, she knew that. He'd saved Tobias. He'd been caring when she'd fallen down the steps, when she'd mentioned her mum, she could see it, in his eyes. His kisses had been demanding, forceful, passionate, yet affectionate. He'd been full of remorse when he'd thought he'd hurt her feelings, and, oh, how he had. If she'd just 'fancied' him, maybe she wouldn't have felt so crushed. The truth was, though, Sienna liked him, which, common sense told her, meant she probably shouldn't go through with this. Desire, though, now pooling hot in the pit of her tummy, told her she very much wanted to. She wanted him. She would never have him. It was quite clear he didn't do emotional commitment, but still, she wanted him. He'd ignited her senses, touched every nerve in her body, right down to the core of her. She wanted him to make love to her, whatever he chose to term it. Her tummy fluttered excitedly at the thought of it. Her heart, though, constricted a little.

Calming her nerves, she climbed out of the car and followed him in. The cottage was just as pretty on the inside. The lounge was beautiful, white walls and high ceilings with natural wood beams.

Adam was standing by the sofa. He was looking at her, at last, but Sienna couldn't interpret his expression. 'Better close the door,' he said quietly.

Sienna did as bid. She had no clue what to do. What he'd expect. She'd just have to follow his lead, she supposed.

'Come over here,' he said, his expression still inscrutable as she turned back.

'It's a very pretty cottage. The décor's lovely, and the furnishings. I might steal some ideas for my place,' she said, stumbling over her words and very nearly her feet as she walked towards him.

He didn't answer, just continued to look at her, his demeanour poised, his dark espresso eyes fixed hard on hers. 'Closer.' He beckoned her.

Sienna stepped further towards him, right in front of him.

His eyes growing disconcertingly darker, he reached out and slid the straps of her top slowly over her shoulders, the straps of her bra. Sienna caught a breath in her throat as he slid the garments further down, exposing her breasts completely. Instinctively, she moved to wrap her arms about herself.

He caught them, lowering them back to her side. 'Don't hide yourself, Sienna,' he said softly. 'Never be embarrassed in the company of a man. You're an exceptionally beautiful woman.' He cupped her face in his hand. Sienna turned her cheek to his touch, her desire spiking as he dragged a thumb over her lower lip.

'Your face, your body, you're beautiful, totally,' he assured her, sweeping his gaze down over her, looking back at her, a flash of heat now in his eyes. Or was it anger? His tone gave nothing away. 'Come closer.'

Sienna moved further towards him, her heart pitter-pattering against her ribcage as she watched him lower his head to take a nipple into his mouth. She gasped as he sucked her, slowly and sweetly, alternating between each breast as he circled gently with his tongue.

She couldn't breathe. Between her legs she was on fire, yet melting at the same time. A low moan escaped her as Adam trailed his tongue lower, planting soft kisses over her torso, his hands behind her, urging her still closer. Oh God, he was going lower, easing the button on her shorts, peeling them down, kissing her belly button, lingering with his tongue. Pressing feather-light kisses on her hips, first one then the other, he moved lower.

She held her breath as he peeled her clothes further down, freeing first one foot of the restricting garments, and then the other. Wordlessly, he kissed his way back up her body. Then standing, his eyes on hers, a smouldering intensity now therein, he guided her towards the sofa. Brushing her lips teasingly with his, he took hold of her arms, gently urging her down.

Her top still around her midriff, feeling foolish, excitingly intimidated, yet wildly wanton, Sienna obliged. Was he going to take her here? Get it over and done with?

Nervously she watched as, lowering himself to his knees, he grasped her hips and eased her towards him.

'Beautiful,' he repeated, his eyes roving over her body, before coming back to hers, never moving from hers, as he eased her legs apart. Her breath coming in short sharp gasps, Sienna watched as he dipped his head, pressing his face to her most secret places, gently exploring, probing; pressing his warm tongue into her wetness.

She gripped the edge of the sofa, panting out a breath as he found her most sensitive spot, softly licking, circling; increasing the pressure, nipping with his teeth, until a white hot spasm of exquisite pleasure shot through her.

Tracing his way back up her body, caressing her warm skin with fingers and tongue, he paused again at her breasts, before seeking her mouth. His kiss was less forceful this time, slower, softer, almost as if he was trying to salve the bruises he'd left there.

'Okay?' he asked, drawing back.

Speechless, Sienna nodded. God, he was beautiful. His dark decadent eyes peppered with concern, she could just eat him. 'I've never, ever experienced anything like it,' she answered breathily.

'Never?' he smiled wryly.

'Never,' she said. 'I've never gone all the way. I've come close but, to be honest, I …' Sienna trailed off, noting his eyes were now smouldering with an intensity of quite a different kind.

'You are joking, right?' He moved away from her, his face paling visibly.

'No.' Sienna blinked at him, stupefied. 'It's no big deal, is it? You sleep with loads of women. You must have had a thousand virgins throwing themselves at your feet.'

'No big deal? *Jesus*, Sienna!' Abruptly Adam got to his feet, now staring at her, astounded. No, horrified, Sienna could interpret that expression all right. She struggled to rearrange herself, to rescue some smidgeon of her dignity, as he dragged his hands through his hair, quite obviously frustrated. And then ... he turned away. Turned his back on her.

'It's not a crime!' Sienna stood shakily behind him.

He didn't say anything for a second, just continued to stand there, his breathing heavy, his shoulders rigid, and then— 'Get dressed,' he said roughly.

'Don't worry, I am.' Sienna was already scrambling into her clothes. 'Thanks for warming me up. I'll find someone else to finish the job.' She headed for the door, hot tears of humiliation stinging her eyes as she pulled it open.

'You bloody well *won't!*' Adam was close behind her, placing the palm of his hand against the door and banging it shut. 'Why didn't you tell me?' he shouted, his eyes impossibly darker, his expression pure thunder.

'Why would you care?' she countered, tearfully.

'Because ...' Adam closed his eyes. 'It doesn't matter. Come back, Sienna.'

'What?' She turned to look at him, flabbergasted.

'Look, I'm sorry, okay. It's just ... It is a big deal. It does matter.'

'You just said it didn't!' Sienna wasn't sure what his problem was. Her, obviously. *She* was the problem, just like her bloody ex-boyfriend had said. She didn't want to do this, cry, in front of a man, again. 'I need to go,' she mumbled, breathing in hard, tying to will back the damn silly tears.

'Sienna, don't. I do care. I ...'

Sienna glanced down, a sob escaping her, despite her best attempts not to give in.

'Sienna.' He lifted her chin. 'I'm sorry. Please believe me.'

She wouldn't look at him. Couldn't.

'Sienna ... I do care.' His face was close to hers, his lips on hers, soft on hers. 'I ... *Dammit*.' He rested his forehead against hers, groaned deep in his chest, pulled in a breath and then picked her up bodily. Sienna was sure she could hear his heart thudding, as he strode through the lounge. Her own heart beat in tandem as he mounted the stairs, carrying her determinedly up to a bedroom. She should protest. What little modesty she had already in tatters, she should leave, but ... she didn't want to.

She half-expected him to throw her on the bed as he pushed wordlessly through the door. Instead, he placed her gently there. 'Are we undressing?' he asked, peeling off his T-shirt.

Sienna opened her mouth and closed it again. He was angry. She could feel it. She should have told him this was her first time, but she genuinely thought it would be no big deal to a man like him. It certainly hadn't been a big deal to her ex, who'd decided she was frigid, because she hadn't been ready to part with her virginity.

She watched as he unzipped, pulling off his jeans, his boxers. *Oh, hell*. She gulped. His erection was eye-bogglingly huge, telling her that he most definitely still wanted to. How though? Her worried gaze drifted back to his face.

'Don't worry.' He managed a smile. 'I won't hurt you. The clothes?' He nodded in her direction.

Her cheeks burning, Sienna squirmed out of them, feeling stupidly embarrassed after what he'd just done to her downstairs.

'That's better.' He walked towards her, his smile warmer now, less forced, yet still uncertain somehow. 'Don't close your eyes,' he said as she instinctively did. 'You're a beautiful, sexy woman, Sienna. There's nothing to be scared about, I promise.'

Sienna opened her eyes, watching as he lowered himself over her. He wasn't just going to … Was he? Oh, no, thank God, he wasn't. She caught her breath as he eased her legs apart and slowly inserted a finger inside her, sliding it gently in and out, over and over, until a groan of pleasure escaped her. Watching her face intently, he slid another finger carefully into her, moving both slowly, his thumb now expertly circling, building her to the heights of pleasure once more. 'Beautiful,' he said as if he really thought she was. Sienna wasn't, she knew, but here, with Adam – seeing herself through his eyes – she believed that she was.

'Oh God,' she groaned again, clamping her eyes shut as he increased the friction, causing her legs to stiffen, her pelvic muscles to almost dissolve.

'Open your eyes, Sienna,' he whispered.

She did as he asked her.

'Much better,' he said as she refocused on him, and then leaned in to kiss her lips, softly, lingeringly. His fingers still inside her he moved down, seeking her breasts. She moaned, pressure building inside her as he circled first one nipple with his tongue, sucking and tenderly biting, then the other. It was like nothing she'd ever experienced, so pleasurable it was almost painful.

'Slowly,' she heard him murmur, as if to himself, as he licked and kissed his way down her body, mapping every inch of her flesh, until her skin tingled and her body ached for him.

She felt his mouth on her, down below. Again, she was fully exposed, open to his probing tongue, his fingers; his teeth softly nipping her most sensitive place. Sienna clawed at the sheets, twisting them in her hands, and then, unable to stop herself, she reached for his hair, raking her fingers through it, pushing him down, lifting her hips to him as her muscles contracted and something dipped and then exploded inside her.

'Beautiful,' Adam growled, and crawled up her body to press his mouth against hers. She could taste herself on his warm lips, his tongue. She was shocked with her own unrestrained lust for this man. With his ability to take her to the heights of sweet ecstasy, yet he hadn't even wanted to.

'Bring your knees up higher,' he said, his voice deep and husky.

She did as he asked, and he eased them open. He looked at her down there, gently stroking a finger over her folds again, and then, 'One minute,' he said, easing away from her.

She waited and watched him, anticipation clenching her tummy, as he opened the drawer and reached for a packet. 'Ever ready,' he said, his smile back to inscrutable.

Sienna felt a pang of sadness, guessing he would be.

He positioned himself back over her. 'Don't tense up,' he said. 'I won't hurt you. If I do, tell me to stop. Okay?'

Sienna nodded, closing her eyes as she felt the tip of his erection press against her.

'Open your eyes, Sienna. I want to see you,' he urged her.

Again, she did as he asked, watching him, watching her as he thrust into her, one long thrust deep and hard. She bit down on her lip and tried to stifle a moan.

Adam searched her face. 'Shit,' he cursed, a look of panic flooding his eyes. 'Are you all right? Do you need me to stop?'

'No. I'm fine,' Sienna assured him, noting his expression was now one of undisguised concern. He *was* an enigma, so confusing. He must be so lonely, making love to so many women but not loving. Never being loved.

He scanned her face again, as if looking for confirmation, then finding what he needed, he drew out and thrust into her again. And again. And again. Slowly increasing the pace, his eyes on hers, building the momentum, until he felt so incredibly deep, he filled her to the brim. She felt full, physically, emotionally. She whimpered, as he picked up the tempo, thrusting still deeper, and deeper, fast sure strokes. She wanted him to. She wanted him to enjoy it, even if he did get paid for it.

She undulated under him, raising her hips to meet him, matching him, thrust for thrust, pushing her tongue deep into his mouth, biting his lips, breathing into him. Digging her fingernails into his back, she felt the wheals previously left there. Adam must have done, too. He caught her wrists, pushing her arms above her head and holding them there while he rode her, plunging into her, until she bucked beneath him, her muscles clenching around him in one flowing contraction, her climax exploding with such ferocity she sobbed out his name.

His dark eyes smouldering above her, Adam thrust one last time, and then, with a throaty moan, he came. She felt his release. Felt a drop of sweat fall onto her forehead. His breathing was ragged. He closed his eyes, exhaling hard, his beautiful dark eyelashes brushing his cheeks. The scar there didn't detract from his masculine beauty. She was sure she could fall for this man, if only …

'Okay?' he asked.

'Perfect.' She could hardly speak.

He studied her for a moment, his look one of uncertainty peppered with anxiety. 'I'm glad you found the service satisfactory,' he said, after a second. Then, smiling that smile that didn't reach his eyes, he eased away from her, climbed off the bed, discarded the used condom and proceeded to get dressed.

'Sienna,' Nathaniel called as she walked from the car park.

'Are you all right?' He caught up with her as she neared her cottage.

'Yes, fine,' she said, forcing a smile. 'I just, um, have to feed Tobias.'

'Are you sure? You seem a bit … down.' He looked her over, his brow furrowed in concern.

'Yes, honestly.' Sienna dropped her gaze. She was sure she must be blushing to the tips of her ears. Her nose was probably red, too. She always looked like a clown when she'd been crying. He promised not to, and hadn't hurt her, far from it, right up until that awful gibe about satisfactory service, his moving so pointedly away from her. She hadn't expected cuddles, not really. She hadn't expected whispered endearments. She hadn't expected him to get calmly dressed without looking back at her, though; to find him waiting by the front door with his keys in his hand when she went down.

She shouldn't have been surprised. She had been just another notch on his bedpost, after all. He needn't have forced the point home, though.

'Right, well, as long as you are,' Nathaniel said, not sounding convinced.

'I am,' she assured him again. 'Just tired. The heat, I think.'

Nathaniel nodded thoughtfully, as she mustered up another smile and turned to go. 'Sienna,' he said behind her, 'if you ever need to talk, you know where I am, right?'

He'd missed his appointment. Didn't matter much, Adam supposed. The lawn would still be there tomorrow. There would always be another woman awaiting his invaluable services. He shrugged and went to the fridge for a much-needed beer. Pulling the ring, he glugged it thirstily, noticing the tossed aside cushion over his can as he did so.

Sighing, he walked across to retrieve it from the floor, and then swallowed, hard. '*Dammit*!' he cursed, hurling the cushion across the boat, closely followed by his can. 'Idiot!' he berated himself, dropping down on the seat and burying his head in his hands.

Why hadn't he just stuck to his guns and let her go? What was the *matter* with him? Maybe it was no big deal, he tried to convince himself. At least this way she didn't end up in bed with some prat who would hurt her and then walk away and not give a damn. But she had ended up in bed with a prat, hadn't she?

He really was a complete waste of space. What kind of man sleeps with other men's wives, blithely sailing through life without caring about anyone? The kind of man a woman like Sienna should steer well clear of. *A thousand virgins throwing themselves at his feet?* Adam clenched his jaw angrily. No, Sienna, in actual fact, two, the second being you. The first? She would probably testify to what a great guy I am, too, if only she could.

Well, that was that, he supposed. Any hope that he might have had a relationship with Sienna was gone. She hadn't wanted that, though, had she? He certainly couldn't blame her. So, where did he go from here? Was he really proposing to crash in on Lily-Grace's life? Turn up out of the blue and turn her little world upside down? Father figure? Yeah right! Some father figure he'd be. About as inept as his own father, screwing around, pretending he was doing womankind a service. His brother, ditto. The psychiatrists had got it wrong. He wasn't suffering from post-traumatic stress disorder. He was delusional, dysfunctional; genetically programmed to be just like the rest of the men in his family.

But ... dear God – Adam prayed earnestly – he didn't want to be.

Feeling someone board the boat, Adam dragged his

hands over his face and tried to compose himself. It was Nate, he guessed, from the considerable sway.

'Happy now?' Nathaniel said, coming down the steps.

Adam pulled in a breath. 'Delirious.' He sighed.

'You really do think you're God's gift, don't you? Just couldn't resist, could you, hey?' Nathaniel seethed angrily, obviously pissed after seeing him drive by with Sienna and drawing conclusions. The right conclusions, as it happened.

'Don't worry, Nate.' Adam wiped a hand over his eyes and got to his feet. 'She only wanted me for my body.'

'*You* are a complete bastard, do you know that?' Nathaniel shouted, glowering at him.

'I do, as it happens.' Adam shrugged, heading back to the fridge. Drinking himself into a stupor seemed like a reasonable idea. At least then he wouldn't have to keep contemplating just how much of a bastard he was. 'Want one?' he asked Nathaniel, helping himself to another beer.

'No, I do not bloody well want one,' Nathaniel fumed. 'Why did you do it, Adam?'

Adam closed his eyes. *Because she asked me to*, he didn't try to explain.

'Just because the only girl you ever cared about screwed around, doesn't mean they all do, you know?'

'Don't, Nate.' Adam shot him a warning glance. 'Drop it, okay?'

'Do you think you're the only bloke in the world who got his heart broken?' Nathaniel clearly wasn't going to.

'Nope.' Adam sucked in a breath and took a swig of beer.

'I mean, we'd all be a sad lot of bastards if we walked around doing what you do because of it, wouldn't we?'

'Nate, drop it.' Adam sat down. It was hot in here. Too hot. He wiped the sweaty palm of his drink-free hand hard against his thigh.

'Shagging every woman in sight and not giving a damn

about any one of them!'

'For God's sake!' Adam got back to his feet, crashing his beer can down hard on the work surface. 'She slept with my brother, Nate! You know she did! You know all this. You know what happened. It's history. Nothing to do with who I am now. Just *leave it*, will you?'

'It's everything to do with who you are now,' Nathaniel said more quietly. 'It's about time you faced it, Adam. You need help, mate.'

'I got help, Nate! It obviously didn't help, though, did it? What I need now is for you to go,' Adam said, breathing heavily.

'Likewise,' Nathaniel retorted, holding his gaze meaningfully, before turning away to head back up the steps. 'Get your engine sorted, Adam. Or get this thing towed, I don't care which. You need to move on.'

'Oh, for … Nate!' Adam dragged his hand through his hair and then followed him. 'I can't overhaul an engine in the middle of nowhere!' he shouted after him. 'I need electricity, access to the workshop.'

Nathaniel turned back. 'Should have thought about that before you decided to turn it into a knocking shop, shouldn't you?'

'Nate …?'

Nathaniel shook his head and turned to walk off. 'You have until the end of the week, Adam,' he threw over his shoulder. 'Move on. And do us all a favour, mate, don't rush back.'

Chapter Six

Home from work early, Lauren had been as worried as Nathaniel when she clapped eyes on Sienna. Obviously it did show when you lost your virginity, in Sienna's case anyway. Lauren's cross-questioning, however, was cut short by the argument they couldn't fail to overhear from Adam's boat.

'Oh, no.' Sienna dashed to the window, her heart plummeting. He had to leave? Because of her? They hadn't mentioned her by name, but ... She shook her head, trying to make sense of some of what Nathaniel had said. What she'd heard Adam shout. His brother? What on earth? Not caring what reception she might get, Sienna flew out of the front door, to see Adam walking back towards the car park, his hand going through his hair, looking thoroughly dejected. She shouldn't care. She shouldn't. But she absolutely did.

'It's him you're upset over, isn't it?' Lauren was by her side, wrapping an arm around her, as Sienna watched him go, stupid tears welling in her eyes, again.

Sienna nodded feebly.

'Come on.' Lauren steered her gently back inside. 'We need wine. We need girl-talk, and possibly a hit man.'

One bottle on the table, one cooling in the fridge and glasses filled, Lauren seated herself opposite Sienna at the kitchen table. 'Well?'

Sienna took a sip of her wine and sniffed.

Lauren handed her a tissue from the strategically placed box. 'Did you sleep with him?' she asked calmly.

Sienna had a blow, while Lauren studied her over her glass. 'Yes,' she admitted, eventually.

'Oh, my *God*!' Lauren banged her drink down so hard

the wine parted company with the glass. 'Have you gone completely insane? Sienna! The man's a one hundred per cent total slut!'

'He has his good points,' Sienna said in his defence.

Lauren folded her arms. 'Such as?'

Knitting her brow, Sienna thought about it, and then, her shoulders drooping, she sighed heavily. She could hardy cite the fact that he'd given her the perfect orgasm *three* times as one of his good points, possibly his only good point.

'You never had sex with anyone else, Sienna! Why would you even contemplate going anywhere near a man like *him* after what happened with your ex?'

Sienna stared at her, astonished. 'He's nothing like him,' she said, bewildered by the fact that Lauren could imagine he was. Sienna couldn't even utter her ex's name without feeling humiliated and ashamed. Every time she thought about him, heard her phone ping knowing it was him, fear clutched at her chest. She hadn't been frightened of Adam. Nervous, yes, but not frightened the way she had been that night.

'But he *is*,' Lauren insisted. 'Just like him. He's taken what he wants, albeit he used a marginally less brutal approach, and now he'll just move right on to his next victim.'

'He is not! Adam would never make a woman feel like that. He isn't capable of it. I know he isn't.'

'Oh, for goodness sake, Sienna, you have no idea what he's capable of.' Lauren blew out an audible sigh of despair.

Yes I do, Sienna was about to say, but couldn't, because actually she didn't.

'Why?' Lauren continued to study her, astounded. 'I mean, of all the men in all the world why would you choose someone who shags anything that breathes?'

Shout it a bit louder, why don't you? Sienna felt a blush creeping up her cheeks.

'Because he *is* experienced,' she pointed out. 'And, whatever you think of him, *I* like him.'

'Experienced!' Lauren shot wine down her nose. 'He's *experienced* practically the whole female race, Sienna. This is what makes him a total bona fide bastard. If you were going to offer yourself on a plate, couldn't you have done it to someone who would savour the dish?'

Sienna flushed down to her toes, then slumped hurriedly down in her seat as an elderly boat owner passed by the window. 'I suppose *your* first time was absolutely earth-movingly shattering, then, was it?' Aware that the earth hadn't moved for Lauren the first time, rather it had ground to an unsatisfactory halt, Sienna eyed her friend accusingly.

Lauren reached for a tissue. 'No,' she admitted, wiping daintily, 'it was all fingers and fumbles and a complete orgasmic wasteland, as you very well know, but that's beside the point.'

'That's precisely the point.' Sienna shuffled up a bit. 'And for your information, he did savour it.' She almost squirmed in her seat, recalling just how mind-blowingly gorgeously he had savoured her.

Lauren's eyes widened. 'He did?' She tried to sound only mildly interested.

Sienna nodded, feeling a flush now of quiet triumph. 'Three times.'

'Three? Bloody hell.' Lauren took a huge glug of wine. 'Well, okay.' She took another. 'I suppose that's a small plus in his favour. So, why the tears?'

Sienna ran her finger around the rim of her glass. Good question. Hadn't he given her exactly what she expected of him, and more?

'You like him, you say?' Lauren said, after a considered moment.

Not sure whether it was a question or an accusation,

Sienna hesitated, then took a breath and nodded.

'Right, I'm going to ask you another question now, Sienna,' Lauren reached for her hand across the table, 'and I want you to answer me honestly.'

Sienna squirmed again, wondering how intimate a question it might be.

'Did he do cuddles?'

Sienna sank back down in her seat. 'No,' she said, shaking her head forlornly.

'A hit man.' Lauren topped up their glasses. 'We'll Google one, preferably one whose weapon of choice is electrodes.'

Adam drove around for a while after finishing up a job cleaning out someone's guttering, which pretty much summed up his skills. He'd driven around a lot since he'd walked out after his blazing row with Nathaniel, slept a couple of nights in the car. It had given him time to think, where he'd fast come to the conclusion that he had nothing of substance in his life, no one of substance, apart from Nate. Nowhere to go, but here.

Adam felt his heart sink as he walked through the door of the cottage. He did have a heart then, after all. He congratulated himself on finally finding it, but sorely wished he hadn't. He didn't want to do this 'friends with benefits' thing with Sherry. He'd thought it was an excellent idea at first. What bloke wouldn't want to have sex on tap? Now, though, the idea didn't seem quite so appealing.

Checking his mobile to find no messages from Nicole in regard to his seeing Lily-Grace, which didn't bode well after two weeks, he sighed and fetched a beer from the fridge, generously provided by Sherry. She'd stocked up: beer in the fridge, condoms in the bedside drawer. He'd been confounded when he'd come across the pregnancy test kit in the next drawer down, until Sherry had confirmed she and her husband had resumed relations. Fair enough, Adam had thought. She obviously wanted children whether the husband did or not. That was none of his business. He'd been somewhat concerned at the sex toys he'd also noticed, figuring she obviously still wanted to maintain 'relations' with him.

Adam swilled back his beer contemplatively. He hadn't wanted to do any of that with Sienna. He could imagine doing it, all and any of it, if she asked him to. Or none of it, if she didn't enjoy it. He hadn't been having sex with her. He *had* been making love to her. And he'd wanted to see her, all of her, not just body bits. To see what she might be feeling. He'd thought he had seen; it was there in her eyes.

And what had he done afterwards? He'd pulled on his clothes and left her in the bed on her own. Why? Why had he done that? To protect her feelings? No, to protect his own. Selfish bastard.

So, what should he do? Tell Sherry the truth and get out of town, he supposed. Nate had made it clear he didn't want him around. Sienna certainly wouldn't want to see him again. She'd been crying on the drive home. Quietly, her face turned away, hoping he wouldn't see. But she had been, and it had cracked his heart wide open. Yet he'd hardly said a word. He hadn't even walked her back to her cottage. Lived right up to his reputation, hadn't he?

Nate was right. He needed help. And he did need to move on, for everyone's sake: Lily-Grace's, Sienna's. It would be pretty difficult to move on without his boat, though, and there was no way his current finances would allow him to get the engine and electrical circuits up to scratch. He'd definitely need to replace some of the old wiring, if he was going to run everything from the batteries. Dammit, he really could do with staying at the marina where he had access to the workshop and mains, for a while at least.

Pondering, he headed to the fridge to fetch another beer. He was beginning to lose track of how much booze he was getting through lately. Too much, he guessed, determined to ignore the sudden cloud of sadness that enveloped him as he returned to the lounge and the shadowy figure that beckoned him from the front door. Emily, again, no doubt here to remind him that making her cry wasn't the way to win a girl's heart.

Sienna declined the beer Nathaniel offered her. 'I've been having a few too many wines lately,' she confessed, a bit guiltily.

'Medicinal purposes?' Nathaniel enquired, raising an eyebrow.

Sienna nodded. He knew, she suspected, what had happened between her and Adam. Probably because he seemed to know Adam better than anyone, which is why, after moping around the last few days, she'd taken up his invitation to 'talk'.

'Me too.' He gave her a smile of commiseration and poured himself a beer.

'Nate, can I ask you something,' Sienna started hesitantly, 'about Adam?'

'He drinks too many of these, for a start,' Nathaniel said, puffing out an agitated breath and seating himself at his desk. 'Have a seat, Sienna, I don't really bite.' He softened his tone, as she fiddled nervously with a strand of her hair.

'Thanks.' She took up his offer gratefully. 'About the argument you and he were having the other day...'

Nathaniel looked uncomfortable.

'... about his history.'

'I said more than I ought to, Sienna.' Nathaniel now looked very uncomfortable. 'You should ask Adam.'

'Please, Nate. I need to understand.' Sienna looked at

him imploringly.

Nathaniel regarded her thoughtfully. 'Yes,' he said with a lengthy sigh, 'I imagine you probably do. It didn't come from me, though, okay? He prefers to keep his business to himself, Sienna, so don't quote me.'

'I won't,' Sienna promised. She wasn't sure she'd ever have a proper conversation with Adam again after their no-conversation journey on the way home from the cottage and the fact that she hadn't seen him since, but she needed to try to understand a little about why he was like he was. 'What happened, Nate, with his brother?'

Nathaniel debated, taking another dink as he did, and then drew in a breath. 'Adam found his girlfriend in bed with him,' he said bluntly. 'His fiancée, to be precise.'

'Oh, no!' Sienna clamped a hand to her mouth.

'It gets worse, I'm afraid.' Nathaniel hesitated, looking her over again. 'Turns out she was pregnant.'

Pregnant? Sienna balked. *With Adam's baby?*

'That's when Adam went on his first bender. Couldn't blame him for that one, though, I suppose,' Nathaniel went on, his gaze on his beer can. 'He was gutted, like a madman. Drunk himself into a semi-permanent stupor. She was his first love, you see. He was bowled over by her the first time he saw her, totally in love with her. And Adam in love is a very different man.' Nathaniel paused, shaking his head sadly.

'What happened?' Sienna's voice came out a croak.

'They split up, no surprise there. Adam wouldn't have anything to do with her. His brother either.'

'But … why would he do it? To his own brother?' Sienna asked, incredulous.

'Who knows?' Nathaniel shrugged. 'Darren and Adam had always been competitive. Truth was, it didn't sit well with Darren that his little brother might be better than him at anything. He was jealous, I think. Adam was the better sportsman, communicator, better-looking. His mother seemed to favour Adam over both Darren and his dad, basically because he wasn't like them. Adam was more like her, caring of people's feelings. At least, he was then. Darren ribbed him about it, mercilessly sometimes, calling him – forgive the expression – a "soft twat". Adam tried to shrug it off most of the time. Finding his brother in bed with his fiancée wasn't going to be so easy to shrug off, though, was it?' Nathaniel stopped angrily.

'Oh God ...' Sienna's stomach knotted inside her. 'He must have been so devastated.'

'Devastated doesn't even come close.' Nathaniel took another drink and then went on. 'Adam and Emily had been at some family do, drink flowing, you know. They'd been having a few problems, quite a few actually. Adam didn't want his old life, you see. He wanted to get as far away from it as possible, once they were married. Unfortunately, he didn't communicate that very well. They argued, a real humdinger of an argument. I'm guessing, because Adam's not inclined to talk about it, that Emily thought he wanted to call the wedding off. Obviously she was pretty upset and pretty drunk, and, from what I gathered, Darren took his chance. He'd always been a womaniser, following in their father's footsteps. Their dad was just the same, cheating on their mother and not even behind her back half the time. Can you believe the man actually told Adam he should just forget about it, that blood was thicker than water and he should put it behind him and move on?' Nathaniel laughed wryly. 'That's exactly what Adam did in the end. Walked away: from his fiancée, his family, the family fortune. Bought his boat, and moved on.'

'And the baby?' Sienna hardly dared ask.

'She had it. Adam heard about the birth. Emily's sister

messaged him. And then, well, Adam surprised me, to be honest. He didn't even know the baby was his, but he said he wanted to see her, Emily, too, try to sort things out in some way.'

'And?' Sienna swallowed back a hard lump in her throat.

'Are you sure you want to hear all this, Sienna? It's not pretty.'

Sienna nodded. Part of her didn't want to hear it; it was too painful. Her heart physically ached for Adam, whose heart must have been shattered into a million pieces. She needed to know though, absolutely. It might not change anything. He was what he was, but at least she'd know some of why.

'Emily had taken off, it seemed. Taken the baby and left her flat. No one had any idea where she'd gone. Her sister was frantic. Turned out Emily was suffering from post-natal depression.'

'Oh, no.' Sienna closed her eyes, her heart plummeting, for Adam and Emily both. 'What did he do?'

'He went to see his brother, hoping he might have some idea where she was. Darren, half-pissed in the pub, apparently didn't know and didn't care. Long story short, they fought. Things got ugly. Darren picked up a bottle.'

'His scars?' Sienna had assumed they were the result of some street fight. Labelled bad, she'd assumed he … She'd judged him, just like everyone else seemed to.

Nathaniel nodded. 'Adam came out on top eventually. He was fitter, stronger. Broke his brother's jaw, actually, serve the bastard right. Pity he didn't do the same to his loving father. Uncaring bastard, he really dug the knife in.'

Nathaniel paused, crushing his beer can in his hand. 'I still can't get my head around it,' he went on, with a disbelieving laugh, 'that a man would tell his own son that if he'd been more of a man, she wouldn't have looked elsewhere.'

'Dear *God!*' Sienna wiped away tears she hadn't realised she was crying. Tears for Adam.

'There's more, I'm afraid. Something Adam will blame himself for for the rest of his life. He needs help, Sienna, but I'm not sure he can be fixed.'

'What?' *What more could there possibly be?* Sienna caught a breath in her throat – then squeezed her eyes shut as Nathaniel's gaze flew to the door.

'Not interrupting anything, am I?' Adam said behind her.

'No! Nothing.' Sienna jumped to her feet, glancing uncertainly towards him. 'Thanks, Nate,' she said. 'I'll settle the plumber's bill as soon as—'

'Don't go on my account.' Adam smiled shortly. 'I only needed a quick word.' He raked his hand through his hair, looking from Nathaniel to her questioningly. 'About my boat.'

He took another step in and seemed to sway on his feet.

At which Nathaniel looked him over suspiciously. 'Are you driving?'

'I'm a bastard, Nate, not an idiot,' Adam told him, and then furrowed his brow. 'On second thoughts ...' He glanced at Sienna.

Sienna dropped her gaze. 'I really should go,' she mumbled, moving towards the door.

'Can I leave it here,' Adam asked Nathaniel, 'my boat? I don't have anywhere else.' He shrugged and waited – and swayed.

Sienna glanced at Nathaniel. He looked doubtful.

'I'll pay the fee. In fact,' Adam fumbled in his jeans pockets and pulled out some notes, 'here,' he said, focussing his gaze to walk unsteadily to Nathaniel's desk. 'It's not all I owe you, but you'll get the rest as soon—'

'Adam, for—'

'Just until I get her seaworthy,' Adam cut in. 'I won't stay overnight, so you won't have to worry about ...' He shot Sienna an awkward glance this time. 'I'll work on her during the day. Just me.'

Nathaniel glanced at Sienna. *Please say yes*, she willed him.

'No exshtra ... extra curricul ...' Adam stopped, furrowed his brow and tried again. 'No women,' he finished.

'Well done, Adam.' Nathaniel shook his head despairingly, as Sienna looked hurriedly down again. 'Okay. Okay, whatever. Just go, Adam.' Nathaniel got to his feet, coming around his desk to steer Adam in the right direction. 'Get some sleep.'

'Right, yep. Will do. Exactly what I'm intending to do.' Adam took a step, and then hesitated. 'By the way,' he said, looking again at Sienna. 'I just wanted to, er ... You know, say thanks.'

'Idiot.' Nathaniel rolled his eyes, as Adam walked through the door – and then promptly disappeared.

'Oh, my God! Adam!' Sienna flew after him.

'Here we go.' Nathaniel sighed, heading swiftly out behind her.

'Shit. Somebody moved the steps,' Adam said, from where he sat outside the office, scratching his head, looking very puzzled, and definitely the worse for wear.

'Adam ...' Sienna moved towards him. 'Are you hurt?'

'No.' Adam held up a hand, clearly not requiring her assistance. 'I'm fine,' he said, and shook his head, probably free of stars.

'Come on.' Nathaniel eyed the skies as he walked past Sienna to hook one of Adam's arms over his shoulders. 'You need to sober up, mate. Permanently, might be a good idea.'

'I'm fine,' Adam insisted, as Nathaniel heaved him to his feet. 'Just a bit ...'

'Drunk?' Nathaniel finished. 'How many, Adam?'

'Two.' Adam held up three fingers.

'At least six then.' Nathaniel shook his head. 'Come on, let's get you to bed.'

'That's what all the girls say.' Adam smiled wryly, as Nathaniel steered him around towards his boat.

'Just for tonight, Adam. I meant what I said.'

Watching their precarious progress, Sienna chewed worriedly on her lower lip. She hated seeing him like this, so dejected, so down, so drunk. If she had made a mistake sleeping with him, it was clear Adam considered he'd made a bigger one. All he'd already been through, and now he was about to become homeless, which was obviously why he'd felt inclined to impart his soul-crushing thanks. Served her right, she supposed. She wished he hadn't though. The way he'd looked at her, half-looked at her, it had felt like a blow to her heart.

He couldn't remember how many he'd had. Adam closed an eye, and then … *ouch!* He winced as he nicked himself shaving. Too many. Nate was right, again. He needed to cut back. Stemming the blood flow with a wad of tissue, he supposed he should collect some stuff while he was here. He'd stay at the cottage, assuming Sherry wouldn't mind. Short-term, though. He really did need to sort himself out, formulate some plan of action. At least he had access to the marina now. Nate had texted him, probably because he'd rather avoid seeing him. He'd made it pretty clear that what he'd said still stood. Adam could come and go, but only to work on his boat. Other than that, he obviously wasn't welcome. Time to move on, Adam guessed. The sooner the better. Nicole still hadn't contacted him and Sienna would be glad to see the back of him, after what she no doubt considered to be the biggest embarrassment of her life. And it was pretty obvious Nate had a soft spot for her, so ... All in all, he'd be doing everyone a favour if he left, which was what he'd intended to do anyway. Wide open spaces and a girl in every port would suit him just fine.

Swilling his face, he grabbed a towel and tried very hard to stop thinking about making love to Sienna. The taste of her, the look in her eyes, one of such sweet ecstasy, his heart had kicked back in surprise. Strange, how he'd felt more of a man at that moment than he ever had when any other woman had huskily assured him how amazing he was.

He'd made love, for the first time in a very long time, and it had been pretty damn incredible. Adam smiled wistfully, wrapping the towel around his midriff and heading out of the bathroom for a second strong cup of coffee.

He didn't notice the envelope until after he was dressed and was tying his laces – a white envelope poking through a slat in one of the air vents on the door. Standing, he finished the dregs of his coffee and went to retrieve it. No stamp, he noticed. His name on the front in elegant handwriting. A woman's handwriting, he guessed. Curiously he opened the envelope and peered inside. Then, puzzled, he pulled out the twenty pound notes – five of them – and the notepaper tucked in there with them.

Yep, definitely a woman's handwriting: Sienna's. Adam looked at the signature first, then read the message, and felt his heart kickback in an entirely different way. *Not sure if this is enough,* he read. *Let me know if I owe you anything. Oh, and thanks to you, too.*

My pleasure. Adam swallowed back a tight knot in his chest. Not such sweet ecstasy, after all then. He glanced at the ceiling and squeezed his eyes shut tight.

He really was a prat, wasn't he? Swallowing again, trying very hard to stay calm, Adam yanked the cushions from the seating area, dug his holdall out from underneath it, stuffed whatever came to hand in it, not much caring what it was, and then headed out of the door, fast, before he was tempted to give in to the almost overwhelming urge to put his fist through it.

'I suppose you think I'm being hard on him,' Nathaniel commented as he and Sienna watched through the chandlery window: Adam throwing his bag onto the bank, then leaping the handrail after it.

Sienna watched him storm off, his hand going through his hair, his expression as thunderous as she'd seen once before, at the cottage, before he'd made love to her so exquisitely. A tremor rippled through her tummy muscles as she thought about the things he'd done to her. She couldn't believe it was no more than casual sex for him.

She wasn't sure what she thought about his having to leave permanently. Adam certainly seemed to be living up to his bad news image. Making sure she knew he considered himself an idiot having anything to do with her, then offering her a casual 'thanks', as if she'd given him a not very inspiring sandwich, rather than her virginity. She really should hate him. After what Nathaniel had told her, though, all she could do was feel wretched for him. She liked him. Despite everything, his reputation, his self-confessed abysmal behaviour, she absolutely knew there was another side to him, a gentle, caring side. Underneath, he was hurting. That was plain to see, to her at least, and she just wanted to hold him, which did make her completely insane, she supposed.

'I probably am a bit,' Nathaniel went on when she didn't answer. 'But he really needs to think about where he's going, Sienna. My seeming to condone what he's doing, being matey with him, well, it's just sending him wrong signals, isn't it?'

Sienna nodded slowly. Her dad would certainly agree. Enabling, he'd call it. Maybe she should ask him about Adam's problems. Yes, marvellous idea. There's this man I know, he drinks too much and he's a sex addict. Any ideas how we can help him? Oh, and I slept with him – and would again at the drop of a hat, if he asked me. But Adam wouldn't, would he? Would never have entertained the idea in the first place if she hadn't done the asking. Hiring, she corrected herself and made excuses to go inside. Tears over Adam were tears wasted, but if nothing else, they might be therapeutic.

Chapter Seven

Adam threw his holdall on the sofa, pulling out the bottle of Merlot he'd found tucked behind the lifebelt on his deck, just where she'd said she'd left it. 'Cheers, Sienna.' He smiled cynically and headed for the kitchen to uncork it.

Dispensing with the glass, the bottle was poised at his mouth when his eye snagged on the wall clock. Ten-thirty. It was half past ten in the morning and he was about to go on a bender? Why? So he could lie about half-soaked, feeling sorry for himself? Which, it occurred to him, was his usual excuse for doing nothing about anything. It even had him seeing things that weren't there. Trying hard to convince himself, once again, that it was all in his alcohol addled mind, he turned away from the ethereal form that seemed to pop up more and more often, insistent on doggedly haunting him.

Was he really going to get his boat up and running if he spent most of his day three sheets to the wind? Make plans and carry them out for once, he chastised himself. Do something about who he was, instead of not liking who he was and making damn sure everyone else did, too. *You know what, sunshine,* he addressed himself soberly, *if I was Sienna, I wouldn't have come near you with a barge pole.*

To top it all off, it looked like Nicole wasn't about to let Lily-Grace anywhere near him either, if the lack of messages over the last couple of weeks was anything to go by. Adam couldn't say he blamed her. Was it likely she'd want a man who odd-jobbed for an income and had no assets to his name anywhere near Lily-Grace? Someone who spent what spare cash he did have on booze and his spare time flitting from woman to woman?

Dammit, he really did need to sort himself out, starting now. He re-corked the bottle. He'd have a beer maybe, later, but not wine, not at breakfast time. He had no breakfast, of course. Sherry had stocked up with every conceivable item that would keep a man happy, apart from food. But then, he was only supposed to be here on a come and go basis, wasn't he? Sighing, Adam headed back for the front door, mentally calculating how much money he had actually got. Money of his own, that was. He'd rather starve than use the payment for services rendered from Sienna. So, did he have enough for a supermarket shop? Probably not.

Oh, no. He groaned inside, noting a car approaching as he walked to his own. Sherry. He hoped she hadn't come with anything more than conversation in mind. After seeing Sienna's not so cryptic note, as much as part of him wanted to say stuff it and carry on the way he had been, there was another part of him that just didn't have the heart.

Fancying it might be a bit bad-mannered if he just climbed in his car and drove off, Adam waited. He kept his hand on his car door, though, hoping Sherry wouldn't hang about.

'Adam, hi!' she said, through her open window. 'I didn't expect to find you here. I brought some things. Some food,' she said, climbing out and retrieving carrier bags from the boot. 'Just a few bits and bobs: bread for the freezer, bacon and eggs for the fridge. I thought you might need your energy levels topping up.' She gave him one of her lingering looks, her eyes coming to rest belt-level. 'Especially as you're going to be here at odd times.'

'Ah, about that, Sherry ...' Adam followed her to the front door.

Sherry looked at him expectantly, once inside.

'I wondered if you would mind if I spent a bit more time here.' Adam shrugged hopefully.

Sherry now gave him a quizzical look.

'Just a few days.' Adam took the bags from her and headed for the kitchen.

'How so?' Sherry followed him.

'Nate, he's, er … Well, he's a bit prickly at the moment.'

'Nathaniel, prickly?' Sherry gawked, astonished. 'With you? I don't believe it.' She set to stowing the shopping. 'What did you do this time, Adam? It must have been something bad to rile Nathaniel. He's generally so even-tempered.'

'Erm, I think it was more a case of what *we* did,' Adam supplied, a bit unfairly. Sherry was one of several women he'd entertained on the boat, but he hoped that might help persuade her to let him stay until he could sort somewhere else out. 'The, er, noise we made attracted a little too much attention,' he elaborated, as she glanced at him, still looking puzzled.

'Oh,' she said, smiling coquettishly as the penny obviously dropped. 'We did a bit, didn't we?'

'A lot,' Adam assured her. 'I thought I might have to gag you at one point.'

'Now, there's an idea.' Sherry took a step towards him, trailing a long fingernail across his chest. Adam eased back an inch. Sex really wasn't on his mind right then, particularly the sort that resulted in physical injury.

'So?' he asked, mentally crossing his fingers.

'Well,' Sherry pondered, 'I suppose it would be all right. But, whatever you do, if James asks, you're paying rent. He throws a wobbly if I let girlfriends have a freebie holiday here. He'd go ballistic if he thought I was letting a man stay here for free. Let alone a man who makes love to me so spectacularly.' Sherry lowered her eyelashes coyly, now rotating a fingernail around his midriff, as if choosing her spot.

Adam gulped, his mind boggling at what a ballistic husband with a shotgun would do if he did find out he was sleeping with his wife, spectacularly or any other way. He wouldn't have any trouble choosing his spot. Adam had no doubt about that.

'You don't have to pay rent, of course.' Sherry plumped for his jaw, her nail possibly giving him a closer shave than his razor had. 'You can pay me in kind. And …'

She grazed the long red-painted nail slowly from his chin to his torso.

'… as you *are* here.'

Crap! Adam caught her hand as she hooked the nail over his waistband. 'Sherry,' he said, wondering how to tell her he'd rather have a bacon sandwich without hurting her feelings, 'I, er … It's a bit early, don't you think?'

'What, for Mr Ever-ready?' She looked at him as if he'd just announced he was celibate, and reached for the button on his jeans.

'Sherry.' He caught her hands firmly. 'I'm really not up to it.'

'Not up to it?' She looked at him bemusedly. 'I thought you were the local Casanova, ready to fulfil a woman's every desire at the drop of a hat.'

'I am, usually,' Adam assured her, though he was definitely beginning to feel a little less ever-ready.

'But not this morning?' Sherry huffed up her magnificent breasts. But tempting though they were, Adam really didn't have the heart. Even though Sienna had 'hired' him, and bloody well paid him – a surge of humiliation flashed through him – after making love with her, all this seemed tacky. Soulless, somehow.

Sherry planted her hands on her hips, clearly peeved. 'So you wouldn't be interested if I offered you a blowjob then?'

Ouch! That was below the belt.

Adam looked her over, noting that flicker of vulnerability in her eyes he'd seen once before, and felt like a complete heel. 'I'd be more than interested, Sherry,' he said softly, 'normally. You're amazing, truly. It's just … I have the mother of all migraines coming on.'

'Oh, no.' Sherry knitted her brow sympathetically.

'Sorry.' Adam smiled weakly and massaged his temples. 'I'd much rather take you to bed, but I really do think I need to lie down on my own.'

'Poor you.' Sherry brushed his cheek with her hand. 'You should have said. I wouldn't have stood here wittering on ten to the dozen, if you had. Go on, you go and tuck yourself up,' she said, genuinely concerned, which made Adam feel even worse. 'I'll bring you some tea.'

'No,' Adam said quickly. 'I, er, don't think I fancy even that. I'll just go and …' He nodded towards the stairs, thinking he really might need to lie down. He'd just been offered a blowjob and he'd said thanks, but no thanks?

Clearly bored with Saturday morning TV, Lauren wandered into the kitchen to peer over Sienna's shoulder at her PC. 'He put his warm tongue *where*?'

'Stop it,' Sienna hissed, scrunching her shoulders forward to cover her screen.

'What's the matter with you? You're writing a script,' Lauren pointed out. 'You're not going to sell it if you don't want people to read it.'

'It's not ready to share yet,' Sienna said, her cheeks burning as she realised Lauren was still helping herself anyway. 'I'm still trying to work my characters out.'

'Looks like your characters are having a thorough workout from where I'm standing.' Lauren leaned closer. 'Did he really do that?'

Sienna squirmed in her seat, embarrassed. 'He's a fictional

character, Lauren,' she informed her, doing her best to look pious.

''Course he is.' Lauren smirked knowingly and read on – out loud, to Sienna's mortification. '*Thumb now expertly circling ... sucking and tenderly biting*. Was he? Tender?' She glanced sideways at Sienna.

Sienna refused to elucidate, but she couldn't quite hide her smile.

Lauren read on, '*I won't hurt you. If I do, tell me to stop. Okay?* Aw, bless.' She sighed dreamily, and read on, '*Open your eyes, Melissa. I want to see you.*'

Lauren sniffled. 'I think I may cry. Melissa doesn't suit you, though, Sienna. You need to change that. Shove over.'

Her bottom perched next to Sienna, Lauren blinked and peered closer. '*Slowly increasing the pace, his eyes on hers, building the momentum, until he felt so incredibly deep ... she whimpered, as he picked up the tempo, thrusting still deeper, and deeper...* Bloody hell, Sienna!' Lauren fanned her face. 'He really does know what he's doing, doesn't he?'

Sienna answered with a long, wistful sigh.

'Well, okay, I can see what you see in him, I suppose,' Lauren conceded, then eyes wide, she read on, '*... undulating ... thrust for thrust ... wanted him to enjoy it, even if he did get ... PAID for it!*'

Lauren paused. She didn't say anything. She didn't look at Sienna. Her expression tight, she continued to read instead, '*pulled away from her, climbed off the bed, discarded the used condom and proceeded to get dressed.*'

Lauren stopped, inhaled deeply, and then exhaled so hard her nostrils flared. 'Bastard,' she said, standing abruptly.

'Lauren, it's fiction,' Sienna called as her friend stomped out of the kitchen, falling over a disgruntled Tobias in the process.

'It's not true, Lauren!' Sienna tried again. 'Lauren, where

are you going?'

'Electrodes,' Lauren supplied. 'I'm going to ask Nathaniel if I can borrow some from the workshop and then I'm going to find Adam and attach them.'

Adam waited until Sherry had driven off and then went back downstairs, now feeling incredibly guilty. He doubted Sherry would have offered him the use of the cottage if she'd realised he actually wasn't interested in using it for anything other than sleeping in. He genuinely wasn't either. He felt about as capable of drumming up the enthusiasm for sex as he could for swimming the channel.

'Yeah, yeah, you can gloat,' he addressed his ghost, which now seemed to be doing just that, ghosting his every bloody step. The sadness he usually felt emanating from her wasn't so overwhelmingly intense, though, he noted. What did she want? Why did she seem to be appearing more and more through this whole mess with Sienna? A mess he'd created, but which, yet again, meant he was losing people he cared for. He sensed she needed something, but he still had no real clue what.

Blimey, he was talking to it now. Adam shook his head, and then addressed the product of his imagination again. 'You're not here,' he told it, walking towards the mist, defiantly through it, and then stopping dead. He could smell her. Emily. He tugged his shirt to his face; breathed the unmistakeable scent of her. The perfume she wore. The same perfume he'd bought for her and which had clung to his clothes for hours after he'd seen her. Nuts. He was going nuts. There was no other explanation. She wasn't *here*.

Adam could still feel her, sense her, watching him. He didn't turn around.

He needed to sleep, he told himself firmly, but headed for the kitchen instead. He needed at least one night's dream-free, Emily-free, unbroken sleep. Yet he knew he couldn't sleep here. Taking advantage of Sherry's hospitality under the circumstances would definitely be taking the proverbial. He'd have to find an excuse and find somewhere else, he realised. He should never have accepted the key, which in itself must have looked like some kind of long-term commitment, however loose a commitment, to Sherry.

So when did he grow a conscience, he pondered as he opened the fridge, retrieving the bacon – and deciding he'd rather have a beer. When he'd made love with Sienna. Slept with, he corrected himself.

He'd thought he'd had everything he wanted, sex in abundance, no complications – though shotgun wielding husbands might come under the heading complication, he supposed. He could come and go as he pleased. Have a drink when he chose to. It suited him. So, why did his life feel so hollow? Adam reached for the beer. He'd stop at two, he promised himself. Why did this all feel so distasteful, and why did he suddenly want to see Lily-Grace, put roots down? Hadn't his last attempt to do that almost destroyed him?

Wasn't going to happen, though, was it? Nicole had obviously had second thoughts and women seemed only to want him for his body. Smiling ironically, he knocked back his beer. Must be worth having, after all, he supposed; the only part of him worth having. A conclusion Sienna had quickly come to. She *paid* him, for pity's sake!

Stuff it. He downed the rest of the can. Who cared? You could love someone with your whole bloody heart and soul. He had. And look where that had got him. Hadn't he found out the hard way that happy endings don't exist? No, he'd stay as he was. He'd get enough money together and move on, get laid, not look back, somehow forget about Sienna. Wide open spaces. That's what he needed, just him, on his own.

'If you were hoping to pen a happy ending, I think your readers are going to be sadly disappointed, Sienna,' Lauren said, grabbing up her Doritos big pack and heading off in her bikini to sun herself outside.

How does she do that? Sienna wondered. Eat everything and anything calorific by the big bagful and still fit in her teeny-weeny bikini? Sienna only had to lick the salt off a crisp and she gained ten pounds. Adam hadn't seemed to mind how her body looked, though. Sienna sighed, a shuddery sigh, right down to her pelvis, which flipped then dipped exquisitely as she thought of his mouth exploring her deepest, most intimate places. Oh God, if only she could stop thinking about him. The panic clouding his beautiful chocolate-brown eyes when he'd thought he'd hurt her. How those eyes had darkened, smouldering with desire, as he'd buried himself deep inside her; his throaty, masculine groan as he came.

Sienna sighed wistfully again. 'I am planning a happy ending,' she called after her as Lauren disappeared through the door. 'I'm thinking of getting my heroine to stowaway in his boat and sail off into the sunset with him.'

'Being thrown overboard is not a happy ending, Sienna,' Lauren replied.

Sienna sighed again, mournfully, and stared at her blank screen. She hadn't got an ending. She hadn't even got a middle. What she had got was writer's block when it came to imagining the other women in her hero's life. What Adam had done with her might not have been driven by passion-fuelled desire, but it wasn't passionless. Naïve she might be, but she wasn't wrong about that, Sienna was sure. She was struggling, therefore, to reconcile Adam-the-super-stud with the man who'd made love to her so sensitively. All of which gave her fodder for her script but, when it came to the writing, her mouth went dry, her stomach clenched, and her mind just couldn't conjure it up. Her characters were copulating camels again. Damn. Sienna jabbed the off button on her PC without even closing her files. She'd take Tobias for a walk before going to work in the pub, she decided.

The man really was an enigma, wasn't he? She pondered this as she pulled on her trainers. Bedding women all over the show, no doubt breaking hearts in the process, when he'd had his own heart so badly broken. No, she simply couldn't reconcile the Adam she'd glimpsed in private with the cocky, carefree man he presented in public. She couldn't save him. With his drinking, his womanising, it would be a hopeless task, but she was positive under there somewhere was a man worth saving, if only he'd realise it himself.

'Come on, Tobias.' She picked up her mobile, quickly deleted this morning's string of upsetting texts from her ex, and reached for the dog's lead. 'Let's go and walk off our frustrations.' She'd have to walk a blooming long way, though, to walk off hers.

Chapter Eight

As usual, Adam felt like the guy in the black cowboy hat as he walked into the pub, all eyes swivelling in his direction and a distinct lull in the conversation as he made his way to the bar. Ah, well, if he was providing the entertainment, fair enough. It was what he was good at, after all.

Ordering a beer and a whisky chaser from the unimpressed looking landlord, he made his way to a quiet corner seat, avoiding cool glances from some of the blokes and eye contact with any of the female clientele, as he did. He wasn't really sure why he was here but, now he was, he didn't want Sienna to see him ogling other women. Which was nuts. She probably wouldn't give a damn how many women he ogled, expected him to, no doubt. Adam wasn't going there, though, not tonight. Despite his promises to himself to forget about her and go back to his lifestyle just the way it was, he was tired, and the tiniest bit inebriated. He didn't want company but, after sitting in the cottage, feeling trapped by the walls and no one to talk to but an uncommunicative waft of mist, he wanted to be *in* company. Did he really want to be in Sienna's company, though? The woman who had sent him possibly the most humiliating Dear John letter ever, and who looked anything but thrilled he was here?

Watching her carefully, jealousy slicing through him every time she smiled that radiant smile at a customer, chatted with someone, Adam noted how she was pointedly not looking at him. What did he expect? That she was going to wave and beam a smile at the local Casanova ... sad bastard, he corrected himself. Not likely, was it?

Adam swallowed and glanced away noticing, as he did,

Sherry sitting across the room, her husband at her side. She wasn't about to wave cheerily either, by the expression on her face. She was staring at him as if she was trying to bore holes in his skull; glancing from him to Sienna and back.

Adam looked away, definitely feeling guilty now as it occurred to him she might have cottoned on to something between Sienna and him, albeit something of little consequence, apparently. But then, Sherry knew the score. She was married, and he was what he was. They were 'friends with benefits,' that was all. They'd both known it was never going to be anything more.

Uh oh, the killer looks were obviously catching. Adam smiled sardonically to himself as Nathaniel walked in with Lauren, both of them pausing only to give him a derisory glance, before walking away to find a table in a more desirable location. He really had got everyone's back up, hadn't he? He supposed he probably would, eventually. It had happened before. He was a bit gutted about Nate, though. Nate was a good mate. He'd been there for him, no matter what. Yes, and Adam had taken it for granted he would always be, no matter what.

Great. Here he was, sitting in a crowded pub, and he felt lonelier right then than he ever had. He should go he supposed. Get out of everyone's hair. One more for the road and he would. He waited a while, choosing his moment to go to the bar when Sienna was busy, for the sake of her embarrassment, as well as his own. How he'd feel if she snubbed him completely, he wasn't sure. Like getting drunk, he supposed. Or rather, even more drunk than he already was, drowning his sorrows, yet again.

Adam noted again Sherry's none-too-friendly gaze on him as he made his way across the lounge. The husband, he also noted, was intently watching her watching him. Realising the situation might get a little awkward, Adam decided leaving sooner rather than later might be wise, and detoured to the exit instead, only to meet one of the gang of thugs who seemed to have it in for him coming in. Unable to avoid him in the small foyer, Adam met his decidedly unfriendly gaze briefly and then reeled inside as he noted the woman at the man's side.

Crap. The penny dropped, resoundingly. Rebekah, the woman the landlord had caught him red-handed with in the car park.

The youth took a swift step towards him as Adam considered whether speaking to her would be prudent. 'If you ever so much as glance in my sister's direction again, you're dead, mate. *Got it*?' the guy snarled in his face.

Definitely not prudent. Adam answered with a short nod, his eyes gliding towards Rebekah nevertheless, which earned him a sharp shove in the shoulder.

'Waster,' the guy said, his gaze definitely malevolent as he backed off to hitch hold of his sister's arm and lead her on into the pub.

Yep, that pretty much summed him up. Offering Rebekah a small smile anyway as she smiled at him over her shoulder, Adam headed on out, almost missed the step down, and then stopped, and sighed.

'Great,' he muttered despondently, and extracted his feet from a very large and very wet puddle. Hunching his shoulders against the lashing rain, Adam felt for the car keys in his pocket, glanced at the car, took a step towards it, then ... Uh-uh, he pulled himself up sharp. He really didn't think he'd bother to swim right now if he took a wrong turn at the river. He wasn't about to ruin anyone else's life, though. Be responsible for someone else's death.

History. Forget it, Adam reminded himself, sucking in a deep breath and turning for the road. It would probably take him fifteen minutes, or ... 'Oops.' He reeled to one side ... forever. He'd be soaking wet as well as legless when he did get there, but at least his conscience would be clear. God, how he wished that could be so.

'Adam!' He heard behind him as he trudged roughly in the right direction. 'Adam!'

He turned back, squinting through the rain to see someone hurrying towards him. Sienna?

'Are you all right?' she asked when she reached him, her coat over her head, mud and water splashed up her gorgeous bare legs.

'Fine.' He smiled, surprised. 'Great, in fact,' he assured her, dragging a hand through his hair.

She looked him over, looking not very convinced.

'Well, not great, but ...' Adam shrugged, '... you know, okay. You?'

'Good,' she said, holding his gaze with those mesmerising green eyes.

'Right. Good,' he parroted, like an idiot.

'I just wanted to check,' Sienna said, glancing down and then back. 'You seemed a bit ...' she trailed off, obviously trying to be diplomatic.

'Drunk,' Adam supplied. 'I am a bit, but I'm okay. Thanks for checking I wasn't lying in the car park, though. And, er, thanks for your note, by the way. It was ... unexpected.'

Sienna looked indignant. 'And *thanks* for your *thanks*. I'm glad you appreciated the goods,' she said, those telltale bright spots flushing her cheeks and a pout on her infinitely kissable lips. If only Adam could lean forward without falling on his face, which though he seriously doubted it, he was tempted to try.

What did she mean, thanks for *his* thanks, though? Puzzled, Adam scrambled through his befuddled brain. Oh, hell. Nathaniel's office! He'd been legless then, too. He hadn't been able to come up with a single coherent word when he'd realised she was there. What a moron.

'That was crass.' Adam glanced sheepishly at his shoes. 'I didn't mean to be flippant. I meant ...' *What?* 'I didn't know what to say, with Nate there. I didn't want you to think ...' *Oh, sod it.* 'It was fantastic, Sienna. The, er ... What we did, together. It was ...'

'Nor did I mean to be flippant,' Sienna said, nipping nervously on her bottom lip. Oh, how Adam wished those were his teeth. 'It was beautiful.' She smiled right at him.

'Really?' Adam's heartbeat ratcheted up a notch.

She nodded. 'Really.'

'Right.' He swallowed. 'I, erm ...' *Say something, twit. Something romantic. Something half-intelligent. Anything.* 'Good,' he said. *Way to go, Adam.* He sighed at his ineptitude, then sighed heavily again as the landlord emerged from the pub foyer.

'Sienna! We've got a bar full of customers,' he yelled. 'Are you going to stand out there all night?'

Sienna rolled her eyes. 'I have to go. Be careful how you walk home, Adam.'

'I will.' Adam nodded. 'Sienna ...' he said quickly as she turned. 'Are you all right? I mean, after ... Are you okay?'

She looked back at him. 'Perfect,' she assured him.

Definitely. Adam smiled. 'More than!' he shouted through the rain, as she hurried back. 'All over!'

She'd spoken to him. Bemused, Adam walked the first few yards slowly. She'd smiled at him. He picked up his pace, pulling the damp air into his lungs as he walked. She'd said it was ... beautiful. Not amazing, with a come-hither look in her eye. Not spectacular, with a coy flutter of the eyelashes. Beautiful. She'd said it was ...

Beautiful, she was the most beautiful woman he'd ever met. Ever made love to. She was ... lovely. Utterly, totally...

Adam stopped and shook his head. Was it possible he was falling in love with her?

Contemplating, his brow furrowed, he started walking again. He was. His heart banged against his chest. Nice to meet you it said, then kicked its heels and did a backflip. Not falling. *Fallen*, hook, line and sinker. He loved her. He really did. *Shit*! He was soaking wet, too drunk to walk straight, and absolutely besotted. Laughing incredulously, he tugged up his collar and increased his pace to a jog.

Catching his breath, he stopped at the bridge over the river. 'I love her.' He practised it out loud. 'I love her,' he said it again, still not quite able to get his head around it. Then hitching himself up on the low-brick wall, he got precariously to his feet and, arms outstretched, shouted, 'Sienna, I bloody well *love* you!'

The cows in the field weren't very impressed. And nor, Adam realised, unaware of the car idling on the road until he turned, was Sherry.

Adam felt a bit of an idiot when he woke up to find he was hugging the pillow. He knew who he'd rather have been hugging. Chances she might reciprocate his feelings, though? Nil, mate, he told himself, ignoring the dull thud in his head and throwing back the duvet. Not unless he did something about himself, now as opposed to maybe, someday.

Reaching for his mobile and finding no message from Nicole, he forced back his disappointment, and went to ferret around in his bag for something suitable to wear. He hadn't done this in a long time. Too long a time. He'd suffer for it initially, but no pain, no gain, he told himself.

'You seem to be hovering a bit lighter,' he addressed his seemingly more buoyant spectre. Was it possible Emily approved of Sienna? More likely she approved of the fact that he'd decided promiscuity and being in love with someone didn't go well together. He'd never have been unfaithful to Emily. He probably shouldn't be thinking of her now, but couldn't quite keep the image of her from his mind, smiling up at him, replete, beautiful, after that first time they'd made love, the sun streaming in through the roof window of her studio apartment, accentuating her perfect nakedness. He hadn't had to make a decision. He'd known there and then that he'd wanted to be with her. He should have told her there and then that he'd been intending to leave home, such as it was, and leave his waste of a family behind him. Adam considered what might have been if only he'd talked to her sooner as he turned away to tug on loose-fitting jogging pants and a vest. Then he realised he had actually turned away, as if there really was someone there, which was crackers, because Emily wasn't actually there.

Insane. Certifiably. Or he soon would be if he kept this up. He really did need to clean up his act, get sober and stay sober. He'd shower when he got back from his run, he decided, pulling on his trainers and heading for the kitchen to satiate his overwhelming thirst. His throat always felt like sandpaper after having one too many the night before, which he was beginning to do most nights. Every night, he admitted. Grabbing a pint glass, he opened the fridge, and then closed it. *No beer*, he told himself firmly, turning to the sink and topping up with water instead. He'd have to get a bottle. An empty water bottle would do. He'd get one later.

Closing the front door behind him, he pulled in a breath – taking in the earthy after-rain smell on the damp country air – and then, bracing himself, he set off at a slow jog, at first, testing muscles he hadn't used in a long time. Didn't feel too bad, he decided, making sure to push his foot into the ground and drive through the balls of his feet. He'd need new trainers if his joints weren't going to suffer. The ones he was wearing had no shock absorbency whatsoever. His feet would be sore, his calf and thigh muscles would too; he'd hit the wall hard, he guessed, but he'd push through it, now he felt he had something worth pushing for. God, he hoped so. Maybe. Someday. Smiling to himself, he notched up the pace a fraction, keeping his body upright, his arms close to his body, positioning his feet carefully to avoid a hamstring injury, and established a comfortable, steady pace.

He should probably have warmed up, done some stretches beforehand, he realised as he ran. He'd make sure to do so tomorrow. Maybe he should join the local gym, he mused, acknowledging two female joggers with a nod as they passed in the other direction.

Nice buttock muscles. He glanced over his shoulder.

No buttocks. Eyes forwards, Adam.

He'd have to make sure to cool down, walk for a while. If he was going to do this, he was going to do it properly: Draw up a reasonable running plan and work through it until he was fit. He felt okay so far, though. Felt pretty good, actually. When had he stopped running? When his world had stopped turning, he reminded himself, stilling a graphic flashback this time. She'd been so still, so cold, so alone.

'So, where do you want dropping off, girls?' Nathaniel asked, glancing in the rear-view mirror at Sienna.

'As close to the High Street as you can get,' Lauren supplied from the passenger seat, bagsied so she could finish applying her make-up through the mirror on the visor. 'We're clothes shopping.'

'Ah.' Nathaniel chuckled. 'Serious shopping then?'

'Deadly serious, as far as Lauren's concerned.' Sienna sighed, thinking of her fragile bank balance. 'I'll be the one gazing wistfully through the windows.'

'She's on the writer's diet, starving for her art,' Lauren elaborated, putting the final touches to her lippy.

'Bloody hell, I don't believe it,' Nathaniel gasped as he crossed the bridge over the river.

'No, me neither.' Lauren gave Sienna a despairing glance over her shoulder. 'You should see what's she's writing.'

'He's up! He's running!' Nathaniel slowed the car. 'Either I'm having a mental aberration or he is.'

'Who?' Lauren glanced idly through the windscreen.

'Adam.' Nathaniel nodded ahead to a jogger coming towards them. 'He hasn't done that since ... In a long time.'

'Adam?' Sienna and Lauren exclaimed together.

'One and the same,' Nathaniel assured them, slowing the car to a crawl as he pulled out to allow Adam to pass on the inside.

'I don't believe it,' Lauren echoed Nathaniel, now gawking through the windscreen.

Nor do I. Sienna peered between the two of them, her eyes travelling the length of Adam as he approached and her mouth all but drooling. Delicious. Muscle-ripplingly, heart-stoppingly, tummy-clenchingly gorgeous. Sienna breathed deeply, her muscles down below luxuriating in another mini-orgasm at the thought of what that body had done to hers.

'Don't strain anything, will you?' Nathaniel shouted through Lauren's hastily opened window, as Adam slowed.

Adam grinned mischievously, his eyes flitting to Sienna. 'I'll try not to,' he said, waving behind him as he jogged on.

'Not the bits that count anyway. Wouldn't want the entire female race to die of disappointment,' Lauren commented drolly, her head twizzling on her neck and her eyes gazing appreciatively after Adam, nevertheless. 'Looks like he'll be charging you more for it now he's honing it,' she said with a smirk, turning back.

'Lauren!' Sienna's eyeballs almost flew out. '*Shhhh.*'

'Oh. Oops.' Lauren looked sheepish this time as she glanced at her. 'Sorry, hon. I thought Nathaniel knew you and Adam were ... *Ouch!*'

Lauren scowled as Sienna tugged on a lock of her hair.

Perfect. Sienna closed her eyes. Adam finally does something his friend approves of and now he's no doubt back in the doghouse. 'He doesn't charge,' she mumbled. 'I told you, Lauren, it was a misunderstanding. The woman wasn't paying him. She was ...' Sienna stopped, searching for a way to diplomatically say what she actually was.

'Giving him money?' Lauren supplied helpfully. Not.

'No! Yes. Oh, for goodness sake, she probably owed him the money, Lauren. And I only paid him some money to get back at him. And since you seem determined to judge him all bad, for your information, Adam didn't do the chasing. I *asked* him. Adam said a flat out no.'

'Oh.' Lauren clearly didn't have a ready smart retort to that. 'And?'

Sienna glanced at Nathaniel. 'So I compromised him,' she said, her cheeks flushing furiously. 'I kissed him, and then one thing led to another and ... well, you know.'

'God, Sienna ...' Lauren sank back in her seat.

Sienna glanced at her knotted fingers wishing she could disappear through the seat. 'It wasn't his fault, Nate,' she said in a small voice and glanced back up. 'It was me who did the chasing, not Adam.'

Nathaniel met her eyes at last through the mirror. '*Did* you pay him?' he asked.

Sienna shook her head, and then nodded. 'To make a point, yes. I was upset. He seemed so distant after we, um ...' She hesitated, realising how immature it all sounded. 'I wanted him to think I didn't care, so I pushed an envelope through his door the morning after you allowed him to stay over.' The morning he'd stormed off, his face like thunder and his body language furious, she recalled miserably.

Nathaniel drew in a long breath. There followed a pause, a very heavily pregnant pause. Would he be furious with Adam? Sienna chewed worriedly on her lip. Ban him from the marina altogether? She so hoped not, when they'd seen with their own eyes Adam trying to pull himself together. Surely that would count for something after all Nathaniel had told her he'd been through.

'Bloody idiot, he hasn't got a clue, has he?' Nathaniel spoke, after an agonisingly long silence. 'Be careful, Sienna,' he warned her. 'He needs fixing, but only he can do it.'

He was out of condition. The sweat was dripping from him in buckets as he came through the cottage door. Adam ran an arm over his forehead and under his chin. He was going to pay for his enthusiasm in the morning, no doubt about it. In which case, he'd just have to run through it, keep going, nice and steady until he was back in shape, he decided, walking to the kitchen to open the fridge.

'Yes, I know,' he raised a hand in acquiescence as he bypassed his misty companion. 'Water. Shower. No beer.'

Filling a glass with something that was naturally thirst quenching and on tap in abundance, he glugged that instead and headed for the bathroom.

So what about his other ... predilection, his inclination towards attached women? He pondered as he let the warm water soothe his aching muscles. See someone about it maybe? Did he need to, though? Despite all his denials, he knew deep down that he'd much rather have what he once thought he'd had, though the prospect of putting his emotions on the line terrified him. He'd been seeking short-term, short-lived satisfaction because he'd been too scared to even contemplate anything else until now, too cynical about the whole rose-tinted love thing. Moving on had been his survival technique, his way of avoiding commitment. He hadn't needed Nathaniel to tell him that.

On that subject, what about his boat? Did he really need to get her under sail in a hurry? Did he actually still want to sail away? No, was the clear-cut answer. He wanted to see Lily-Grace. He'd made up his mind. Nicole was going to have to accept that he was determined to and trust him not to do anything that might upset her. He'd waited long enough. If she wasn't going to call, he'd call her back and move that along.

He also wanted Sienna. A desperate need that almost made his gut ache. But what if she didn't want him? Even if he did manage to clean up his act, what if 'beautiful' sex was just that, and she didn't want more? He'd need to go then. He really didn't think he could cope, seeing her out with other men, knowing what those other men might be doing with her.

Adam's stomach tightened as he recalled the intoxicating smell of her, the taste of her. Her long legs wrapped around him, how she'd clenched him so mind-blowingly tightly. The way she'd called out his name. It was more than sex he was interested in, though. Much more. He loved the way she walked, the way she talked. The way she smiled at him. The way she blushed. The way she looked at him, like she cared, her intoxicating green eyes lighting up when she laughed. He loved her cupid, upturned lips, her red-and-gold-flecked hair, curling so carelessly down to her creamy firm breasts. He loved her body, every desirable inch of it.

He loved her. He wanted her. He wanted to be with her. Might it be possible? Might she love him, learn to love him? Only one way to find out and that was to sort himself out. But then, if she didn't want anything to do with him? Adam pulled in a breath. He'd need his boat ready to go.

And if she did? He would stop chasing women, and getting no satisfaction apart from the physical sort. He'd stop. No question. If Sienna even hinted she cared enough to consider a future with him, he'd drop anchor and stay put. Meanwhile, he decided, towelling himself down, he'd increase the odd jobs, decline the bonuses, and think about looking for an actual job. There must be something he could do that didn't mean being shut indoors nine-to-five. What though? There were no local firms he hadn't already tried.

Okay, so he'd just have to try further afield. It was a semblance of a plan, at least. He pondered as he shaved – and tried to ignore the persistent ringing at the front door.

Coming downstairs for a coffee dressed in only his towel, he realised ignoring the doorbell had been a bad idea. If he'd answered, he might have avoided what looked like an imminent confrontation with Sherry. She'd obviously let herself in with her key. *Dammit.* Noting the thunderous expression on her face, Adam almost about-faced.

'What's up?' he asked her apprehensively instead.

'I might ask you the same question,' she snapped. 'What are you playing at, Adam?'

'Nothing.' He eyed her quizzically. 'Why?'

'So you haven't been fucking the trollop you're in love with then?'

Adam felt his jaw tighten. 'What?' He glanced at her narrowly.

'The trollop you were declaring undying love for last night.' Sherry planted her hands on her hips. Her eyes were full of hostile accusation.

His anger escalating, Adam was sorely tempted to send a derogatory retort back, but … Cool it, he warned himself. He might be a lot of things, but arguing with women, he'd much rather not. 'I was drunk,' he said, walking past her to retrieve his watch from the coffee table. Deflection, he thought, might be best.

'Right, so the barmaid won't be affecting your performance?' Sherry asked, tapping a toe impatiently.

Adam ignored her. 'Sherry, you're going to have to excuse me,' he said tightly. 'I have to—'

'In which case you can make love to me *now*, can't you?' Sherry challenged him.

'No,' Adam said.

Sherry eyed him accusingly. 'No?'

'No, Sherry. I have to go.' Trying hard to keep his temper in check, Adam turned for the stairs. 'I'm due at the marina—'

'Hah!' she said triumphantly. 'No doubt to show the trollop the interior of your boat. This is my cottage you're staying in, Adam. Rent-free, may I remind you? So, if you're about to renege on our—'

'That's enough!' Adam turned furiously back.

Sherry was clearly shocked by his tone. 'I beg your pardon?'

'I said that's enough, Sherry.' Adam's temper was now dangerously close to the surface. 'I don't much like you bad-mouthing Sienna. So don't! Got it?'

'I … Yes,' Sherry stammered. 'I …'

'You need to go.' Adam tugged in a breath and tempered his tone.

Sherry pulled up her shoulders. 'It's *my* cottage, Adam.'

'I'll be out of it by tomorrow,' Adam assured her. 'Don't slam the door on the way out.' He turned away, disgusted, but mostly with himself. If he'd needed a stark reminder of how messed up he was, this was it.

'You're a bastard,' Sherry said behind him.

Adam didn't turn back. 'I know,' he said quietly. 'But then, so did you, Sherry.'

Chapter Nine

He was here! Sienna peeped through her window, a thrill of excitement running through her as a glorious sight greeted her eyes: Adam, stripped to the waist, his toned torso on show, his beautifully sculpted calf muscles; the bit in between wasn't too disappointing either, sexily packaged in distressed denim. Sighing dreamily, she watched as he fed himself into his engine well, his movements supple, languid, pulse-racingly sensual; he really was enough to stop hearts.

Her excitement was soon replaced with trepidation, though, as she noticed Nathaniel emerge from his office. She watched as he looked over towards Adam's boat, shaking his head, his expression one of tired resignation, which didn't bode well.

Damn. Sienna so wished Lauren hadn't spouted her mouth off in Nathaniel's car like that. Lauren had been contrite, of course, treating Sienna to a new bralet top with little diamante studs and a gorgeous pair of denim hot pants embroidered with little flowers. She'd even offered her her last chunk of whole nut chocolate, before she'd gone off to meet her boyfriend, an indication of how truly sorry she was. Sienna really wished she hadn't felt compelled to share the details of her sexual encounter with Adam with his best friend, though, someone whose support Adam badly needed. Lauren didn't know, of course, how badly he did need that support. She'd been appalled at Adam's tragic history when Sienna had filled her in afterwards, saying she'd hold off on the electrodes, at least for a while.

The damage was done however. Sienna could only pray Nathaniel wouldn't be so despairing of Adam that he would wash his hands of him completely. She almost wished she'd never asked Adam to have sex with her – manipulated him into it, more like. The fact was, though, Sienna didn't regret it, nor would she ever. Losing her virginity to Adam, bar the emotional anticlimax afterwards, had been one of the most beautiful experiences of her life. Closing her eyes at night she could feel him making love to her; holding her with his dark eyes, intent on tipping her over the edge and driving her to a climax that would touch the very core of her. And he had.

No, she would never regret it. She just hoped Nathaniel wouldn't do anything that … Hang on? Was he taking him a beer? Sienna strained her neck as Nathaniel strode past, heading for Adam's boat, a stony, determined look in place of his normally cheery one, and a beer in each hand. But hadn't he said Adam needed to cut down? Hadn't he seen him out jogging, stone cold sober, obviously trying to do exactly that? What on earth?

Flip! 'Stay,' she told Tobias, who was curled contentedly in his basket anyway, and headed swiftly to the front door. Nathaniel was testing him, that's what he was doing. And if Adam failed that test? Well, everyone else might want to wash their hands of him, but Sienna wasn't about to. If Adam needed a friend, she'd be that friend, because she'd grown to know a different man under the surface. A lonely, gentle, caring man, who did seem to want to fix himself. He was going to fall at the first fence though, if someone dangled a huge distracting carrot in front of him.

Reaching the quayside, Sienna stopped as Adam popped up from his engine hole.

'Afternoon,' he greeted Nathaniel with a smile. Then, seeing Sienna behind him, he gave her a sunny smile, too.

Nathaniel nodded shortly. 'You look purposeful,' he commented.

'That I am.' Grabbing a cloth to wipe his oily hands,

Adam squinted up at his friend.

'Got your piston pin?' Nathaniel asked him.

'Yep,' Adam said, dragging an arm over his brow. 'Needs a new oil filter and the fuel injection pump's going to be a bit of a bugger, but she's coming along.'

Nathaniel nodded thoughtfully again. 'Thought you could use this.'

Sienna held her breath as Nathaniel extended the beer. *Don't take it*, she willed him.

Adam cocked his head to one side, looking at Nathaniel curiously. He looked from Nathaniel to the beer, eyeing it thirstily, then, 'No, thanks, Nate, I'm good. Given it up for Lent.'

'Oh, right,' Nathaniel said, not sounding as impressed as Sienna thought he might. 'Not given up taking the heights of prattishness to whole new levels, though, hey, Adam?'

Oh, no. Sienna closed her eyes, guessing what might be coming next.

'Sorry?' Adam caught hold of the handrail and heaved himself up to standing.

'You're accepting payment for sex?' Nathaniel gawked at him.

Shoot! Sienna took a step back and tried to blend in with the nearest boat.

Adam dragged his hand over his neck. 'Yeah, well.' He glanced quizzically towards Sienna. 'I'm obviously good at something, hey, Nate?'

'I don't know! I haven't had the dubious pleasure!' Nathaniel bellowed. 'For God's sake, you'll be sending their husbands a bloody invoice next!'

Adam laughed. 'Now there's an idea.'

'I don't bloody believe this. I really don't.' Nathaniel blew out an exasperated sigh. 'Have you got one single grain of common sense in there anywhere, Adam? I mean, are you looking to get yourself shot, or what?'

'Erm, what?' Adam shrugged hopefully.

'It's not funny, Adam. Someone's going to get hurt. It's very likely to be you, and I might just be the one to do it!'

Adam sighed and raked a hand through his hair. 'I know it's not funny,' he said, more seriously. 'I do know, Nate. Look, I'm not charging for it, for Pete's sake. It was just a misunderstanding, that's all.'

Nathaniel didn't look convinced.

'I'm not, I swear. I'm trying here, Nate. Give me a break.'

'What, you mean another one?' Nathaniel looked him up and down despairingly. 'Look, Adam, if you really want to get your act together, use your brains, why don't you, and use your hands.'

Adam knitted his brow, puzzled. 'Come again?'

'You're a mechanic. You're surrounded by boats,' Nathaniel supplied, not very enlighteningly.

'Your point being?' Still clearly confused, Adam looked again past Nathaniel to Sienna, who dearly wished the ground would open up and plop her in the river.

'Boats have engines, Adam. Engines that constantly need tweaking and fixing. If you could stay away from the booze and the customers' wives, you'd have a ready-made clientele; right here!' Nathaniel pointed a beer can demonstratively at the ground, shook his head, and turned back to his office.

'I suppose I should offer you congratulations on getting the jogging shoes on rather than your kit off,' he added reluctantly over his shoulder. 'It's a start, at least.'

'Cheers,' Adam called after him. 'So does that mean I can stay, or what?'

'The former,' Nathaniel said, giving Sienna a sly smile as he passed. 'But if that boat sways other than from the natural ebb and flow of the water, you're gone, Adam. And

I mean permanently.'

Adam crouched down to close his engine well half an hour later, concentrating on making sure the decking of the boat was sitting right.

'I brought you a drink,' Sienna said from behind him. 'Some lemonade. I'm not sure you like lemonade, but I thought as you've been working so hard, and with it being so warm; and you obviously won't have much in the way of supplies on board, so I ...' She paused for a necessary breath. 'Well, I thought you could use one.'

Adam turned and looked up at her from where he was crouching. 'I could.'

He stood up then. He looked taller on the deck, looming over her where she stood on the bank. She dropped her eyes from his inscrutable gaze, and found herself admiring his glistening torso instead. *Damn*. She twanged her eyes back up again.

He was scrutinising her, his head tilted to one side and his hands on his hips. Was he annoyed with her? 'It wasn't me,' she said quickly, in the absence of any conversation forthcoming from him.

Adam looked perplexed. 'Sorry?'

'It was Lauren,' she added, guiltily sacrificing her friend to save herself. 'She didn't mean to. It just slipped out when we were in the car with Nathaniel and she saw your honed muscles, and ...' Sienna trailed off. That didn't come out right.

'Erm ...?' Adam scratched his head. 'I think I'm losing the plot.'

Ah, yes, that was it, the plot! 'My script!' Seizing the lifebelt he'd thrown her, Sienna attempted to turn her gibberish into some kind of apology. 'Lauren read it and she assumed, you know, and I did explain to her but ...

Anyway, I'm sorry.'

'You are?' Adam narrowed his eyes.

'Yes.' Sienna nodded earnestly.

'Don't be,' Adam said after a second, his beautiful mouth curving into a smile. 'I'm not.' He pressed his hand to the handrail, to leap over it in that easy way he did, and drop down beside her.

'You're not?' Sienna asked hopefully.

'Not if you're not,' he assured her, his smile widening. 'I am sorry I was a bit of a bastard, though,' he added, his decadent chocolate-brown eyes clouding with concern.

'You weren't,' she lied, trying to still an urge to lean forward and kiss his unfairly long eyelashes.

He laughed. 'You reckon? You're probably the only one who doesn't think so. And actually, I think I was. So, how about you accept my apology, I'll accept yours, and we'll call it quits?'

'Deal.' She nodded, relief washing through her.

'I'll accept that drink, too,' he said, indicating the glass still in her hand. 'And the sandwich, if it's on offer,' he indicated the cheese sandwich she'd forgotten she was holding in her other hand, 'before it curls up and dies.'

Adam was making coffee when Sienna dropped another bombshell. His first thought was to reach for a beer. His second: *no beer*. The first few days were the hardest. He knew that. He'd done it before though, survived without alcohol, only to fall off the wagon when he'd discovered Emily … Stopping his thoughts short, he grabbed up the coffee and turned back to Sienna, who was sitting in his seating area, munching innocently on a bag of cheese and onion crisps, having just casually asked him if she could write about his past sordid sex life.

Adam shook his head and looked her over quizzically.

What was this really about? Might she be trying to find out whether he lived up to his womanising reputation? If so, why not just ask? Probably because she imagined he'd lie. And if he wanted her to have anything to do with him in future, he probably should.

He wasn't going to lie though, he decided. Knowing someone is cheating on you was bad enough. It was the lies that hurt more. The realisation that someone didn't even respect you enough to stop piling pain on top of pain, that's what twisted the knife. Adam knew it. He'd watched his father destroy his mother's confidence, inch by excruciating inch. Walking in on Emily and his so-called brother, *he'd* almost been destroyed, incapable of doing anything but focussing on the anger festering away inside him, mostly because of the deceit. He was wiser now, might handle it better, but it was too late to turn back the clock. Too late for Emily. Whatever she'd done, she'd needed someone, particularly once the baby was born, someone to just care. He hadn't been there. So no, no more lies. Sienna would find out anyway, about his past exploits. It was better she heard it from him.

'Let me get this right,' he eyed her bemusedly and parked himself at the opposite end of the seating area, 'you're saying you only want me for my mind, right?'

'Well, I'd quite like your body as well, but I can't afford it.' Sienna waggled her eyebrows mischievously and continued to munch on her crisps.

You can have it for free, Adam almost joked, but stopped himself. If it opened up the conversation to her saying she wasn't interested in anything more, gutted wouldn't even begin to describe how he'd feel. He could cope if a sexual relationship was all she wanted – he watched, mesmerised, as she licked the salt from her lips with the succulent tip of her tongue – but he quietly hoped she might want an actual relationship.

'Right, so ...' he coughed awkwardly, '... you want me to talk about my sexual encounters so you can write about them in your script?'

'Describe how you felt, yes,' Sienna confirmed, inserting her index finger in her mouth, sucking the salt from that, and slowly drawing it out. Did she have any idea what that was doing to him?

'I want the male point of view,' she said, reaching for her pad and pencil, then drawing her legs up underneath her and turning to face him, 'what you're actually thinking when you're, you know, with a woman.'

Sienna, you really do not want to know what I'm thinking right now. Adam tugged in a breath.

'Are you okay with that?' Sienna smiled, waiting expectantly.

Adam steepled his hands under his chin and studied her thoughtfully. 'Okay,' he said at length, steeling himself. 'Where do you want me to start?'

'Just pick one encounter at random,' she suggested. 'But not me,' she added quickly. 'I've already written that one.'

'Right.' He nodded slowly. 'I'll start with my first casual encounter then, shall I?' He worded it carefully, because other than two, including her, he'd never had meaningful encounters.

'Perfect.' She jotted hurriedly on her notepad. 'So, where did this encounter take place?' She looked back at him, her expression all business.

'A pub,' he supplied, glancing down and then back. 'Er, *the* pub, to be precise.'

Sienna's eyes grew wide. 'The Fish and Anchor?'

'Afraid so.' Adam smiled, contrite. 'Sorry. I wouldn't have said, but I thought as you work there, you'd be bound to find out sooner or later. I, er, got caught, in flagrante, as they say.'

'Oh God, Adam.' Sienna laughed, incredulous. 'I wondered why the landlord looked at you like something the cat dragged in.'

'Yeah.' Adam rolled his eyes. 'Doesn't exactly extend the warm welcome, does he?'

'So, you …' Sienna glanced over her shoulder, for what Adam wasn't sure, and then lowered her voice to a whisper, '… had sex in the pub?'

'Well, you have to admit the place could do with a bit of livening up,' Adam quipped, 'but not the actual pub, no. The car park.'

'Why?' Sienna looked at him, surprised. 'Why there, I mean? It's not exactly the most romantic place in the world, is it?'

'No,' Adam conceded, 'but it was the only place available at short notice. And the woman was definitely up for it, so …' He shrugged in embarrassment.

Sienna didn't look overly impressed. 'So you grabbed your chance.'

'Yes, I did. Like I say, she'd made it obvious she was up for it, and I …' Adam paused, now feeling distinctly uncomfortable. 'I'd been abstaining for quite a while,' he went on awkwardly, 'let's put it that way.'

'Oh, right.' Sienna nodded, giving him a long, searching look. 'Do you mind if I ask why?'

Definitely fishing, Adam realised. Did he mind? He did and he didn't. He supposed he'd do the same in her shoes. He wasn't ready to share details, though, because he simply couldn't. God knows, it was enough it haunted his dreams, dogged him every single day, no matter how hard he tried to push it away.

'A bad experience?' Sienna probed gently.

Adam drew in a breath. 'Yes.' He nodded tightly. 'And

some.'

Sienna nodded, in turn. 'Fragile things, aren't they?' she said softly. 'Hearts?'

'Very,' Adam replied quietly.

'So what happened?' Sienna urged him on.

Adam closed his eyes. He really wasn't sure he could do this. He was happy to answer her questions, but not about that. 'Sienna,' he started, 'I ...'

'I mean, I assume you didn't just say do you fancy a quickie in the car park?'

'What? Oh, no.' Adam blew out a relieved sigh. 'She did.'

Sienna blinked at him, astonished. 'You're joking.'

'No.' Adam resisted a smile. 'I know it's not usually the done thing for a woman to proposition a man, but ...' He let it hang, locking amused eyes on hers.

'Oh, ho-di-ho, ho.' Sienna blushed to the tips of her extremely nibbleable ears. 'And?' she asked, casting him a touché glance.

Adam shrugged. 'I said yes. She was attractive. I was lonely, so ...'

'Oh, I see.' Sienna looked down, jotting quickly on her notepad again 'Did you know her?' She glanced back up, trying for a confident smile. It wasn't working. Adam saw the swallow slide down her slender neck and badly wanted to trail his lips down after it.

'Yes, vaguely,' he said, not wanting her to think he was into one-night stands. 'I'd cut some trees back at their house.'

'Their house? She was married?'

'They usually are,' Adam confided. 'Er, scratch that,' he added quickly. 'I should say were. I'm trying to clean up my act.'

'You are?' Sienna's mouth curved into a delighted smile. 'Why? I mean,' her eyes flickered down again, 'I thought you liked having sex?'

Adam nodded contemplatively. 'I do,' he admitted, 'but I'm beginning to think soulless sex isn't good for the soul.'

She smiled that radiant smile again, which somehow lifted his spirits and had Adam wanting to smile, too. 'So,' she said, arranging her face back to serious researcher, 'it was a no strings thing, then? No commitment, the way you prefer it?'

'The way I *did* prefer it, yes,' Adam answered honestly.

'Good.' Sienna's shoulders sagged with – relief? 'I mean, this is good. Go on.'

'Yes, ma'am.' Adam gave her a small salute. 'Okay, so she's been watching me all evening, smiling, fluttering her eyelashes. You know the sort of thing.'

'I don't actually.' Sienna looked po-faced.

Good sign? Might she be jealous? Adam wasn't sure. 'Then she's standing at the bar, ordering a drink, and she presses a note into my hand: *Car park. Two minutes.*'

'And you went?' Sienna's eyes were agog again.

'Wouldn't you?'

'No!' She was back to po-faced.

Adam chuckled. 'Do you want me to tell you about this, or not?'

Sienna pulled herself up and tried to look less affronted. 'Yes, go on.'

'At your request, my lady.' Adam dipped his head reverently. 'I must admit I did debate, for a second. Her husband was sitting at the table, so—'

'Her husband was there?' The wide eyes were back.

'Engrossed in the football on the flat screen TV,' Adam replied. 'But I thought, why not? She obviously wanted to.'

'Obviously,' Sienna said, followed by an audible humph.

Adam hid a smile. 'So I waited two minutes and then followed her out.'

'I can't believe you were willing to take the risk with her husband sitting in the bar. *Or* her.' Sienna shook her head, disbelieving.

'Me neither. In retrospect, I probably shouldn't have, but—'

'Too tempting?' Sienna arched an eyebrow.

Adam smiled. 'Extremely.'

'Oh.' Sienna's eyes dropped back to her notepad. 'And was she worth the risk?' she asked, running the tip of her tongue over her lips, as she looked back at him. Adam seriously wished she wouldn't.

'Yes,' he confirmed, awkwardly. 'Like I said, it had been a while.'

Sienna nodded, and coughed. 'How did you, um …? Where did you …? *Ahem.* I presume you didn't actually do it in the car park?'

'Erm, actually we did. I was drinking. I'd left my car at home, so it was the car park or nothing.'

'Not in her car then?'

'Well, I did consider asking her old man for his car keys, but somehow I didn't think he'd be very obliging,' Adam joked. Then wished he hadn't.

Sienna didn't look any better impressed. 'So you followed her out, then what?'

Adam narrowed his eyes, regarding her curiously. 'You want details?' he asked warily.

'Not a blow by blow account,' Sienna assured him, her cheeks colouring up again.

Thank God for that. Adam trailed his hand over his neck. Talking dirty to Sienna might be a bit of a turn on, but only if he was talking about what he'd like to do with her.

'Tell me how you felt,' she went on. 'What you were thinking.'

Adam furrowed his brow. 'Thinking?' He hadn't thought

much about what he thought while he was having sex. He scratched his head, feeling now definitely self-conscious. 'I was terrified,' he said, glancing back at her. 'Turned on by the illicit thrill of it, but scared, absolutely.'

'Of getting caught?'

'Some.' Adam hesitated. 'But more of, erm, not performing well.'

'Ah, a man's ego thing.' Sienna nodded understandingly.

Adam met her eyes. 'More a *my* ego thing. It got damaged somewhere along the way,' he admitted, and couldn't quite believe he had. She was certainly her father's daughter, he decided, a psychiatrist in the making. He doubted he would admit that to any other woman.

Sienna studied him. Her expression was thoughtful, puzzled. And well she might be. He was a puzzle to himself most of the time. 'Tell me what you thought,' she pressed him. 'What you were thinking while you made love to her?'

Adam sighed inwardly. Made love? If only she knew that he hadn't, not in a very long time, until her. 'That she was pretty,' he said. 'That her mouth was kissable,' he went on, honestly, but cautiously, 'that I wanted to push my tongue into it, stroke her breasts; taste her.' Leaving out his distinctly remembered thoughts around biting and sucking, he paused, watching Sienna carefully. She blushed, but her gaze didn't flinch. 'That I needed to make love to her from behind.'

Sienna's eyes pinged wide. 'Behind? Why?' she asked, now clearly shocked.

'We were in the pub car park,' he reminded her. 'There were cows in the field beyond. The grass was wet. The ground was wet. There was a brick wall behind her. I didn't want her to graze her back, so ...' He stopped, shrugging apologetically as she continued to stare at him. 'You did ask.'

Sienna scanned his face, her head cocked prettily to one side. 'You're an enigma, Adam,' she said, after a pause. 'Do you know that?'

'There's a coincidence.' Adam smiled, holding her gaze. 'I've been thinking the very same thing about you.' He had been too. She was a gorgeous, baffling enigma, and, right then, he desperately wanted to make sweet, meaningful love to her.

'Can I ask you something?' Sienna shifted awkwardly in her seat. 'You don't have to answer, if you don't want to.'

Adam nodded hesitantly. 'Ask away,' he said, praying it wasn't anything too invasive.

'What were you thinking when you made love to me?'

Adam swallowed. 'That I very much wanted to,' he said softly. 'But most of all that I didn't want to hurt you.'

Sienna searched his eyes. Hers were glassy, wide, disbelieving, beautiful. She was beautiful, every distracting, delicious inch of her. She glanced down, then back, a smile playing at her too tempting lips. 'So how was the, um, car park performance?' she asked as Adam continued to drink her in, wishing he could watch her all day and all night. Lie next to her while she was sleeping. Listen to her breathing; feel her heart beating.

'Ah,' he said, smiling awkwardly. 'Cut short, unfortunately. Guess you could call it a case of premature interjection. The landlord postponed emptying his bin in favour of punching my lights out.'

'Oh, no.' Sienna blinked at him, aghast. 'He knocked you out?'

'I definitely saw stars. No permanent damage, though, much to some people's disappointment.'

'What did you do?' Sienna asked, a concerned little 'v' furrowing her brow.

'Nothing.' Adam shrugged. 'Apart from the fact the

guy's a hell of a lot heavier than me, I figured I'd got what I deserved. The husband's a regular, a friend of his, so ...'

'But weren't you upset?' Sienna asked, incredulous. 'Angry? It wasn't his battle to fight, after all, was it?'

'Not angry, no. I was bloody sore. Feeling guilty, because of the consequences for her, but not angry,' Adam confessed. 'So, did that do it for you?' he added quickly, before they got onto the subject of guilt, one he really didn't want to explore his feelings around.

'Sorry?' Sienna said distractedly, her eyes locked on his.

'Your notes,' he said, searching her face, wondering how long it would take him to kiss every freckle, 'you haven't written many.'

'I've committed it to memory,' she said, her gaze travelling to his lips. 'And I can always pop by if I need you to, um ...' She smiled uncertainly, and leaned towards him.

'Clarify anything?' Adam took her cue and moved closer.

'Demonstrate,' Sienna breathed. And Adam was drawn, like a magnet. He wanted to feel her warm breath on his face, her tantalising tongue in his mouth. He wanted to hold her. Caress her. Be with her.

'*Hell!*' His lips a millimetre from hers, he moved faster than he'd ever done in his life.

'Anybody home?' Nathaniel called, banging the door wide.

'Thanks, Adam,' Sienna said cheerily, heading swiftly up the steps to leave Adam under Nathaniel's suspicious scrutiny.

'Discussing engines, my eye,' she heard Nathaniel say behind her. 'Do you really expect me to believe you were discussing the intricacies of your turbocharger?'

'Injector,' Adam corrected him. 'She's into mechanics, what can I say?'

'I gathered, Heaven help her,' Nathaniel's voice drifted

after her as Sienna flew mortified back to the cottage.

She was still all hot flush and fluster as she tiptoed inside, to be greeted by Tobias bounding gleefully towards her. 'Hello, sweetie.' She bent to plant a kiss on the top of her faithful friend's head, and couldn't help wishing it was Adam's hot sensual mouth instead. That he'd rock his flipping boat with her in it. *Oh God*, she groaned quietly as her insides turned once again to gloop. She wanted him, any which way and anywhere. Did he want her? He'd admitted he'd had a bad experience. That his ego had suffered. That must have taken a certain amount of courage, and it was definitely progress. At least he'd opened up a little. He'd clearly been struggling, but he had talked, and it was plain to see he wasn't the couldn't-care-less Lothario everyone thought he was, expected him to be. He cared about women. It was obvious he did. He'd just erected a fortress around his fragile heart, that was all.

She still wasn't sure whether he wanted to take things further, though. He'd been going to kiss her. His gaze on hers, uncertainty this time in his eyes, he'd been going to press his beautiful warm lips against hers. Would they have done more than kiss? Would she have allowed him to? And, if she had, would he have walked away again when he'd finished? Sienna thought not, but ... She just wasn't sure.

He'd said he was trying to clean up his act. That he was beginning to think soulless sex was no good for the soul. That he *had* preferred no strings. He wouldn't have said those things to try to seduce her into bed when she'd already leapt gaily into it with him, would he? He'd said he hadn't wanted to hurt her. She swallowed back a tight lump of emotion.

He cared about her. He did. She cared about him, too. She more than liked him, possibly even loved him. Sienna felt it again, that little flutter in her chest whenever she thought about him. Foolish it might be – he obviously had issues – but she couldn't help it. Her heart had soaked him up like it was wet cotton wool. She wanted to make love with him, again and again. She'd wanted him to kiss her, not because she'd compromised him, but because *he* wanted to. She wanted to feel his mouth hot on hers, his hands on her body, exploring, touching her so exquisitely tenderly, so passionately.

What she also wanted though, she conceded, as her heart dipped in conjunction with her constantly clenching pelvis, was Adam to do cuddles. To hold her afterwards. Yes, to bask in the afterglow, although it sounded corny. She wanted him to spoon her with his hard body; she wanted to lie satiated in his arms, limbs entwined, until they were almost as one. Could a man who was broken, a man who drank to excess and had affairs with other men's wives ever really do that, though? Could he ever be faithful to one woman?

She contemplated this as she climbed the stairs, meeting Lauren coming out of the bathroom as she did, who was wearing a scowl, gone-to-bed hair, and not a lot else. 'Where on earth have *you* been?' she asked, looking Sienna up and down accusingly.

'With Adam.' Sienna squared her shoulders defiantly.

Lauren balked. 'Adam?'

'*Talking*, Lauren,' Sienna said, miffed at the assumption that anyone who went near Adam would fall prey to his sexual depravities. Not that he had any sexual depravities she was aware of. 'And, no, he didn't charge for it.' She thought she'd get that droll witticism in before Lauren did.

'Yes, well, he obviously doesn't do *verbal* intercourse quite as well, does he? He's more wham-bam, yes I do take credit cards, ma'am.' Lauren settled on another equally droll quip.

'Stop it, Lauren.' Sienna sighed. She really was getting fed up with people taking every opportunity to thrust Adam's womanising in her face. She *knew*. Not being completely cerebrally challenged, Sienna was well aware he might just be that way inclined, it was the old nature versus nurture conundrum, but still, she didn't need reminding of his shortcomings every two seconds. 'I've told you he has some issues to work through.'

'What, shagging every woman he meets?' Lauren chose a more barbed unwitty remark this time.

'He doesn't!' Sienna snapped, bypassing Lauren for her bedroom, where she could ponder Adam and his issues in peace, assuming she could stop fantasising about him and his body for five consecutive minutes.

'For God's sake, Sienna.' Lauren sighed exasperatedly behind her. 'I know you're infatuated with the man, but open your eyes, will you?'

'They are open.' Sienna gave her a blinky-eyed demo over her shoulder. 'I'm well aware he's bedded a string of women, Lauren. It doesn't mean he's on a mission to bed the entire female race.'

'Right, so assuming it's only the bazillion or so fool enough to fall for his charms, what does this indicate, Sienna?' Lauren wouldn't let it drop. 'That he either loves women or he hates them, as far as I can see. Either way, he's addicted to sex, isn't he? He's at it at every opportunity. You know very *well* he is.'

'Unlike some,' Sienna observed, glancing archly over her shoulder at her minuscule bra and knickers clad friend and then back to Lauren's open bedroom door. 'Hi, Josh,' she greeted the blushing boyfriend in Lauren's bed and walked on.

'He's bad news, Sienna,' Lauren pointed out, yet again. 'That's all I'm saying.'

'Yes, I know!' Sienna closed her own bedroom door and leaned back against it.

Of course she knew. She wasn't blind *or* stupid. She was aware he might be incurably broken. But try as everyone might to force the 'bad news' point home, she didn't truly believe it, not deep down, not after hearing him talk tonight, after seeing his tenderness, albeit sandwiched between anger and abruptness. And hadn't he had every right to be angry with her that first time? Even then his lovemaking hadn't been unfeeling or abrupt, anything but. He hadn't tried to force her to do anything she hadn't wanted to do, unlike the bastard boyfriend who'd texted her yet again this evening, *five* times: *Please text me back. I'm desperate. I love you. Have you found someone else? Is he good in bed?*

He quite plainly had issues. Sienna closed her eyes, nausea churning inside her. She could still smell it, his drunken breath on her face, see the contempt in his eyes. *He'd* had no qualms about driving under the influence. A supposedly respectable man, a trainee solicitor, he'd had no qualms about groping her in the car either, pushing her down, insisting that he'd waited long enough. He'd been cruel, unkind and uncaring. He'd had no concerns about hurting her. He had hurt her.

Adam had not!

What Adam had done was confirm what she knew to be true but couldn't quite make herself believe: that there was nothing wrong with her. He was a caring person, Sienna knew it. She pondered his comment about abstaining from sex for 'quite a while'. That had to be something to do with the awful nightmare of finding his fiancée in bed with his own brother. And then there was a child! What happened, she wondered. Where was that child now? Where was his fiancée? Sienna had no idea, nor would she ever, unless Adam felt confident enough to tell her. To trust her.

He might not want to. He might prefer to stay as he was. He might hate women. It was possible. Sienna didn't believe that though, not after the way he'd been with her. Wasn't it more likely that he was choosing women who were already committed, precisely because they were? Moving on whenever his emotions were in danger of becoming embroiled? As far as she could see Adam seemed to be abstaining still from normal loving relationships, because he'd had his heart so badly broken and couldn't risk that kind of pain again.

Now he was 'trying to clean up his act', which surely counted for something. He'd cut back his drinking, too. He hadn't had a single one today, Sienna could vouch for that. She wished other people would at least give him a chance, instead of assuming he was bad news, through and through.

Sighing, she headed to the window. His boat was rocking, but that was because Adam had obviously just climbed on top of it. He was lying on his back, his head resting on his hands, quietly contemplating the stars. Would a man who was emotionally disconnected do that?

Chapter Ten

Adam was pulling on his trainers when his phone rang. Hoping it was the returned call he'd been waiting for, he jumped to his feet and almost fell over his laces in his rush to grab up the phone. 'Nicole?' he said, seizing on it before his voicemail picked up.

'Yes, hi, Adam. Sorry I didn't get back. Phil has been tied up running a training course abroad and I needed to talk to him properly before I spoke to you.'

Adam pulled in a tight breath. 'And?'

Nicole paused before answering, causing a trickle of apprehension to run the length of his spine. 'You can see her tomorrow,' she finally said.

Yes! Adam allowed himself to breathe out.

'But a short visit only, Adam,' Nicole reminded him. 'Lily's shy of strangers, so we need to take things slowly. We'll see how it goes from there, yes?'

The 'stranger' comment hit home. Adam swallowed back a mixture of guilt and trepidation. Now it was actually going to happen he was suddenly more nervous about meeting this particular little lady than he'd ever been about meeting any other female in his life. 'Yes, no problem,' he assured Nicole.

Lily-Grace's interests were paramount here. They simply had to be. However it worked out, Adam had made a promise to himself: he would keep in touch. If it went badly, maybe he could try again when she was older. When she could understand a little more and learn to accept him. Hopefully, even to like him. 'Should I bring anything?' he asked, wondering what on earth a man did bring a two-year-old child.

'Just yourself. Twelve o'clock, if that's okay with you. That gives me a chance to get some shopping before I pick her up from Mum's,' Nicole said over a timely yawn, reminding Adam she'd probably just got back from her shift. She was still nursing, then. It couldn't have been easy for her, taking on Lily-Grace with her own two children already at school. But then, in the absence of any other available parent, she'd had no choice. Adam's guilt multiplied threefold.

'Twelve it is.' He nodded, determined to try to do this right.

Nicole yawned again. 'See you tomorrow, then. Oh, and Adam, make sure to be on time. She's got an appointment with the nurse in the afternoon. Just routine, but she'll need to have her lunch.'

'I will be,' he promised. 'Thanks, Nicole.'

'Like I say, don't thank me yet. She's a handful, Adam. Let's just play it by ear.'

Adam rang off and flicked to his photos. 'Nice to be meeting you, Lily-Grace,' he said, his mouth curving into a smile. How would she look now, he wondered again, and made a mental note to ask Nicole to send him some new photos. He should have done that before, too. Despairing of himself, of the time he'd wasted, going nowhere and doing absolutely nothing with his life, Adam smiled at his now almost constant ghostly companion, whose sorrow he sensed definitely wasn't so heavy. Time he stopped looking for reasons not to and started making something of himself, he decided, bending to tie his laces good and tight.

He'd made sure to warm up this morning, got some quad, calf and hamstring stretches in, giving Nathaniel cause to poke his head suspiciously out of his office door. His curiosity had obviously been piqued by the unnatural ebb and flow of the boat. Adam was only grateful he'd let him stay onboard. He needed to be out of the cottage but the prospect of a hotel room even for one night … Apart from the fact that he couldn't afford one, Adam doubted he'd have been able to face staying in a soulless hotel room on his own. It was way too stark a reminder.

Forcing back the inevitable image his mind conjured up, Emily, so still, so cold, Adam sucked in a breath, plucked up his bottle of water, and headed quickly for the door. He needed to be out running, not thinking.

Despite the dreams – the hallucinations, he supposed that's what they were – he was definitely feeling better. That was probably more to do with having Sienna in his life than the short time he'd been off the booze – though he wasn't sure she was, or even wanted to be. Also Nicole returning his call might mean he'd have another person he cared about in his life. Was he being over-optimistic, he wondered? Possibly, but it felt a bloody sight better than being pessimistic.

'All right?' Nathaniel called across the marina as Adam leapt his handrail to the bank.

'Yep, good,' Adam called jauntily back. 'You?'

'Astonished,' Nathaniel answered, looking him over, perplexed. Understandably, Adam conceded. It wasn't often he emerged hangover free this early in the morning. 'Are you off running?'

'Thought I might now I'm dressed for it. Fancy joining me?'

'Do I look as if I need to?' Nathaniel indicated his physique with a sweep of his hand.

Adam laughed, noting the slight but definite paunch his friend was sucking in. 'Erm, from this angle, truthfully, yes.'

'Cheers.' Nathaniel waved him on. 'Don't fall down any potholes, will you.'

Adam gave him a cheery wave back and set off at an

even jog, running at a comfortable pace for two minutes at a time, then walking for two minutes times five. He thought that was sensible for the first week.

Not too disastrously breathless after his fifth sprint, he took a drink from his bottle, wiped the sweat from his forehead with his vest, and slowed his last two-minute walk right down, which should bring his heart rate back to resting level. As long as his mind didn't wander in a certain other direction, that was. He could swear his pulse kicked up a notch every time he thought about Sienna. He still couldn't believe the conversation they'd had, that he'd actually recounted details of his not-very-savoury first casual encounter after Emily. Why Sienna hadn't recoiled in horror, he had no idea. Instead, she'd encouraged him, somehow making him feel safe to admit things he'd never imagined telling to anyone. She really was an enigma, sexual, sensual, innocent, shrewd, caring, kind; beautiful, inside and out. He'd be mad not to be in love with her. Adam smiled as he realised how easy it was becoming to admit that, too.

He wished Nathaniel hadn't turned up at the crucial moment last night, checking up on him. He'd been a heartbeat away from pressing his lips against hers, possibly more terrified of kissing a woman than he'd ever felt; scared that she might pull away. Would she have? She'd have been wise to. She should have nothing to do with a waster like him, but Adam sensed that for some unfathomable reason, she wanted to. And, as much as he'd tried to tell himself he didn't want to go there, didn't need love and commitment and all the heartbreak that went with it, he knew now that he did want to, very much.

He wanted Sienna, in his bed, in his heart, in his life.

He wanted to hold her in his arms. Talk to her, lie with her; dream with her. He wanted to make love with her, and this time he wanted to do it right.

She'd said it was beautiful. He'd taken her virginity, treated her abysmally afterwards, and still she'd said it was beautiful. It had been. She was. Amazingly beautiful with her wild hair splayed against that pillow, her eyes holding his, smoky with sated desire. The way she called out his name ...

Dammit. Seeing Sherry's car parked outside the cottage, Adam stopped short. He'd aimed to collect his stuff but no way was he going in there while Sherry was around. He wasn't sure he'd be able to hold his temper if she started bad-mouthing Sienna again.

She was probably about to put his stuff on the doorstep anyway, now whatever it was they'd been doing together was over. It should never have started, any of it, using women and then emotionally abusing them just as surely as their husbands were. What the bloody hell had he been thinking?

Had he abused Emily? Neglected her feelings in some way before the arguments had started? His mind drifted back to a place he didn't usually dare let it dwell. He didn't think so. He'd never been aware she'd been so unhappy that she'd want to seek affection elsewhere, with his own *brother*, who really didn't give a damn about the women he bedded, just like the old man. Adam had tried to be like them, once his mother had left, to be one of the lads. He just didn't get it, though, especially once he'd met Emily. Booze, women, booze, women and more booze, it just didn't appeal. He'd done all right since though, hadn't he? The old man would be proud.

Why? Adam asked himself the same question he'd asked himself a million times as he headed back the way he'd come. Why his brother? Yes, she'd been drinking, more once they'd started to argue, but had she been *that* drunk?

Had Darren coerced Emily in some way? Had she been in love with him? He'd never know, would he? As hard as Adam tried not to think about it, his mind had played it over and over, searching for answers. Waking in the dead of night when the nightmares came, he searched. Sensing the emotions of the presence he either imagined or genuinely encountered, he searched.

He never found them.

What he had come to realise, though, was that he'd been running ever since. He'd run away on that godforsaken day, and he'd kept on running because he was truly scared he might meet someone he loved as much as he had Emily – and his love would never be enough. He'd put his cards on the table ever since, been honest with women, or so he'd kidded himself, making it clear he didn't do commitment. He'd told himself he'd been ensuring the woman's feelings didn't get hurt. He'd been lying. It was his own feelings he'd been protecting. And now he wanted out. He had no clue what the future might hold, but he didn't want to live like this anymore, every conversation he had with a woman peppered with sexual innuendo; every relationship nothing but physical. Whatever happened, he would be more grateful to Sienna than she could ever know for helping to open his eyes to that fact.

'Are you decent?' Sienna shouted down from the deck of Adam's boat.

'Er, yep,' Adam shouted up. 'Come on in, Sienna.'

'How did the run go this morning?' Sienna came down his cabin steps and then, 'Oops, sorry,' she said, averting her eyes and twirling around as she realised Adam was dressed in only a towel.

'Erm, Sienna,' he said, so close to her ear it sent goosebumps the entire length of her spine, 'I realise it might not have been the most thrilling sight ever, but you have seen it all before, you know?'

'It was,' Sienna said, whirling back around to see his delicious, dark eyes filled with uncertainty. He was self-conscious? Adam-the-super-stud? Sienna was momentarily speechless.

'Glad to hear it,' Adam said, his gaze drifting towards his torso. 'My ego was on a serious downslide there for a second.'

But his body, despite the scar, was the sexiest thing Sienna had ever laid eyes on. Did he really not realise what women were lusting after? She couldn't quite believe it. 'You have a gorgeous body,' she assured him, helping herself to a leisurely perusal of it. 'It's just a pity it has to keep flaunting itself in front of every passing female.'

'I'm trying to restrain it.' He smiled embarrassedly and turned to reach for his shorts. 'So what can I do for you?'

'I, um …' *Whew*, Sienna felt a definite hot flush, high up and lower down, as he whipped off his towel and tugged the shorts on '… wondered if you'd like to come over to my place?'

'Sorry?' Adam turned back, a curious look in his eye now as he plucked his shirt from the seating area.

'Later. For a drink, maybe? A soft drink, obviously, as you're, um, you know. And a bite to eat, possibly? That's if you're free, of course. No pressure. I haven't got anything special in or, um, anything …' Sienna trailed hopelessly off, her tongue tying itself in an inarticulate knot.

'Oh, right.' He looked a little uncertain, causing Sienna's heart to go into crestfallen free fall. 'I'd love to,' he said, still not looking overly enthusiastic, 'but won't Lauren mind?'

Thank God for that. Sienna's heart started its laborious ascent back up her chest, one of many it had undertaken since she'd first set eyes on him. She'd thought he was about to say he'd got other, more interesting plans. 'She's out,' she assured him, 'nightclubbing with her new boyfriend, so ...'

'Great,' Adam said, looking relieved. 'Death by killer look is a painful one, I'm told.'

So is death by electrodes, Sienna thought but didn't volunteer. 'So, you'll come?'

'I'd like nothing better,' he said, his mouth curving into a lovely warm smile. It suited him, it really did. He should do that more often. 'Do I have to dress?'

'Um ...' Sienna eyed his still bare chest. No, she thought, absolutely not, ever. 'Casual's fine,' she said, scooting around and heading for the door before she drooled on his toes.

'What time do you want me?' Adam asked.

All the time. 'Sevenish,' Sienna said shrilly, trying not to trip up the steps. 'I'll give you a guided tour of my interior. I mean ...' *Oh God.*

'Can't wait.' She heard Adam chuckle softly behind her.

Making sure Tobias was watered and fed and comfortably tucked up in his bed in the kitchen, Sienna checked the general ambience and decided the lighting still wasn't right. Growing more nervous by the minute, she flicked off the lamp in the lounge, and then clicked it back on again. They were just going to be talking, she reminded herself. She'd invited Adam over for a social get together, that was all. So she could hopefully get to know more about him, which might have been better relationship protocol than offering him her not-very-inviting virginal self on a plate before they'd even had a proper conversation.

If she was going to establish whether he might really be interested in her, mind and body, she had to stop compromising him – which she blatantly had – and have some kind of dialogue with him. Blowing out a tea light on the coffee table, she headed for the hall in search of her ringing mobile, her mind completely ignoring her will to resist and conjuring images of Adam doing terrible things to her with his tongue, as she answered it without first checking the number as she usually did.

Shoot! 'Hi, Dad.' Sienna blanched and blushed in turn. 'Yes, yes, I'm fine,' she said, attempting to moderate her tone to something other than choking.

'So, how's the script coming along?' her father asked, probably imagining she'd written something equivalent to *Gone With The Wind* at the very least, inspired by her new surroundings – requisite inspiring surroundings her reasons for renting the cottage, she'd told him.

'Um, yes, good,' Sienna assured him, fancying that disclosing the actual inspiration behind her latest efforts might not be a terribly good idea. 'How's the training going? Five miles? Fabulous! Well done you.'

Her father continued to bombard her with questions. 'Huh, huh, absolutely. Five a day,' Sienna dutifully answered him, but when the conversation hinted at heading towards her love life: 'Got to go, Dad. I'm expecting a friend.' At which point, thank goodness, the doorbell rang right on cue.

Still on the phone, Sienna opened the door and gestured Adam on in. 'Yes, a girlfriend.' She gave him a smile and carried on talking to her dad. 'She's just arrived.'

Adam furrowed his brow and glanced back over his shoulder.

'Byee! Good luck with the training tomorrow. Speak soon.' Sienna ended the call and rolled her eyes. 'My dad,' she explained as she led the way to the kitchen. Bad enough that she'd been caught unawares by her dad but it would have been even worse if the caller had been her increasingly bothersome ex.

'Ah, I see,' Adam said. 'I think. Training?' he asked as Tobias bounded up to greet him, clearly thinking his hero was worth getting out of bed for.

Sienna smiled as Adam gently discouraged the dog from jumping up on his creaky hips, crouching down to his level instead to give him a good fuss.

'He runs,' Sienna said as, duly stroked and patted, Tobias went back in search of his creature comforts. 'He's training for the London Marathon in aid of mental health awareness. You two would have a lot in common.'

'Wow.' Adam looked impressed. 'He must be pretty fit, then?'

'He's a former Physical Education instructor,' Sienna said, turning to the cooker to check the Bolognese sauce.

'Sounds like a formidable man to cross.' Adam furrowed his brow, looking the tiniest bit concerned.

'No, not really.' Sienna smiled. It was true, her dad was a man's man, tall and fit for his age, but he was actually as much a puppy as Tobias was, most of the time. 'He's lovely,' she assured him, 'despite outward formidable appearances. He took up running after Mum died. I think it was his way of coping, you know, focussing his energies – on his running, his career, his daughter's virtue.'

'*Rrrright,*' Adam said, dragging his hand over his neck, now looking very concerned.

'Oops.' Sienna chewed on her lip, and then laughed out loud as Adam gulped demonstratively. 'Don't worry, I won't tell him you stole mine,' she said, pouring them both a lemonade. 'I'll tell him I gave it to you.'

'Erm, I actually can't see that making him want to kill me any less, Sienna,' Adam pointed out as she passed him his glass. 'So, er, how fast can he run, exactly?'

'Fast,' Sienna said, and then laughed again, as Adam made a great show of loosening his T-shirt collar.

'I think I'd better up my jog to a sprint.' He frowned worriedly, his mouth curving into a slow smile nevertheless. 'You do that beautifully, you know?' he said, scanning her face.

'What?' Sienna asked, feeling suddenly self-conscious under his gaze.

'Laugh,' he said softly. 'It lights up your eyes.'

His eyes were locked on hers, dark and searching, that same hungry desire she'd seen there once before. Sienna looked away. He was burning a hole in her soul, he really was – and superheating other parts of her.

'Shall we, um …?' She nodded towards the lounge and stepped past him to lead the way there, brushing his bare arm with hers as she did, which shot a sizzling fission of heat right through her.

'So, what happened with your mum?' Adam asked as he followed her. 'If you don't mind me asking.'

Sienna shrugged. She didn't mind him asking. She did mind that her answer might make her seem needy, though. She was, of course. Wasn't everyone who'd lost someone too soon? But no more so than he, she supposed, albeit in a different way. 'She committed suicide,' she said as matter-of-factly as she could, turning away to rearrange a cushion lest she see a '*Holy crap, I'd better get out of here*' look in his eyes. Sienna had seen that look before. Sadly, some people just weren't comfortable dealing with such an emotive issue, so she didn't generally share it.

'She was bipolar,' she went on, focussing on the rearranged, and rearranged again, cushion when Adam didn't speak. 'It's an awful illness, little understood. I don't think you can understand it really, unless you live with it. More awful for the person suffering, though. I don't think Mum understood it.'

She paused, remembering with crystal clear clarity the

147

look of bewilderment in her mum's eyes, the disillusionment – with herself – that she'd slipped back into her dark place, not even knowing why. Nothing triggered it. Her mum would always be at great pains to tell Sienna that she was never the cause of it. Nothing in particular ever was. That's why it was such a terribly cruel affliction, taking a sunny, caring person and draining the happiness out of her, leaving only dark thoughts and desolation.

'She was fabulous when she was on a high,' she continued quickly, catching a lump in her throat, 'upbeat, bubbly, fun, the life and soul of the party, but when she was down … She was always consumed with guilt, mostly because she didn't know why she was down. Maybe if they'd ever managed to get the medication right …'

Sienna swallowed and chatted on, wanting to just get it out there and hoping Adam wasn't already contemplating his escape route, possibly thinking he might have to handle her with kid gloves.

'Dad found her. He blamed himself, I think, because he hadn't realised how desperate she was to just be "normal". That's why he decided to study psych—'

Catching a movement behind her, Sienna stopped and turned around, to see Adam not so much sit down on the sofa, as drop down, like a stone. 'Adam, are you okay?' she asked, stepping towards him.

A faraway look in his eyes, he didn't even seem to see her. 'Adam?'

Adam shook his head. 'What?'

He seemed utterly bewildered. 'You look as if you've seen a ghost. Are you all right?'

'I …' Adam dragged his hands over his face and through his hair. 'I did,' he said quietly, looking back at her.

Sienna scanned his face. His complexion was ashen.

'I, er … *shit*.' Adam got to his feet, shaking his head

again and tugging in a sharp breath. He looked back to Sienna, and then moved towards her to pull her wordlessly into his arms.

'I am so, *so* sorry, Sienna,' he murmured, holding her close. 'That's hard.' He buried his face in her hair. 'So fucking hard.'

Sienna heard his voice crack and felt a splinter pierce her heart. He knew. He knew how hard it was. Her mind strayed to his circumstances. His loss. She didn't ask him. She didn't know how, given the secrets Nathaniel had told her were just that, secret. '*There's more*,' Nathaniel had said. '*Something Adam will blame himself for for the rest of his life.*' Sienna didn't know what, but she had a sick feeling she was beginning to guess.

She let Adam hold her instead, pulling her impossibly closer, his arms tight around her. Sienna waited, feeling the steady rhythm of his heartbeat next to her own, his hand weaving softly through her hair.

He eased back after a moment, bringing his hand around, under her chin, lifting her face to look directly at him. Slowly, he searched her eyes, the same smouldering intensity she'd seen once before darkening his own. There was something else there though, uncertainty, fear, longing.

Hesitantly he leaned towards her, tentatively seeking her mouth with his, parting her lips so softly, Sienna felt something beyond physical dissolve inside her. His kiss was slow, deep and passionate, his tongue finding hers, exploring her, tasting her. Sienna reciprocated, her tongue more demanding, more wanting than his, as he welcomed her eagerly into his mouth.

Stopping, out of necessity of breathing, he looked back into her eyes, and then pressed his forehead to hers. 'I want you, Sienna,' he said, his voice low and husky. On its own it sent a wave of white-hot desire right through her.

He looked back at her, relief flooding his beautiful features as Sienna nodded. You have me, she wanted to say, but stopped herself. Would he ever want all of her?

'Excellent,' he said quietly. He didn't seem cocky; over-confident that she would have said yes. She would have, though, however he'd asked her.

Sienna closed her eyes, a thousand butterflies taking off inside her tummy as he cupped her face in his hands. Closing his mouth back over hers, his kiss was bolder this time, deeper, sensual, plunging his tongue into her as if he was making love to her mouth.

His hands were in her hair, gliding down her back, over her bottom, everywhere. Sienna caught a gasp in her throat, wove her own fingers through his hair. She wanted him too. Like nothing she'd ever felt before, she knew that Adam making love to her was the only thing that could satiate her burning need. Her body ached for him. Her breasts tingled in anticipation of him, as he trailed his lips down her neck, his hands now sliding the straps of her top urgently over her shoulders.

Sienna heard the low moan in his throat as he bent to suck a nipple into his mouth, circling with his tongue; savouring the taste of her so gently she was near to coming from that sensation alone. She was almost ready to fall over the precipice into sweet oblivion, when his teeth, nipping, softly biting, increased the sensation, and when he moved to take her other nipple into his mouth, she groaned out loud. Her tummy was melting, literally, she could feel it.

'Adam,' she groaned. Her voice, thick with need, was alien to her ears. She opened her eyes to look down at him. The sight of this man at her breast made her head swim and her muscles down below contract in need of him. A need that was taking her breath away.

Adam found her mouth again, his hand seeking her

bottom under her shorts, gliding up over the restricting fabric, seeking her waistband. His breath was ragged, frustrated, as he fumbled with the button. '*Dammit*,' he cursed. 'Sorry,' he added quickly, and then, pulling in a breath, he scooped her into his arms and carried her upstairs, following Sienna's guidance to her room.

Laying her down on her bed, he ran his hands over her body, freeing her first of her top, then, his scorching eyes holding hers, he made short work of the button. Crawling over her, he eased the shorts down. Sienna lifted her hips allowing him to remove them all the way, and then waited, watching in awe, her breath coming in short, sharp gasps, as he peeled off his shirt.

His body truly was heart-stoppingly beautiful, the scar on his chest where he'd fought for his woman somehow making it more so. Unzipping his shorts, his erection was just as full of promise as before. Sienna wanted him now. She wasn't sure she could wait another second. Oh, but he was going to make her wait. And he was going to do terrible things to her while he did.

She could barely breathe as he climbed back on the bed, easing her legs open as he did. She watched, her chest tight with yearning as he bent to trail his mouth slowly along her inner thigh.

'I'm rushing,' he said. 'Sorry,' he repeated. 'I need to … Want to make love to you.'

Sienna gasped out loud as he ran his tongue along the secret folds of her flesh, lapping at her, expertly circling her sensitive place, until her hips undulated beneath him. 'Oh God, Adam, *please* …' she eventually cried out. She didn't know whether to scream stop or don't stop. She wanted him so badly.

Adam didn't stop. Intent on administering pleasure that would surely kill her, he eased his hands under her bottom and pressed his tongue deep into her, drawing it slowly in and out, nipping at her, pleasuring her – until she came so hard she screamed and convulsed beneath him.

'*Shhhh*,' he whispered, pressing his mouth urgently back over hers and inserting one finger inside her, then two, his thumb paying meticulous attention to her now hyper-sensitive spot as he did. 'I want to make love to you,' he repeated hoarsely. 'Open your eyes, Sienna. I need to see you.'

'Oh God.' Sienna let out a long, throaty moan. He was making love to her. He was making love to her with his words. She loved him. She absolutely did. And if he couldn't ever love her back, she'd still love him, for making her unashamed of her body and showing her how beautiful sex could be.

She opened her eyes, to see him watching her intently as he slid his fingers slowly in and out. She was so wet. So unbelievably wet.

'You're beautiful, Sienna,' he said. 'You should see. You should watch what your body can do to a man.' He kissed her lips again tenderly, and then kissed his way down to her breasts, circling attentively again with his tongue. She stroked his hair, tugged his hair, entwined her fingers through it and yanked it hard.

She couldn't watch. Couldn't keep her eyes open. It was impossible. Her back arched and her tummy muscles contracted and melted again in sweet, exquisite ecstasy.

Adam brought his mouth back to hers. 'I think we might be in trouble,' he said as he peppered her face with kisses.

Sienna's eyes sprang wide. 'Why?'

'Contraceptives,' he whispered, holding her gaze. 'I didn't think that you … That we, er …'

'Lauren's room, next door, bedside cabinet, top drawer.' Sienna nodded him there, her heart now physically swelling with love as she realised he hadn't been ever ready, that he hadn't assumed.

Adam was gone and back in seconds, it seemed. 'Have I spoiled the moment?' he asked worriedly, positioning himself back over her.

Sienna shook her head. Looking as impressively magnificent as he did, as concerned, how could he ever?

'Beautiful,' Adam said huskily, finding her mouth again with his. 'I want to see you, Sienna. Don't close your eyes. Let me see you.'

Sienna did as he asked, watching him, watching her as he pressed his erection against her, and then slid slowly all the way in, deep inside her.

'Okay?' he checked. She loved him for that, too.

She swallowed. 'Perfect.'

Closing his own eyes briefly, Adam smiled, withdrawing from her and thrusting slowly into her again.

'Do you like it like this?' he asked.

'Yes.' She could barely draw breath as he plunged deeply again.

'Faster?'

'*Yes.*' She squeezed her answer out, her excitement spiked by the sound of the husky urgency in his voice.

Stroking her hair from her face, he locked his eyes on hers and increased the pace, deep, sure strokes, plunging into her over and over. Sienna raised her hips to meet him, matching his tempo, pushing her tongue into his mouth, her fingernails finding his back.

This time he didn't seem to mind. Weaving his hands through her hair, he kissed her hungrily back. 'You're so beautiful,' he whispered, thrusting harder and deeper until she bucked beneath him, a guttural moan escaping her. 'Tell me when, Sienna?' he said, holding back. He was holding back, so he could …

'Now!' she cried, a tear escaping her eye as a white-hot spasm clenched her muscles around him, followed by another and another, as Adam groaned throatily and jolted inside her.

'Unbelievable,' he murmured, exhaling hard and sweeping his beautiful dark, concerned eyes over her face. 'Okay?' he asked.

Sienna nodded, too scared to speak. If she answered, what would he say? *Glad to be of service*, and then walk away?

He brushed her lips with his. 'It was a bit rushed,' he said, kissing her eyelashes. 'Sorry, we'll go a bit slower next time.'

Next time? Sienna blinked as he moved away from her. To climb off the bed and get dressed, she fully expected. But he didn't. Instead, he excused himself to the bathroom, then came immediately back and settled back beside her.

'Bed's a bit small, isn't it? Girl sized,' he said after a moment, observing the edge, which he was perilously close to. 'Roll over.' He turned to face her.

Sienna blinked again, bemused.

'Don't worry, I'm not going to molest you.' He smiled, his eyes roving suggestively over her body. 'I'll need at least five minutes.'

'Five whole minutes?' She widened her eyes in mock-horror.

'Okay, four.' He laughed. 'Roll over on your side,' he said, a definite twinkle now in his eye. 'Tuck that gorgeous bottom into me. That should hurry things up a bit.'

'You're bad,' Sienna scolded him, turning to nestle into him. Bliss, she thought, wanting to preserve these few precious moments forever. He'd be gone soon, she supposed, back to his rocking boat.

'I know,' Adam said, finding her ear beneath her mad

mess of hair and brushing it with his lips, 'but I am trying not to be.'

'I thought we were spooning,' Sienna said after a second, realising he was perched on his elbow, now studying her obviously really interesting ear.

'We are. I, er ...' Adam settled back behind her, circling her waist and pulling her close. 'I just wanted to dispel any illusions you might have, while we do.'

'Oh.' Sienna's blissful contentment evaporated.

'I am bad news, Sienna. You know that, right?'

Sienna nodded. Her voice seemed to have deserted her again.

'So, if I asked you to do this officially. If I asked you to go out with me and you told me to get stuffed, I just wanted to say, I'd completely understand.'

Chapter Eleven

'You've gone completely insane.' Lauren imparted her thoughts on Sienna's state of mind, yet again, the next morning. 'You need help, Sienna, you really do. You should speak to your dad. I'll speak to your dad. You can't possibly—'

'Don't you dare!' Sienna stopped attempting to scrape the burned Bolognese sauce from the pan and stuffed it wholesale in the bin instead. 'My love life is my business, Lauren, not anyone else's.'

'But it will be, won't it? Do you think God's gift to women is going to do the gentlemanly thing and *not* announce to his mates he's notched you up on his bedpost, twice?'

He doesn't have that many mates, Sienna didn't bother to reply. 'He's not like that,' she said, resisting the urge to point out that Lauren had also had quite a rigorous night, judging by the inside-out top she'd arrived home in and the now considerable hangover. Rather than give her the third-degree, though, as Lauren seemed intent on giving her, Sienna was doing what friends did, making her a very strong coffee and providing the aspirin, although why she should bother ...

'No, of *course* he's not.' Lauren accepted the aspirin, wincing as she swallowed them. 'He's just so caring of women's feelings he's probably dashing out to buy you flowers right now as we speak – on his way to his next shag.'

'Stop it, Lauren. That's not fair.'

'No, Sienna. It's Adam who's not being fair. He's an emotion-abuser, you know he is. He's just messing with—'

'He's not!' Sienna gave up on her toast and scraped that

into the bin, too. 'He's asked me out! Properly out.'

Lauren rolled her eyes sky-high. 'Because he wanted to get you into bed, Sienna, don't you see?'

'No, Lauren, I don't see, because I'd already gone to bed with him, hadn't I? And just so you have all the facts before coming to your oh-so-not-correct conclusions, it was earth-movingly orgasmic, *both* times, and I would hop into bed with him again in a flash.'

Sienna plucked up Tobias's lead and huffed towards the door. 'Come on, Tobias. Let's get some air.'

'You have a self-worth problem, Sienna,' Lauren said behind her. 'You must have to get involved with someone who doesn't give a damn about anyone.'

'Yes, he *does*!' Sienna turned angrily back. 'He was lovely when I told him about Mum. You don't know him, Lauren, so stop judging him.'

'Oh, Sienna, Sienna …' Lauren slapped her hand against her forehead. 'You really don't see, do you? He's playing games with you, sweetie. You confide in him and he just knows all he has to do is offer you a bit of sympathy and affection, and then it's wham-bam.'

'Why on earth would he need to do that? I approached him for the pleasure initially, Lauren, remember? And it was!' Sienna shouted, her face flaming.

'To shore up his bloody ego! The thrill of the chase and all that crap. That's what men like him are like! And when he thinks he's got you, he'll drop you like a hot brick. He doesn't care about you, Sienna. For God's sake, open your eyes.'

'They are open!' Sienna headed for the hall. 'It's you who can't see, Lauren,' she threw, over her shoulder, 'past the spiteful gossip.'

Outside, Sienna pulled in a breath, notched up her chin and set off at a march. *I don't care what they think.*

They were wrong, all of them. They simply refused to give Adam a chance. Yes, he had a terrible reputation, obviously deserved, but while there were no real excuses for his behaviour, there were reasons. It wasn't just her who thought so either. Nathaniel did, too. And Adam was trying to change his ways, wasn't he? Why couldn't people give him the slightest benefit of the doubt and acknowledge he was?

He did care about her. Would a man who didn't care take her hand, his beautiful eyes clouded with worry, as he'd asked her if she was absolutely sure she wanted to go out with him? If she was sure she wanted to be seen *with* him? That wasn't cocksure, confident Lothario Adam. That was a different Adam, a lonely, uncertain man. Sienna was as sure of that as she was that she absolutely *did* want to go out with him.

She stopped in her tracks as the man himself leapt his handrail and dropped down in front of her like a vision from Heaven.

'Hi,' he said, looking tanned and toned, temptingly edible in his jogging gear, and extremely nervous. As if he thought she might have slept on it and decided she wanted no part of him. 'How are you?' he asked hesitantly.

'Good.' She smiled. 'Better than.'

'No regrets then?' he asked, and there it was again, that look. A mixture of uncertainty and fear; Sienna just knew she wasn't wrong.

'None,' she assured him. 'It was beautiful.' She felt herself blush, and didn't much care.

'My thoughts entirely.' He smiled, his face flooding with obvious relief. 'In fact, I hold you personally responsible for the fact that I didn't sleep a wink for thinking how beautiful you were.'

Sienna laughed. 'Flatterer.'

'It's one of my better qualities,' Adam said, falling into step with her as she walked.

'Can I ask you something though, Adam,' she said, after a pause, 'about last night?'

'Ask away,' Adam shrugged easily, 'as long as it doesn't dent my male ego too much.'

'It won't.' Sienna laughed. Adam-the-super-stud's ego, she suspected, was probably much more fragile than it seemed. 'About what I told you ... My mum ... What were you thinking about? You seemed ...' overwhelmed with emotion, she thought, '... shocked.' She opted for.

Adam stopped walking.

'Adam?' Sienna turned to face him.

Adam glanced at his trainers. 'Ghosts,' he said quietly. 'Someone I lost. Someone I should have been there for.'

His fiancée? Noting his downcast eyes, the reticent body language, Sienna hesitated. 'Do you want to talk about it?' she asked carefully, not wishing to force him into telling her what he might not be ready to.

'I, er ... Sometime.' He shrugged again, awkwardly this time, and looked back at her.

Sienna scanned his eyes. Haunted eyes, she saw immediately. Eyes where a thousand dark shadows danced, those of a man who was more than scared, she realised, her heart constricting for him. He was terrified.

Blow them all, she thought angrily. They could think what they liked. She *would* go out with him and world condemnation be damned. 'In case you were wondering,' she stepped towards him, 'I still want to see you again and still want to be seen with you.' She stood on tiptoe to brush his lovely lips softly with her own.

Adam's mouth curved into a delicious, bone-melting smile. 'Excellent,' he whispered, folding her into his arms to kiss her thoroughly back.

That should give the gossipmongers plenty of fodder, Sienna thought, as his tongue slid deliciously into her mouth to say good morning to hers.

Adam kept jogging until he ran out of steam, finally grinding his euphoric run to a stop as he rounded the bend to the cottage. He'd probably crucified his quad and calf muscles. Adrenaline still pumping through him, he bent his head, clasping his thighs and taking deep breaths. He'd done it. He tugged in a slow breath and held it. He'd asked her out. And she'd said yes.

Yesss! Bloody good! Punching the air, and then waving to some bloke who obviously thought he was a complete loony, Adam set off again at a jog, careless of his escalating heartbeat.

She wanted to go out with him. He still couldn't believe it. History, bad-news reputation and all, Sienna wanted to be with him. She was actually comfortable being seen in public with him, confirming it with a steamy, tongue-duelling kiss that had possibly given Nate apoplexy, judging by the stunned expression on his face. Peering out of the window of the cottage, Lauren's expression had been a bit shocked, too, before she'd disappeared from view.

She'd probably passed out in horror. Adam was sure she'd been about to keel over or self-combust when she'd come through the kitchen door last night to find him half-naked and up close to Sienna. Very close. Sienna's fault. She'd insisted on spoon-feeding him the salvageable bits of the Bolognese sauce.

Smiling to himself as he recalled how she'd also insisted on licking up any inadvertently spilled drips, Adam checked his mobile in case of last-minute changes regarding his meeting with Lily-Grace. Relieved when he found none, he made sure Sherry's car wasn't parked outside the cottage and headed up the path. He wanted to get in and out as fast as he could. He was sorry he'd got involved with her, sorry he'd hurt her feelings. He hadn't set out to do that. He had hurt her, though. He'd obviously hurt other women, too, in the past. If only he hadn't been such a self-centred bastard, too preoccupied with his own problems and needs, he might have realised it. He'd hurt Emily, too concerned with his own future to consider her. He could have made changes once they were married, applied for jobs elsewhere, rented a house under his own steam instead of being beholden to his father. He could have manned up and talked to her, before the wedding, after they'd split – there was a child involved, for God's sake. Instead he'd turned his back on her, ultimately driving her to do what she had. Had she meant to? Truly meant to leave her child without a mother? Adam would never know the answer to that either. Yet, he knew she was sorry. Seeing her last night at Sienna's, he'd felt the weight of her sorrow, and his heart had broken twice over: for the woman he'd once loved – and for the courageous woman he now loved, standing right beside her.

Reaching the front door, he paused to fish in his pocket for the key. Maybe he should apologise to Sherry, he pondered. But then, the mood she'd been in when he'd last seen her, if he went anywhere near the farm in the foreseeable future, Sherry would probably be the one brandishing the shotgun.

Still debating, Adam opened the door, stepped in and … *oh, crap* … found himself looking down the barrel of it.

'Inside.' Sherry's husband fixed him with hard, uncompromising eyes.

Jesus. Adam swallowed back his racing heart, which felt as if it was clawing its way up his oesophagus. He tried to think, to move, follow his inclination to run, but his legs refused to respond to his brain's instructions.

'I said, *inside*!' The guy fumed, an angry bubble of spittle forming at the corner of his mouth.

'Look, I'm not sure what your problem is,' Adam tried, 'but—'

'Shut up, you little shit, and get inside!' The guy seethed, raising the gun and bringing the butt of it down hard.

Fuck! Adam sucked in a sharp breath as an excruciating pain seared through his shoulder.

'Inside!' The guy grabbed a fistful of his vest, as Adam's knees buckled, twisting it around his hand and dragging him bodily in. 'Sit!' he snarled, shoving him in the direction of the sofa.

Adam's head reeled. His gut lurched. Righting himself on his feet, he gulped back a sick taste in his mouth and looked back at him.

'Sit,' the guy grated again, indicating his requirements with the gun. Panic knotting his insides, Adam glanced past him to the still open front door.

'Don't even think about it,' the man warned him, his tone pure venom, his face tight with rage.

Shit. He meant it. A trickle of sweat snaking its way down his spine, his heart thudding so loud he could hear it, Adam raked a hand shakily through his hair and did as requested.

The guy watched him for an agonising few seconds, not speaking, not moving, the gun cocked and poised. 'Not nice, is it, being assaulted?' he asked eventually, his tone calmer.

Adam swallowed repeatedly. He had no idea what to say.

'My wife didn't like it, Adam. That is your name, isn't it?'

Adam stared at him, stupefied. His wife …? Sherry? Assaulted? What the *hell*?

'I asked you a question,' the guy said, his tone still calm, chillingly so.

Adam blinked back a salty bead of sweat. Which question was he supposed to bloody well answer?

'Is that how you get them to comply, Adam?' the guy went on, his steely-eyed gaze never leaving his. 'Your renowned many sexual exploits?'

Adam shook his head, bewildered. 'I ...' he started.

'By bullying them?' the guy yelled, causing Adam to jump in his seat. 'Forcing them?'

'*What?*' Adam stared at him, terror mounting inside him. He was going to do it. The madman was going to shoot him.

Adam's eyes flew to the kitchen doorway, and his stomach turned over. Another man blocked that exit. Arms-folded, feet splayed in a silent display of aggression, he was broader than Adam, taller than him, and from his expression he would take great pleasure in making sure he went nowhere.

Petrified, Adam looked back to her husband. 'I didn't ... I have no idea what—'

'Quiet, Adam,' the guy said, 'if you know what's good for you.'

Jesus. Adam closed his eyes. Lily-Grace was all he could think of. He was supposed to be seeing her. He was going to let her down. He was going to fail to show up, and she would never know ...

'Sherry begged me not to do anything,' the husband went on as Adam steeled himself for whatever was to come. 'Me, I was all for shooting you, since you're obviously illegally on my property. What I decided on, Adam, was a compromise. First we're going to beat the crap out of you, and then we're going to have the police come and pick you up.'

Adam pulled in a breath and glanced back to the kitchen.

'Tut, tut, where are my manners. Michael, meet Adam. Adam, Michael, Rebekah's husband. I believe he has a score to settle with you, too.'

That was it. He was dead. Or soon going to wish he was. Adam braced himself, as Michael moved into the room, and then prayed.

Sienna watched Nathaniel approach the cottage over the book she wasn't reading. She was trying to, but she had the attention span of a gnat. However hard she tried to concentrate, her mind kept sliding right back to Adam. The things he'd said to her. His own emotions obviously in turmoil, he'd sought only to offer her comfort, selflessly, caringly. The way he'd folded her into his arms; made such special, sweet, sensual love to her, as if trying to caress her pain away. The way he'd held her afterwards, his firm body pressed close, his arms tightening around her as he'd asked her out. He'd joked about it, as if it wouldn't be the end of the world if she said no, but he'd stopped breathing for a second. She was sure his heart had stopped beating.

He'd said it was rushed. Not in her book it wasn't. If that was his version of a quickie, he could rush away with her any old day. Sienna smiled gloopily, then straightened her face as she realised Nathaniel was regarding her curiously.

'Morning,' he said.

'Morning.' Sienna beamed him a smile.

Nathaniel offered her a small smile back and then seemed to hesitate.

Sienna waited.

'So, it's official then?' Nathaniel finally asked. 'You two are definitely an item?'

'Most definitely,' Sienna assured him.

Nathaniel nodded slowly. 'And you're certain about this, are you, Sienna?' He glanced down and back as Sienna regarded him questioningly. 'I mean, I love the bloke to bits. He's my mate, but ...'

'But?' Sienna narrowed her eyes.

'He has issues, Sienna.' Nathaniel obviously felt obliged to point out, again. 'I'm not sure he's—'

'I know he has issues!' Sienna snapped. 'You know I do, Nate. I thought you were on his side?'

'I am on his side.' He sighed and parked himself on a spare patio chair. 'I've always been on his side, even when he was being a complete prat. I'm just concerned, that's all; for both of you.'

'Nate, I'm a grown woman,' Sienna pointed out. 'I know what I'm doing, honestly. There's no need to worry about me.'

'Do you, though?' Nathaniel looked her over thoughtfully. 'Could you really handle it if he couldn't give up the booze, Sienna? If despite his best intentions, he couldn't commit to one woman?'

'You sound as if you expect him to fail.' Bracing herself for yet another anti-Adam barrage, Sienna closed her book and parked it on the ground.

Nathaniel blew out a long breath. 'That's the trouble, Sienna, I don't know what to expect. Adam's predictable in a lot of ways, but this is a new one on me.'

Predictable meaning doing everything they expected of him, meaning he was 'bad news'. But he wasn't doing everything as expected, was he? He *had* stopped drinking, started running. 'He is trying, Nate,' Sienna reminded him. 'You have to give him some credit.'

Nathaniel looked abashed. 'I know.' He nodded, and mopped the sweat from his brow with his sleeve. 'I know he is. It's just … it's early days yet. I'm concerned he'll struggle with emotional commitment, I suppose, and end up letting you down. Then he'll be off on one of his guilt trips and the drowning-his-sorrows and womanising thing will start up all over again.'

'You mean it's stopped?' Lauren piped up through the

open kitchen window.

Sienna ignored her. 'You sound like a mother hen,' she addressed Nathaniel kindly.

Nathaniel rolled his eyes. 'That's what Adam calls me.'

'It's nice,' Sienna assured him, 'that you care about him, I mean.'

'Someone has to.' Nathaniel smiled stoically and got to his feet. 'The man's a hazard to himself and everyone else.'

'So everyone keeps saying.' Sienna dropped her gaze and plucked up a strand of hair to fiddle with.

'Sorry.' Nathaniel shrugged apologetically. 'I know you care about him, Sienna. It's hard to be objective, though, when you're ...' He paused, searching for the right word.

'Shagging him,' Lauren supplied.

'I'd better get back to the chandlery.' Nathaniel blushed purple and about-faced.

'He's a heartbreaker, Sienna,' Lauren felt obliged to comment again as Nathaniel walked off. 'I hope you've got your loins girded, girl, because he's going to break yours sooner or later, mark my words.'

'And *you* sound like my grandmother. Shut up, Lauren.'

'Just saying.'

'Well, don't.'

He wasn't going to break her heart. He'd never hurt her intentionally, Sienna was sure. She wished people would stop predicting he'd let her down and being generally so down on him. You'd think they would at least try to reserve judgement. Retrieving her book, she glanced at her watch, aware that it was now a good hour past the time Adam said he'd ring her. He'd suggested they go out later. He had job-hunting plans he wanted to tell her about, he'd said. He wasn't sure what time he'd be back, but he'd give her a ring to confirm. Strange that he hadn't.

Chapter Twelve

'Blimey, he's a bit of mess, isn't he?' Adam heard one of the officers addressing James.

'He broke into my property. I was using reasonable force to protect myself,' James pointed out irritably. 'Are you going to sympathise with him, or arrest him?'

'Better get him down to the station, Steve,' the same officer said, presumably to his partner. Adam didn't look up as the officers walked across to him.

'Adam Hamilton-Shaw, we are legally obliged to inform you that we are arresting you on suspicion of breaking and entering with intent to commit a crime.'

'Intent?' James laughed scornfully. 'The bastard bloody well attacked my wife!'

'You do not have to say anything,' the officer went on as his partner cautioned James to quieten down. 'However, it may harm your defence if you do not mention when questioned something which you later rely on in court. Anything you do say may be given in evidence. Do you understand, sir?'

Adam swallowed and nodded. He was in so much pain he couldn't have answered if he'd wanted to. He was still breathing. He supposed that was something to be grateful for.

The cuffs hadn't been necessary, the police had decided, when he'd been struggling to even stand up. Adam had badly wanted to run though, as fast and as far away as possible. Wasn't about to go anywhere now, was he, apart from the cells probably. A shiver ran through him as he responded to the on-call doctor's prodding, poking and questions with a nod or a shake of his head.

He'd done it again. Adam sighed inside. Let everyone down. Nicole, little Lily-Grace, who at least wasn't old enough to know he had – yet. Sienna, the only good, decent thing to have happened in his life in a long time. *She* should have run, should have avoided him like the plague. Would now, Adam was certain of that.

'Is he done?' the detective inspector asked, once the doctor had established he didn't need hospitalising and had bagged up the various swabs.

'All done,' the doctor confirmed. 'No strenuous activity, though,' he addressed Adam. 'The ribs are definitely cracked.'

'Oh, I doubt he'll be undertaking any strenuous activity for a while,' the detective commented drolly, perching himself on the table to Adam's side as the doctor took his leave.

Too close. Adam felt suddenly very claustrophobic in the confines of the soulless interview room.

'So, Mr Hamilton-Shaw …' the detective said companionably. 'Or should I call you Adam, God's gift to womankind,' his voice took on a mocking tone, 'because you obviously think you are, don't you?'

Adam fixed his gaze on his hands in front of him on the table. He didn't answer. After the kicking he'd taken back at the cottage, he wasn't sure any answer he gave wouldn't be a wrong one.

'Seems you've bedded every woman in the vicinity, Adam,' the detective went on, idly plucking a piece of fluff from his trouser leg.

Adam flinched as a hand was slammed down in front of him, and then gulped back a hard lump in his throat as he felt the man's breath inches from his cheek. Adam didn't move. He didn't dare.

'Did you do it, Adam?' The detective got suddenly to his feet and paced slowly around behind him. 'Assault the man's wife?'

Adam closed his eyes.

'Wasn't going to take no for an answer, is that it?'

The guy waited. Adam swallowed.

'I've been doing some digging around, Adam.' The detective walked around in front of him. 'Seems you have a history of violence. Your brother wasn't very happy with you, by all accounts. Your fiancée either.'

The man paused, glowering down at him.

Adam tried to concentrate on the simple act of breathing.

'Couldn't have been really, could she? Did you treat her with the same respect you treat all women, Adam?'

Adam tugged in a painful breath, and tried hard to still the flashback: Her eyes were open, empty; her spirit flown. *No!* He couldn't do this.

'Well?'

Saying nothing, Adam tried to control his insistent shaking.

The detective planted his hands on the table and pushed his face up close to his. 'You either cooperate, Adam,' he growled menacingly, 'or you are going to be here for a very long time. Now, I asked you a question. It's a simple yes or no answer.'

Adam swallowed again, hard, and looked up at him. Her spirit ... His heart jolted. Not flown. Here, still. Could it really be that she'd been waiting, watching, appearing more and more often, until he *had* to acknowledge he could see her? He *could* see her. He squinted hard past the detective. Indistinct still, but she was there. Emily. She was shaking her head. There was no sadness there, only ... determination? He could feel it. It was right there inside him.

Adam focused back on the copper, scanned his merciless,

mocking eyes, and took a breath. 'Can I phone a friend?' he asked, deliberately flippant. He might be going insane, probably was. Whatever this 'defender of the law' did to him, though, he wasn't going to give in. Not here. Not now.

'Cocky little bastard,' the detective seethed. 'You really are a piece of work, aren't—' He stopped as the interview door opened behind him.

Adam wasn't sure if he should feel relieved or whether to brace himself all over again, as the duty officer came back in.

Relieved, he supposed, as the detective switched to professional police mode. 'I'm going to ask you some questions,' he said, his tone detached, but borderline respectful. 'You do not have to say or do anything if you do not want to. Do you understand, sir?'

Having worried and wondered for several hours, Sienna finally decided to ask Nathaniel if Adam might have mentioned going on somewhere after his run this morning. He hadn't spoken to Nathaniel before he'd left, but he might have rung him, Sienna supposed. She hoped he had, because the only place she imagined he might be was the cottage. That thought causing a flutter of uncertainty in her chest, she tapped lightly on Nathaniel's open door and went on in. 'Sorry to bother you, Nate,' she said, 'but—'

Sienna stopped as Nathaniel continued his conversation on the phone, beckoning her stay put with his hand, rather than beckoning her on in, as he normally did.

'They're charging you with *what*?' He looked up at Sienna, his face visibly paling. 'Don't say anything. I'm on my way.'

Sienna felt a sinking feeling in the pit of her tummy as Nathaniel banged the phone down and scraped his chair back. 'Nate …?' She eyed him quizzically.

'Adam,' Nathaniel supplied, snatching up his mobile and jabbing a number into it as he scrambled around his desk. 'He's in police custody.'

'Police custody?' The floor shifted under Sienna's feet. 'But why?' Her alarm escalated as Nathaniel headed fast for the door. 'Nate? Why? What are they charging him with?'

Nathaniel stopped, tugging in a terse breath as he turned to face her. 'Breaking and entering, and ...' he glanced evasively down, '... they're claiming he assaulted someone's wife. I'm sorry, Sienna.'

Shaking his head, Nathaniel turned agitatedly back to the door. 'Bloody idiot,' he muttered as he left. 'I warned him something like this would happen.'

'I'm taking you to the hospital.' Nathaniel glanced sideways again at Adam as he drove.

'No,' Adam insisted. 'I'm fine.'

'*Fine?* You look as if you've gone ten rounds with Mike Tyson. You look like shit, Adam.'

'Feels like it.' Adam laughed wryly. He actually felt like crying, like crawling in a hole and dying. He just wanted to get home. Wash off the stench of hours at the station – being prodded, poked, questioned and basically disbelieved – from his body, climb into his bed and stay there. He wanted to close his eyes. Close his eyes and not think or *see* anything.

'Bastards,' Nathaniel seethed. 'Are they charging them?'

'For restraining an intruder? A violent intruder? Not likely, is it?' Adam shook his head, and then winced as a searing pain ripped through his chest.

Nathaniel pulled in a breath, as if to say something, but didn't.

They drove on for a while in silence, the only noise the purr of the engine and the rhythmic swish of the window wipers, which was actually quite soothing. Adam was immensely relieved Nathaniel hadn't decided to launch into a sermon. He much preferred quiet. Craved it, in fact. He really didn't want to answer any more questions. Didn't want to talk anymore. There just didn't seem to be any point.

'Did you do it?' Nathaniel finally asked the one question Adam definitely didn't want to answer. The one Nathaniel had obviously been bursting to ask since they'd released him.

Adam watched the wipers slosh hopelessly against the deluge of rain, his heart sinking. 'Do you think I did?' he asked quietly.

Nathaniel shrugged. 'No, but ...'

And there it was, the 'but', which meant that even Nathaniel doubted his innocence. If the one person who knew him better than anybody didn't believe him, what chance Sienna would? What chance Nicole would? History, he told himself. *Forget it.* 'I didn't assault her, Nate, no,' he said, swallowing back a tight lump in his throat.

'Okay,' Nathaniel said, after a loaded pause. 'In which case, they'll probably have little in the way of evidence. I doubt they'll be able to make a strong enough case to—'

'I had sex with her,' Adam cut him short. 'And I was staying at the cottage.' He didn't say anymore. He guessed Nathaniel didn't really need him to.

'Idiot,' Nathaniel muttered, his eyes fixed frontwards as he drove on.

'Can I ask you another favour, Nate?' Adam asked hesitantly, as they approached the marina, though he guessed he'd probably used up his quota of favours where Nathaniel was concerned.

Nathaniel nodded shortly.

'Can you lose the lights and park as close as possible to

my boat?'

Nathaniel glanced at him, sighed, and switched off his headlights. 'You'll have to face her sometime, you know?'

'I know.' Adam sighed wearily. 'Not now, though. Not like this.'

'Hot chocolate,' Lauren said kindly, planting a mug on Sienna's bedside cabinet.

Sienna didn't want it. She wouldn't be able to swallow it. She didn't want to do, say, drink or eat anything. All she wanted was to stay curled up with Tobias until she knew what on earth was going on. She needed to know Adam was home safe. She needed to *know*.

'Come on, sweetie, drink it. It'll make you feel better.' Lauren perched herself on the edge of Sienna's bed. Her 'girl-sized' bed, where she had lain with Adam. Where he'd made such tender, beautiful love to her, awakening parts of her she hadn't even known existed. Could that man, who'd crossed no boundaries she hadn't agreed on, really have assaulted a woman?

'Do you think he did it?' she asked, running a hand under her nose.

'Your eyes are swollen, Sienna,' Lauren answered evasively. 'You need to get some sleep.'

'Do you?'

Lauren reached out to brush Sienna's now totally bedraggled hair from her face. 'We don't know anything yet, sweetie.'

'But do you *think* he did it?'

Lauren glanced down. 'You have to admit his morals are a bit skewed, Sienna. And, from what you've told me, he has every reason not to like women very—'

'He didn't!' Sienna shot up. 'He's not skewed. He's not anything. He's just a lonely person who got hurt.'

'All right, Sienna.' Lauren looked at her worriedly. 'I didn't say I did believe it. Now, come on, calm down. You're frightening Tobias.'

Sienna glanced at her poor dog's cocked ears and puzzled wide eyes, but still she pushed on. She had to make people see. He couldn't have done it. He *hadn't*. 'His affairs were his way of dealing with his hurt, don't you see?' she tried to explain. 'His way of working through it? His sleeping with women doesn't make him a violent attacker.'

'It does make him a sex-addict, though, Sienna,' Lauren pointed out quietly. 'A man who uses women, ergo, doesn't really care about them.'

Sienna jumped off the bed. 'You'd have him hung, drawn and quartered. All of you! You won't even give him the benefit of the doubt. You *never* would.'

'Sienna, you need to calm down.' Lauren stood to face her. 'Come on, come and sit back down. I'll ring your dad. He can come and collect you. You'll be better off at—'

'Don't you dare, Lauren! This is *my* life. I love Adam, and I'll stand by him, even—' Sienna stopped as she heard a car door slam. *He was here!*

She needed to see him. She needed to tell him. She didn't believe it. She *didn't*. Heedless of shoes or coat, she flew downstairs and straight out of the front door, heading for Adam's boat, Lauren two steps behind her.

'Nate?' Realising Adam had already gone inside, Sienna stopped dead. Bewildered, she glanced from Nathaniel to Adam's closed boat door.

Nathaniel's smile was forced. 'He's okay,' he assured her. 'Just needs some rest.'

Sienna glanced at Adam's boat again, where no lights came on, then back to Nathaniel. 'Did he say anything?' she asked him, her voice quavering, though she was trying very hard not to crumble, right there in front of everyone. He must have said something? Left some kind of message for Nathaniel to pass on to her, surely?

Nathaniel shrugged uncomfortably. 'He said he'd talk to you soon.'

'That's very thoughtful of him,' Lauren mumbled facetiously.

'Lauren! Just stop!' Sienna whirled around, hot angry tears coursing down her cheeks. '*Please* stop.'

Shaking her head, concern etching her face, Lauren stepped towards her. 'Come on, Sienna, come back to the cottage,' she urged, wrapping an arm around her shoulders. 'It's pouring with rain and you've got no shoes on.'

'Tell him, Nathaniel, will you?' Sienna begged him as Lauren attempted to steer her back towards the cottage. 'Tell him I want to talk to him. Tell him I'll always want to talk to him, no matter what.'

No matter what, Adam repeated the words in his head. Sienna obviously also thought he might be guilty then. Guilty. Seated on the floor of the cabin, the hull supporting his back, he rolled that word around for the umpteenth time too, and then gulped back his heart, which felt as if it had been shot into shards.

He couldn't blame her. Couldn't blame anyone but himself. He didn't even blame Sherry. He'd gone into their 'arrangement' with his eyes open. Whatever she'd wanted from him, he'd used her entirely for his own gratification. He still wasn't sure why she was corroborating the husband's claims. Presumably he'd found out, been aggressive, physically possibly. In which case, judging by his own encounter with him, she'd probably be terrified enough to go along with anything he wanted her to. The man was a vicious bastard, that much was clear.

There was a way he could prove he'd been granted

permission to use the property, disprove the breaking and entering claim; it had occurred to Adam when the police had been questioning him. The husband had relieved him of the key, obviously, and made sure there were visible signs of forced entry, but Adam had a witness. Someone who had seen him with a key, but absolutely no way was Adam about to ask Sienna to verify it.

She loved it here, in her own little cottage overlooking the water. She had her part-time job here. And there were people here who would make her life a misery if they knew she'd been associating with him, been at that property with him; the pub landlord for one, who'd only ever tolerated his drinking at the pub since the car park incident, probably with his profit in mind.

Then there was the gang of thugs, noisy and intimidating at best, the ringleader of which Adam now knew to be Rebekah's younger brother. Adam had noticed them eyeing Sienna up, smirking and nudging each other. He had no doubt they would take great pleasure in winding her up once this got out. Possibly even pushing things further. No, he wasn't going to get Sienna involved.

He'd made his bed. He was bad news. A useless bastard. No way would he ever have been good enough for her. At least Sienna's eyes had been opened to that fact before he screwed up her life as well as his own. She'd be better off without him. Fighting back the gnawing pain in his chest, Adam grappled his mobile from his pocket and checked his messages, several from Sienna wondering if he was okay, each growing more concerned, the last simply reading *please talk to me*. Adam would. He owed her that much, but not yet. He wasn't sure he could cope with the disappointment in her eyes.

Two messages from Nicole, pretty much what he expected: *I hope you have a bloody good explanation*, read the first. *Second thoughts, save it. We don't want to hear it,* said the second.

No, you really don't, Nicole. Adam pulled in a slow breath, which stopped short of his chest. The sadness was back, he realised, suffocating, heavy, all around him; inside him. Closing his eyes, he breathed slowly out, and willed himself not to cry out in pain.

He didn't bother to flick to his photo of Lily-Grace. Not much point, he guessed. He needed a beer, he thought vaguely. He needed to lie down. The lying down bit might be tricky, given he was now struggling to even sit back comfortably. The beer he could manage, if only he could force himself to stand up.

Sienna had watched the boat all night. He hadn't put a light on. Not one. There'd barely been any movement. He'd been sitting in there on his own in the dark. Drinking on his own in the dark?

She couldn't save him, she knew that. Contrary to Lauren concluding she hadn't got a brain cell in her head, Sienna knew that ultimately Adam would have to help himself, but she couldn't just sit by and watch him drink himself into a stupor; a permanent stupor probably. He must be feeling so down, so alone. Might he do something worse? It was probably her paranoia at play, but now that the awful thought had occurred, she couldn't just sit here and do nothing. Guessing Lauren was still sleeping, she pressed a finger to her lips and mouthed, 'stay' to Tobias, then slipped on her trainers and made her way to Adam's boat.

'Adam?' she called as she boarded, not wanting to scare him. No answer, she tapped on the door and called again. Still there was no answer, no movement; no signs of life at all.

Foreboding growing inside her, Sienna rapped hard and

called again. He must be able to hear her. If he'd been asleep, she would have woken him by now, surely? He might be ignoring her, wishing she'd go away and leave him alone, but she couldn't shake the feeling he might not be *able* to hear. 'Adam!' she shouted, and banged on the door. 'Adam!'

Nothing. Not a sound. Frantically, Sienna looked around, unsure what to do next. His curtains were drawn. He'd been in there all night, barely moved, and no one seemed to give a damn. People were poking their noses out of windows now, though, she noticed. Other boat-owners, people from the neighbouring cottages, who never normally gave Adam more than a derisory, disinterested glance. They were interested now, weren't they? More anxious they might miss a juicy bit of gossip than about Adam. Sienna had no doubt about that. So much for neighbourly concern, she thought angrily. It was no wonder Adam had shut himself away.

Ignoring them, Sienna went back to the door. This time she hammered, shouting so loud Adam couldn't fail to hear her. Still, he didn't answer. He would if he could, she was sure he would. He wouldn't just lie there ... *Dear God*, panic clutching icily at her insides Sienna whirled around, leaping from boat to bank to fly towards the office. Nathaniel would have spare keys. She tried to still her racing heart. He had spares to all the boats, in case of emergencies. *Please, please, don't let this be one.*

Obviously having heard the commotion, Nathaniel was already out of the chandlery, hurrying towards her, keys in hand. 'Nate ...?' Sienna said tremulously, meeting him halfway across the marina.

'I'm on it,' Nathaniel assured her, bypassing her, his face white, in his eyes palpable panic.

'Adam?' he yelled, clambering up onto the deck, fiddling the key into the lock. 'Adam! For God's sake, open up!'

He still wasn't answering. *Why* wasn't he answering? Feeling sick to her soul, Sienna watched from the bank, as did the gongoozlers, who'd now gathered for a ringside seat.

'Adam!' Nathaniel shouted urgently again, finally thrusting the door wide. 'Adam!'

Sienna was up on the deck, right behind him. 'Sienna, wait!' Nathaniel turned, catching her shoulders, trying to prevent her going down into the boat. 'Let me go in first. He won't want ...'

Sienna wasn't listening. Desperate, she pushed past Nathaniel and half stumbled down the steps, and then stopped. Dear *God!* What had they done to him?

'Adam!' Sienna screamed, flying to where he was slumped on the floor, his head lolling awkwardly back against the wall of the boat. He had a pillow clutched to his chest. Where was he hurting? She couldn't see where he was hurting!

'Adam,' she repeated tearfully, dropping to her knees to brush his sweat-dampened hair from his forehead. His beautiful dark eyes flickered open and then closed. He didn't seem to see her. His face was bloody and bruised. His complexion was pale; as pallid as death.

The absolute bastards! Swiping a tear from her cheek, cursing whoever had done this to damnation, Sienna shuffled closer, and heard a distinct rattle in his chest. He couldn't breathe properly! He was struggling to get air into his lungs. 'Nathaniel!'

Nathaniel was already there, right next to her. 'Adam?' he said, reaching to gently shake his shoulder, but Adam's head just slumped forwards.

'Idiot,' Nathaniel grimaced. 'I told him to go to the hospital, but would he?' One arm across Adam to support him, Nathaniel fished in his pocket and passed Sienna his phone. '999,' he instructed.

Adam was sleeping when she arrived at the hospital, his long, dark eyelashes brushing his cheeks, his eyelids flickering as his mind chased his dreams. God, he was so pale. Normally tanned, smiling, outwardly confident, he looked so troubled, so ill. Pleurisy, Nathaniel had told her it was, an inflammation caused by the fractures to his ribs. Why had they done this to him? Did he really deserve this?

Some people would say so, based on the assumption he was guilty before proven innocent. Sienna had heard one of the boat owners commenting as the ambulance had taken Adam away. '*Deserves that and more,*' a man, who probably didn't even know Adam other than by reputation, had said.

'*He'll get his comeuppance,*' another boat owner had imparted. '*Scum like him get a taste of their own in prison.*'

It was wrong. All wrong, condemning him without even knowing. Sienna had wanted to scream at them, he didn't do it! But what was the point? They'd obviously already judged him.

His breathing was easier, she noticed. Shallow, but that awful rattle she'd heard wasn't there. He was sweating, still, though. Tentatively, she reached out, to brush his hair from his forehead, and Adam was wide awake in a flash, seizing her hand, cold fear in his eyes that chilled Sienna to the bone.

'Adam, it's me!' she said, her heart wrenching for him.

Adam blinked, his fear ebbing as he finally managed to focus. '*Christ,* sorry,' he said, relaxing his grip and falling back on his pillow. 'I, er ... bad dream.'

'I gathered.' Sienna smiled. 'I'm not surprised. Does it hurt very—'

'I didn't do it,' Adam said over her.

Sienna's eyes flickered down.

'I didn't do it, Sienna,' he repeated, quiet desperation in his voice. 'I swear to God.'

Sienna looked back at him, trying to read what was in his eyes. Eyes she knew he'd learned to hide emotions behind.

Had he had sex with the woman, she wanted to ask. She knew he had with many women. Her eyes *were* open. She knew Adam was what he was. Had he had sex with *this* woman, though? Sienna steeled herself. 'Did you have … relations with her?' she ventured, cautiously.

Adam closed his eyes. 'Yes.' He nodded wearily.

'Who is she?' Sienna felt as if she were judging him now, cross-questioning him, but then, she did have a right to know. Didn't she?

Adam swallowed. 'The woman you saw on the boat.'

In which case, he could hardly deny he'd had sex with her. Sienna swallowed in turn, the conversation she'd overheard between the two springing to mind, reminding her that people often played games in the bedroom. Had Adam, with this woman?

'The same woman whose cottage you were staying in?' she managed, though the words almost got wedged in her windpipe.

'Yes,' he admitted, shamefaced, and glanced down. 'I'm sorry. I … didn't think.'

Sienna nodded, and dropped her gaze to her hands. She hadn't given him much room to think, had she? And she hadn't objected to his taking her there.

'Do you believe me?' Adam asked quietly.

Sienna hesitated. There was another question she had to ask. She didn't want to, but her former bully of a boyfriend in mind, who clearly couldn't read the signals, she simply had to. 'Is it possible the lines might have got blurred, Adam?'

Adam's head snapped up 'What?' He stared at her, incredulous.

Sienna took a breath. 'That maybe rough sex got a little too rough?' she clarified quickly, and then dearly wished she hadn't.

Adam's expression went from stunned, through bewildered, to utterly crushed. She might as well have taken a knife to his heart.

'I thought you were going to ring me,' Nathaniel said, walking over to him as Adam paid off the taxi driver.

'It's okay, Nate, I've got legs.' Adam smiled, half-heartedly. 'Got a voice, too, but it looks like no one's hearing me.' He glanced over to Sienna's cottage as he walked to his boat.

'She came to see you, then?' Nathaniel obviously got the gist.

'Yep,' Adam said, climbing aboard with a little more care than he normally did. 'I wish she hadn't. Wish this bloody thing was up and running.' He looked towards his engine compartment despairingly.

'And then what would you do? Sail off half a mile upstream and moor up in the middle of nowhere?'

Adam was grateful Nate hadn't actually reminded him he wasn't supposed to leave the area. 'Sounds like a plan.' He shrugged.

Alone definitely sounded like a plan. He'd stopped at the off-licence on the way, and wondered if the two blokes in there, regulars from the pub, were going to trip him up on the way out. The grapevine had obviously been working overtime. Seemed he was headline news and at the top of everyone's hit list, the men anyway. The women? Adam didn't even consider going there.

'Give her a chance, Adam. It's a lot for anyone to get

their head around, you've got to admit.'

'What?' Adam eyed him questioningly as he unlocked his door. 'That I assault women and I'm such a shit, I don't even admit it?' He let it hang, watching Nathaniel carefully as he did. 'Yes, I suppose it is.' He smiled cynically, as Nathaniel's cheeks flushed a telltale red.

'Cheers, Nate.' Adam headed down his steps, the bottles in his carrier clinking as he went.

'Oh, come on, Adam,' Nathaniel said despairingly. 'You're not going to start boozing again, are you? What good will that do?'

'It'll take the edge off,' Adam assured him.

'Until you wake up,' Nathaniel reminded him.

Adam turned around. Nathaniel was a good friend, even if he also apparently thought he'd 'blurred the lines'. 'Nate, I'm okay,' he assured him. 'I'm going to have a drink, several possibly, but I'm not going to go OTT. I just want to be on my own for a while; think things through, that's all.'

Nathaniel didn't look convinced. 'Heard that one before, haven't I? Are you on tablets?'

Adam ran his hand through his hair, which was a bad idea. Lifting his arm was painful. His chest still felt as if it was being slowly crushed by a truck. 'Nate, I'm fine. Bugger off and stop mothering me, will you?'

'Just don't overdo it.' Nathaniel couldn't help himself.

'I've only got four, Nate. You really do need to find another case to get on, you know?' A less hopeless case, he added mentally. 'Look, I'll see you later. I'll be fine, I promise.'

Nathaniel sighed heavily and turned away, then turned back. 'Do you remember that day on the locks at Tewksbury when we skipped school to go boat spotting,' he asked Adam, his eyes narrowed nostalgically, 'and that Sheerline 950 came through?'

Adam thought about it. 'Aft cockpit, four cylinder diesel engine with bow thruster and stern thruster?' Adam nodded. 'Yep, I remember it well.'

'You should do. You fell in trying to get a better look at the engine,' Nathaniel reminded him.

'Yeah, you didn't help much.' Adam's mouth twitched briefly up at the corners.

'What? I threw you a lifebelt!' Nathaniel said defensively.

'It hit me on the head, Nate.'

'Didn't knock any sense into you, did it?' Nathaniel smiled wryly and paused. 'Don't give up on your dream, Adam. You have to have something to hold onto. Everyone does.' He looked him over, smiled sadly, and turned to head back to the chandlery.

Adam watched his friend walking off, shaking his head as he went. Nate had always been there, right by his side, Adam the one getting into trouble, Nate fishing him out, or trying to. There was nothing much he could do to help him out of this hole, though, was there? He couldn't blame him for not believing him, Adam supposed. Pity he hadn't heard the conversation he'd had with Sherry the day before her caring husband had kicked the crap out of him. Adam doubted a woman who he'd supposedly attacked would have been asking him to reconsider their arrangement. She'd even texted him: *When you decide you still want sex with a real woman, you'll know where to find me.* There were other texts, too. All confirming they'd had a sexual relationship. Adam was glad he'd remembered those texts, because up until then, he'd been wondering whether he *had* blurred the bloody lines.

Glancing despondently towards Sienna's cottage once more, Adam sighed and closed his doors. He doubted Nathaniel would have gone for the whisky he'd also bought being for medicinal purposes, but as far as Adam was concerned, medicinal was exactly what it was. He needed anaesthetising. Drinking himself into a deep, dreamless sleep seemed a much preferable option to lying wide awake tonight, seeing things that didn't exist, thoughts going around in his head, until he was halfway out of his mind.

Chapter Thirteen

A week he'd been holed up, a whole week, only emerging when the police turned up to take him in for more questioning. And here they were again, in a patrol car of course, advertising they were here, why they were here.

'He looks so pale,' Sienna said, watching from the window as Adam came out of his boat, looking neither left nor right as he walked across to where the two officers were waiting.

'Nice of them to send him an escort,' Lauren observed, pausing in her soup making efforts to come and have a nose alongside her. 'It's obviously something important. Or else they're making sure he doesn't do a runner.'

Sienna ignored her. Lauren seemed to reinforce her low opinion of Adam even more now she thought Sienna had seen the light. She hadn't seen anything, apart from the fact that she'd opened her mouth and put her foot squarely in it that day at the hospital. Adam had looked close to tears. He wouldn't meet her eyes, not even when she'd said goodbye. 'See you around,' he'd said as she'd left, leaving Sienna in no doubt he didn't want to see her any time soon.

She'd texted him, even slipped a note under his door, nothing too pushy, just a casual enquiry: Was he okay? Did he need anything? He hadn't responded. She needed to explain why she'd asked the question she had, a stupid question borne of her own insecurities, but it wouldn't take away the fact that she'd doubted him, would it?

'He's all crumpled. He's usually always clean-shaven and showered,' she said worriedly, noting Adam's creased T-shirt and jeans and his unshaven chin. The unshaven look suited him, made him look even sexier, if that were possible, but it wasn't him. She wished she could find the courage to just go out there and speak to him, whatever his reaction. He probably wouldn't appreciate it though, not with the police waiting for him.

Lauren didn't miss her chance. 'Yes, well, he probably had to shower a lot, didn't he, given his various *activities*.'

'Lauren ...' Sienna sighed despondently.

'Just saying.' Lauren went back to her soup. 'He did do a lot of *odd* jobs, after all, didn't he?'

'Please don't, Lauren,' Sienna asked her, yet again. She was seriously tempted to hit her with the serving ladle, if she could have found the energy.

Lauren gave her a look, clearly not getting how hurtful her remarks were. She wouldn't, Sienna supposed. They were mostly true, after all.

'Come on,' Lauren said, dishing up the soup. 'You haven't been eating enough to keep a mouse alive. You look as pale as Lothario does. Eat up. And I mean all of it, Sienna, not just a spoonful.'

Sienna tried, but she just wasn't hungry. Every time she thought about food she felt dreadfully sick. She wished she could just go over to Adam's boat, curl up in his arms and stay holed up with him forever. But Adam didn't want her. He couldn't have made it any plainer, could he? Sienna couldn't really blame him.

Her soup barely touched, she was halfway through the washing-up when she noticed them again, the horrible brats belonging to the equally horrible boat owner who'd made the awful comment about Adam deserving all he got. And there they went again, removing Adam's lifebelts from his boat, about to throw them in the river just for the spiteful fun of it.

God, they really were loathsome. Sienna stormed to her front door. If she had children, she'd make damn sure to bring them up to respect other people's property. Their idiot father had even seen them doing it and not said a word.

'Oi!' she shouted from the quayside. 'Put those back, you little brats.' They weren't that little actually, but Sienna had had enough. Five times she'd fished the lifebelts out now. They even had the nerve to do it while Adam was on board, curtains drawn, bothering no one. Couldn't they just leave him alone?

'And who's gonna make us?' the bigger of the two boys drawled, obviously aware that Nathaniel was off at a boat show and therefore not about to intercede.

'Me!' Sienna stepped forwards, probably not looking much of a threat, but she meant business.

'Yeah, right, you and whose army?' the kid sneered and proceeded to lob one of the lifebelts out as far as he could.

'You little … *shit!*' Sienna seethed, stomping across to him, then stopping short to try to stop his brother from hurling the other lifebelt out, only to land heavily on her backside as the boy yanked it from her grip and threw it anyway.

'You're vile,' Sienna said tearfully, scrambling to her feet and noticing she'd drawn an audience as she did. Well, she would, wouldn't she? They just couldn't resist an opportunity to gossip about other people's misfortunes, could they?

And there, gloating as per usual, was the father who'd spawned the horrible brats. 'Tyler, Dylan, inside,' he called, nodding the sniggering teenagers towards his own boat.

'Aren't you going to say anything?' Sienna asked, astonished.

'Why?' The man shrugged.

'Because it's someone else's property!' Sienna pointed out, as if he didn't know it was – and whose it was.

The man shrugged again. 'Tough,' he said.

What? Sienna couldn't believe her ears. Was he really just going to let them do this and not say a word? Obviously he was. He just stared at her, hands in pockets, a couldn't-care-less look on his face. 'Those kids of yours ought to be locked up!' she fumed, her cheeks burning with anger.

'No, luv, it's him who ought to be locked up,' the man said, pointing at Adam's boat.

That did it. Sienna's tears sprang forth, damn her treacherous eyes. She looked at him bewildered, at other neighbours gawping from doorsteps and decks, revelling in the gossip and doing absolutely nothing about it. If it was one of their properties, one of their flashy yachts, they'd move fast enough to make sure these kids didn't run riot. 'You're all the same,' she shouted. 'All of you! You just can't resist kicking a dog when it's down, can you?'

Dragging her arm across her eyes, Sienna tugged in a breath and set determinedly forth for Adam's boat. No offers of help, naturally, she struggled to get the little dinghy off the top of it on her own, just about managing it by the time Lauren appeared from the cottage, an alarmed look on her face and a towel on her head. 'Sienna, what on earth's going on?'

'Ask them.' Sienna nodded angrily over her shoulder as she dragged the dinghy to the water.

'But ... where are you going?'

'To fetch Adam's lifebelts. It's the least I can do since he dived into the ice cold water to save my dog's life!' Sienna yelled the latter, in hopes the nosy neighbours might get the message.

She was straining over the edge of the dinghy trying to reach one of the lifebelts caught up in another boat's mooring ropes with a paddle when she heard him. 'Sienna!' Adam shouted from the bank. 'What the *hell* are you doing?'

'Trying to reach your lifebelts,' Sienna shouted back. 'They fell off.'

'Sienna, leave them! That water's bloody deep. Come back in.'

'I've almost got it.' Sienna strained a little bit further. If she could just reach the rope with her hand, she could pull herself in, grab the lifebelt and … '*Shoot!*'

Her first sensation was that it was blood-freezingly cold. Blinking against the swirling green murkiness, she couldn't get her bearings, but she sensed she was going down. Instinctively she kicked, flailing her arms, trying to push herself upwards, but her trainers felt like concrete blocks and her limbs seemed so very heavy. Where was the sky? She tried to glimpse a patch of light through the darkness but she couldn't see anything.

Trying not to panic, not to think about how long she could hold her breath, she pushed up with all her might, only to meet hard surface above her. *Oh God. Oh God.* It was a boat. She was under the immovable hull of it. Blinking wildly, Sienna palmed the bottom of the boat, trying to feel her way. It was so long. She was going the length of it. She needed to get to the side. But not the inside! It would crush her against the bank like a fly. *Shit!* She was going to die under it. She needed to breathe. She had to find a way out! Terror gripping her, she thrashed about wildly, fighting for a gap in the lid of her tomb. There was none. Feeling her strength slip from her body, the air ebb from her lungs, Sienna stopped flailing. She was going to die. She blinked slowly against the darkness, noting a soft, white light floating towards her. An angel, she thought blearily, feeling a strange calm envelop her. She'd come to take her. She was very beautiful.

She felt his fingertips first, and then his mouth was on hers. He pinched her nose and breathed deep into her mouth. Adam. Sienna felt her heart beat. She wanted to cry, but you couldn't cry under water. Could you? His arm was around her. He was holding her tight, feeling his way out of her watery grave with his other hand, kicking out, strong, sure kicks. Carrying her like a limp little fish to the surface.

Many hands tugged at her. Someone grabbed her hair. Adam heaved her up from behind and, gasping for life-giving air, Sienna found herself being dragged onto the bank, turned over, feet and legs and people milling around her.

'Is she all right?' someone said.

'Give her some room,' the father of the teenagers said, leaning over her, his expression no longer couldn't-care-less. You should tell your children, Sienna thought woozily.

And then Adam was there, looming over her, kneeling beside her to brush her wet hair from her face. He searched her eyes, his face white and tight. His beautiful eyelashes were wet, again, little droplets of water dripping from them to mingle with the tears on her cheeks.

'Okay?' he asked.

Sienna nodded and spluttered.

His jaw tensed. 'Don't ever do that to me again, Sienna,' he said hoarsely. His gaze was stern. His eyes ... they were blazing, his pupils so large there was no chocolate-brown there at all.

'He was furious,' Sienna said, still shuddering from the inside out, as Lauren tucked the duvet up under her chin.

'He wasn't furious, Sienna,' Lauren assured her, adamantly. 'The man was terrified. You almost drowned! For the sake of a lifebelt? Honestly, Sienna ...'

'He said not to ever make him jump in again. Twice he's had to go in because of me. He could have drowned.'

'"Don't ever do that to me again", I think you'll find he

191

said, Sienna; as in please don't give him a double coronary.'
Lauren reached for the soup she'd re-heated, determined
that Sienna should get something hot inside her. 'Come on
swallow a little bit for me. It'll warm you up.'

The spoon was barely at Sienna's lips, before another
sweeping wave of nausea washed over her. 'I can't, Lauren,
honestly. I feel terribly sick.'

Lauren frowned and parked the bowl on the bedside
table. 'You've been feeling sick a lot lately, haven't you?' she
asked, her head cocked curiously to one side.

Sienna slumped down in her bed, heartily wishing she
could crawl under the duvet and stay there.

'Is there something you want to share, Sienna?' Lauren
asked, clearly guessing there was something that Sienna
would rather not share.

She wasn't even sure herself. She had no idea how. No
idea what she was going to do; absolutely none, when the
only person she'd wanted to confide in didn't want her.
When he might even end up in prison. Oh God, she didn't
want Adam to go to prison! He was an outdoor person. A
free spirit. It would kill him.

'Sienna?' Lauren pressed her, her tone growing more
concerned.

Sienna gulped back a hard lump in her throat. 'I missed
my period,' she said quietly, slow tears sliding down her
cheeks. She didn't look up. She didn't dare. She didn't want
to see yet more condemnation of Adam. 'Please don't say
anything horrible. Please don't ask me how. We did use
precautions. I ... don't know what happened.'

Obviously stunned, Lauren didn't say anything for a
second, and then, 'You're pregnant?' she spluttered.

Sienna heard her bedroom door squeak open. Tobias,
she thought, looking past a thunderstruck Lauren. Come to
offer the kind of comfort only a dog can and not stare at

her with horrified, admonishing ... Oh, no. Sienna closed her eyes, feeling sick now to the very depths of her soul.

'You're *what*?' her father said, standing tall in the doorway, his face pale and his eyes utterly horrified.

'OhmyGod!' Lauren shot off the bed as Sienna looked from her father to her accusingly.

'Oh, Lauren ...' Sienna peeled her gaze away from her, attempting to heave herself out of bed.

'I didn't phone him, Sienna. Honestly, I didn't,' Lauren said, reaching to help her.

Sienna met her eyes. How could she? How *could* she? Now of all times?

Lauren obviously read the disappointment in hers. 'He was on the phone when you fell overboard, Sienna! What was I supposed to do? Tell him you'd popped out for a swim?'

Sienna plopped back down on the bed. What did she do? What could she say? She couldn't look at her dad; couldn't bear to see the disillusionment she would be bound to see in his eyes. She gulped back another tear, and another. *God!* She wished she bloody well had drowned.

Crying in earnest now, big fat choking sobs, she felt the bed dip beside her, a strong arm slide around her. 'Come on, sweetheart,' her father said emotionally. 'Worse things happen.'

Sienna blinked at him, bewildered. He looked shocked, his ruddy tan faded white, and, yes, there was disillusionment there, but most of all concern.

'We know they do, don't we?' He gave her shoulders a reassuring squeeze. 'It's not the end of the world.'

Sienna nodded snottily. They did. He'd lived through much worse things. And yet, he'd forced himself on, stayed strong, for her. Always there. Playing father and mother, worrying about her; trying to offer her a shoulder, even though she'd been adamant she didn't need one. She wanted to be independent, wanted to be on her own. But she didn't, not emotionally. Everyone needs someone. Sienna snorted back another sob and relaxed into a much-needed hug. Over-protective he might be, but she loved him, absolutely, and it was about time she made more effort to make sure he knew it.

'Adam, could you please open up, before I die of hypothermia?'

Blimey, she was persistent. Adam sighed and parked his glass on the work surface. After almost having a heart attack out there, the last thing he needed was killer-look-Lauren reading him the riot act, presumably what she'd come to do, but he supposed he had better let her in. At least she'd be able to tell him how Sienna was, before she told him exactly what she thought of him.

He was surprised, actually, that she'd risk coming anywhere near him, given his reputation. 'Lauren.' He smiled tightly, opening up the doors. 'What can I do for you – apart from dive back in and make sure to drown?'

'Oh, dear,' Lauren said, coming down the steps as he moved back to allow her access, 'we are feeling sorry for ourselves, aren't we?'

Adam ignored that. 'Watch the steps,' he said. 'They tend to be slippery.'

'Thoughtful, aren't you?' Lauren looked him over narrowly as she came into the seating area.

That was a double entendre if ever Adam heard one. 'No comment,' he opted for his right to silence when faced with a loaded question, a policy he'd adopted right up until his last police interview.

'I brought you some soup,' Lauren said, her unnerving gaze going from him to the bag she was carrying.

'Come again?' Adam thought he must have misheard. Soup? What, spiked with cyanide?

'Soup,' Lauren repeated, bringing a flask from the bag. 'I thought it would warm you up after your bracing swim, but I see you already have something.' She glanced pointedly to the tumbler, which was half full of whisky.

Adam shrugged indifferently. 'Any objections?' After seeing Sienna under that water, her beautiful eyes wild and terrified, the life-breath about to drain out of her, he really had needed a medicinal drink. He'd needed several, not that it was anybody's business but his.

'No, no objections,' Lauren assured him, placing the flask next to the glass. 'If you want to drink yourself to death, feel free.'

Adam laughed derisively. 'Cheers,' he said, retrieving the whisky and taking a drink.

'Can I ask you something before you do, though?'

'Ask away,' he said, taking a seat. He wasn't exactly at death's door yet, no doubt to many people's disappointment, but he was beginning to feel a touch unsteady on his feet. 'As long as you don't mind me not answering if it's anything to do with trumped up charges.' He took another swig.

'It's not. Do you mind if I sit?'

'Not if you don't mind who you're sitting next to,' Adam quipped.

'Very cheerful, aren't you, considering.' Lauren perched herself on the seat next to him.

'No, Lauren, not cheerful,' Adam assured her, taking another slug of whisky. 'Definitely not that. So?' He waited for whatever question she had, which was bound to be a prequel to her suggesting he didn't go within a mile of Sienna ever again.

Lauren gazed around. 'It's a bit of a mess in here,' she observed.

'I know.'

'You should open the curtains.'

'Better left closed when you're on a par with the local fairground attraction. Lauren, did you have a question? It's just that I'm a bit busy right now.'

'So I see.' Lauren eyed his drink pointedly again. 'Do you care about her?' she asked suddenly as Adam was trying to work out how to politely ask her to leave.

That caught him off guard. Adam looked at her curiously. Another loaded question, he wondered. Probably, but ... 'Yes,' he said, 'very much.'

'Do you love her?'

Adam hesitated, not sure how much he should admit to, and then nodded.

'How much?' Lauren shuffled around to face him.

Here it came. Enough to get out of her life, he guessed would be next. But then, he was already, wasn't he? Did it matter what he said, then? Adam supposed not. 'Enough to want to spend the rest of my life with her,' he said, contemplating the contents of his glass. 'Not much chance of that now, is there?'

He looked back at Lauren, fully expecting a *maybe you should stop ruining her life instead* comment, but Lauren just nodded and got to her feet.

'Is that it?' Adam asked as she headed for the door.

'For now, yes.'

'Right.' Adam watched her go, perplexed. 'Lauren,' he said, standing up as she mounted the steps, 'is she okay?'

Lauren hesitated. 'Still a bit shocked,' she said finally, 'but, yes, she's okay.'

'Good.' Adam breathed, relieved. 'Lauren,' he stopped her again, 'will you tell her ...' What? That he was sorry for the pain he'd caused her? The uncertainty? Sleeping with her? The two former he was. The latter? His only regret was that it wouldn't happen again. He couldn't say any of that to Lauren. 'Tell her thanks,' he said lamely instead, 'for batting in my corner when nobody else would.'

Lauren considered. 'You should tell her yourself,' she suggested, 'but not tonight. Her dad's visiting. And not when you've been drowning your sorrows in that.' She nodded at his glass. 'Her dad doesn't drink. He'd probably skin you alive if you rolled up drunk to talk to his daughter.'

Adam had a sneaking suspicion he probably would however he turned up. 'One last thing.' He stopped her again. He hadn't been going to say anything, assuming that most people's opinion of him wouldn't change, based on the no smoke without fire theory, but … 'Did you know?'

'Know what?' Lauren looked at him as if she didn't relish having to know anything about him.

'That the charges had been dropped?'

Lauren now looked stunned.

'She retracted her statement,' Adam went on cautiously, aware that a woman retracting her statement might make people wonder why. 'I thought you must have found out somehow.' Because you're being almost nice to me, he didn't add.

'No, I didn't. Why did she?' Lauren asked the inevitable.

'Not under duress,' Adam stated categorically. 'Texts she sent me, it cast doubt on the allegations. The police decided it wasn't worth investigating.' He didn't elaborate further.

Lauren looked him over for a long moment, her mouth eventually curving into something resembling a smile, nothing earth-shattering, but definitely a smile. 'Talk to Sienna, Adam,' she said. 'Tell her how you feel. You need to.'

With that Lauren departed, leaving Adam puzzled. If she didn't know the charges had been dropped, did that mean she didn't think he was the biggest piece of scum that ever walked the earth?

Shaking his head, he pondered, and then shook it again as Nathaniel appeared, obviously beaming himself onto Adam's deck as Lauren had left. With his ghost permanently floating about, it was beginning to get very crowded in the small confines of Adam's cabin.

'Everything all right?' Nathaniel asked, eyeing him curiously as he came on down.

'Yes, Nate.' Adam sighed. 'The lady's virtue is intact.'

'That's not what I meant.' Nathaniel puffed out a sigh. 'I heard about the incident earlier. I just wondered if you were all right, that's all.'

'Getting there,' Adam said, still pondering why anyone should care.

'Looks like it.' Nathaniel nodded at the whisky bottle, not looking very impressed. He looked around then, at the general clutter Adam had let build up. 'This place is a dump, mate,' he commented. 'You need to clean it up.'

'I know. I will.' Adam poured himself another drink, a shorter one this time. 'Why do you care, Nate?' he asked, eyeing his friend bemusedly. 'I mean, why do you give a damn?'

'Because I'm a bigger idiot than you are, obviously.' Nathaniel shrugged good-naturedly. 'Someone's got to, haven't they? They won't if you don't, though, Adam.'

Sienna knew she was being unfair, about to ask her dad a question that he couldn't answer honestly without giving her cause to think he might have regretted having her. He had been a little older than her, twenty-five when he became responsible for another life, but three years didn't make much difference in the great scheme of things. If he could, then she could. She wasn't even sure she was pregnant yet, though all the signs were there. She wasn't sure how things would turn out, whether Adam might be the slightest bit interested.

She recalled the terrible situation with his fiancée; the baby. Adam hadn't even known whether he was the father. Had he ever found out? Had he traced the child? Been in contact? Sienna felt she knew some of the awfulness of what had happened, after Adam had opened up a little, but she didn't know the whole story. He hadn't told her. She couldn't help wondering, however, even though they'd been as intimate as it was possible for two people to be physically, that maybe he really couldn't do emotional intimacy. He'd closed part of himself off and Sienna understood why. She didn't find it easy to share either, with strangers, people she didn't trust.

She was hardly a stranger, though, and if he didn't feel he could trust her … He might never trust anyone again, she could understand that too, but without trust a relationship could never flourish. It was the very foundation relationships were built on.

Sienna pulled in a shuddery breath. She'd have to tell him, eventually. She would. Whatever his reaction though, there was one thing she knew for certain; if she didn't keep this baby she would regret it, bitterly. If Adam wasn't interested, so be it. At least she would have given him the choice. How she'd tell him when he was barely ever seen lately and then barely ever sober …? She'd just have to cross that bridge when she came to it.

Looking across to her father sitting in the armchair, who'd been quietly studying her she realised, she steeled herself to ask, 'Do you think I'll regret it, Dad?'

Understanding the question, her dad sighed long and hard. 'We're all different, Sienna,' he finally said. 'I didn't regret it, if that's what you're asking.'

Sienna searched his face. 'Never?'

'Not even when you were working at being the world's stroppiest teenager.' Her dad managed a smile. Sienna felt so ashamed that she'd almost reduced this big, strapping man to tears with her news. 'Things were difficult, Sienna, as you know, with your mum's illness,' her dad went on, 'but there was never a day when either of us regretted having you. You were always wanted.'

Sienna was hesitant. 'But not planned?' She watched him carefully, aware that she'd been 'a surprise baby'. A lovely surprise her mum had always said, but still she'd been young, too. Sienna couldn't help wondering.

Her dad's brow furrowed. For obvious reasons he was reticent to answer. 'Not planned, no,' he eventually said, his smile now a little on the sad side. Because he'd guessed where this was leading, Sienna knew. 'You've made up your mind then? You're definitely going to have it?' he asked gently.

Sienna nodded thoughtfully, and then more decisively. 'Yes. Definitely.'

'Can I ask why?' he probed a little deeper.

'Because I'll regret not having it,' Sienna answered as honestly as she could. He would understand, Sienna knew that too. He was hurting. It was obvious in his eyes, but he would understand.

Her dad nodded slowly in turn, as if he'd already reconciled himself to it. 'A baby is a huge commitment, Sienna,' he warned her, 'full-time, twenty-four seven, and for life.'

'I know.' Sienna stroked Tobias as he rested his snout faithfully on her lap. It wouldn't be like taking care of a not-so-well-trained dog, she knew that, but Sienna was sure she could care for a child as much as a child needed to be cared for, that she would love that child unconditionally. She already did.

'Particularly without a partner's input,' her dad added as if reading her thoughts. 'He doesn't know yet, you say, the father?'

'No.' Sienna shook her head, adamant he wouldn't, at least for now.

'And you're not ready to introduce me to him?' Her dad looked her over with a mixture of suspicion and worry.

'Not yet, no.' In truth Sienna wondered if she ever could.

'I take it you think he might not be interested, then?'

'I honestly don't know, Dad. We've only … We haven't known each other that long.'

'Long enough, obviously,' he said, not quite able to hide his annoyance. 'Right,' he said with a sigh, 'well, if you're sure it's what you want, Sienna, I'll be there. You know I will. However, if the bastard isn't interested, at least enough to support you financially, he'll have me to answer to. Tell him that when you pass on my regards, will you?'

Adam was bleary-eyed when he finally managed to answer the door the next morning. 'Yes?' he said, squinting to focus on the father and the two brats who'd lobbed his lifebelts into the water. The older one had pissed up the side of his boat, too. Adam had seen him, but knew from the father's hostile glances that any attempt to do anything about it would only incite violence, him on the receiving end of it. He wished he had done something, though, seeing Sienna go into that water.

'They've come to apologise,' the guy said. 'Haven't you boys?'

Apologise? Blimey. Adam glanced from the father to the two belligerent-faced youths, bemused.

'Haven't you boys?' The father placed a hand on the back of each of the boys' necks and squeezed.

'Dad, geddoff,' the older one said. 'That hurts.'

'Not half as much as it will if you don't do as you're told,' the guy growled in his ear. 'Now, say you're sorry boys.' Forcing a smile, he looked back to Adam.

'Sorry!' the boys both blurted together, obviously under a bit more pressure.

Adam raised his eyebrows. 'Apology accepted,' he said, though he had an idea the 'boys' might not be quite such sweetness and light once their old man's back was turned.

'Right, get back over there and get busy with buckets,' the guy said, pointing them back to his boat, which they'd obviously been allocated cleaning duties of.

His sons dispatched, the guy turned back to Adam. 'We're not thrilled about having your sort moored here, you've no doubt gathered that, but I don't condone what they did, just so you know.'

Right, cheers, Adam thought, as the guy climbed off his boat, having delivered the most insincere apology he'd ever heard in his life.

Sighing, he closed the door, glancing towards Sienna's cottage, as he did, and got the biggest fright he'd ever had in his life. The man emerging from the front door was at least six-two, and built like a brick outhouse. If that was her father and he found out what he'd been doing with his daughter, Adam had a feeling he'd most definitely be fish food.

Chapter Fourteen

It was now or never. Adam braced himself to walk into the pub, and then wondered whether to about-face and walk straight back out again. This time the vibes were palpable. There wasn't so much a lull in the conversation as deadly silence, all heads turning in his direction. Adam tried to avoid the open stares as he made his way to the bar. The sneers, though, he couldn't avoid hearing. The village drums clearly hadn't yet dispatched the latest instalment of his life, then.

'Scum,' one of the gang of thugs muttered as he passed.

Yep, definitely a problem with the old grapevine, Adam decided, righting himself on his feet after tripping over the leg the guy 'accidentally' stuck out in front of him.

Sienna was behind the bar, her face so white and her eyes so huge, she looked like a little China doll. Adam felt a familiar kick in his chest as he saw her.

Ignoring the mutterings behind him, he smiled uncertainly. 'Hi,' he said.

Sienna smiled hesitantly back and stepped towards him, only to be ushered aside by the landlord.

'I'll deal with this, Sienna,' he said, his not-overly-welcoming eyes locked hard on Adam's. 'Did you want something?' he asked him brusquely, pulling himself up to his full height as he did.

'A drink would be nice,' Adam suggested, with a hopeful shrug.

'Not here. You're banned, Shaw. Find somewhere else to drink.'

Adam watched him as the guy reached for a glass, wiping it demonstratively, his stony gaze fixed on him the whole time. *Right, fine.* Guilty until proven, obviously. Maybe he should share his good news. He might even get offered a congratulatory drink then. Yeah, not likely. Not worth it, he decided.

He glanced at Sienna, wishing he'd braved her old man instead of coming here, where he really hadn't been welcome anyway. Her father couldn't do much more to him than had already been done, after all. 'Talk later,' he said, running a hand through his hair and turning to walk the gauntlet back to the door.

'Piss off, Shaw. And don't bother coming back,' a member of his fan club imparted as he went.

'Yeah, sling your hook in some other port,' another lout shouted, hilariously, as Adam slammed through the exit, the jibes following him out right through the foyer.

'Prats,' he muttered, quickening his pace away from the place. It didn't matter, he told himself. Apart from Nate, he'd been pretty much a loner for years anyway. He didn't need anyone else's company. As for the pub, plenty more boozers around, he thought, swallowing back his humiliation as a car, obviously from the pub, cruised past, the idiot thugs therein glaring aggressively at him.

'Stuff it.' He sighed and walked on, and then stopped, as he heard a familiar voice behind him.

'Adam!' Sienna shouted. 'Wait!'

Adam stopped walking and tried to compose himself. He didn't want Sienna thinking his embarrassment was due to being thrown out of the pub. The fact that it had happened in front of her, humiliated her, too, was what was getting to him most.

She didn't say anything as she reached his side, just stopped and slipped her hand quietly into his. Adam didn't speak. He actually didn't think he could formulate any words to speak, right then. Instead, he squeezed her hand back as they walked on in silence. He hadn't thought love like this was possible. Not for him anyway. He didn't deserve her, though, did he? And she definitely didn't deserve him.

'Sienna ...' Adam stopped again. He loved her name, the way it rolled off his tongue. The vision of the amazingly sensual woman he knew her to be it evoked. 'We need to talk,' he said, turning to face her.

Sienna looked at him. 'I know,' she replied, glancing down and then back up. 'My dad's staying at the moment, but we could talk as we walk.'

'You're better off without me, Sienna,' Adam said quickly, determined to do the only decent thing he probably ever would in his life, before his courage failed him.

'What?' Sienna stared at him, her grass-green eyes wide with shock.

Adam closed his own eyes and swallowed. 'You need to find someone else, Sienna,' he said firmly.

Sienna pulled her hand from his. 'I don't want anyone else!'

'Someone wholesome, decent,' Adam went on, trying to look anywhere else than at her. 'I'm never going to be any good for you, Sienna. I'm bad news. It's who I am. Everybody knows it.'

'I don't *care* about everybody. I care about you!' Sienna shouted, her cheeks flaming deep red, tears welling in her beautiful eyes.

Jesus. Adam scrunched his own eyes closed. He couldn't do this. It was killing him. It would kill him, slowly inch-by-inch, to live his life without her. And if he didn't do it, he'd mess up her life as sure as God made little green apples.

'I want to be with you, Adam,' Sienna insisted, tears now spilling down her face, 'don't you see?'

'But I don't want *you*, Sienna!' Adam said forcefully.

He looked directly at her, working to keep his tone dispassionate, his eyes devoid of emotion, and his heart from cracking completely in two.

Sienna blinked at him, bewildered, and then took a faltering step away from him. 'Why?' She choked back a sob.

'I'm a free spirit, Sienna,' Adam said with a shrug, gulping back his own emotion. 'I don't want to be tied down.'

'Oh God.' Sienna clamped a hand to her mouth and then, dragging her wounded gaze away from him, she stumbled back another step, and turned away.

He had to let her go. Swallowing hard, Adam willed himself not to go after her as she walked back towards the pub. Watching her go, he didn't register the car cruising up behind him, until a door slammed, then two, three ...

Adam turned around as the fourth door slammed.

Fuck! The louts from the pub, he recognised them immediately. And one of them, the ringleader, was wielding a chain.

'Are you all right, sweetheart?' the guy called past Adam to Sienna.

Adam didn't dare take his eyes off the guy long enough to look back.

'What?' he heard Sienna say tremulously. 'Yes!' she added quickly. 'I'm fine.'

'She doesn't look fine to me.' The guy glanced from her to Adam. 'Does she to you, Matt?'

'Looks a bit upset to me,' Matt concurred, accusing eyes also on Adam. Adam took a step back, glancing past them to the little used country lane. Chances of getting past them, nil, he realised. 'Go back to the pub, Sienna!' he shouted.

'Tasty little thing, isn't she?' the chain wielder observed. 'Nice legs.'

God, no. Adam's gut twisted as he watched the

guy openly leering at Sienna, running a hand over his disgustingly salivating mouth as he did.

'Adam?' Sienna said tearfully behind him.

Risking a glance back at her, Adam shouted again, loud. 'Go, Sienna! Now! Use your phone!'

Making sure she was on her way, Adam turned back, moving quickly to block him as the letch with the chain took a step forward. One more step, just one in the direction of Sienna and Adam would kill him – and quite gladly do time for the bastard. 'You're not seriously going to take me on, are you?' he said scornfully, baiting the guy and hoping to God he would take it.

'You what?' The letch's eyes twanged incredulously back to his.

'Don't look as if you could fight your way out of a paper bag, mate,' Adam said glibly.

The guy gawked. 'Is he having a laugh, or what?' He glanced back at his mates, then back to Adam, disbelieving.

'Do I look like I'm laughing?' Adam said, deadly serious.

'*You* are kebab meat,' the guy growled, advancing towards him, cocksure with his chain in his hand and his 'gang' backing him.

Good. Okay. That was exactly what Adam wanted. Quickly checking Sienna was within reach of the pub, he breathed slowly out. All eyes were on him. He was what they wanted. Purposefully, Adam took a step back, keeping them engaged, keeping them focussed. The letch kept coming.

Guessing his suspect martial arts skills would be pretty useless against four, ergo he would be kebab meat if this didn't work, Adam took the only option he could. Calling on all his skills from his rugby days, he waited for the guy to raise his arm ready to swing that chain – and then he went for him, diving for his midriff and bringing the man down so hard he almost spat out his lungs.

Winded himself as he went down, Adam didn't pause to draw breath. He moved, fast. Rolling sideways, scrambling to his feet, he leapt the five bar gate into a field in one, and then, praying his chest would hold out, he ran as if his life depended on it.

Looking back only once, to check the bastards were where he wanted them, on his tail, Adam regulated his breathing, and picked up his pace. The ground was good. Not too soft. Not too hard. Tricky probably, when he hit the ploughed fields beyond, but he could do this. He had to do this. He had no doubt his life *did* depend on it.

'What the *bloody* hell's going on?' Nathaniel asked, ramming the passenger door wide to allow Adam to throw himself inside.

'Is Sienna okay?' Adam managed, panting hard and craning his neck to see the two persistent buggers who'd managed to keep up a fair pace with him slowing to a frustrated halt on the road.

'I don't know. You tell me. She was hysterical when she phoned. What in God's name have you done now, Adam?'

Adam sank back in his seat, breathing heavily. 'What I'm best at, Nate,' he said with a sigh, and tugged his shirt up to mop the sweat from his face, 'getting people's backs up.'

Nathaniel glanced sideways at him. 'Are *you* okay?'

'I've been better.' Adam leaned his head against the headrest and tried to get his breathing back to somewhere near normal. God, his chest hurt.

'Well? What happened?'

Adam shrugged. 'Seems like there's some people who would much rather I left town.'

'But didn't you tell them the charges have been dropped?'

Adam smiled wryly. 'Somehow I don't think they were in

the listening mood, Nate.' He hesitated, glancing warily at his friend. 'One of them is the brother of someone I, er …'

'Shagged,' Nate finished, with a despairing shake of his head. 'So he was defending her honour, was he? How very valiant of him,' he added cynically, unusually for Nate.

'Looks like they're standing in line. I'm guessing there are a few more blokes around here who'd like to take me aside and point out the error of my ways after the thing with Sherry. Mud sticks, I guess.'

'So you are going to move on then?'

'Yep. As soon as.'

'And Sienna?'

'It's over.' Adam ran his hand over his neck, recalling Sienna's wounded expression as he'd casually informed her he didn't give a damn about her. He didn't think he'd ever forget it. 'I told her I didn't want to see her again.'

'Right.' Nathaniel emitted an exasperated sigh. 'Way to go, Adam. That has to be the shortest relationship in history.'

'Not for me,' Adam reminded him drolly.

'And that's the truth, is it? You really don't want to see her again?'

'What do you think?' Adam glanced at Nathaniel, who probably knew him better than he knew himself.

'I think you're a prat, but that aside, why, for pity's sake? You obviously care about her.'

'More than,' Adam admitted, swallowing back a tight lump in his throat.

'So why?'

'Because I'm no good for her!' Adam pointed out the obvious, frustrated. 'I'm a complete waste of space. You of all people should know that. And now *this*. Those bastards could've done anything. I couldn't have fought four of them off if they'd decided to go after Sienna. Anything could have

209

happened. She deserves better, Nate. You know she does.'

'Right.' Nathaniel drummed his fingers on the steering wheel. 'You don't choose who you fall in love with, unfortunately,' he said, after a second.

Adam sighed despondently. 'I know.'

'So that's it, then. You're just going to go.'

'Like I said.'

'Whatever.' Nathaniel shrugged. 'You've obviously made up your mind. Word of advice, though, Adam, unless you want to explain to her father, I'd make yourself scarce tonight. His daughter's upset and I suspect if he finds out why, he might just be looking for blood.'

'He might have to join the queue,' Adam joked, half-heartedly.

'So where do you want me to drop you?' Nathaniel asked.

'My car, I suppose. I'll find somewhere for tonight, and then ...' God only knew.

'What happened?' Lauren asked, holding Sienna's hand as her sobs juddered to a stop.

'Four men,' Sienna managed, in between hiccups. 'They followed Adam from the pub.'

Standing over her, arms folded, Sienna's dad raised an eyebrow. 'Adam?'

'Adam,' Lauren repeated, with a weary sigh.

'The obvious-by-his-absence father, I take it?'

'One and the same,' Lauren supplied.

'I thought they were going to kill him!' Sienna dissolved into a fresh bout of tears. 'They were vile to him, sneering at him in the pub, tripping him up. It was just awful.'

'Yes, well they haven't killed him,' Lauren assured her. 'Nate rang to say he picked him up on the road.'

'He made sure I was safe.' Sienna ran a hand under her

nose. 'He just stood there, waiting for them to do whatever they were going to do to him until I was out of harm's way. One of them had a chain! God knows what they would have done if they'd caught him.' Sienna shuddered at the thought. With his already cracked ribs, Adam would have stood no chance at all. 'It's so unfair. Why can't they just leave him alone?'

Lauren handed her a tissue. 'I've no idea. You'd think they'd let up a bit now the charges have been dropped. They're obviously just idiots with nothing better … *Hell*!' Realising she'd said too much, Lauren clamped her mouth shut, her gaze drifting worriedly from Sienna to her dad.

'Charges?' he repeated, his jaw tightening demonstrably. 'Explanations, Sienna!' he barked, his tone brooking no argument. 'Now, please! And make sure it's the truth, young lady, because I'll find out anyway.'

Oh God. Sienna closed her sodden eyes. 'Burglary and assault,' she whispered hoarsely. 'But he didn't do it!' She looked beseechingly at her dad. Her dad looked as if he was about to self-combust. 'He didn't, Dad. I promise he didn't. There's proof he didn't, I swear. Some woman gave Adam a key to the place he was supposed to have broken into, and then her husband found out and they said he was there illegally, and then they beat Adam up and—'

'Stop.' Her dad held up his hand. 'I think I've heard enough.' His tone was now troublingly quiet. 'Tea, I think, strong and sweet.' He nodded to himself and headed from the lounge to the kitchen.

'I thought they were going to kill him, Lauren, I really did.' Sienna turned to Lauren. 'Everyone's been so bloody awful to him.'

'Your dad probably *will* kill him, if you keep crying,' Lauren whispered. 'Stop, for goodness sake. I've told you he's fine. Nate said—'

'He finished with me,' Sienna blurted.

'Address, please, Sienna!' her dad boomed up the hall. 'I think it's time I made *Adam's* acquaintance.'

Praying to God that Adam's lights not on meant he really wasn't at home, Sienna watched through the window as her dad hammered on Adam's door. The gongoozlers were just going to love this. Poor Adam. She really should hate him now, with a vengeance. She didn't understand him, probably never would. She'd been on the verge of telling him about the baby, too, now she'd done the test. Thank God, she hadn't. The hard look she'd seen in Adam's eyes had been crushing enough. She didn't dare imagine how he might have looked if he'd thought she was trying to trap him in some way. He'd hurt her so badly. Her heart ached, physically, but she didn't want Adam to be hurt anymore.

'Nate's going over to him,' Lauren said, giving her a nudge and easing the window wider.

Sienna felt a huge surge of relief. If anyone could dissuade her dad from doing Adam permanent damage, Nathaniel could.

'He's not in,' they heard Nathaniel venture, standing a safe distance off.

Sienna's dad turned to glare at him. 'And *you* are?'

'Nate Brooks, Marina Manager,' Nathaniel introduced himself. 'I saw Adam go out earlier. I doubt he'll be back tonight.'

'Just as well he's *not* in,' Sienna's dad growled. 'He'll be mincemeat when I've finished with him.'

'Not a lot of him left to mince,' Nathaniel imparted, with a dispassionate shrug.

'Is the man a complete prat, or what?' Her dad turned to Nathaniel, his expression a mixture of furious and confounded.

'Er ...' Nathaniel diplomatically declined from answering. 'Do you fancy a drink?' he asked instead.

'I don't drink, thank you.' Finally concluding no one was at home, Sienna's dad climbed agitatedly down from Adam's boat.

'Ah, right.' Nathaniel nodded. 'Me neither, much. I have some excellent Earl Grey or Assam tea, though, if you fancy a chat over it, about a certain prat you're obviously keen to have a word with.'

Chapter Fifteen

Moving on seemed like the sensible option, his only option. Also the easy option, Adam had realised. Running away, as he usually did, pushing people away – and hurting people along the way. He'd worked hard to keep the past in the past, shut it off; pretend it never happened. But it had happened. Lily-Grace was a reminder of that: a tiny, fragile human being, her whole future ahead of her, whose feelings around her parentage might shape who she was. If he could do one thing to prevent her going through life with the kind of self-doubt that comes from thinking you might not have been wanted, loveable enough, good enough ... If he could do anything to allay the kind of hurt and the emotional loneliness that went with it, then he owed it to Lily-Grace to at least try.

Checking his watch, he glanced again at the doors from the cubicles into the hospital waiting area, and then got nervously to his feet as Nicole swung through them, looking not overjoyed to see him there. 'Nicole, hi.'

'Adam?' Nicole regarded him incredulously. 'What on earth are you doing here?'

'Apologising.' Adam shrugged, hopefully.

Nicole folded her arms, her look now disparaging. 'Again,' she said, her voice loaded with cynicism.

'Look, Nicole, I am sorry.' Adam ran a hand through his hair, realising how glib a word sorry really was. 'I didn't mean not to turn up. I—'

'Without a word or explanation as to why you didn't,' Nicole cut in, angrily.

Doubting she'd want to hear his explanations and not blaming her, Adam glanced around at their eager, variously injured audience, realising that, yet again, he seemed to be providing the entertainment. 'Is there somewhere we could talk?' he asked, desperate to say what he'd come to.

'Adam, this is an Accident and Emergency department. We have emergencies to attend to.' Nicole splayed her hands, demonstrating thus. 'I don't have time.'

'Nicole, please hear me out,' Adam called as she turned back towards the cubicles.

'Why?' Nicole turned around. 'Why should I, Adam? She's just a child. You let her down! She's too young to understand, thank God, but what about in another two years? You can't just flit into her life when it suits you. You could do irreparable damage.'

'I know.' Adam eyed her levelly. 'That's the last thing I'd want to do, Nicole. I just—'

'She lost her mum, Adam! Don't you think she'll have enough to deal with?'

'I know! Of course I bloody well know, Nicole.' Adam agitatedly kneaded his temples, then sighed and studied the ceiling. 'That's why I'm here, Nicole,' he said, more calmly. 'Why I think it's important I make contact. My life is a mess. It has been since Emily died. I'm trying to do something about it.'

Nicole folded the arms again. 'Trying?'

'Trying,' Adam answered honestly. 'I ran away, Nicole. I know I did. I convinced myself seeing Lily-Grace, acknowledging she might not be mine, would be too painful. I was wrong. This is too painful. Not seeing her, knowing how painful it will be for her when she's old enough to wonder whether her parents cared about her. I do care, Nicole. It doesn't matter whether she's mine or not. I feel her, in here.'

Adam punched a hand against his heart. He closed his eyes. He didn't know what else to say. He was a mess.

He knew he was. Definitely needed more help than he'd thought he did, feeling the emotions of some ethereal being that no one else could see. But didn't that child deserve to know he did care? If he wasn't her father, he was her uncle, and that was the one thought that really did pain him. He'd got past it though. He had acknowledged it, finally.

Nicole studied him. 'So, why didn't you turn up?' she asked finally. Her tone was weary, her expression wary.

'I … got detained,' Adam said, not wanting to dramatise it. Definitely not wanting to appear to be seeking sympathy, given how and why he'd got detained.

Nicole sighed and shook her head. 'Goodbye, Adam.' She turned away.

Adam drew in a breath. 'By someone's husband,' he admitted, embarrassed. He could have lied, but lies had a habit of catching up with you. He'd learned that much.

Nicole turned back. Arms still folded, eyebrows raised.

Adam shrugged, despondent. 'Hospital food's not great, is it?'

Nicole cocked her head curiously to one side.

'I've made some mistakes, Nicole. Big mistakes. I won't do that where Lily-Grace is concerned. I don't want to upset her. I don't want to take her away from you. I just want her to know …' Adam stopped, running a hand over his neck. 'I loved Emily.' He swallowed and pushed on. 'I wasn't there when she needed me. I want to be there should her child ever need me, that's all.'

Nicole looked him over, long and hard. She didn't say anything.

'I'd better go,' Adam said, concluding she'd prefer him to. 'Leave you to attend to your patients.'

'I know you loved her,' Nicole said quietly as he turned away. 'I just want what's right for Lily.'

Adam stopped. 'Me too.' He shrugged, turning back.

'I'll think about it.'

Adam swallowed, and nodded. 'Thanks, Nicole.'

'I'll be in touch. Make sure to pick up this time,' she warned him as he headed towards the exit.

'I will,' he assured her, then smiled as an old lady reached for his hand, squeezed it and said, 'Well done, son.'

Adam hadn't been able to stay in his hotel room. The memories it evoked were just far too damn painful. Parking himself in the hotel bar to escape being shut in his room hadn't been such a good idea. Buying a bottle to help wash away the memories wasn't a great idea either. Walking back to the marina in the dead of night in the pouring rain had definitely been a bad idea. Pulling his jacket tight around himself, Adam looked over to Sienna's cottage again from where he sat on a wall in the car park; sat very damply on a wall in the car park.

So what did he do now?

Get sober. The much-neglected sensible part of his brain kicked in. *Get a life and be the kind of man Sienna does deserve*. Which might also mean he'd be the kind of man a child would benefit from having in her life.

Adam sighed. Plenty of Dutch courage inside him, he'd intended to just go right on over and knock on the cottage door. Face the wrath of her father, beg Sienna's forgiveness for his stupidity, for hurting her so badly; beg her for another chance, grovel if he had to. Now he'd finally managed to register through his haze what time it was, that didn't seem to be one of his better ideas either.

Should he text her? He would, he decided. The worst that could happen is she'd send him a succinct two word text back, beginning 'f' and 'o'. Searching for his phone, he fumbled it from his pocket and realised he'd received an incoming text. Hopefully, Adam checked it and his heart sank. 'When I said tell her how you feel, I didn't mean that. You're a total shit. Lauren.'

Dammit! Adam squeezed his eyes closed. What did he think Sienna was going to do when he'd dumped her out of the blue? As if what had happened between them meant nothing, when it meant everything? Say *cheers, nice knowing you but not that nice*, and then go off and find someone else? Idiot! He cursed himself. What did she ever see in him? Adam really couldn't fathom. Why would a girl like Sienna choose him? Someone who was so determined happy endings didn't exist he'd make sure they didn't? Because love *isn't* choosy. Nathaniel was right. She *did* love him, Adam was sure. She might have doubted him over the assault thing, had every right to doubt him. She could never doubt him as much as he doubted himself, but ... God, he really was a prize prat.

Squinting, he re-read Lauren's text and clumsily thumbed in a reply.

Is her did sill there?

No clue what he'd do if he was, what he'd do if he wasn't, Adam rested his head against the wall he was now propped against and waited, then breathed a sigh of relief when his phone pinged a reply.

Yes and if u can't spell u'd better not come here. L.

What? Adam checked his message. She was right. He couldn't even see to text straight. Twit. Berating himself, Adam hesitated, and then, figuring he'd got nothing to lose except everything, he risked phoning Lauren instead. He needed to know. If there was any chance at all Sienna still wanted him ...

'What are you doing?' Lauren rasped in his ear.

'Phoning,' Adam supplied, then righted himself, realising he was reeling to one side.

'Wait,' Lauren said crisply.

Didn't have a lot of choice really, did he?

'What?' she came back on. 'And make it quick, Adam. I've had to come outside the cottage.'

'Oh, yep, right. I can see you, just about.'

'I'm surprised you can see anything at all. You've been drinking, haven't you?'

'I, er … Yes, a bit.'

'A lot,' Lauren huffed. 'You really are completely bloody hopeless, aren't you?'

'You say the nicest things, Lauren. D'y'know that?'

'Where are you?'

'Erm … around.'

'Well, you'd better not come around here like that, Adam. I mean it. Sienna's dad is not a happy man.'

'No, I know.' Adam tried again to straighten himself up, scowling at his unworldly hovering companion as he did, who also seemed to be despairing of him. 'I didn't mean to hurt her, Lauren, I swear. I just … I don't know. You're right, that's the thing. I am hopeless. I love her, but—'

'You know, for a man so determined – and you must be to have bedded the entire female race – I really thought you had more spunk, Adam. Fight for her, if you want her! Sort yourself out, get help if you need to, and bloody well tell her! I've got to go. I'll see you whenever, if her dad doesn't catch sight of you first.'

Adam picked up his bottle of whisky as Lauren rang off. *Liquid nectar.* He swirled the amber contents around. Liquid poison, he corrected himself, tipped the bottle upside-down and ditched it.

Sienna was tucked up in bed with Tobias when she heard him. Was it him? Hardly daring to breathe, she cocked an ear and listened.

'Sienna!' She heard again. It was! Scrambling out of bed,

much to her dog's chagrin, Sienna flew to the window and yanked it open.

'Sienna,' Adam shouted from down below. 'I love you!'

Oh, no. Sienna closed her eyes, realising her dad was outside her front door, looking from Adam and then up to her, astounded.

'I love you, Sienna!' Adam repeated, loudly.

Sienna peeled an eye open, risking another peek at the inebriated man, declaring his love for her in the rain. Oh God, he was swaying on his feet. He wasn't even facing the right window.

'I love your mind,' Adam went on, now addressing the entire boatyard, including Lauren, who'd joined her at the window, and Nathaniel, who'd appeared, bewildered and bleary-eyed, from the chandlery.

'I love your body.' Adam stopped and glanced down at his feet. 'God, I love your body,' he reiterated, throatily.

Lauren sighed and rolled her eyes. 'Perfect. Well done, Adam.'

'I love you, Sienna! I don't not want you. I don't not want you more than anything in my entire life. I'll sort myself out. I promise!' Adam went on determinedly – and drunkenly, turning around and heading in the vague direction of his boat. 'No more booze, no more women, no more ... anything.'

Pausing, Adam stopped, and turned back. 'I'm sorry,' he said, more quietly. 'If you don't want me, Sienna, I don't blame you. Totally, absolutely undersh ... under ... get it.' With which Adam turned to reach for his handrail, and missed it.

Jolting awake as something pressed heavily down on his chest, Adam coughed and spluttered, puking up a bellyful of river, as he did.

'I see you're back with us,' the man looming over him, looking mightily unimpressed, said. 'David Meadows, Sienna's father,' he introduced himself, smiling the kind of smile an executioner who enjoyed his job might. 'I've promised Sienna I'm not going to break your legs. If I'm going to keep that promise, your explanations had better be good.'

The boat dipping violently to one side was nauseating this time. Adam rolled over onto his back wondering if he did manage to make it to the bathroom whether he'd have anything left to actually bring up. He'd heaved last night until he was sure he'd turned his stomach inside out. Yet again, he thanked his lucky stars for Nathaniel, who'd rescued him from Sienna's father, who looked all too ready to carry out his threat to hurt him – in a permanently disabling sort of way.

Sienna's father. Oh, hell. Draping an arm over his face, Adam groaned inwardly and tried to remember some of what he'd actually said. Any of what he'd said.

'Awake at last, are we?' Nathaniel enquired, sounding not too pleased as he lumbered down the steps.

'I think I might be dead,' Adam mumbled.

'If Sienna's father has his way, dead you might well be,' Nathaniel warned him, tersely.

Nope, definitely not pleased, Adam gathered by the tone of his voice. Feeling guilty and more hung-over than he could ever remember being, he waited for Nathaniel to commence the sermon, starting with his usual observation that he was a complete prat, but none was forthcoming. Curious, Adam peeled his arm away from his protesting eyes and blinked up at his friend, to see Nathaniel looking dispassionately down at him.

'You're on your own this time, Adam,' Nathaniel said

flatly, his expression unflinching.

He meant it, Adam realised. With some effort, he raised himself to sitting, swinging his legs around in hopes his feet might find floor. Whether he could stand up on them was a whole other matter. 'I, er, think I owe you an apology,' he said, closing one eye and squinting back at Nathaniel.

'Save it, Adam. I've heard it all before. Never has any substance to it, does it?' Nathaniel pushed his hands in his pockets and shrugged.

'Right.' Adam now felt very guilty. He dropped his gaze and raked his hands through his hair.

'If you can manage to stagger as far as the kettle, you'll need plenty of black coffee.' Nathaniel turned back towards the door. 'And I suggest you take a long shower and a good, hard look at yourself, once you're compos, Adam. There are one or two other people you do owe an apology to – and this time you'd *better* bloody well mean it. My office, one hour. Sienna's dad wants a word.'

Adam had an idea Sienna's dad might impart two words, actually, and given his diabolical performance last night, his unforgivable treatment of his daughter, the man had every right to. Daunted at the task ahead, and very much doubting any kind of apology would be accepted, Adam tested his legs and got shakily to his feet.

Coffee, he instructed himself, trying to still the sway underneath him which was nothing to do with the natural ebb and flow of the river. He'd never touch another drop of whisky ever again, he vowed, searching through the general debris for painkillers, which he doubted would make a dent in the mother of all headaches he'd deservedly got. No booze, full stop.

Did he mean that, though? Or was this another half-hearted attempt to climb back on the wagon? Noting the slight shake to his hand as he swallowed down the tablets with a pint of cold water, Adam cursed himself liberally. He was an idiot. A total bloody idiot. He hadn't been running away from his past. He'd been using it as an excuse not to give a damn about anyone but number one. He really didn't deserve the time of day. Not Nathaniel's. Not Sienna's father's, who was probably only about to spare him as long as it took to wipe the floor with him anyway. Definitely not Sienna's.

Adam guessed that whatever he said or did, he couldn't put things right, but he had to try. Not try, Adam corrected himself furiously. Bloody well do it! For once in your pathetic life, do something right. He had no idea whether Sienna wanted anything more to do with him. Whatever, he owed it to her to tell her he loved her with his whole damaged heart; that he would walk away, but only if she wanted him to.

Two extremely strong coffees, fifty-five minutes later, and still very shaky, Adam checked out his appearance in the wardrobe mirror. 'Yes, I know,' he said out loud, feeling despairing vibes from his misty lodger behind him.

She was right. He looked about as good as he felt, a complete mess. His eyes were bloodshot, dark shadows underneath. His head was pounding. And he'd managed to cut himself shaving. That was a given. Maybe he should have gone the whole hog and saved the executioner the job.

Saying a silent prayer to a God who'd also probably given up on him, Adam smoothed down his clean T-shirt, ran his hands through his permanently unruly hair, then squeaked the door open. *Ouch!* Crap, it was bright out there. Shielding his eyes, he climbed the steps, thought better of leaping the handrail, and set out across the boatyard to face the music.

Shoot! Arriving back from walking Tobias to see Adam

approaching the chandlery door looking deathly pale, Sienna chewed worriedly on her lip. Unable to dissuade her father from his intention to have a 'quiet' word with him, she'd been hoping to warn him beforehand. Aware of the delicate state he would no doubt be in, she'd decided to allow him half an hour's extra sleep and speak to him on her way back from her walk. Clearly he'd already been summoned. *Damn.* Why hadn't she texted him? Texted him what though? *My dad wants to have a word with you. Oh, and, by the way, I'm pregnant.*

What would his reaction be, she wondered nervously? What would any man's reaction be to a woman who he'd slept with twice, and taken all the right precautions with, announcing she was pregnant? Shock, obviously. Would he even believe it was his? He would. Of course he would. She still didn't know all there was to know about Adam, but she knew him well enough to know he wouldn't doubt her. Would he want to be involved though? He was a free spirit, when all was said and done. Would he really want a child to tie him down?

She should have insisted her dad wait until she'd spoken to him. He'd been so furious though. After Adam's shenanigans last night, Sienna really couldn't blame him. He was her dad, after all. Naturally, he'd want to protect his daughter, even if she was a grown woman. Hadn't he always? And, after learning all he had the last few days, she understood why his protective gene had gone into overdrive. She'd made him swear not to say anything about the pregnancy. It was up to her to do that. With or without Adam, she was having her baby. She had to tell him in order for him to make the choice though, didn't she? She had no intention of being a string, if 'no strings' was what he wanted. She'd be quite open to a bit of bondage, but she wouldn't tie him down. She wouldn't want to. She didn't want him on that basis. It would crush her to lose him. She couldn't even bear to contemplate that, but she could do this without him if she had to.

'Can't I, Tobias?' she asked the ever-faithful male in her life, as she heaved his hindquarters up over the doorstep. 'If he's not interested, then I'll bring the baby up on my own.' She nodded determinedly. She might possibly need to ask her dad for a little help initially. In which case, she really shouldn't be berating him for doing what he saw as his responsibility as a father. Oh, dear. Men, they really were a conundrum, Adam the biggest conundrum of all. She would tell him, as soon as she saw him. If, please God, there was anything left of him.

As for *him* ... Sienna was sorely tempted to reply succinctly to another more aggressive incoming text from her ex, but thought better of it. The man was clearly disturbed, absolutely believing he'd done nothing wrong. Frighteningly, still trying to convince her that *she* had. What frightened her more was the thought of what he might do if she did reply, telling him exactly what she thought of him. A cold shudder ran through her as she recalled the look in his eyes, flat and cold; there was no caring there, and then ... utter contempt. Sienna shakily deleted the message. If he didn't stop soon, she really would hire a hit man, or else send in Lauren.

Adam went nervously through the chandlery and into Nathaniel's office, not sure what to expect. Two not-so-polite requests to do the decent thing and disappear, he supposed. He glanced to where Nathaniel was sitting at his desk, arms folded, pointedly not looking at him and not saying anything, which spoke volumes.

Sienna's dad was at the window, his hands in his pockets and his back towards him. Even from where he was standing, Adam could feel the distinctly hostile vibes. Uncertain what to do next, he swallowed and waited. Then dragged a hand through his hair and waited some more. If one of them didn't say something soon, neither of them would have to go to the trouble of decking him. Feeling as ill as he did, Adam was pretty sure he'd pass out where he stood.

'You'd better sit down,' Nathaniel finally spoke.

Wary of what might be about to happen, Adam had a feeling he might need to. Keeping an eye on Sienna's father as he did, he walked over to the visitor's chair. If the man was going to hit him, he would only need to do it once. Adam was in no position to fight back, that was for sure. Sweat tickling his forehead, he sat down, wiped the palms of his hands against his thighs and continued to wait.

Nathaniel did look at him then. Shaking his head, he leaned back in his chair and just looked, wearing that same dispassionate expression he had earlier, which only increased Adam's nervousness further.

'You've got bottle, turning up, I'll give you that,' David Meadows spoke eventually, without turning around.

Feeling an agreement wouldn't be an appropriate response, Adam kept quiet.

'David Meadows,' the man reminded him, after another uncomfortable pause. 'Sienna's father, I assume you've remembered?'

Pleased to meet you also not being quite the correct response, Adam coughed and mumbled, 'Yes,' instead.

The man turned to face him at last, looking him over before locking furious eyes on his. 'Start talking!' he barked suddenly, causing Adam to almost have apoplexy.

Start talking where? He tried to quash his rising panic.

'Well, come on then, Romeo. We've had the ineloquent balcony scene, let's have the story behind it, shall we?'

Meadows said, more quietly, which really wasn't any less intimidating.

Adam glanced desperately at Nathaniel, who shrugged and gave him nothing in the way of guidance.

'Struck dumb, are we, lad!' Meadows boomed.

Shit! 'I, erm …' Adam ran his hand over his neck, no clue what to say.

'Thirsty possibly? Need a hair o' the dog to cure your hangover and give you some Dutch courage?'

'No!' Adam said quickly. 'No, I don't,' he added, more quietly. 'I shouldn't have … That was stupid.'

David Meadows arched an eyebrow.

Adam thought better of commenting further.

'Right, well, as you seem at a loss where to start, I'll get the ball rolling then, shall I?' Meadows didn't wait for an answer. 'I won't ask what your intentions are. It's quite clear from what I've heard so far, from your friend,' he glanced at Nathaniel, 'and your fan club around town, you don't have any; friends or intentions.'

Adam pulled in a breath. He didn't look at Nathaniel. They'd obviously been discussing him. Fair enough, after his idiotic behaviour, but if Nate had told this bloke what he thought of him, he really had washed his hands of him. That hurt.

'You let your balls rule your brain and fuck everything up, don't you, Adam?'

Adam winced. 'Pretty much.'

Meadows folded his arms. 'I'm told you had a devastating experience a while back,' he said, left-winging Adam completely. 'One which apparently set you off on this immature path of destruction.'

Astonished, Adam did look at Nathaniel then, a long quizzical look. How much of his history had he felt at liberty to discuss, exactly?

'Don't worry, he didn't give me details,' Meadows went on. 'Apparently, he respects your wishes that you'd rather he didn't.'

Adam nodded, immensely relieved. He'd stand still while Nathaniel took a pop at him. Several. He ought to. That wouldn't hurt as much as knowing the one person he'd always trusted had broken that trust.

'So, I'm going to ask you to provide details instead, Adam. You've got one chance to convince me there's a shred of decency in you, assuming you want to. This is it. Convince me.'

What? Adam's stomach clenched like a fist. He looked incredulously from Meadows to Nathaniel and back. Was he serious? A psychiatrist he might be, but did he really expect him to confide something he'd tried to block out every day since it happened? Just trot it out? Something he couldn't even think about without feeling as if someone had ripped his guts out? Something he *couldn't* talk about? Nathaniel knew he couldn't. Swallowing back a hard lump in his throat, Adam shook his head. 'I can't.'

Meadows considered. 'Right,' he said. 'In which case, please don't try to see Sienna again, because from what I do know about you, you're a self-centred little shit who'll destroy her life. Goodbye, Adam. Nathaniel, Sienna and I will be leaving in half an hour.'

Adam sucked in a long breath as Meadows walked towards the door. 'Wait!' he said, panic gripping him as the man reached for the door handle.

Meadows turned slowly back.

Adam looked at him and then down. 'My fiancée ... she ...' he started falteringly.

'You were due to be *married?*' Meadows sounded incredulous.

Adam hesitated. 'Yes.'

'And?'

Again Adam faltered, not sure where to even begin explaining.

'Let me guess, you got cold feet?' Meadows now sounded unimpressed.

'No,' Adam denied quickly. 'Yes. No, I ...' Stammering, he stopped and wiped a bead of perspiration from his cheek.

Meadows waited.

'Not about marrying her, no,' Adam went on, though the words were threatening to choke him. 'About the wedding. My family, the property we'd be living in. I did want to marry her. I just ...' Trailing hopelessly off, he tugged in another tight breath.

'So, what happened?' Meadows forced it.

'We argued.' Adam breathed raggedly out. 'Kept arguing. Couldn't seem to talk without arguing eventually. We were at a family function and ...'

'You argued,' Meadows supplied as Adam trailed off again.

Adam nodded, trying hard to still the pictures in his head. 'Emily. She and my brother, they ...' He paused, and breathed. 'She ... got pregnant, somewhere along the line. I ...'

Dragging an arm across his forehead, Adam felt compelled to glance up. She was here. His eyes flicked to the side of Meadows. Tangible, almost. He could see her; her form, her face, pale, mournful, her features etched with such sorrow it seared his very soul.

Somehow sensing she wanted him to, Adam gulped back the jagged pieces of his heart and pushed on. 'I didn't know whether it was mine. I walked away. Ran away. Drank myself into oblivion. I ...' *Shit, he couldn't do this.*

Meadows was silent for a moment, then, 'She had the baby?' he asked softly.

Adam answered with a tight nod.

'And?'

Adam ran a hand shakily through his hair. 'I went to her flat. I wanted to talk, to see the baby, try to … She wasn't there. She'd left, taken the baby. She…' Again, he stopped, his voice cracking. 'I can't.'

'She committed suicide,' Nathaniel picked up, gently. 'She'd been depressed. Adam found her. She'd booked into the hotel they often stayed at; the hotel where he'd proposed to her.'

The ensuing silence was heavy, punctuated only by the tick of the office clock. Loud, ominous, it emulated precisely the sound that Adam could never shut out. He could hear it now. He'd never forget it, the steady, drip, drip, drip: a slow trickle of blood, staining the white bathroom tiles crimson.

'The baby?' Meadows asked after a moment, his voice low, shocked.

'Safe,' Nathaniel supplied, glancing at Adam.

Adam didn't speak. He couldn't. Seeing in his mind's eye the tiny form of Lily-Grace, little limbs flailing, lost and alone amid a sea of white bed linen, he felt something brush his cheek, soft, like a single snowflake. Emily. Adam wiped away a tear, wrapped his arms about himself and closed his eyes.

Nathaniel offering him a glass of water snapped him back to the present, away from the baby's bewildered cries, Emily's lifeless form. 'Take it,' he said. 'You'll be dehydrated.'

Blinking, Adam heaved himself up in the chair and took the glass. His hands were still shaking, he noticed vaguely, and then realised he was shaking all over.

'Two more questions and then subject closed,' Meadows said, more kindly.

Adam swallowed and nodded.

'Do you see the child?'

Adam took a gulp of water. 'I didn't, no,' he answered, struggling to keep his voice in check. 'I was too messed up. I've been in touch recently. I'm hoping Emily's sister will agree to me seeing her soon.'

'Well done, Adam,' Nathaniel offered, sounding surprised – and impressed for the first time in a long time.

'Last question,' Meadows went on. 'Have you flitted from woman to woman ever since to avoid getting hurt, Adam, or is it some form of love 'em, leave 'em retribution?'

Adam nodded again, realising it was a fair question. 'The former,' he replied honestly.

Meadows paused, seeming to assess him. '*Do* you love Sienna?'

Adam met his gaze. 'For the rest of my life,' he stated emphatically.

Seemingly satisfied, Meadows nodded in turn and walked across to him. 'I've taken some leave from work to be with my daughter. I'll give you two weeks, Adam. Two weeks to show me you want a life worth living. But ...' He leaned forward to press his hands on the arms of the chair either side of him, 'if you slip up ...'

Chapter Sixteen

Watching nervously from her window, Sienna saw Adam emerge from the chandlery to walk towards his boat. His face was white and tight, that same angry expression he'd worn once before. He was dragging his hand repeatedly, agitatedly through his hair and his breathing was heavy. She should go to him. Go now and talk to him. Sienna pulled herself from the window to dash outside, just in time to see Adam swing towards the back of his boat, where he leaned over the water and was violently sick. Dear God, what had her dad said? What had he done?

Sienna hovered, torn between going to see Adam, whatever reception she got, and going to tell her father to *please, please* go home and give her some space.

'Sienna.' Her dad came out just then, calling towards her.

Sienna flew over to him. 'What did you do?' she demanded, glancing frustrated from her father to Nathaniel close behind him.

'Do?' Her dad looked at her, puzzled.

'He's been sick.' Sienna flailed an arm in the direction of Adam's boat, which he'd now disappeared into. 'He looked absolutely dreadful. What did you say?'

'Sienna, calm down.' Her dad placed a hand on her shoulder. 'I didn't do or say anything dramatic. I just told him he needed to sort himself out, that's all.'

Sienna glanced warily from her dad to Nathaniel, who offered her a reassuring smile. 'He's just feeling a bit hung-over and emotional, Sienna. Give him—'

Nathaniel stopped as a loud crash from inside Adam's boat echoed across the marina, followed by a voluble expletive.

Sienna took a step towards the boat, which was now most definitely swaying, only to be stopped by Nathaniel. 'Give him some time, Sienna. He's just trying to sort some things out in his head.'

'What things?' Sienna looked at Nathaniel imploringly. She needed to know. Surely he must know she did, for Adam's sake, as well as her own. 'Nate, what did you talk about?'

Nathaniel looked at her thoughtfully, and then nodded. 'Emily, amongst other things. That is, Adam did, for the first time. I'm not sure how much you know?'

'I know,' Sienna told him. Adam had never spoken the words, it was true, but she knew.

'Adam found her,' Nathaniel said gently, confirming the most awful detail. 'He's never been able to talk about it before. He's bound to be overwrought. I'll go and check on him when—'

Nathaniel stopped again as Adam reappeared, his face still wearing the same thunderous expression, his chest heaving. He didn't leap the handrail. He just stepped heavily down. Then, not even glancing in their direction, he walked away.

'Any ideas?' her dad asked coming up behind Nathaniel, as Adam stormed on out of the marina.

Nathaniel sighed. 'None, but he's left his car wherever he was drinking last night, which means he's on foot. I hope he's *not* heading for a hair o' the dog, because the nearest pub is the same one the idiots who went after him frequent.'

Sienna was sitting outside an hour later reading the same paragraph of a book over and over. She glanced at her dad, who was reading his newspaper. She'd been so upset with him, taking it upon himself to corner Adam like that.

Her dad flapped his newspaper, pretending to be

absorbed. He wasn't. Sienna could tell. He had that little v in his brow, which was always there when he was worrying, mostly about her. 'Sorry, Dad,' she offered eventually, knowing she owed him much more than an apology.

Her dad lowered his paper. 'Me, too.' He mustered up a smile. 'Look, Sienna, I know you think you're old enough to make your own decisions—'

'*Dad*.' Sienna sighed.

'The thing is, Sienna, I don't think any of us ever are, when it comes to matters of the heart.'

'But he's not all bad, Dad,' Sienna tried to point out, again. 'He does have some good qualities. Lots, really he does. Under all that … stuff … he's a warm, caring person. He's just lost and lonely. I'm not ready to give up on him because he can't find his way, not yet.'

Her dad's expression was pensive, as if he doubted Adam could possibly have a single good quality. 'I think he might well be,' he said, at length.

Sienna smiled, hopefully. 'You do?'

'After our chat, yes. Possibly.' Her dad back-pedalled a little. 'He obviously did care enough about the woman he broke up with to try to do the right thing. He's still working through his issues, though, Sienna.'

'Like you had to?' Sienna asked gently, not wanting to remind her dad of what he called his 'black' period, when his life seemed to have no purpose, other than to be there for her.

Her dad looked her thoughtfully over. 'Yes,' he conceded, with a sad smile. 'I can empathise, to a degree. I'm not heartless, Sienna. I realise the man's hurting. He's not going to find his way viewing the world through the bottom of a whisky bottle though, is he? Whether he's an addict or not, remains to be seen, but he obviously uses alcohol as some kind of crutch. As for the womanising,' he paused to look gravely at her, 'he might love women, preferring short relationships to avoid getting hurt. On the other hand, it's possible he hates women.'

'He does *not*.' Sienna scowled. Why did everyone have him down as a woman-hater? They couldn't possibly understand. They didn't *know* him.

'It's a harsh observation, but the fact that he talked about it does give me a shred of hope.' Her dad offered her another small smile, this time of reassurance. 'He claimed the former incidentally. But then, I doubt he would have readily admitted to the latter.'

He really had grilled him, hadn't he? No wonder Adam had looked so distraught when he'd come out of the chandlery. Sienna's heart twisted for him. 'He doesn't hate women, Dad,' she reiterated, confident that, after the way Adam had touched her, every part of her, he simply couldn't.

'A man might be a competent lover, Sienna, but it doesn't mean he's competent at loving relationships,' her dad pointed out, eerily psychic. 'He has to be able to change, sweetheart,' he went on, kindly. 'To do that, he has to want to enough to start making those changes. If I can see any evidence he's capable of trying, I'll preach from a distance. For now though—'

He stopped as Nathaniel came across from the chandlery. 'Just thought you'd like to know, he's back,' he said. 'And he's driving.'

'I take it this is a good sign?' her dad asked, following Nathaniel's gaze back to the car park, where Adam was indeed climbing out of his car.

'Very,' Nathaniel assured him. 'He doesn't drink and drive.'

Her dad looked marginally impressed. 'What? Never?'

'Never.' Nathaniel gave Sienna a sly wink.

Sienna beamed. 'A good quality?' she asked her dad.

'I concede he's not *all* bad.' Her dad gave another inch.

Smiling, Sienna watched as Adam walked back to his boat. He still looked broody, and very tired. But he no longer looked furious. Sienna so hoped that was a good sign. The information her dad had dragged out of him, that was personal and painful. Too painful for Adam to easily talk about it, she'd seen that for herself. It must have been hard, yet he'd done it. He was trying, he really was. How could she not love him?

She tried to catch his eye as he neared his boat, but Adam's gaze was once again averted, which struck Sienna as *not* a very good sign. Feeling her own eyes filling up, she glanced quickly down. Hormones, she told herself firmly. They would be bound to be flying all over the place. She was reading too much into it, overreacting, that's what she was doing. She gave herself a good talking to. She still didn't feel any less like bursting into tears, though.

'All right, sweetheart?' her dad asked as Tobias heaved himself from where he was lying at her feet to plant his head in her lap and look dolefully up at her.

'Yes,' she assured him, cheered a little by her ever-faithful friend.

'Your hormones will be a bit wobbly,' her dad imparted, spookily. 'I'll get you a nice cup of tea, shall I?'

'Thanks.' Sienna smiled, now grateful for his unerring intuition.

'Nathaniel?' her dad asked, standing up.

In answer to which, Nathaniel said, 'Bloody hell!'

All eyes followed his astounded gaze to where Adam was now climbing back off his boat. About to clean it, judging from the buckets and cleaning paraphernalia he deposited on the bank. They watched on as he went to unroll the water hose and proceeded to wash the dust and mud from the hull.

Nathaniel grinned at Sienna and then nodded in Adam's direction and wandered across to him. 'Need a hand?' he asked him.

'Nope,' Adam said, concentrating on his efforts.

Nathaniel looked a bit deflated.

'I could use the vacuum, though, if that's okay?'

'Vacuum?' Nathaniel repeated, boggle-eyed.

'Yep, and some bin bags if you've got any spare, to do the inside.'

'Bloody hell,' Nathaniel repeated, shaking his head. 'Don't need some aspirin, while I'm at it, do you?'

Adam laughed. 'No, just the vacuum and bin bags,' he assured him. 'Throw me the keys and I'll fetch them in a sec.'

Nathaniel shook his head again, turning back towards the chandlery. 'Definitely not himself,' he said, stopping to allow a van to pull up.

Fleur's Flowers' van from the village, Sienna noticed, watching Nathaniel with interest as he chatted to the driver, then looking curiously at Adam, who seemed to be completely oblivious. Flowers not for her, then, she assumed, a bit dejectedly, and then looked at the bouquet with as much surprise as Nathaniel as the driver walked up to her.

'Sienna Meadows?' the delivery girl asked.

'That's her,' her dad said, Sienna being temporarily gobsmacked.

Sienna swallowed as the girl deposited the flowers into her arms. 'Thank you.' She laughed, looking at Adam, who was still cleaning his boat.

God, they *were* from him, weren't they?

Adam stopped and glanced towards her, his expression unreadable for a second. And then he winked, his mouth curving into his delicious, bone-melting smile, before he went fastidiously back to his cleaning. She loved him. She absolutely did. He was utterly edible. Trying not to think about the parts she'd like to eat, Sienna smiled a gloopy smile and pulled the little handwritten card out of the envelope.

In case I slurred my words, I LOVE every inch of you, it read. Give me two weeks to prove it. Then, when my psychiatrist has gone, I'll prove it all over again. XXXXX

PS. I'm sorry. PPS. We need to talk. PPPS. Liked what you did with the Bolognese sauce. What flavour ice cream do you like?

Oh God. Sienna flipped the card over, realising her dad was peering over her shoulder. Had he seen it? Her cheeks no doubt scarlet, Sienna peeked up at him. Phew, no, judging by his unmoved expression. 'Two good qualities?' she ventured.

'Hmm?' Her dad didn't look convinced. 'Let's see how the next two weeks pan out, shall we?' He glanced across to where Adam was still hard at it, polishing metal until it shone. Then, shaking his head bemusedly, he went off to make the tea.

'How goes the battle?' Sienna asked when Adam grabbed up his phone an exhausting two hours later.

Adam smiled, glad to hear her voice, relieved she was speaking to him. He wasn't entirely sure she ever would again after his deplorable behaviour. 'Which one?' he joked, searching his small under sink cupboard in hopes of a clean cloth.

'Sorry about my dad,' Sienna said quickly. 'He means well, but ...'

'Don't be. If I was him I probably would have left me to drown. It's me who should be apologising. I'm sorry, Sienna. I just ...' Drawing in a breath, Adam gave up on the cloth, wanting to give her his full attention, wishing he could be with her, talk to her properly. 'The thing is, he's right. I am a mess. I'm going to change things, though, I promise.'

Sienna went quiet for a moment, causing Adam's heart to skip a beat. 'You do believe me, don't you?' he asked, feeling suddenly panicky. He still had no idea what she saw in him.

'Yes,' Sienna replied after a pause. 'I believe you want … *Whoops*. Got to go. My security guard's coming in. Catch you later.'

'Okay. Sienna, is it okay to ring you?' Adam asked, trying not to wonder how she'd been going to finish that sentence. With a 'but' probably. 'I wasn't sure whether your father might be censoring all calls.' As well as keeping me under constant surveillance, Adam didn't add. Given why he was under surveillance, the situation was probably more embarrassing for Sienna than it was for him.

'You'll have your very own ring tone,' Sienna whispered. 'Speak later.'

Two weeks. Adam pondered as he pocketed his phone, his lifeline. He'd got two weeks to prove himself, or he'd lost her. Sighing, he glanced around at his only earthly possessions, and wondered where the hell he even started. By finishing the cleaning, he supposed. Clearing out his old life and then somehow showing Meadows that he did want a life worth living, no 'buts'.

Finding a spongy cloth, finally, Adam turned to the fridge, the last thing on his list. Would one really hurt, he debated, eyeing the cold beers inside which looked mightily tempting. He'd worked hard, cleaning the boat so thoroughly inside you could eat your dinner off the floor. He'd recycled his recyclables, opened the curtains, giving every passing person in the marina a chance to ogle inside. He'd even scrubbed the cooker, working up a mighty thirst as he did.

Just one, he considered again. He could take the rest over to Nate, keep one back and … And then he'd be off down to the pub, one further afield, and have one hell of a walk back. Sore feet and soaking wet, he could cope with. Sienna's old man on his back, he'd rather not. The guy was a little late protecting his daughter's virtue, but from hereon he obviously meant business. Adam had to admire him for it, even if he had forced him to dig up old ghosts he would much rather have left buried. They weren't, though, were they? He didn't really need his constant hovering companion to tell him that.

Where was she anyhow? He glanced over his shoulder. Gone to powder her nose, he guessed, or more likely checking out his cleaning efforts in the bathroom. Adam shook his head as she floated through the bathroom door. She seemed lighter, somehow, as if some of the sadness had been lifted. He wasn't sure why she was here, *if* she was, but, though she seemed determined to be on his back, at least she wasn't trying to psychoanalyse him. Adam really didn't think he needed to go that route again. He'd been trying to shut off the memories with booze and sex, he knew that. Sex had a whole new impetus now, though. And it was pretty damn good. His mouth curved into a slow smile. He wasn't sure how he was going to cope with abstinence, but he was going to have to, he supposed, until her father had gone, assuming Sienna wanted a future with him.

Meanwhile … *No beer.* Steeling his resolve, Adam shoved cans and bottles into the carrier, including another half-drunk bottle of whisky, and headed for the door.

Leaping the handrail, and wincing as the contents of his carrier clinked, he headed over to the chandlery and Nathaniel's office, where he knocked and then went on in.

'What's up?' Nathaniel asked, eyeing him warily.

Adam looked at him curiously. 'Nothing. Why?'

'You're smiling.'

'Still? Damn.' Adam straightened his face.

'Thinking about anything in particular?' Nathaniel enquired casually. 'Sex? Booze?'

'Sienna,' Adam assured him, dumping the carrier on his desk. 'Do me a favour, Nate, drink that or ditch it.'

Nathaniel peered in the bag then looked up at Adam, astonished. 'Blimey, you really are serious, aren't you?'

'Totally,' Adam assured him, turning back for the door.

'Right, well, will do then. Adam …?' Nathaniel stopped him short.

Adam turned back again. 'Yep?'

'Well done. It's been a long time coming, but well done.' Nathaniel stood up and offered him his hand.

Adam smiled and shook it. 'We're still mates, then?'

'Stuck with you, aren't I?' Nathaniel rolled his eyes. 'At least until someone's fool enough to take you off my hands.'

'Cheers, mate. In case I forgot to mention it, you're a good one.'

'I know,' Nathaniel said, plonking himself back down and turning back to his laptop. 'Not too many cheers, though, hey? And no falling off the wagon the minute you hit the first bump in the road. Roads are full of potholes, Adam, it's a fact. Don't drink if you drop down one. Climb out again and bloody well get on with it.'

'Blimey, that's your most concise sermon yet. Constructive too. You're improving.'

'Bugger off.'

'Yes, mother.' Adam gave him a wink and whistled on out.

'Evening,' he said to David Meadows, who was back on duty, watching him like a hawk as he walked back to his boat. Adam was only surprised the man hadn't got binoculars. He really was going to be on his back, wasn't he?

Shaking his head, Adam climbed on board, and then stopped, glanced across the marina and did a double take. Nicole? He squinted. She'd come here? Looked like she had. And, what was more – he took a faltering step back down – she'd brought Lily-Grace.

Astounded, Adam walked out to meet them, immediately sweeping his eyes over the child in Nicole's arms. She was beautiful – he swallowed back a tight knot in his chest – a miniature replica of Emily, apart from her eyes. Framed by luxuriant, dark eyelashes and crystal clear with the innocence of childhood, Lily-Grace's eyes were brown; rich velvet brown, he noticed. His brother's eyes were blue. Adam's mind raced. Emily's had been blue. He was no expert on genealogy, but he supposed blue-eyed parents could have a brown-eyed child. The thing was, Adam now knew with certainty, it really didn't matter anymore. What mattered now, what should have always been paramount, was this child's happiness.

'I hope you didn't mind us just turning up,' Nicole said, bringing his attention back to her. 'We had a spare couple of hours, so …'

'No. God, no, not at all,' Adam assured her. 'But how did you know where to find me?'

'Nathaniel,' Nicole supplied. 'I still have his number from … before, you know. I wanted to surprise you, so I rang him earlier.'

Surprise him as in catch him in his natural habitat, Adam guessed, and thanked God for Meadows' timely intervention which had galvanised him into tidying it. 'I'm glad you did.' He smiled, uncertain what to do next.

Nicole smiled back. 'Lily, this is Adam,' she said. 'He's Mummy's friend.' Her gaze strayed meaningfully to Adam.

Mummy being her, Adam understood.

'She's gorgeous,' he said, 'adorable.' He took in her tiny cupid lips, her soft peachy cheeks, her hair, similar in colour to his, a halo of baby-soft ringlets. She was perfect. He felt his heart swell. She was his. Adam pulled in a breath and dipped his head in a small nod, sensing her birth mother needed that affirmation. Whatever her genealogy, she was his flesh and blood, and he'd turned away from her. So much time wasted. Feeling dangerously close to tears, Adam quickly ran his forearm over his eyes and offered the little girl a smile, rather than stare at her, like the idiot he was.

Plugging a thumb into her mouth, Lily regarded him curiously.

'That's Adam's boat,' Nicole said, nestling her cheek close to Lily's. 'Shall we ask Adam if we can see inside?' She hoisted the little girl, who was obviously growing heavy, higher in her arms.

Lily's eyes flicked from Adam to his boat. 'Boat,' she said, around her thumb, one little sausage arm now outstretched towards it. 'Want see.'

Adam laughed. 'Certainly, madam. Your wish is my command. Here let me,' he said, reaching for her as Nicole hitched her up again.

'Careful,' Nicole warned him. 'She's a bit shy of strange—' She stopped, raising her eyebrows in surprise as Lily reached both arms out and slipped easily into Adam's.

'Well, that's a first.' Nicole smiled, falling into step alongside them as Lily, inhibitions clearly forgotten, latched herself around Adam's neck.

'It's my natural charisma.' Adam gave Nicole a wink and pressed his free hand to the child's back, making sure she was secure, praying she always would be. Emily was hovering directly in front of him as he walked, nervous, Adam felt. Not half as nervous as he was. She's beautiful, he mentally addressed her, something close to contentment settling inside him. Just like her mother. At which, Emily appeared to actually smile.

Smiling back, briefly, lest Nicole catch him smiling at nothing, Adam turned his attention to Lily. 'I don't have a name for my boat yet,' he confided. 'What do you think we should call her?'

Lily pondered, her little brow knitted in thoughtful concentration. 'Boat,' she plumped for, turning her face to his, her naïve child's eyes looking into his eyes with such open trust, it flipped Adam's heart right over.

'Great name.' He nodded, swallowing back his emotion. 'I thought something a bit prettier, though. How about … Lily-Grace?' he suggested, climbing carefully up onto the deck with her.

Lily had another think. 'Lily-Glace,' she lisped at length, nodding contentedly.

Nicole laughed. 'Well, you certainly have a way with the ladies,' she observed, stepping up behind them.

'Er, some.' Adam glanced sideways to where David Meadows was still watching him.

Nicole gave him an inquisitive glance, as Adam motioned her on in ahead of him. 'Anyone special?' she asked, perceptively.

Adam supposed she would want to know if he was seeing anyone, Lily-Grace in mind. He glanced uncertainly at Meadows again, whose expression was troubled at best. 'I hope so.' He sighed, following her in.

Sienna had watched proceedings from her usual vantage point at her kitchen window. Surprised when the woman and child had turned up, mesmerised as Adam had reached for the little girl, she'd almost gone out. Almost. Assuming that this was Emily's child, though, she'd decided against it.

This was a private, personal moment for Adam. One that he didn't need her crashing in on. He'd looked so natural, seemed so comfortable with that little girl, as if she belonged in his arms, in his heart. Her hand strayed to the soft round of her tummy.

Sienna watched on as her dad, still on vigil outside, shook his head, bemused, and then headed back to the cottage. What would he make of all this, the timing around Adam being reunited with his lost daughter, Sienna wondered? He knew about her, having dragged the information from Adam. Would he see the way he'd interacted with her so naturally as a plus in Adam's favour? Sienna did, absolutely. Her heart had swollen with pride, watching him carrying the child, holding her so instinctively caringly, as only a father could. Or would her dad see this as another negative, the fact that the child would now be a part of Adam's future? Of her future, too, if Adam did want to be involved in the life of the child growing inside her.

Would he?

Sienna chewed on a stray strand of hair, examining her own feelings. Would she want to take on board responsibility for his child? Could she make room in her heart for her? Would Adam want her to? She felt she knew him, but they'd known each other for such a short time, in reality. Sighing, she glanced over her shoulder, as her dad came into the kitchen. 'A good quality?' she asked him.

Her dad came to stand alongside her. His hands in his pockets, he looked over towards Adam's boat, looking pensive. 'Given the circumstances,' he said thoughtfully, 'I'd say, yes, definitely a good quality.'

Sienna leaned into him, glad of his shoulder.

Her dad wrapped an arm around her and pulled her closer. 'Are you going to tell him?' he asked her, after a moment.

Sienna didn't answer. She wasn't sure how to.

'You know, Sienna, if he does feel trapped into commitment then—'

'He's not worth having.' Sienna nodded, and swallowed. 'I will tell him. Soon,' she said, knowing that Adam's reaction when she did tell him would be a defining moment in her life, her child's life.

Her dad didn't say anything, just squeezed her shoulders, communicating he understood she needed to decide when the timing was right. Now wasn't that time, clearly. When would be, though?

Chapter Seventeen

'Does he usually get up this early?' Sienna's dad asked the next morning. He'd obviously noted the movement on Adam's boat as he took in the view whilst drinking his coffee, the view being Adam's boat, which his eyes were still permanently on.

Sienna spied out alongside him, her hormones panting themselves into a frenzy as she also took in the view. And what a beautiful one it was, too. Adam had just come up on deck, topless. 'When he runs, yes,' she said, her voice sounding a bit shrill.

'He runs?' Her dad looked at her, astounded.

'Yes.' Sienna wondered why it would be such a surprise. 'He's actually quite fit.'

'Hmm.' Her dad nodded thoughtfully and turned to head for the hall.

Very fit, Sienna thought, taking the opportunity for another surreptitious peek and trying not to openly drool. God, she wanted him. Her breasts literally tingled every time she even thought about him. Seeing him half-naked, they were almost on fire. Ooh, it was just *so* frustrating. Here she was, pregnant with the man's baby and she was being chaperoned by her father, for goodness sake!

Yet, still she hadn't told him. How could she have, though, when Adam had been so obviously delighted at having been reunited with Lily-Grace, besotted with her – rightly so – and relishing every minute of her company? She'd watched Adam take the little girl's tiny hand in his strong man's hand, smiling down at her, talking gently to her as she'd tottered alongside him to her cottage. Sienna's heart had almost burst at the sight of this beautiful, supposedly uncaring man, so openly embracing his nurturing side.

She'd been so pleased he'd decided to bring Lily Grace to see her. A twinkle in his liquid brown eyes, he'd introduced his daughter to his 'special friend'. He'd seemed so genuinely happy, like a big kid himself, his mouth curving into its gorgeous smile as he'd looked from her to Lily-Grace, who would steal any man's heart in an instant.

He'd brushed her cheek with a kiss as he'd left, any too-intimate gestures out of the question with her dad looking on. She couldn't have mentioned anything, not then. It would have been so unfair, giving him her news like a thunderbolt out of the blue. She needed to see him on his own. Oh, how she needed to see him on his own, to look into Adam's eyes; to see *him* when she told him. Have him hold her, touch her; bring her to such sweet heights of …

'He obviously does,' her dad observed, alarmingly telepathically as he came back into the kitchen.

What? Sienna gulped and immediately censored all thoughts.

'He looks like he's quite serious about it.' Her dad nodded through the window, to where Adam, now kitted out in his vest and track bottoms, leapt athletically over his handrail and set off at a jog.

God, but he was beautiful. He'd be all sweaty when he got back. Sienna closed her eyes, her tongue involuntarily trailing over her lips. 'Like I said, he's very fit,' she squeaked, heading to the stairs to shower, which she doubted would help wash away her lustful thoughts.

'Think I'll go with him,' her dad said behind her.

Oh, no. Was he really going to shadow Adam *every*where? Sienna turned worriedly back.

'I was going for a run anyway.'

'Oh, right.' Sienna nodded as her dad bent to tie the laces of his trainers. Looked like there wasn't much she could do to dissuade him. 'Well, I'm sure Adam will be glad of the company.'

Not. Oh, dear. Watching her dad leaving, she immediately texted Adam, wanting to warn him her dad was on his tail as well as his back.

Are you OK? She typed and pressed send.

Excellent. Adam pinged back. Are you sexting me – hopefully?

I need to see you. He immediately texted again, as Sienna was typing in her 'dad alert'.

Sienna backspaced. Why? She sent apprehensively instead.

2 talk 2 u. Adam sent back.

About? Sienna thumbed worriedly back.

Phoning u. Male. Rubbish at multitasking.

Oh God. To say what? Sienna immediately went into worry overdrive. That he was fed up probably. He'd slept with her twice, and now he had to answer to her father regarding his every move? He was a grown man, for goodness sake, with a child. Yes, and he had another child on the way. She steeled herself to tell him so. He loved her. It was obvious he loved Lily-Grace. He would love this child, want to be part of its life, she was sure.

Hurry up. Sienna jiggled, waiting for him to phone. Her dad was fast. She wanted to give Adam fair warning he was about to be ambushed, but most of all she desperately wanted to talk to him, to hear his voice, to feel reassured. She always did when she saw him. Spoke to him. Saw the undisguised longing in his lustful dark eyes. Impatient, she was selecting his number, when her phone rang. Adam's tone, thank goodness.

He didn't wait for her to speak. 'Why me, Sienna?' he asked outright.

'What?' Sienna said, feeling not at all reassured.

'Why me? Why did you sleep with me, without knowing

me? Why did you ask me?'

Sienna's tummy flopped down to her toes. 'Because ...' she faltered '... I liked you.'

'How?' Adam sounded confused, short even. 'How could you like me? You didn't know me.'

'I *did*,' Sienna protested, feeling very confused. 'We'd talked. I didn't just knock on your door and ask you—'

'But you'd already made up your mind.'

It was a statement, not a question. Why was he doing this – Sienna's eyes filled up – being so blunt? Making her feel like a complete tart? Like she'd thrown herself at him? Because she bloody well had. She swiped at a stupid tear on her cheek. And now she was pregnant. And he was going to hate her. He was bound to think that she'd set out to trap him.

'I hadn't made up my mind, actually,' she said, trying to sound calmer than she felt. 'I'd thought about ... fantasised about you, yes, because I did fancy you and, let's face it, you weren't exactly shy, flaunting yourself all over the show.'

'Flaunting myself?' Adam laughed.

'Yes, flaunting your far too tempting torso and your far too distracting shorts. It's bound to fuel a girl's fantasy, isn't it, when—'

'She fancies me,' Adam finished, chuckling merrily.

Now she felt silly. Sienna debated whether to hang up. Apart from the fact that he was totally embarrassing her, if he was cross-questioning her now, hinting she'd coerced him, then he'd obviously be less than delighted when she presented him with the consequences of their sexual exploits. 'I have to go,' she said. 'Tobias needs his—'

'No, don't,' Adam said quickly. 'Don't go, Sienna, please. Look, I'm sorry. It's just that I can't seem to get you on your own, and I needed to know. It was your first time. What the hell did you see in me?'

'I told you, I fancied you. And, once you'd decided to stop being obnoxious and we talked, I realised I liked you. I felt I could trust you and ...' Sienna stopped, hesitant to impart information that would make her look completely foolish.

'And?' Adam coaxed her.

Sienna drew in a breath and scrunched her eyes closed. 'And I wanted to find out if there was something wrong with me.'

Adam paused. 'Wrong with you?' He laughed again, incredulously.

'I thought someone experienced might know.'

'Know what, Sienna?' Adam asked gently.

He waited.

Sienna hesitated.

'Whether I was frigid!' she blurted.

'*What?*'

Adam slowed his jog to a walk. 'Why the bloody hell would you think—'

'Because my last boyfriend told me I was, before he tried to ...' He heard her catch a sob in her throat. 'I have to go, Adam.'

Before he ...? It didn't take a genius to work out what he'd *tried to*. 'Bastard!' Adam ground to a halt, his jaw clenching.

'I have to go,' Sienna repeated, tearfully. 'I'll talk to you—'

'Sienna, there is *nothing* wrong with you!' Adam said angrily. 'For God's sake, Sienna, you blew me away. You're the most beautiful, sensual, sexual woman I've ever met.' He stopped talking, panic gripping him as he wondered whether she'd ended the call.

'Sienna?'

She didn't speak. He heard her sniffle, though. She was

crying. That was down to him. Again! *Dammit!* He ran a hand furiously through his hair. 'I fancied you the second I set eyes on you, Sienna,' he told her, wanting her to know, wanting her to realise how utterly desirable she was. 'I mean fancied you in a way I really didn't think I could cope with. I tried to tell myself I didn't. That's why I avoided speaking to you, why I was being so obnoxious that day at the marina, because I felt destabilised, out of my depth. I wanted to make love to you more than I had any woman. I enjoyed making love with you more than I have any woman – and when I did, I realised I was *in* love with you. Does that answer your question?'

'Um ...?' Sienna emitted a strangulated laugh.

'That's better.' Adam breathed, relieved, and made a mental note to try to find out where the little shit who'd dared lay a finger on her without invitation lived. 'Do you know what I'd like to do to you, right now? What I'd give to be there with you?'

'I'm all ears,' David Meadows said, behind him.

'*Jesus Christ!*' Adam almost died on the spot.

'No, just me,' the man assured him, catching up. 'Anyone interesting?' He nodded at Adam's phone.

'Sienna,' Adam supplied, with a roll of his eyes.

Meadows turned to squint mistrustfully at him.

Adam went back to the phone. 'Your dad says to say hello,' he said, and then held the phone in Meadows' direction.

'Don't break his legs,' Sienna shouted down the phone. 'He needs them for running on.'

Meadows' mouth tugged briefly up at one corner. 'He has a temporary reprieve, Sienna,' he called back. 'Very temporary,' he added, more quietly, as Adam pressed the phone back to his own ear.

'Talk later,' he assured Sienna, 'okay?'

'Sorry,' she said sheepishly. 'He insisted.'

'No problem,' Adam replied.

'Liar.' Sienna laughed. 'I love you, Adam Hamilton-Shaw, do you know that?'

Adam smiled. 'Ditto,' he said, then, glancing sideways at her dad, added, 'More than words could ever say.'

Meadows didn't comment once Adam had ended the call. He just set off at a jog, beckoning Adam to do the same. 'If you're going to talk dirty to my daughter,' he said, when Adam caught up, 'it's probably better to do it in private.'

'I, er … ' *thought I was in private*, Adam was going to say. 'Sorry,' he said instead.

Meadows nodded, and went quiet.

'You're going to have to run faster than this, if you're going to outrun me, Adam,' he said, after a pause.

'I'm not trying to outrun you,' Adam assured him, keeping his eyes fixed forwards and concentrating his efforts on driving through the balls of his feet.

'Glad to hear it,' Meadows said, matching his footfalls.

He hadn't warmed up, Adam reminded himself. Aching muscles and dodgy chest in mind, he should make sure to stick to his run/walk programme. This guy was a marathon runner, he also reminded himself, a determined man, who'd given him two weeks to prove himself. Adam decided to keep going.

'I'm pleased the visit with the child went well,' Meadows said, after another lengthy pause.

'Me too,' Adam said, not bothering to hide his smile.

Meadows nodded. 'Will you continue to see her?'

'I intend to, yes.' Adam guessed that information wouldn't hurt.

'Not knowing whether she is actually yours?'

'That's right.' Adam could feel the burn through his thigh muscles. He kept running.

'No paternity test?' Meadows glanced sideways at him.

'No point.' Adam kept his eyes front. 'She's family. I love her.'

'Will you try for custody?'

He didn't give up easily, did he? 'I don't intend to do anything that might be detrimental to Lily-Grace's welfare.' Adam maintained a steady pace. 'Certainly not without full discussion with Nicole and her husband. They were there for her when I wasn't. They've loved her, fed her, nurtured her.' He shrugged and kept running.

Meadows matched him, pace for pace. 'Commendable,' he said.

'You reckon?' Adam smiled wryly. Commendable would have been acknowledging her existence before now, he personally thought.

'Are you still in touch with your family?' Meadows asked, after a short silence.

Adam's stride faltered. 'No.' He tugged in a sharp breath and hoped the man wouldn't pursue it.

'Your parents didn't condone what your brother did, though?' Meadows ventured, obviously determined to pursue it. For Sienna's sake, Adam knew, and resisted telling him he'd rather not 'share' any more personal stuff.

'On the contrary.' He laughed scornfully. 'My *father* probably gave him a pat on the back and bought him a new car.'

Meadows glanced curiously at him.

'Chip off the old block,' Adam offered, hoping that piece of information might give the guy pause to ponder and leave it alone.

'Not like you, then?'

Fell into that, didn't he? Adam sighed, knowing there was no right answer. Telling Meadows his brother's only interest in women was notching them up on his bedpost made him exactly like him, he supposed.

'Your father's well off then, I take it?' The enquiry was casual, but Adam suspected Meadows was hoping he had at least one redeeming feature, for example a family fortune behind him.

'Yep.' Adam ran on. 'Owns half of Worcestershire; land, property,' he elaborated only as much as he needed to. 'And, just so you know, I'd rather starve than touch a penny of his money.'

Meadows fell silent then, but not for long. 'Your mother?' he asked, intent on opening up the whole ugly can of worms.

Adam understood why, but he dearly wished he wouldn't. 'She left, years before,' he imparted, reluctantly. His gut twisted every time he remembered her walking out of the door. Aged fifteen, he'd seen enough, understood enough to know why she was going. It didn't hurt any less, though.

Meadows nodded. 'Did you blame her?'

'Nope.' Adam dragged his forearm across his brow, feeling now very hot and clammy. 'The only thing I blamed her for was not taking me with her.'

'Do you see her?'

'Nope,' Adam said, tightly again. 'She didn't keep in touch. With her oldest son following in his father's footsteps, assuming I'd be the same, I suppose she'd had enough.'

'You blamed your dad for her leaving, though, I take it?'

Adam shrugged and focussed on his running. He really didn't think he needed to answer that one.

Right by his side, Meadows' step didn't falter. 'So you wouldn't blame Sienna, then, if she walked away from a serial womaniser?' He finally got to the point.

'No,' Adam said quietly. He wouldn't, if she had cause, but he didn't intend to give her that cause.

'Tell me, Adam,' Meadows went on, after another brief pause, 'do you feel your fiancée let you down in the same way your mother did?'

'What?' Adam shook his head, no idea now what the man was talking about.

'Well, you obviously felt you loved the girl if you were thinking about lifelong commitment.'

'I did,' Adam answered brusquely. Did the guy really need to go down this route? *Again.*

'Is it possible you poured all the love unrequited by your mother into her, only to realise it wasn't enough?'

Adam didn't answer that. Psychiatrist? The man was a fruitcake.

'I imagine you felt your mother had abandoned you. Your fiancée abandoning you, too, must have evoked old ghosts. Might that be part of the reason you reacted so badly, blaming yourself, as you probably did as a child, carrying the guilt? Why you haven't been able to move on?'

Adam drew in a breath. 'Maybe,' he conceded, at length. He felt almost as if he was betraying Emily. 'I never really thought about it that way.'

'Did you seek professional help, Adam? You've obviously been struggling for some time.'

'I did. It didn't.'

Meadows nodded slowly. 'It must have been extremely traumatising, finding her. Forgive my probing, but did she take tablets?' The question was asked sympathetically, but still Adam felt like screaming at him to stop. He couldn't say the words. Couldn't bear the images in his head. He'd slipped trying to lift her out. His clothes had been soaked, a thin, stark red stain, seeping slowly through his clothes right down to his skin. Dear God ... Adam squeezed his eyes closed ... why wouldn't the man let it drop?

'Adam?'

'No!' Adam's answer was short.

'You're angry,' Meadows observed.

Adam was tempted to a facetious comment, but refrained, just. 'Yes, I'm angry,' he managed, more moderately.

'With?' Meadows just wouldn't let up.

Adam focussed on the road ahead. 'Me,' he supplied, with a shrug. 'If I'd reached out sooner, arrived earlier ...' He stopped, assuming the man could fill in the gaps.

'When you sought this help, what conclusion did they come to?' Meadows changed tack. 'I assume they gave you a diagnosis?'

Adam sighed inside. He needed that information, he supposed, though he doubted it would do him any favours in the man's eyes. 'They told me I was suffering from depression related to post-traumatic stress disorder,' he gave him what he wanted. So, now it was out there. His whole ugly past. He was a depressive, an alcohol abuser, a womaniser, a loser. Someone Meadows was probably considering couldn't prove himself in two lifetimes, let alone two weeks.

They went on in merciful silence for a while, Adam hoping the guy had asked all he needed to. Apparently not. 'This good hiding you took,' Meadows started up again as they rounded a bend, 'do you think it taught you a lesson?'

Good hiding? Adam almost laughed. 'Did it make me see the error of my ways, you mean?' He blew a trickle of perspiration from his eyelashes. 'Honestly, no. I already knew the error of my ways, Mr Meadows. Falling in love with your daughter reminded me of that.'

Meadows fell silent again, thankfully. Adam used the time to try to moderate his breathing. He was definitely unfit and this guy was quite plainly fit. Crossing swords with him, Adam realised, would certainly be unwise.

'I heard about the pub incident,' Meadows continued,

annoyingly.

Which one? Adam cast him a worried look sideways.

'Wielding chains was pretty low.'

Adam's jaw tensed. 'Sienna should never have been involved,' he grated, angrily.

'No,' Meadows agreed, glancing leisurely at him. 'Right, inquisition over,' he said suddenly.

Thank God for that, Adam thought, relieved.

'Come on then, Adam, let's see if we can push ourselves, shall we?' Meadows notched up the pace. 'Make sure next time you can leave the bastards standing.'

You have to be kidding? Adam's eyes boggled as the guy took off ahead of him. *Dammit*, pushing him was about right. He'd be too stiff to walk, let alone run, in the morning. Determined to try to prove himself in any way he had to, particularly after what he'd just told him regarding his mental issues, Adam sighed and then sprinted after him. If the man was trying to commit the perfect murder, he thought, now feeling every step through his limbs, death by jogging was probably it.

Chapter Eighteen

Sienna just knew he'd do that, throw down some sort of a challenge. Fuming, she headed outside, as her dad jogged towards the cottage.

'Dad!' She stopped him short of the door. 'What are you doing?' She nodded towards where Adam had ground to a halt by his boat, panting and clutching his thighs.

'Just running.' Apparently oblivious, or couldn't-care-less, her dad shrugged nonchalantly.

'Just acting like a juvenile, you mean.' Sienna stepped huffily past him as Adam sank to his haunches, his hands draped between his knees and his chest now visibly heaving.

'Sienna?' Her dad turned around, obviously shocked by her tone.

'What are you trying to prove, Dad?' Sienna turned back, her cheeks flaming. 'That he's got stamina, staying power? Or are you just trying to kill him off, rather than scare him off?'

Her dad furrowed his brow, glancing past her to Adam. 'It's okay, Sienna,' he said, with a shake of his head. 'He's still breathing.'

Sienna glanced back, relieved to see Adam standing up. 'But that's the point, Dad, he might not have been,' she said, eyeing him despairingly.

'Sienna, I know you think you're in love with him,' her dad's voice took on a patient tone, 'but don't you think you might be a bit over-zealous, jumping to his—'

'He's just had pleurisy! They had to take him to the hospital! Those bloody, bloody animals very nearly did kill him!' Sienna seethed, furiously.

'Ah.' Her dad looked contrite.

'Pushing him physically makes you just as much a bully as they are, Dad,' Sienna pointed out, trying to moderate her tone to something less than absolutely livid.

Her dad now looked very contrite. 'He never said anything.'

'No, well he wouldn't, would he? He's a man, spelt s-t-u-b-b-o-r-n. I think you two have much more in common than either of you imagine.' So saying, Sienna gave her father a reproving glance and turned back towards Adam, to see him now at the water hose, liberally drenching himself in cold water.

'I think he's still functioning,' her dad commented, coming to stand by Sienna's side as Adam sloshed back towards his boat, dragging a hand through his sopping wet hair and waving wearily in Sienna's direction as he went.

Oh, no. Adam groaned, delving in his soaked track bottoms for his phone – his only means of communication with Sienna while the anti-Adam brigade was on vigil twenty-four seven. Finding it decidedly wet, again, he sighed and tried a text message. How R U?

Missing you. Sienna immediately texted back. Thought U wanted phone-sex?

Adam's mouth curved into a smile, despite his aching limbs. I do, but you'll have to be gentle with me.

Phoning U :) Sienna pinged back.

'How sore are you?' she asked, when Adam answered.

'Very,' he assured her, heading for the seating area, and then thinking better of soaking that, too, he slid down the wall of the boat onto the floor.

'Would you like me to come and give you a massage?' Sienna asked teasingly.

'Erm ...?' Adam laughed. 'What do you think?'

'Where would you like me to start?' Sienna asked,

alerting Adam to the fact that, even with debilitating muscle fatigue, a certain part of his anatomy was still keen to function where Sienna was concerned.

'With you taking all your clothes off,' he suggested. In agony or not, if her old man wasn't around, he'd go over there and do terrible things to her, right now.

'What, in broad daylight?' Sienna sounded alarmed.

Adam supressed a chuckle. 'I've already seen you in broad daylight,' he reminded her, 'every tempting, extremely beautiful, kissable inch of you. Are you okay?' he tacked on, quickly. 'After what you told me, I mean? That must have been hard for you to do.'

'Oh.' Sienna paused. 'Yes, yes, it was. I wasn't going to tell you. I didn't see any need but you kept pushing, so ...'

Bullying, Adam mentally corrected her. He'd forced her to confide stuff she didn't want to. Adam didn't like himself much for that. He was no great catch, but he hoped he would never be anything like his father, constantly bullying his mother, emotionally, physically, reducing her self-esteem to nil. If he ever turned out to be like that, then he would deserve to be shot. 'Did he hurt you, this ...' *bastard*, he thought '... bloke?' he asked gently.

Sienna paused before answering, which pretty much confirmed that he had. Anger bubbled up inside Adam like bile. 'He was ... rough,' she said, eventually. 'It was more groping and slobbering than anything, though. He didn't ... you know.'

Adam felt his gut clench. 'What did you do?' he asked tightly, fervently hoping she'd managed to knee the bastard where it hurt most.

'I managed to get the car door open and I ran.' Sienna's tone was light, but Adam heard the tremor in her voice, and prayed earnestly one day he would meet him. 'I'd only got one shoe on, though. One came off in the struggle. I must have looked like a complete pathetic mess. He didn't bother to come after me.'

No, Adam thought, disgusted, didn't sound like the sort who would, other than for the wrong reasons. 'Bastard,' he uttered out loud. 'You could never look a mess, Sienna. You're beautiful, inside and out, trust me.'

She gave a small, disbelieving laugh. 'What, not even half-drowned?'

'Never,' Adam assured her. 'When you walk by the flowers hang their heads in shame, I swear.'

'Ooh.' Sienna laughed again, delightedly, 'I do love it when you flatter me.'

'I love it when you do that,' Adam said softly.

'What?'

'Laugh.' He smiled to himself, loving how infectious her laugh was. It lifted his spirits, reminding him of the sunnier things in life. 'You should never be sad,' he told her, promising himself that he'd never do anything to make her be.

'I'm not,' she said. 'Not anymore.'

'Good.' He nodded, wishing he could go over there and physically reassure her how irresistibly, frustratingly sexy she was.

'What about ...' her tone now genuinely lighter, she paused to ponder '... covered in Bolognese sauce?'

'Okay.' Adam laughed, remembering their brief experimentation with food as an aphrodisiac. 'I concede, messy but most definitely mouth-watering. Still think I'd prefer ice cream, though.'

'Fudge,' Sienna said. 'My favourite flavour is fudge.'

'Now that *would* be messy.' Adam played along, his taste buds tingling at the prospect.

'Smeared on all over,' Sienna went on.

'And licked off very slowly.' Adam closed his eyes

imagining his lips on hers, his tongue trailing the long slender length of her throat, tracing the contours of her breasts, the soft curve of her stomach; the sharp jut of her hips. He swallowed. 'I want to taste you,' he said huskily. 'I want to come over there and —'

I don't bloody believe this. Adam stopped abruptly as he felt the boat shift to one side, and then almost passed out while sitting when he saw who it was. 'I think I left it in the kitchen,' he finished.

'Pardon?' Sienna said, puzzled.

'My watch.'

'Um?' Sienna was clearly clueless.

'Mr Meadows,' Adam said pointedly as the man himself peered suspiciously through his door, 'what can I do for you?'

'Ooh, flip!' Sienna gasped, and hurriedly rang off.

Adam might have laughed, visualising those two cute bright spots on her cheeks, but for the fact that her father might have overheard that last bit. In which case, smiling like an imbecile probably wasn't such a good idea. Looking Meadows over worriedly as he came down the steps, Adam levered himself up from the floor.

'It's on your wrist,' Meadows pointed out.

'Sorry?' Adam followed his gaze to the watch he was obviously wearing. 'Oh, right, yes. It's, er ...'

'Wet?' Meadows suggested.

'Yes.' Adam tugged in a breath and nodded, fancying he looked very much like an imbecile.

Meadows looked him archly up and down. 'You're wet pretty much all over,' he observed, coming to stand in front of him. 'Do you always take a shower with your clothes on?'

Adam allowed himself to breathe out. 'No.' He risked a smile. 'Only when I'm in danger of expiring from heat exhaustion.'

Meadows studied him again, his look now inscrutable, which was unnerving. 'You didn't mention anything,' he said, now eyeing Adam narrowly, which was definitely unnerving, 'about your recent illness.'

Adam looked at him quizzically, wondering where this was leading. 'No.' He shrugged. 'Given what caused it, would you have been very impressed if I had?'

Meadows considered. 'No,' he said, at length. 'You're right. I wouldn't,' he acquiesced, with a short smile.

Wondering if that was it, or whether Meadows was going to continue with the Spanish Inquisition, Adam waited, though he'd much rather not. Standing around in wet clothes, he was rapidly beginning to cool down.

'Should you be running?' Meadows asked.

Adam shrugged again. 'I'm not exactly fit, but it helps keep me focussed.'

Meadows nodded slowly. 'We'll go at a slower pace tomorrow,' he offered.

Very magnanimous of you, I'm sure. Adam sighed inside, realising the guy was probably going to shadow him for the length of his stay, which meant his chances of getting anywhere near Sienna were nil. In which case, he'd be cold showering on a regular basis. 'Right. See you then.' He mustered up a smile.

'It's David, by the way, the name,' Meadows said, throwing Adam completely and offering him his hand.

'Er, right.' Adam shook his head, and then reached out and shook the man's hand. 'Cheers,' he said, bemused. Did he detect a slight thaw in his attitude here?

'I'll catch you around, no doubt,' David said. 'Meanwhile, you'd better get out of those clothes.'

Adam glanced down at his attire, his brow furrowed in confusion. Was the guy actually looking out for him?

'Oh, and Adam,' David said as he turned to leave, 'if you're going to try to encourage my daughter out of hers, in private, please.'

Shoot! 'Right, yes, will do. Er ... *ahem.*'

Despairing of ever getting anything right in the man's eyes, Adam tugged off his vest. 'I'm glad someone's amused,' he said, tossing it at his definitely more cheerful floating guest. It didn't hit anything, of course, just dropped right through her to the floor. So how come he was still having the hallucinations even though he'd given up drinking, he wondered, as he headed for the shower?

He considered *taking up* drinking again when he returned. The vest wasn't there anymore, on the floor. It was on the seating area, neatly folded in two.

Adam stopped towelling his hair and dropped down next to it, disbelieving. If he hadn't folded that himself, and conceivably he had and forgotten, without doubt, that was Emily. Her constant nag was for him to stop leaving his clothes where he'd stepped out of them. What in *God's* name did she want? He swallowed, feeling for the first time since she'd appeared something akin to fear. Would she ever go away? Was it possible he really was going slowly out of his mind?

Arriving back at the marina the next morning, breathless but at least still able to stand, Adam detoured away from his jogging companion, as Nathaniel beckoned him over. 'Way to go, Casanova. Well done.' Nathaniel grinned as he neared him.

At which Adam cringed and glanced over his shoulder. David Meadows had ears like a bat and eyes like a hawk. Had he heard? Yep, inevitably. David glanced back in his direction and shook his head as he carried on towards the cottage.

'Cheers, Nate.' Adam sighed, running his forearm over his sweat-beaded brow. 'The guy's just got through suggesting that odd-jobbing isn't the best way to earn a gym membership fee.'

'Oops, sorry, mate.' Nathaniel looked sheepish. 'Force of habit.'

'One I'm trying to break, Nate,' Adam reminded him.

'Still giving you the third degree then, is he?'

'And some,' Adam replied despondently. 'He wonders if it's wise turning my back on my inheritance. I suppose he's wondering at my future prospects. Can't say I blame him, given my prospects are currently nil, along with my bank balance.'

Nathaniel nodded thoughtfully. 'So you are considering a future, then, with Sienna?'

Adam ran his hand over his neck. 'Yes,' he admitted, still somewhat surprised at his emotional U-turn. 'Yes, I am.' Given Emily's manifestations didn't sabotage everything that was. God only knew what Sienna would think if he confessed to seeing ghosts.

'And Sienna?' Nathaniel enquired, his eyebrows raised curiously. 'Is she considering a future with you?'

Good question. 'I don't know.' Adam sighed. 'I hope so.'

Nathaniel's eyebrows arched a fraction higher. 'You mean you haven't discussed it with her?'

Adam shrugged awkwardly. 'Not yet, no.'

'Right.' Nathaniel eyed the skies. 'Tell me if I'm being a bit dense here, Adam, but don't you think this might be a bit of a hindrance to your plans?'

Adam smiled dejectedly. 'Haven't had much chance, have I?' He glanced again in the direction of Meadows, who'd just disappeared through the front door of the cottage. 'I'm fully expecting him to mount a gun on the turret if I attempt to go anywhere near her.'

'Just a thought,' Nathaniel mused, his eyebrows now meeting in the middle, 'but did it occur to you he might *not* want you to keep away from his daughter?'

'Come again?' Adam laughed, bemused. The guy had shadowed him everywhere but the bathroom. It's a wonder he hadn't intercepted his texts. Blimey, he hoped he hadn't intercepted his texts.

'Well, I'm just guessing here, not being an expert on what women really want, like you,' Nathaniel paused, casting Adam a somewhat facetious glance, 'but don't you think he might be wondering whether you're actually going to court the girl? That Sienna might even be wondering whether you are?'

Adam frowned. 'You reckon?'

Nathaniel shook his head, a smile creeping across his face. 'You know, I've never seen you uncertain in a woman's company. Not once. You really have got it bad, haven't you?'

Adam glanced down, his mouth twitching into an embarrassed smile.

'Take her out, Adam.' Nathaniel placed a hand on his shoulder. 'One bunch of flowers does not a courtship make. Wine her, dine her. Impress her, and her old man into the bargain. And while you're at it, do something about your finances, yes?'

'What? Sell my body, you mean?' Adam couldn't resist.

'Ho, ho.' Nathaniel looked highly unimpressed. 'See that guy over there ...' He nodded towards one of the yachts. A beauty Adam had admired when it cruised in, a hundred grand's worth, at least. 'He asked me if I knew of a good mechanic I could recommend.'

'You mean ...' Adam eyed him, surprised, '... you would?'

'A few weeks ago, in all honesty, no, I wouldn't. Now

267

though …' Nathaniel looked him over and then gave him an approving nod. 'You obviously are trying, so, yep, I'm prepared to recommend you.'

'Excellent.' Adam brightened considerably. If he had some work, at least he might actually be able to afford to take Sienna out. 'Cheers, Nate. You're a diamond.'

'I know.' Nathaniel smirked as Adam turned towards his boat. 'If you let me down, though, Adam …'

Adam turned back. 'I know,' he said, his hands raised in acquiescence, 'mess up and I up anchor and move on.'

'Pronto,' Nathaniel assured him. 'Oh, and, Adam,' he called as Adam walked on, 'if you really want to impress her, wear something decent when you do take her out.'

Adam glanced down at his track bottoms, which had seen better days and which were about as suitable attire for a restaurant as his cut-offs. His jeans were reasonable, he supposed, teamed with his good T-shirt maybe? Blimey, he was debating his wardrobe. Adam smiled as he walked. Nathaniel was right. He had got it bad. For the first time in a long time, his dreams didn't haunt him, ceaselessly waking him in the dead of night. Even aware of Emily's presence, he went to sleep thinking about Sienna; he woke up and his first thoughts were of her. His only nightmare was envisioning life without her.

Would she want to be with him, though? If she did, how the hell would he ever find the courage to consider the marriage route again? Assuming she would want a future with him, could she understand that, where he'd once been reluctant to go the white wedding route, the prospect of marriage actually now terrified him? The whole choosing the ring thing, booking the church, planning the reception; the fear that fate, human frailty, whatever, would intervene and it would all go tragically wrong, Adam couldn't imagine how he'd cope with that again.

He had been going to go through with it. Despite his unwillingness to be beholden to his father – who naturally had thrown money at the wedding, attempting to pay his way out of everything as he usually did, the havoc he created in people's lives, the pain, physical and emotional – Adam had never intended to call it off. He couldn't have if he'd wanted to. Everything had been organised. They'd even hired the band. He'd rehearsed his speech, over and over. That had been one of his recurring nightmares, that he'd be reading it, having never yet managed to memorise it, and he'd look up to see the wedding breakfast turning to dust and decay, the whole thing covered in cobwebs, crumbling right before his eyes. It was like something straight out of a Charles Dickens novel. As much as Adam might want to, he wasn't sure he could get past it.

Despite the heat, which was heavier than ever, indicating thunderstorms brewing, Adam felt a distinct chill as he descended the steps into his cabin. It was back, the sadness. He could sense it.

Chapter Nineteen

'You mean you're not going to haul the engine out and charge me a fortune?' The owner of the yacht looked at Adam incredulously.

'I'd like to,' Adam answered honestly, 'but, nope. It's definitely a fuel contamination problem.'

'So what causes it?' the guy asked, peering confusedly into his engine well.

'Air in less-than-full fuel tanks contains moisture. It condenses over time, ergo, water in the fuel,' Adam explained, hauling himself out of the well. 'It can also seep in through poorly-sealed fuel caps and vents during boat fueling.'

'It's quite common then?'

'Very,' Adam assured him as he replaced the decking. 'Black smoke pouring out of the exhaust, lack of power, hesitation in acceleration, or outright stalling are all pretty good indicators.'

The guy – obviously new to boating – nodded. 'And you reckon replacing the filters is enough to cure her?'

'I've done a visual inspection of the tank,' Adam told him. 'It looks pretty clean, no corrosion or sediment, so I don't think you'll need to polish the fuel.'

The guy looked nonplussed. 'Polish it?'

Definitely new to boating, Adam decided. 'Hire a specialist fuel filtration company,' he translated. 'I'd bear water contamination in mind in future, though. Check your filters regularly, add a fuel stabiliser, make sure to top off your tanks with fuel when she's resting.'

'Bugger, I would have done if I'd known.' The guy sighed. 'I had no idea it could cause such problems.'

'Afraid so.' Adam grabbed his cloth to make sure he'd left the decking as clean as he'd found it. 'In diesel engines, a good ninety per cent of all problems are fuel-related. Water or debris in the fuel can lead to damaged fuel tanks, blown engines. Algae can flourish, which leads to corrosion of tanks, pumps, and injectors ... You definitely need to keep an eye on it.'

'I'll make sure to.' The guy looked relieved, and a little daunted. 'So, how much do I owe you?'

'With the filters, call it a hundred.' Adam gave him a fair price. 'I'd recommend you keep a couple of extra filters on board. You'll need to change them at least every two hundred hours. I'll get Nate to order some in, if you like?' Adam couldn't actually see the guy getting down there and changing them, but at least he'd have them when needed.

'A hundred?' The man seemed astounded.

'Well, I did give her a quick check over,' Adam reminded him uncertainly. 'I—'

'God, no, I'm not querying it,' the guy stopped him. 'I'm ecstatic. It's a darn sight cheaper than however many thousand for a new engine.'

Several thousand, Adam smiled, relieved. 'Excellent,' he said.

'Thank you, Adam.' The man offered his hand and gave Adam's a heartfelt shake. 'I'll shoot up to the cashpoint and drop the cash over to you later.'

'Cheers.' Adam nodded, and collected up his tools.

'Oh, Adam,' the guy called as he crossed the marina. 'Let me have your contact numbers, will you? I'll call you when my next service is due.'

'Will do.' Adam waved behind him, and then grinned at Nathaniel, who'd appeared eagerly from the chandlery.

'New client, Adam?' he shouted over to him.

For Sienna's dad's benefit, Adam guessed, who inevitably

had eyes on proceedings from his chair, strategically placed in front of the cottage.

Meadows hadn't been impressed with the single rose Adam had left in the milk bottle for Sienna this morning. Probably thought he'd nicked it. He hadn't. He'd run into town very early, not much caring about eyes swivelling in his direction, and bought it. With the last of his money, unfortunately, which is why there weren't twelve. Still, at least her old man had taken it in and given it to her. Sienna had texted him saying it was the most romantic gift she'd ever had. A rose in a milk bottle? Adam very much doubted it. He also doubted his having secured one customer would majorly impress her father either, but at least it was a start. Now to get cleaned up and go and ask him if he could escort his daughter out.

Adam mentally shook his head, feeling like a sixteen-year-old kid about to go out on a first date, and actually feeling as nervous as. Where was he going to take her, though? He still had no clue. A hundred pounds wouldn't cover the cost of theatre tickets and dinner, which was where he'd like to take her, because he most definitely wanted to impress Sienna. Having noticed the theatre guide pinned up in her kitchen, he'd figured putting a little thought into the evening might go some way to doing that.

Another time, he supposed, climbing onto his boat, stowing his tools and heading straight for the shower; when he'd secured another couple of jobs, though that wasn't going to be easy now his gardening services weren't so much in demand around town.

He was still pondering as he headed towards Sienna's cottage, freshly showered, shaved and wearing a clean white T-shirt that probably made him look like a soap-powder advert. Guessing Sienna wouldn't fancy a meal at the pub he was banned from anyway, it was either a pub further afield or a restaurant. Indian, he debated. Chinese? Italian, he decided, a smile curving his mouth as he recalled Sienna's penchant for pasta sauce.

Adam was Googling Rossini's when his phone rang. Noting the number he immediately answered. They'd arranged another meeting next week, including her husband this time. Adam's first thought therefore was that there might be a problem with Lily-Grace. 'Hi, Nicole. What's up?' he asked, with a degree of trepidation.

'Hi, Adam. How are you?'

'Er, good, yes. Why?'

'Don't sound so wary, Adam.' Nicole laughed. 'It's not a loaded question.'

'Right, no. Sorry. I'm fine,' he assured her. He'd had that many loaded questions fired at him lately his first instinct was to brace himself he supposed. He really did need to rid himself of the bad-things-are-bound-to-happen-attitude, though.

'I had a chat to Phil, that's all,' Nicole went on.

'And?' The trepidation was back.

'And, as it's my night off and my two kids are over at Phil's mums, we wondered whether you'd like to bring your girlfriend to dinner tonight? Nothing formal, just a nice casual get together. It will give you a chance to see Lily-Grace on home territory, too. What do you think?'

'Oh, great, yes,' Adam said, relieved and pleased. 'I'd love to. I'll have to check with Sienna, though. I was just about to ask her out. I mean, book a table; the Italian.' Adam took a breath, realising he was tying himself in knots.

Nicole chuckled. 'Ooh, you little romantic, you.'

'Trying to be.' Adam shrugged self-consciously. After so long telling himself he could live without romance, he was definitely out of practice.

'You like her, then?' Nicole probed, gently.

Adam smiled to himself. 'And some,' he admitted.

'Bring her round.' Nicole was adamant. 'Phil's cooking. It won't be haute cuisine, but it will be edible, just.'

'I'll text you,' Adam promised, pocketing his phone and nervously preparing himself to ask David Meadows if he could start courting his daughter.

It didn't bode well that Meadows didn't answer him from behind his newspaper. Adam coughed and waited, as Meadows rattled the newspaper and carried on reading.

'Would you like to run that by me again?' The man eventually peered over it, as Adam considered whether to dig a hole and drop down it.

'I was asking for permission,' he repeated, pulling in a nervous breath. 'I wondered if I could, er—'

'Permission?' Meadows barked, now giving his newspaper a demonstrable rattle. 'You're a bit late for that, aren't you?' He stared at Adam, a look of bemused incredulity on his face, which didn't make Adam feel any more comfortable.

He ran his hand over his neck, acutely embarrassed as he noticed the father of the two brats who'd thrown his lifebelts in the river looking on. 'Yes, probably,' he conceded.

'Probably?' Meadows repeated loudly, ensuring anyone within earshot was privy to the conversation. 'You really are clueless, aren't you?' He sighed and shook his head.

Clearly, he was. Adam shrugged, feeling definitely confused. The guy had banged on at him this morning, giving him a sermon about taking his responsibilities seriously that Nate would have been proud of, and now he was trying to, Meadows was talking in riddles.

Meadows narrowed his eyes, appraising Adam curiously. 'She hasn't said anything, has she?'

'About?' Adam cocked his head to one side. He really

was losing the plot here.

'Oh, for God's sake, man!' Meadows snapped. 'She's—'

'Plaiting her hair!' Lauren shouted, shooting through the front door, closely followed by, 'oops,' as the door hit her in the backside. 'Hi, Adam,' she greeted him with a sardonic smile. 'Come to try to redeem ourselves, have we?'

Adam smiled tolerantly back. 'Yes, Lauren, as it happens. I thought I'd try to redeem myself in Sienna's eyes, though, if that's all right with you?'

'Perfectly.' Lauren nodded, and folded her arms.

Adam dipped his head in turn and continued to wait, no choice but to with her bodyguard plus one in full anti-Adam mode.

'She shouldn't be long,' Lauren assured him.

'No problem.' Adam smiled again and glanced at Meadows, who was back to leisurely reading his paper.

'So, where are you taking her?' Lauren asked.

She'd obviously been eavesdropping then. No change there. 'I thought the Italian, Rossini's,' Adam supplied.

'Blimey.' Lauren raised a perfectly plucked eyebrow. 'As well as giving her a whole single red rose? What did you do, win the lottery?'

Adam's smile was now rather forced. 'No,' he sighed, wondering whether he should write them up a daily diary of his activities and supply them with all his details including his blood group. 'I got a job in this morning.'

Lauren swept derisory eyes over him. 'Oh, *yes*?'

'Fixing a boat engine,' Adam clarified, glancing again at Meadows, who returned his glance briefly. A congratulatory glint therein, did Adam detect? Possibly. He obviously wasn't top of the guy's list of favourite people, but it was possible he might have slipped off the top of his hit-list.

'OhmiGod!' Lauren said suddenly, her eyes pinging wide. 'She'll need un-plaiting and re-dressing.'

Do what? 'Sorry?' Adam furrowed his brow.

'If she's going for posh nosh, she'll need some wardrobe advice. Serious wardrobe advice, unless you want her flashing the waiters in her shorts. And shoes, she'll need heels.' Lauren nodded determinedly and twirled around.

'Whoa,' Adam said, behind her, 'We're not going tonight. Something else came up and I—'

'Gosh, there's a surprise,' Lauren drawled facetiously, turning back.

'I got a call and I ...' Adam started, and then stopped, a genuine smile tugging at his mouth. 'I wondered if you'd do me the honour of escorting me to Nicole's as my partner for dinner?'

'Excuse me?' Lauren looked at him as if he'd gone quite barking mad.

'Not you, me,' Sienna said behind her, giving Lauren a less than subtle nudge sideways as she emerged from the front door.

Adam's smile broadened as he looked her over. *You'd be hard-pushed to improve on that, Lauren*, he thought, his stomach doing a somersault inside him. Wearing pink plimsolls, a short, white flared skirt with a loose strappy top over, she looked fabulous. Her pretty cheeks were flushed. Her green eyes were sparkling deep emerald. Her hair, obviously 'un-plaited', tumbled gloriously over her shoulders. Her breasts ... He twanged his eyes back up. She looked totally ... Sienna: natural, achingly desirable, edible. What would he do, her old man, Adam wondered, if he took her in his arms right now and kissed her senseless?

'Hi,' he said, stepping towards her, his eyes on hers, drinking her in. She really was a breath of fresh air, the look in her eyes so warm Adam felt as if he could bask in the glow of it forever. 'You look radiant,' he said, at which point her dad dissolved into a hearty coughing fit.

'Hey, Shaw!'

'*Grreat!*' Adam ground to a halt halfway across the marina.

'What does *he* want?' Sienna glanced past him, to where the horrible father of the equally horrible teenagers was standing on his boat deck, looking across to them.

'I have no idea, but if he intends to cause trouble ...' Adam tightened his grip on her hand, and turned to face the man, steering her behind him as he did.

Instinctively protecting her, Sienna knew, and loved him for it. Little did Adam know, though, it would be that excuse of a man who would need protection if he did intend to cause trouble. One smart remark, that was all; one derogatory comment aimed at Adam and she would be seriously tempted to go over there and lob *him* into the water.

'Nice job you did on Richard's yacht,' the man said, to Sienna's astonishment. 'It's running as smooth as a whistle.'

'Oh.' Adam ran his hand through his hair, clearly confounded by the compliment. 'Right, thanks.' He nodded and turned back to Sienna.

'Wonders, never ...' he said, waggling his eyebrows and reclaiming her hand.

'Don't fancy giving me a service sometime, do you?' the man shouted.

'Erm?' Adam glanced at Sienna. 'Not a lot, no,' he whispered. 'Can do,' he stopped to address the man again. 'When were you thinking?'

'Tomorrow? She's leaking oil into the sump. Sooner the better.'

'Ten o'clock suit?'

'Perfect. I'll make sure the tea's on.' The man smiled and gave him a cheery wave.

'See you then.' Adam smiled back. 'Blimey,' he said to

Sienna as they walked on. 'Do you reckon it'll be safe to drink?'

Sienna beamed from ear to ear. 'I reckon you've gone up in the popularity stakes,' she said proudly. She knew he could do it, if only he wanted to enough. Oh, she did love him, absolutely. She could just eat him.

'Yeah, not sure I've gone up in your father's estimation, though,' Adam said glumly.

Sienna squeezed his hand. 'It might take a bit of time,' she said. *Under the circumstances*, she didn't add, 'but he'll come round. You'll see.'

Adam parked the car, hopped out, and then scooted around to open the door for Sienna. 'What?' he asked her, doing his best to look wounded as she laughed. 'I'm trying to be romantic here, Sienna, a gentleman. You're not supposed to dissolve into a fit of the giggles.'

'I'm not. I'm impressed,' Sienna assured him, rearranging her face to demure and extending her hand in a ladylike fashion.

'Clearly.' Adam gave her a mock-scowl, assisted her out and pulled her towards him. 'I think madam might need teaching a lesson in manners,' he growled.

'Ooh, yes please.' Sienna waggled her eyebrows and planted a fat kiss on his cheek. Assertive with Adam she could quite easily do.

'Later,' he promised her, a devilish gleam in his eye as he leaned around her to close the car door and then lovingly took her hand in his.

Much later, Sienna thought gloomily as they headed towards Nicole's and Phil's house, given her dad didn't score him nil points in regard to his attempts to prove himself that was. He was doing pretty well in her book, staying sober, securing jobs, impressing those who were determined not to be. He'd even managed to win Nate over. Her dad must see how hard he was trying.

'Are you sure you don't mind?' Adam asked, sounding nervous as they approached the front door.

'No, you can hold onto my hand forever, if you like,' Sienna joked, attempting to allay his apprehension.

Adam tightened his hold. 'I intend to,' he said softly, turning to give her such a warm smile, Sienna's heart just melted. And then constricted a little at the thought of the news she still had to tell him. Would her unplanned pregnancy give him pause for thought regarding his forever plans?

'About coming here with me tonight, I mean.' Adam stopped walking and turned to face her. 'It's just, to be honest, Nicole's the closest thing to family I have since …' he faltered, his eyes closing briefly, reminding Sienna how painful his past still was for him to talk about. 'I wanted to grab the opportunity to spend more time with Lily-Grace. I'm going to see her regularly and I hoped … Well, it's early days yet, I know, but if we're together, given you'd want to be, then …'

He stopped again, searching her face, his soulful brown eyes so full of uncertainty, Sienna felt her tummy flip over. 'Lily-Grace would be part of your life, I know,' she finished, seeing he was struggling. 'I'd be more concerned if she wasn't, Adam.'

Adam breathed a visible sigh of relief. 'So you're okay with it, then?'

'She's gorgeous,' Sienna assured him. 'She looks just like you. How could anyone not adore her and want to spend time with her?'

'She does, doesn't she?' Adam's mouth curved into a delicious self-conscious smile. Sienna could almost see his chest swelling with pride. 'A little, around the eyes?'

'A lot,' Sienna corrected him.

Adam's smile widened. 'But you are absolutely sure? I wouldn't want you to feel obligated in any —'

Sienna pressed a finger to his lips, and then followed it with a soft kiss. 'I love you, Adam Hamilton-Shaw,' she reassured him, sensing that that was what he needed. 'I want what you want. That little girl won't be hard to love.'

Adam blew out another sigh, glanced heavenward, and then reciprocated her kiss, hungrily, fervently, right there on the garden path, right outside the front door.

The open front door, Sienna realised mortified, as their lips finally, reluctantly parted. Standing at the door, Emily's sister, Nicole, quickly dropped her gaze. She looked back up after a second, a bright smile fixed in place, but her expression, just briefly, had been haunted, reflective; heart-wrenchingly sad. Sienna understood, completely. She knew all about loss. Kissing Adam on her doorstep, she was treading in the wake of the woman's sister. What ghosts must she have evoked?

Smiling timidly back, Sienna took hold of the hand Adam offered again and walked with him to the door. 'I'm sorry,' she said immediately, letting go of Adam's hand to take hold of Nicole's, 'about your sister. The pain lessens but it doesn't go away, does it?'

Nicole scanned her eyes, her own questioning, curious. 'No,' she said, after a second, 'no it doesn't.' Her smile now warm and genuine, she gave Sienna's hand a quick squeeze and Sienna sensed her approval. She was pleased, for Adam's sake.

Nicole's gaze travelled from Sienna to Adam. 'I'm glad you could make it, Adam,' she said, moving to give him a tight hug. 'And I'm really glad you're okay. I worried about you, you know, incessantly.'

Adam hesitated and then wrapped his arms around her.

'Getting there,' he said emotionally. 'With the help of two beautiful women,' he added, giving Sienna a mischievous wink as he pulled away.

Sienna glanced pseudo-despairingly at Nicole. Nicole shook her head. 'Flatterer,' they both said together.

'It's one of my better qualities,' Adam quipped, as was his wont. There was sadness there still, though, Sienna could see, in his eyes.

'Come on in.' Nicole stepped back to allow them access. 'Lily's been desperate to see you,' she said, closing the door and then leading the way up the hall.

'She has?' Adam looked dubious.

'You've obviously made an impression. She's even named her best beloved soft toy after you,' Nicole assured him, showing them to the lounge.

'This is Phil,' she introduced her husband, who was holding Lily-Grace in his arms. 'Phil, you know Adam. This is his girlfriend, Sienna. Make yourself at home, guys. I'm just going to check the oven. Won't be a tick.'

'Phil.' Adam nodded and smiled uncertainly at him.

Phil smiled in return, his smile warm and welcoming, Sienna noted. They were obviously good people, a strong unit. Little Lily-Grace's start in life might have been tragic, but there was no doubt she was a contented, happy child.

'Hey, Lily. How's my favourite girl, hey?' Adam smiled at her, a smile that definitely reached his eyes. Sienna swallowed, her own eyes filling up and her heart all but bursting.

'Want Adum,' Lily said excitedly, unhooking little sausage arms from around Phil's neck and immediately outstretching them towards Adam.

Adam eyed Phil questioningly.

'Oh, the fickle female heart.' Phil sighed melodramatically. 'Here, take her. She's a lump. Grown two inches every time

281

I see her, I swear. Drinks, guys?' he asked, his lump safely deposited in Adam's arms.

'Just a soft one, thanks, Phil,' Adam said, his gaze on Lily-Grace, taking in every little detail, counting every eyelash, it seemed to Sienna.

'Oh?' Phil glanced surprised at Sienna, and then gave her a wink, meaning Adam had scored another little point, Sienna guessed, offering Phil a warm smile in return. 'Right you are. Sienna, what's your poison?'

'Same for me,' she said, her own much smaller lump in mind.

Phil looked her over approvingly. 'You're obviously a good influence,' he commented as he headed for the kitchen.

'I try,' Adam said, behind him. 'She's very wilful though, Phil. Isn't she, Lily, hey?'

'I am not,' Sienna retorted, indignantly.

'Yes, you are,' Adam said, a soft twinkle in his eye as he glanced back at her. 'And I think I'll be eternally glad that you are.'

Sienna felt herself blush, particularly as Nicole, coming back from the kitchen, had caught the exchange. 'Looks like love is in the air.' She smiled indulgently at Sienna. 'Do you want to take her upstairs, Adam?'

'Er?' Adam looked momentarily flummoxed.

'Lily.' Nicole laughed, coming over to plant a kiss on Lily's overripe cheek. 'It's her bedtime. I wondered whether you wanted to read her a story?'

'Oh, right. I'd love to.' Adam turned back to Lily, who'd been as good as gold in his arms, studying him as intently as he had her. 'Would you like that, Lily?'

Lily studied him a second longer, then, 'Yeth,' she articulated around the thumb she had wedged in her mouth.

'So, what story shall we read, hey, Lily?' Adam asked her as he headed to the hall.

'Phil usually makes it up as he goes along, which bores her to sleep in two seconds flat,' Nicole called after him.

'I heard that,' Phil boomed from the kitchen, followed by, 'ouch!' as a pan clanged worryingly loudly.

'He's better at cooking,' Nicole assured Sienna, beckoning her over to sit with her at the dining table. 'She likes *Animals Around the World*, Adam,' she shouted. 'It's on her dresser. Hers is the second room on the left.'

'Got it,' Adam called. '*Animals Around the World* it is. What animals are they, hey, Lily? Tigers? Lions?' The two women heard him chatting on to her as he went.

'Adum,' Lily answered.

'Oh, right. Okay.' Adam sounded a little puzzled.

'Adum!' Lily sounded a little stressed. 'Want Adum!'

A second later, Adam reappeared, a now tearful toddler in arms. 'Want Adum,' Lily insisted, her bottom lip wobbly, jiggling body language indicating imminent tantrum.

'Erm?' Adam looked helplessly to Nicole.

'Ooh, cripes.' Nicole shot off her chair to toss cushions arbitrarily from the sofa, revealing a soft toy buried beneath them. 'Adum,' she announced, handing the toy to an immediately placated Lily.

'Ah.' Adam looked the Peppa Pig over as Lily squished it lovingly close. 'I can see the likeness.' He nodded and about-faced.

Sienna was struggling with the, 'So, how did you two get together?' question when Adam came back down.

'She propositioned me,' Adam supplied blithely, sailing across the lounge.

'I did *not*.' Sienna shot him a look and blushed down to her décolleté.

Adam walked around behind her. 'It was a hard proposition to turn down,' he said, brushing her hair aside and planting a soft kiss on the nape of her neck.

'I can see why,' Phil observed, from where he sat next to Sienna.

'*Ahem.*' Nicole cast him a withering glance as she placed the garlic bread on the table.

'Not that she could hold a candle to you, of course, light of my life,' Phil added quickly, giving Sienna a wink and reaching to steal a chunk of bread.

Nicole slapped his hand away. 'You'll be in the spare room if you don't reel your eyes in,' she warned him; cheerfully though, Sienna noticed. She was nice. They both were. Despite the link to Emily, the sad memories they would all undoubtedly share of her, she was glad Adam had found them again. They truly did seem to be like his family.

'We haven't got a spare room, sweetness,' Phil pointed out, stealing the bread anyway.

'There's always the dog kennel,' Nicole assured him.

Phil sighed heavily. 'She's a hard woman,' he said, reaching for the ladle and removing the lid on the dish.

'It's just spag bog,' Nicole said. 'Hope that's okay with you two?'

'Perfect.' Adam caught Sienna's eyes across the table, a slow smile curving his mouth and a mischievous glint in his own. 'Love Bolognese, don't we, Sienna?'

Nicole obviously noted the look, glancing between them as Sienna blushed furiously again. 'Sienna's just been expounding your virtues,' she said, smiling indulgently and passing plates.

'She did say she'd struggled to find any, mind,' Phil chipped in.

Adam smiled good-naturedly. 'Yeah, she would a bit.'

'She's been telling us how you gallantly saved her dog from drowning,' Nicole went on.

Adam glanced at her, amusement now dancing in his

eyes. 'Not sure about the "gallant" bit. I think she might have been being kind.'

'Must be love.' Phil emitted a wistful sigh as he offered the bread around. 'So,' he turned to Adam, 'do I hear wedding bells on the horizon?'

At which, Adam immediately glanced down. 'Erm ... I, er ...' His eyes flicked back to Sienna. 'Not sure,' he said, now toying with the food he'd just swallowed several hearty mouthfuls of.

Uncertain what to say or where to look, particularly when Nicole shot her husband a now furious glance, Sienna fixed her eyes on her plate.

'Damn. Sorry, Adam,' Phil apologised over the ensuing awkward silence. 'I didn't think.'

'It's okay.' With an obvious struggle, Adam regained some of his composure. He glanced at Sienna, as she looked cautiously back at him. His expression was apologetic. Extremely apologetic, she noted, a wave of icy trepidation washing over her.

Chapter Twenty

'I think I might just need to pop to the loo,' Sienna said as they were about to leave.

'Must be all those soft drinks.' Phil smiled and stood aside to allow her access to the stairs.

'I'll go and start the car,' Adam said, shaking Phil's hand and giving Nicole a hug as Sienna nipped on up.

She had to tell him, she decided. Tonight. She couldn't leave it any longer. He'd notice something anyway soon. The meal had been lovely, but she'd felt terribly nauseous after what was clearly a thundering faux pas on Phil's part. She did have to tell him. Given the speedy change of topic after what must have been the most awkward moment ever, she also had to ask him, what on earth had it been all about?

Emergency bathroom call attended to, Sienna was halfway down the stairs when she heard Nicole from the kitchen. 'He's obviously in love with her,' she commented.

Uh, oh. They were undoubtedly talking about her. Feeling like a rabbit caught in the headlights, Sienna debated whether to go up or down, then, curiosity getting the better of her, plumped to stay where she was.

'Definitely,' Phil agreed. 'Couldn't take his eyes off her. Young love, hey?' He sighed nostalgically.

'*Ahem,*' Nicole coughed, presumably to alert her husband to the fact that she wasn't much older than Adam.

'Reminds me of how I feel about you, my sweet.'

Sienna smiled as Phil neatly rescued himself, and risked another step down, then stopped again as Nicole said, 'Do you think he will ever think about getting married again?'

'Not sure,' Phil replied. 'I can't imagine it being top of his list of favourite things to do after what happened.'

'No.' Nicole sighed thoughtfully. 'Nathaniel said he's had a string of relationships,' she went on, over the clink of dishes. 'Not very savoury relationships, apparently.'

'Running scared,' Phil observed, astutely. 'I can't say I blame him. To be honest, I'd be surprised if he found commitment of any sort easy. I know I would.'

Nicole emitted another troubled sigh. 'I do hope he doesn't mess that girl about. She seems lovely, doesn't she? Really pretty, too.'

'Very,' Phil agreed enthusiastically. 'Lovely, that is,' he added, followed by, 'Ouch.'

Sienna took the opportunity to thump noisily on down, catching the pair in a mock tea towel and rubber glove duel as she poked her head around the kitchen door. 'Thanks both,' she called. 'Better dash. Adam has a boat to look at in the morning. Byee.' She forced a cheery smile and skidded on out.

Sienna glanced sideways at Adam as they drove. He really was handsome, his strong profile and high cheekbones making him classically beautiful. He was kind, thoughtful, not the brash bullying person she'd thought him to be, but his dark eyes were clouded with such confusion sometimes, such uncertainty. He had ghosts to deal with, Sienna knew that. But after his reaction to Phil's comment around marriage ... Would he ever be free of them enough to trust a woman again, she wondered, to trust her completely and give all of himself?

'Nicole's lovely, isn't she? They both are,' she commented, making conversation in the absence, yet again, of any from Adam.

'They are,' he agreed. 'I should have kept in touch, but ...'

'You found it difficult?' Sienna finished, aware that he must have had reasons why.

Adam sighed. 'Very,' he admitted, 'particularly as they have such a strong relationship.'

Sienna hesitated. 'Because it reminded you of what you should have had?' she ventured.

Adam nodded tightly and signalled left, unfortunately instead of right and got hooted from behind for his efforts.

Sienna waited until he'd made the turn safely and then pushed on, hoping he'd open up and talk to her about his relationship issues. 'It must have been hard for you tonight, seeing them with Lily?'

Adam pulled in a long breath. 'It was,' he said, glancing quickly at her. 'Sienna, about earlier … *Damn!*' Swerving abruptly, Adam cursed quietly again, and then waved his apologies to the driver he'd inadvertently cut up at the roundabout.

Sienna waited until they were back safe on the road, and then cautiously urged him on. 'You were saying?'

'I, er … Nothing. It wasn't important.' Adam turned to give her a reassuring smile. But it wasn't reassuring. It wasn't reassuring at all. It didn't reach his eyes. There was something else there.

Smiling tremulously back Sienna averted her gaze. He'd been about to mention what Phil had said, she was sure. But he couldn't even talk about it. Did that mean he truly couldn't contemplate long-term commitment?

'Sorry about that. Anyone would think I had been drinking,' Adam joked, referring to the roundabout incident, and neatly deflecting the conversation away from anything emotive.

'It's fine,' Sienna assured him, and allowed him to drive on in silent contemplation, which Adam seemed to prefer while he was mulling things over. As he had the first time she'd ridden in his car. The first time she'd been with him, when, despite his reluctance, he'd made such passionate, all-consuming sweet love to her. It had felt so right, so as if it was meant to be. Somehow, Sienna wasn't sure how, they'd made a baby together. She'd felt, naively probably, that that might have been meant to be too … until now. Swallowing hard, Sienna turned her gaze to the passenger window.

What did *he* want, she wondered? When he'd said he intended to hold on to her hand, talked about them being together, had he meant he needed a hand to hold for the now? Might Adam have wanted to present himself as a couple tonight, the thought occurred. Prove he was in a steady relationship to secure access to his daughter? Sienna wouldn't have minded that. If he'd asked her, she would have done anything within her power to ensure he had future contact with his daughter. Had he considered his future with *her*, though, his whole future?

Fear gripped coldly at Sienna's insides. Why would he have? They'd been together such a short time. It was *her* making big commitment plans. How would Adam have been considering them, if he simply couldn't? And now, he no doubt knew she'd gleaned that he couldn't. Announcing she was pregnant, it *would* look like she was trying to trap him, expecting more of him than he was capable of giving, the pain of his loss still being so obviously raw. She did have to tell him. He had a right to know. But, before she did, *she* had to know, did she really figure in his forever plans?

'Lily's beautiful, isn't she?' she said, after a while, attempting to steer the topic to the one she wanted to discuss.

'She's perfect,' he agreed wholeheartedly. 'Amazing. Did you see the way she smiled at me?' he went on enthusiastically. 'I can't believe she actually remembered my name.'

'You love her, don't you?' Sienna asked gently, though her heart seemed to be folding inside her.

'Irrevocably.' He smiled, a genuine smile, which lit up his whole face. 'God only knows why I've wasted so much time.'

'You'll see much more of her now, though,' Sienna reminded him. They were nearing the marina. She had to say something. Now. She just had to. She couldn't spend another night on her own in the dark, worrying, wondering, tossing and turning.

'I hope so,' Adam said, his voice catching with emotion. 'Thanks for tonight, Sienna. I really appreciate it.' He reached for her hand, squeezing it, but only briefly.

'My pleasure,' Sienna said, swallowing back a stab of pain. He was being distant, impersonal almost. He hadn't said anything deliberately hurtful. It was more what he wasn't saying. Debating, she took a breath, and took the bull by the horns. 'Do you want more children, do you think?' she asked, making sure to keep her tone casual.

'God, yes,' he said, signalling to turn into the marina. 'Eventually.' He glanced at her as he pulled into the car park.

Eventually. The word hit Sienna like a slap in the face. She closed her eyes as an almost overpowering wave of nausea swept over her.

Adam killed the engine. 'Do you?' he asked, turning to look properly at her, at last.

His look was quizzical, that same uncertainty there she'd seen so many times before. 'Loads,' Sienna said. It came out more stridently than she'd intended.

'Me, too.' Adam smiled, but still there was hesitation in his eyes. 'Enjoyable though it might be making them, though,' he reached again for her hand, grazing his thumb contemplatively over the back of it, 'I think I might need to spend some time getting to know Lily-Grace before I go that route.'

His kiss was sweet, like stolen candy, his lips soft on hers, his tongue gently exploring her mouth. Sienna thought her heart might explode, so full was it of overwhelming sadness. She kissed him back, her tongue seeking his, a long, soul-crushing goodbye.

Adam felt the sadness weigh down on him like a lead weight as he entered his boat. 'Idiot!' He thumped his forehead with the heel of his hand. What the hell was wrong with him? *What?* She'd opened the door a mile wide. All he'd had to do was ask her, but how? How do you say, *I love you with my whole heart and soul. I want to be with you for the rest of my life, but I don't want to do the wedding bit, so will you come and live with me on my* … 'damn, fucking, stupid boat!'

Sighing heavily, cursing liberally, Adam sank to the seating area. It was time he faced facts. He ran his hands through his hair, wishing he had a beer in the fridge, glad that he hadn't. The fact was, Sienna's father was right. He had absolutely nothing to offer her. So what did he do? Get in touch with his father, gloss over the past as if it didn't matter, thereby ensuring access to family funds? His old man might have been tight with his affections but he was never tight with his money where his sons were concerned. Adam thought about it, felt bile rise in his throat thinking about it. Would it really kill him to swallow his pride? He needn't take money from him, but he could ask him if he could move into one of his rental properties. He couldn't contemplate going back to work with his brother in the boat building business, but he'd have a base to look for work from, a place to call home, a decent place to bring Sienna, which might gain her father's approval. He'd have his inheritance eventually, security for Sienna and the children he absolutely did want to have with her, given she wanted him; for Lily-Grace. The old bastard wasn't going to live forever, particularly downing the amount of booze he did on a daily basis.

Adam weighed it up. Yes, right. He'd go and shake hands with his father, in so doing condoning the way the man had treated his mother, the way he and his brother treated people in general. As if they didn't matter. It did matter. Emily *had* mattered. Lily-Grace mattered. Sienna mattered.

Not happening, he decided, immediately feeling the almost oppressive sadness lift as he did. He'd rather starve to death than go anywhere near them. He'd just have to work harder and smarter, starting with the boat in the morning. He wouldn't overcharge, that really was a sure-fire way to a bad reputation. He'd just make sure to do a good job. He'd get referrals, eventually. Had already, hadn't he, proving to him that reputation was actually all.

Yep, that's what he'd do. Adam got to his feet to make coffee. He'd turn things around. He might have to do it the hard way, but it was the only way, if he was going to live with himself. As for Sienna, it was about time he opened his mouth and told her how he felt. If she loved him – and Adam was sure she did, it was right there in her beautiful eyes – she'd understand. He'd talk to her, tomorrow. He'd do the job, get cleaned up, take her out to lunch and just talk to her. And if she had got her heart set on the whole white wedding thing ... Adam tugged in a breath and then blew it out hard ... he'd just have to man up and find a way to get through it; all this assuming Sienna did want a future with him, of course. Adam dearly hoped so. Now she'd come into his life, he wouldn't know how to be without her.

Adam hated to break the news, but ... 'I can't be certain

until I can get a better look, but I suspect it might be the crankcase seals,' he said, noting the steady drip of oil from under the engine.

'Damn, thought it might be.' The guy sighed. 'I suppose that means the engine has to come out?'

Adam nodded. 'Afraid so,' he said, relieved that the guy obviously knew one end of his boat from the other, ergo wouldn't think he was trying to fleece him. 'They're right at the bottom.' He indicated thus. 'The only way to access them is to lift the engine out and dismantle it.'

'Which I suppose means I have to haul the whole boat out of the water and get it transported to the boatbuilders, which will cost me an arm and a leg.' Shaking his head, the guy puffed out another exasperated sigh.

'You could limp her there,' Adam suggested, climbing up from the well. 'She'll probably get you there as long as you don't push her.'

'Upstream?' The guy didn't look overly thrilled at that prospect. Given the rain the last few days, Adam guessed why. The river would be on high amber alert pretty soon, which would be bound to put a strain on the engine. Brats his sons might be, but Adam doubted he'd want to drown them.

'I could do it in situ,' he suggested. 'Given I get Nate's agreement.'

The guy looked at him, surprised. 'Really?'

'I'd have to get a pulley and jig in but, yes, I don't see why not.'

'How much?' The guy eyed him suspiciously.

'The whole job?' Adam paused, really hating to break this news. 'Well, obviously, I'll give you a fair quote, but if you do decide to get her transported, it could run into thousands.'

The guy's shoulders drooped. He sighed again, long and

hard.

'You need to get the head gasket checked first, though.'
Having decided honesty was his best policy, Adam made
sure the man had all the information he needed, should he
decide to go elsewhere. 'Could be that that's the problem.
The top part of the engine would still need dismantling to
get to it, but it wouldn't need lifting out. In which case,
you'd be looking at hundreds.'

The guy nodded slowly, looking slightly less daunted at
that news. 'Is it worth it?' he asked, the age of the boat
obviously in mind.

Adam debated. 'It's not an unusual problem for an older
boat, but it's very unlikely to reoccur with this type of
engine, once it's fixed. Given the market value of the boat,
I'd say, yes, definitely.'

The guy thought about it, glanced at Adam, seeming to
weigh him up, and then, 'Do it,' he said.

It was Adam's turn to look surprised now.

Obviously noting the look, the man's mouth twitched
into a smile. 'You needn't have offered the information
about the head gasket,' he said. 'I appreciate it.'

Adam nodded, outwardly professional, underneath so
ecstatic he could cheerfully have kissed the guy. Bearing
in mind the bloke's tattoos and macho attitude, though,
he doubted it would have gone down very well. 'I'll have
a word with Nate,' he said, preparing to lay the decking
back, lest the brats drop down the engine hole and break a
leg.

'Cheers, Adam.' The guy moved to lend him a hand. 'I
thought you'd tell me I'd need a new engine, at least.'

Adam smiled wryly. 'What, with my good reputation to
consider?'

Showered and freshly shaved, Adam booked a table

at Rossini's. It would mean taking his car, but he wasn't drinking, so that wasn't a problem. He wasn't either, hadn't touched a single drop in … He'd stopped counting, he realised. That had to be progress. Smiling to himself, he tried to comb his hair into something near tidy. Apart from the passing urge he'd had last night, he hadn't had that much inclination to drink, he realised. What's more, he hadn't really missed it, which meant he didn't have to add alcoholic to his long list of faults. He felt better; a lot better, managing to climb straight out of bed this morning, rather than the ritual half hour trying to summon up the energy to heave himself out. Looked better, too. Bound to, he supposed, minus the bloodshot eyes and shaky shaving endeavours.

The exercise helped, kept him focussed. Adam gave up on his hair and reached into his wardrobe for a clean shirt, relieved to notice as he did that the one he'd discarded on the seating area hadn't miraculously folded itself up.

Sienna, what he felt for her, that definitely helped keep him focussed. He'd never imagined it possible, never dared hope he might feel whole again, like a part of him wasn't missing. And now, after years floundering around, satiating sexual urges, but never, ever acknowledging he might have emotional needs, he was in love; hopelessly, unequivocally in love.

He *was* scared. Terrified, when he stopped to think about it, realising he was opening himself up to the kind of pain a person surely couldn't survive twice. He had no idea how he'd cope losing someone he loved all over again. He didn't intend to lose her, though. Whatever it took, whatever he had to do to make it work, he'd do it, because for the first time in too long a time, Adam felt he did have a life worth living, and he wanted to live that life with Sienna.

Yet, he hadn't told her.

True to form, he'd behaved like a complete idiot last night, doing what he'd always done, employing avoidance techniques. He should have pulled the car over, looked her in the eyes, and told her he loved her, with every fibre of his being; admitted he was frightened, that any uncertainty he might have was only about failing her because of those fears. Instead of which, he'd whammed up the shutters again.

He shook his head despairingly. Time they came down. Without complete honesty there would be no relationship anyway, he knew it. It was time to lay his soul bare and pray Sienna wouldn't give up on him. Adam gave himself a quick check in the mirror, and then, sensing approval from the person he hoped *was* only in his head, he dragged a hand nervously over his neck and headed for Sienna's cottage.

Adam stepped away from the front door, taken aback when Lauren yanked it open and greeted him with a curt, 'What?'

'Good afternoon.' Adam dipped his head and tried a smile. That worked. Her look was still cool enough to freeze over an ocean.

'It's not,' Lauren replied shortly.

'Right.' Adam nodded. Clearly someone had got out of bed the wrong side this morning. 'Must be only me who's noticed it's not raining then.'

Lauren folded her arms, obviously not impressed, by him or the cloudless blue skies.

Fine. Adam glanced past her in hopes of salvation. 'Erm, would you like me to go and come back again?' he asked, perplexed by her attitude. He'd gathered he was never going to be flavour of the month where Lauren was concerned, but hadn't she addressed him at least halfway civilly when they'd last had the pleasure?

'*Go*, yes,' Lauren retorted, her expression still ninety

degrees below zero.

'Nice to see me but not that nice, hey, Lauren?' Adam shook his head.

Lauren sighed and rolled her eyes.

He'd obviously rubbed her up the wrong way, again, but Adam was blowed if he knew how. Whatever, it didn't look like she was about to invite him in, so ... 'Can I see Sienna, please?' he asked, now feeling like a six-year-old kid come to call for his friend.

'Not from here, no,' Lauren observed drolly.

Adam forced a smile. 'It's just that I've booked a table at Rossini's and—'

'She's not here.' Lauren cut him short.

'Oh, right.' He hadn't seen Sienna out walking Tobias, come to think of it, or Meadows with eyes on him from a distance. 'Not here as in where?' he asked, assuming they'd taken a father and daughter trip somewhere.

'Not here as in gone,' Lauren imparted, her expression unflinching.

Adam's heart missed a beat. 'Gone?' he repeated, incredulous. 'Gone where?'

'Gone home, Adam,' Lauren clarified, her gaze still locked stonily on his, 'with her dad.'

Home? 'But ...' Adam swallowed back his rapidly escalating panic '... why?'

Lauren rolled her eyes again, infuriatingly. 'As if you didn't know,' she muttered. 'You really are a complete—'

'Lauren, for God's sake!' Adam shouted, fear knotting his stomach. '*Why?*'

Her arms still folded, her expression guarded, Lauren searched his face and her antagonism seemed to waiver.

'Lauren, please ...' Adam begged, '... tell me.'

Lauren glanced down and then back to him, the look in her eye now somewhere near compassion. 'I'm sorry,

Adam,' she finally relented a little. 'I can't say. I promised I wouldn't. She said she'd write to you.'

Write to him? Adam's heart dropped like a stone. *Another Dear John letter?* 'You're joking,' he managed, past the tight lump in his throat.

Lauren's gaze flitted down again. 'I wish I was.'

Adam ran a hand shakily through his hair. She'd gone? Without saying a word? No, she wouldn't … Couldn't have! Why would she? Why wouldn't she have …? Adam's confused thoughts screeched to an abrupt halt. He knew why. Knew exactly why, because he'd been too concerned with his own feelings, too wrapped up in himself; too bloody selfish to consider hers. All he'd needed to do last night was explain, open his mouth and spit the words out. Sienna would have understood. Wouldn't she? 'I need her address,' he said, his mind racing, his head reeling. He had to see her. He had to talk to her. Now.

Lauren shook her head adamantly. 'I can't say, Adam. I'm sorry.'

Adam stared at her, disbelieving. 'There's not a lot you can say suddenly, is there, Lauren?' he asked, a hard kernel of anger growing inside him. 'Pretty damn amazing when you couldn't resist sticking your oar in at every other opportunity!'

'Shouting at me won't help your cause much, Adam!' Lauren eyeballed him, equally angrily, and then pulled up her shoulders, clearly determined not to go behind Sienna's back and share anything she didn't want her to.

Because that's what friends do, Adam reminded himself, guilt at raising his voice vying with heart-crushing despair. She wasn't going to tell him. Who was *he*, after all, other than someone who'd apparently taken advantage of her friend? Hurt her. Made her cry more often than he'd made her laugh. Adam closed his eyes. 'Where's Nate?' he asked, his very soul sinking.

'I don't know. I'm not his keeper either,' Lauren replied caustically, obviously upset, with every right to be.

'Right.' Adam dropped his gaze. 'Thanks.' He swallowed, pulled in a breath and turned away.

'You should have talked to her, Adam!' Lauren shouted behind him. 'About her, about what Sienna might want, instead of concentrating all of your efforts on what *you* wanted!'

'I know,' Adam said quietly, feeling the ground shift underneath him as he walked unsteadily to the chandlery. Nathaniel would have the address. Adam tried to focus, to stay focussed, to not drop down on his knees right there and just … stop fighting.

Chapter Twenty-One

The chandlery was closed. Adam had guessed it would be. He recalled Nathaniel saying something about an appointment. Adam couldn't think where. Couldn't think straight. Fumbling his phone from his pocket, he turned towards the car park. Stay calm, he cautioned himself, trying to still his trembling hands as he searched for Nathaniel's number. There had to be some explanation. Had to be a way ...

Should he phone her? Blinking hard, he scrolled down his phonebook. But what if she didn't answer? His thumb hovered over Sienna's details. What then? What the hell would he do then?

Selecting Nathaniel's number instead, Adam dragged an arm across his eyes and waited for him to answer. *Please, please, pick up, Nate.* He prayed harder than he ever had. He was falling, free-falling. He didn't want go there, to sink back into the pit of despair. Yet, it was beckoning him, like a soft, suffocating, dark blanket.

Stop! Kneading his temple with the heel of his hand, Adam willed himself not to give in, not to do what he was best at and give up, again. He tried to remain rational, though his thoughts were colliding, his heart close to exploding. Nathaniel would have her address. He'd rented her the cottage. He *had* to have the address.

'Nate, I need to speak to you,' Adam choked the words out when Nathaniel finally did answer.

'Adam?' was Nathaniel's curious reply. 'What's up?'

'I need to speak to you, Nate.' Adam could hear the desperation in his own voice; feel everything he'd thought he'd had slipping through his fingers. He couldn't do it.

Couldn't do this again. He needed to know. If there was any chance at all, he *had* to know.

Nathaniel's tone was wary. 'You're not in trouble, are you?'

'No,' Adam assured him quickly. Yes, he wanted to say, deep trouble – and this time I'm not sure I can hold on.

'I can't right now, Adam,' Nathaniel answered cautiously. 'I'm having lunch with a customer. I can see you straight after. Can it wait?'

Adam gulped in a breath, forcing himself not to do what he wanted to do, sit down where he stood and sob like a baby, or drink until he couldn't think anymore. 'I really need to speak to you, Nate. I'll come and meet you.'

'Not a wise idea, Adam,' Nathaniel cautioned him. 'I'm in The Fish and Anchor, and the customer is James.'

Sherry's husband, Adam's heart sank.

'Sherry's with him, Adam. I wouldn't, if I were you.'

Adam nodded, feeling the ground drop away another inch. Nathaniel was right. He couldn't barge in there and pull him out of his meeting. Nathaniel needed the sale. His showing up would probably blow it for him. Quite possibly cause further trouble for Sherry, too. 'I'll wait outside,' he said, knowing he needed to be in touching distance of someone he knew. The only other place he'd go if he didn't go there would be to another pub. He didn't want to do that. Didn't want to let go.

They weren't flashbacks, more like slow motion stills, this time. His mess of a life playing out in staccato before him; his father's sneers, his mother's quiet sobs, his baby's bewildered cries. Swaddled in a duvet that must have seemed like a desolate wilderness, she'd been so tiny, so vulnerable. Emily lying still and cold, the lifeblood seeping from her body, the bathwater, deep, dark, impenetrable red, her life over, finished. She'd been desperate, lonely, alone, all because his damaged pride had steadfastly refused to allow him to contact her.

Yet she was here, beside him. She'd always be here, right inside him, driving him quietly insane. Didn't he deserve it? Whatever had happened between them, for the sake of the child, a whole new, innocent human being, he could have tried. Couldn't he? To be there. To be a friend when she'd needed one, if nothing else? Instead, he'd walked away to lick his own wounds. God alone knew how she'd ended up in his brother's bed. Scratch that. Adam knew. Darren had always fancied her, fancied himself, chatted her up; flattered her. Adam, weak specimen that he was, unable to stand up to his brother or his old man and say 'enough', he'd made her cry. Darren would have moved in, switched on the charm; mopped up her tears.

How many times had they … Adam closed his eyes, his stomach clenching, as he recalled walking past his brother's bedroom door, hearing sounds from within that drew him like a magnet: Emily, unmistakably Emily, with Darren.

He could never have forgiven his brother, but he should have tried to forgive Emily, not turned his back on her. Finding out she was pregnant, in all probability with his child, still he'd refused to have anything to do with her, with anyone. Darren had taken his chance, taken advantage of her, Adam knew it. Emily had played her part. Maybe she'd wanted to hurt him in the most painful way possible, and she had, but how much had *he* hurt her? Ultimately, he'd destroyed her. His love had destroyed her. He didn't deserve forgiveness, a future, the love of someone good and wholesome, like Sienna. Adam would never forgive himself.

'*Jesus*. Just stop!' Trying to vanquish the memories, Adam dragged his hands over his face, wrapped his arms tight about his chest and waited. Watching the clock, willing

Nathaniel to appear from inside, he continued to wait, knowing where he'd end up if he didn't stay put: drowning his sorrows. Sorrowful bastard, he needed to fight. For once in his life, he needed *not* to run away.

He needed Emily to leave him alone, to stop feeling her feelings, hear her softly calling his name. *You're not here!* Adam sucked in a breath, clamped his eyes shut and silently begged. *Get out of my head. Get out of my life. Please. I loved you, Emily, with all of my heart, but I have to let you go. You have to let me go.*

Hearing someone emerge noisily from the pub, Adam pulled himself up in his seat and squinted through his windscreen. Not Nathaniel, one of the Neanderthal louts from the lane. He'd recognise them anywhere. So what was he doing, moving across the car park as if he was being chased by the Devil himself? And why – Adam looked harder and then reached for his door – did his shirt appear to be covered in *blood*?

Foreboding creeping through him, Adam was out of the car, sprinting towards him. 'Whoa,' he called, causing the guy to falter. Glancing panic-struck over his shoulder, the guy pushed on, stumbling as he ran, and Adam was on him. Clutching the scruff of his neck and not much caring if there were fifty other thugs to back him up, Adam dragged him bodily backwards. 'What happened?' he growled.

'Rob,' the guy spluttered. 'He's gone mental.'

Adam twisted the guy's collar tighter. '*What* happened?' he repeated, more than ready to choke the information out of him if he didn't talk.

'Some bloke, he mouthed off,' the guy rasped. 'Rob ... He's got a knife ...'

Nate! Adam stopped listening. Dropping the guy, who fell heavily to his knees, he turned and ran flat out towards the pub. It could have been the rustle of leaves. Yet, there was no wind. The swish of car tyres on the road? It wasn't. Adam heard it clearly this time as he ran. '*Soon, Adam,*' Emily whispered a promise. '*Soon.*'

The only person who noticed him as he came silently through the back entrance of the pub was the landlord. He was on the wrong side of the bar, his look this time one of wary confusion as he made eye contact with Adam.

Adam quickly shook his head hard and cast his gaze down, hoping the man would get the message and look away. He did, thank God. Nodding almost imperceptibly, the landlord turned his gaze back to the gang-leader, the chain-wielder. But now it wasn't a chain he was wielding. Hardly daring to breathe, his adrenaline pumping, his heart pounding a steady drumbeat in his chest, Adam looked from the knife the guy was brandishing to the body on the floor. A male, he could see from the feet visible at the end of the bar, but who? The bar obscuring the rest of his view, Adam had no hope of knowing without making himself known.

'He needs a doctor.' Nathaniel's voice, from the side of the room. Relief flooding through him, Adam almost reeled where he stood.

'No doctor!' the knifeman yelled, his voice frantic, hysterical almost. 'I said, don't move!' Adam took a step back out of sight, as the guy whirled around, jabbing the knife in Nathaniel's direction.

'Mobiles!' the guy shouted, dragging his free hand across his mouth. 'I told you to throw them on the floor. Do it!'

Dammit, the police? Why the hell hadn't he called them? Adam reached carefully into his pocket. Pulling out his own phone, he checked it was on mute, then quickly keyed in 999. Easing down slowly, desperate not to attract attention, he rested the phone on the floor, hoping they'd realise something was seriously wrong and stay on the line.

Standing, he risked a step back towards the bar. Then another step closer, but it still didn't afford him much of a view.

'You!' The guy gestured in Nathaniel's direction again, pointing the knife, the blade of which Adam could now see was coated in blood. 'You're coming with me.'

'She's going nowhere.' The landlord stepped towards him from the opposite side.

Sherry? Adam prayed it was her, which hopefully meant she wasn't hurt. There'd only been four cars in the car park, including his. He'd recognised Nathaniel's and James' four-wheel drive. The other presumably belonged to the landlord.

'Says who?' the guy snarled, dragging his hand once again over his mouth, seriously scared, Adam imagined, if he'd just used that knife in full view of everyone – and probably very close to losing control.

'Me,' Nathaniel said. 'You want someone, you take me.'

Oh, no … Adam closed his eyes, knowing that that's exactly what his friend would do. Always there for anyone who might need him, always respectful of women, Nathaniel would probably allow him to take her only over his dead body.

'You must be joking, mate. Do you seriously think you can stop me?' the guy sneered, reinforcing his authority with his weapon. 'Well, *do* you?'

Spitting at the mouth, the man moved forwards, towards Nathaniel, towards Sherry.

Uh-uh, no way. Adam moved faster. Pressing one hand on the top of the bar, he was up, on top of it, and over it in two seconds flat, landing firmly and determinedly behind the assailant. 'Don't,' he said simply, as the guy twirled round to face him.

'*You?*' The guy gawked, disbelieving.

'Yep,' Adam assured him. 'And trust me, you go anywhere near those two, and I *will* stop you.'

'Get out of my way.' Breathing hard, the guy dragged a hand over his mouth again.

Not a nervous twitch, Adam learned. James had obviously landed one good punch to the bastard's jaw, before he'd gone down. 'No can do, sorry,' Adam said, his tone light, his intent, he hoped the guy realised as he fixed his gaze hard on his, deadly serious.

The guy looked away first, his eyes flitting this way and that, specifically towards the door. And then he did what Adam had fervently been hoping he wouldn't. Bringing the knife higher, he took a step back, closing in on his victims. Adam shadowed him. The guy took another step, catching hold of Sherry's wrist with his free hand.

Sherry whimpered. 'Adam,' she implored, trying to wriggle out of the man's grasp. Adam's gaze flicked to hers. Her face was tear-stained, her eyes wide, she was petrified.

Adam brought his gaze back to the bastard who'd caused her to be. A bully, no backbone, hiding like the coward he was behind his knife. Fury burned in Adam's chest, stuck in his craw.

'Adam, don't!' Nathaniel warned as he advanced.

Adam wasn't hearing him. He was focussed now, totally focussed. He locked eyes with the piece of human flotsam before him, intent on bringing the man down.

'Adam!' Nathaniel shouted as the man lunged, loosening his hold on Sherry as he did.

But Adam was quicker, marginally, back-stepping as the blade swished a hair's breadth from his chest.

His own breathing heavy, Adam studied the man, guessing he had seconds before his fetid mind remembered his only real chance was a larger shield than his knife. He needed a body. He needed someone he could manhandle. He needed Sherry. *Not happening*. Adam didn't waste any more time debating. Bracing himself, he took a purposeful step forwards ... and then stopped, his disbelieving eyes travelling upwards.

There in the air, suspended right above the guy's head, was Emily. Astonished, Adam tried to look away, but he couldn't take his eyes off her; her aura was mesmerising, so dazzlingly bright it was almost blinding.

Watching him, the guy's malevolence faltered, and then he gave a humourless laugh. 'Nice try,' he spat, looking Adam over contemptuously. 'Did you really think I'd fall for that?'

Astounded, confounded, Adam continued to watch as she hovered, drifting silently downwards, bypassing the man and floating towards him. He felt her, not cold, not terrifying, comforting somehow; she reached out her hand, brushed his cheek lightly, and then moved to stand right beside him.

Seeking confirmation, Adam looked around. All eyes intently on the knife-wielder, it seemed no one was aware of her presence but him. Shaken, he looked back to the guy, and his heart almost stopped as the door he'd come in by slammed.

Instinctively, the guy spun around, pointing his knife in that direction.

Adam didn't hesitate. Stepping in behind him to his side, he grabbed the knife wrist with his right hand, dead legging the man from behind with a knee as he did, and bringing the knife arm swiftly and violently back across his own body, forcing the elbow to break sickeningly across his chest. Simultaneously, he brought his left arm up and under the man's chin, forcing the man backwards over his leg.

The guy landed heavily, twisting on to his side. Adam

wasted no time there either, dropping down fast after him, his bodyweight pinning him down, and forced his knee hard into the squirming man's shoulder.

Better, Adam thought, wiping a hand across his own mouth and then grabbing a fistful of the guy's hair. 'Not nice, is it, you piece of scum,' he seethed, 'getting a taste of your own medicine?'

The man reasonably subdued, Adam turned his attention to the landlord, who was looking on stupefied. 'Towels!' he yelled, nodding towards James, who was still bleeding out onto the floor. 'Press them to the wound!'

'I'll call the emergency services.' Nathaniel bent to retrieve his discarded mobile as Sherry, shocked though she was, flew to her husband's assistance.

'Don't bother.' Adam smiled wryly, indicating the police presence swarming into the bar area. 'The cavalry's arrived.'

Chapter Twenty-Two

'Move over Bruce Lee.' Joining him at the bar, once police procedure was complete, Nathaniel gave Adam a congratulatory slap on the back. 'Where the hell did you learn to do that?'

'Darren, my hero and my nemesis.' Adam shrugged, reminding Nathaniel of his not-so-friendly martial arts spars with his brother. 'He was quite fond of breaking my arm.'

Nathaniel nodded, furrowing his brow. 'Not great hero material really, was he?' He smiled sadly in Adam's direction as he parked himself on a bar stool.

'Nope.' Adam shrugged again, preferring not to think about him.

'Well, whatever, you were pretty impressive, mate. I have no idea how you avoided serious injury. You've obviously got someone on your side.'

'Yeah.' Adam smiled ruefully. 'Unfortunately, not the person I'd like to have.' Even as he said it, Adam was mentally apologising to Emily. He had no doubt that without her timely intervention, he would have been in A&E nursing stitches, or worse. He wasn't about to claim to have his very own guardian angel looking out for him to Nate, though, who would naturally assume he'd been hitting the hard stuff.

'You never cease to amaze me, you know, Adam,' Nathaniel looked him over approvingly, 'taking him on like that. I'm not sure I would have had the bottle. Well done, mate.'

Adam just shrugged again. Despite the coppers looking at him with respect, rather than like something that crawled out from under a stone, Sherry thanking him and apologising for her husband kicking the crap out of him, he didn't feel like much of a hero. Where the women he loved were concerned, he was obviously a complete let-down.

'Me either,' the landlord commented, with a touch less hostility than he usually did. He was still cleaning his glass, Adam noted. Probably the same glass: his 'reserved-to-eyeball-him-menacingly-over' glass.

Adam went back to studying his hands on the bar in front of him, debating what to do next. Text Sienna? Nathaniel had offered to ring her and report back to him. He'd even offered to go and see her, data protection preventing him giving out her address. Adam really couldn't blame him for that. He had no doubt David Meadows would go for Nathaniel if her useless boyfriend turned up where he wasn't wanted, which might hurt Nate's business. He never was her boyfriend, though, was he, in Meadows' eyes? Probably not in Sienna's eyes either.

God, he could use a drink. Adam ran a hand over his neck and then snatched his gaze up sharp, half-expecting to see a certain someone hovering, as a brandy glass slid towards him.

'I owe you one,' the landlord said, his expression a mixture of puzzlement and appreciation. 'I suspect James will probably want to buy you one, too.'

'Oh, right.' Adam looked from the extremely large brandy to the landlord, surprised. 'Cheers,' he said, picking up the glass and swirling the contents around. He could almost feel it sliding down his throat, hitting the spot, numbing the pain, at least for a while. And therein was the problem. How many would he drink then? Enough to render him incapable of being anything but what everyone expected him to be, including Nicole and Phil? He'd seen the look when he'd opted for a soft drink: disbelief. And what about Sienna? Would she seriously have contemplated a future with someone who would buckle every time there was an emotional crisis? Someone so needy, he couldn't function without her? She obviously had contemplated it. She wasn't here, was she?

Still at his side, Nathaniel coughed, loudly. 'You going to drink that?' he asked, his wary tone back.

Adam tugged in a breath. 'No,' he said, planting the glass firmly back down and getting to his feet. 'I have Lily-Grace to consider, don't I? Thanks.' He offered the landlord a smile. 'I appreciate the gesture, but I'm on the wagon.'

Please God, let me stay on it, he thought, heading for the door. Alone on his boat without the woman he loved all over again and no bottle to keep him company, that was going to be a hard place to be.

Adam felt something brush his arm, soft, like a passing bird's wings. Reluctant to open his eyes, elusive sleep having claimed him despite it being only early evening; vaguely aware he was still on the seating area, he ignored it, preferring to hold onto his dreams. The dreams were sketchy, foggy, mostly of Sienna, her smile content, her mesmerising green eyes filled with a mother's love as she cradled a baby. Lily-Grace? Adam couldn't see clearly. And then he sensed danger. He couldn't see where or what the threat was, but it was there somewhere swirling around her.

Adam called her name, but no sound came from his mouth. He could hear his heartbeat, loud and fast; feel her heartbeat, a steady thrum next to his own. He wanted to go to her, fold her into his arms, keep her safe, but, try as he might, the distance grew wider, the fog grew denser, and he couldn't quite reach her.

'Sienna!' he called her again, heard himself call this time, the name drawn out and slurred, but he hadn't been drinking, and yet the fog in his mind kept getting thicker and thicker. 'Sienna!' he shouted, swatting away the bird that flapped at his face, pulling away from the feather-light fingers that touched him, tugged him, urged him … *Adam, wake up!*

'*Jesus!*' Jolted to consciousness, Adam sat bolt upright, sweat pooling at the base of his neck and tickling its way down his torso. She was here. Her aura was strong, all around him, he could smell her perfume. 'Emily?' He blinked against the semi-dark and then he felt it, saw it clearly, etched into her features, ice-cold fear.

Stumbling to his feet, Adam reached for his phone. No messages. He hadn't expected any. He hadn't rung her. Why hadn't he damn well *rung* her? Selecting Sienna's number, he let it ring, only to reach her voicemail. What the hell good was that?

'Sienna,' he said, 'it's Adam. I need you to call me. I …' What? What did he say that didn't make his concern seem only for himself? 'Sienna, whatever's happened, whatever you've decided, please call me. I just need to know you're safe, that's all.' He left it there, not knowing what else to say. She might think he was mad. He might well be mad, but this feeling in his gut, in his soul, it was too strong to ignore.

Stopping only to scramble into his trainers, he crashed out of the boat, leaping the handrail, tripping as he did. '*Fuck*,' he uttered, dragging himself up from the sodden grass and racing on.

The river was high, heaving, swollen. Adam caught the name whispered on the wind above the rush of the water, *Sienna*, she said over. It was soft, melodic; urgent. Trying to still his panic, quiet his heartbeat, now a rat-a-tat-tat in his chest, Adam hammered on the chandlery door. 'Nate! Nathaniel!' He hammered again, pushing his weight against it. He needed him to answer. He needed that address. Now!

'Sienna, she's in trouble,' he said breathlessly as Nathaniel yanked the door open.

'What?' Nathaniel whirled around as Adam pushed past him. 'What do you mean, in trouble? In trouble how?'

'I don't know.' Adam banged into his office, careering around Nathaniel's desk, pulling out drawers, attempting to find the information himself. 'Nate, I need her address.'

'I can't give it to you, Adam. I've told you. How do you know she's in trouble? Have you spoken to her?'

Adam pulled in a breath, breathed out hard, and banged a drawer shut. 'No.'

'So how do you know?' Nathaniel watched his frustrated progress through filing cabinets. 'Have you been drinking?' he asked inevitably.

'No!' Adam opened another drawer and ferreted uselessly through it.

'Right.' Nathaniel sounded unconvinced. 'So, enlighten me,' he said as Adam searched fruitlessly through paperwork on top of the cabinet. 'How do you know she's in trouble, if you haven't spoken to her?'

'I don't bloody well know how I know!' Adam turned to face him. 'I just do! Nate, please ...' Adam's shoulders sank. Something had happened. Or was going to happen, he could feel it. How was he supposed to explain that? 'I don't know how, Nate, I just do. She's in trouble. I have to go to her. Please help me.'

Nathaniel narrowed his eyes, studying Adam for a long, hard minute, then, 'Come on,' he said, turning for his chair to grab his jacket. 'The address is in my phone.'

'What time is it?' Adam asked again as they drove.

'Two minutes past the last time you asked, Adam.' Nathaniel glanced worriedly sideways at him. 'It's nine-forty seven p.m., precisely.' He nodded at the clock on the dash. 'I can't see Meadows being very thrilled to find you hammering on his front door at this time of night.'

'I can't either,' Adam conceded. He'd no doubt tell him to get out of Sienna's life and stay out, and Adam would, if that's what Sienna wanted, but only after he'd established she was all right. If she was, well he'd definitely look like an idiot, but he'd rather that than ignore the gut-wrenching certainty that she wasn't.

Dammit. Why hadn't she returned his call, if only to tell him she'd thought about it and considered him a tosser? At least then he'd know she wasn't incapable of returning the call. With that idea knotting his stomach, Adam selected Sienna's number and tried her again, sighing heavily as her voicemail picked up.

'So, are you going to tell me what this is all about?' Nathaniel asked, as Adam keyed in a text. Please let me know you're OK. One word.

'I wish I knew,' Adam said, growing more anxious by the second. 'Can't you go any faster?'

'Not if you want to get there in one piece, no. It's raining, Adam. The roads are wet.' Nathaniel glanced sideways at him, for about the tenth time. 'So, you haven't had any contact with Sienna, her dad, or Lauren, you say?'

'No.' Adam shook his head, adamant, and willed the car on.

Nathaniel glanced at him again. 'You're just acting on intuition then?'

'Something like that.'

'Right.' Nathaniel nodded. Adam heard the audible sigh that went with it. 'And this intuition hit you when exactly?' he asked, the insinuation implicit, how many drinks had he had *exactly* that had him rambling like a madman?

Nathaniel probably thought the booze had addled his

brain. Maybe it had. Adam couldn't get his head around any of this himself. The psychiatrists would have a ball, including David Meadows. He couldn't deny it any longer, though. Emily was here for a reason. Something terrible was going to happen. He knew it. He prayed to God it hadn't already.

Adam ran a hand over his neck and tried not to think about worst-case scenarios. 'I have dreams,' he said, no idea how else to explain.

Nathaniel twizzled his neck to look at him. 'What? Premonitions, you mean?'

'Not exactly, no. More feelings. Watch the road, Nate.'

Nathaniel turned his attention back to the windscreen. 'So,' he said, over another loud sigh, 'I'm driving around in the pouring rain at ten o'clock at night because the man's finally discovered he has feelings.'

'Strong feelings,' Adam tried, aware of Nathaniel's distinctly unimpressed vibes.

Nathaniel shook his head. 'I have no idea what's going on here, Adam, but if this turns out to be you manufacturing a way to see Sienna when, for whatever reason, she doesn't want to see you, this will be the absolute last favour you get from me.'

'It isn't,' Adam assured him, his apprehension increasing as the satnav announced they'd reached their destination.

'What the hell do *you* want?' David Meadows greeted him not-over-enthusiastically after Adam had almost banged the front door down.

'Sienna,' Adam said shortly, no inclination for explanation. 'Is she here?'

'You really are the limit, aren't you?' David Meadows folded his arms over his broad chest and regarded Adam with a mixture of incredulity and ill-repressed anger.

'Mr Meadows, I—'

'You sleep with my daughter, string her along, for kicks, presumably, as good as tell her there's no future in it, and then you come looking to ... *What*, Adam? Try your luck again, is that it? Sweet-talk her into bed because you've run out of other women whose lives you can ruin?'

'No!' Adam refuted angrily, breathed in, and tried to temper his tone. An argument on the doorstep would get him nowhere, and he needed to be wherever Sienna was. The sense of urgency he felt now was practically choking him. 'I didn't tell her there was no future, I just ...' He struggled for an explanation.

'She's pregnant, you bloody idiot!' David Meadows boomed. 'How scared do you think that makes my daughter?'

'*What?*' Adam's heart jolted violently in his chest.

'Pregnant, Adam. With child. *Your* child!' Meadows spelt it out as Adam shook his head and then stared at the man, utterly stupefied.

'I'm working on the assumption you didn't know before you announced you'd rather wait before having children. Frankly, if I'd suspected you had known, *Mr Shaw*, you'd have been nursing far more than broken ribs. Now, I imagine even someone as completely self-obsessed as you are will be able to glean you've caused enough trouble. I think you should leave, don't you?'

A baby? Adam tried to get his head around it. She was having ... No, not possible. Unless ... *Sherry?* His mind flicked back to the pregnancy test. Had she interfered with ... Meant him to father a ... 'Wait!' he said as Meadows made to close the door. 'Are you sure? I mean, is she sure?'

Meadows yanked the door back open, now looking very close to hospitalising him. 'Be careful, Adam. If you value your life, be very careful indeed.'

'No, not about me,' Adam said quickly. 'My being the … I mean, is she sure she's …? *Jesus*.' Winded, Adam swallowed back his confused emotions. Overriding his bewilderment, his absolute bafflement as to why she didn't tell him was a deep-seated terror. Sienna was in danger. Every second spent talking here, was a second wasted. 'I need to see her,' he said, eyeing Meadows levelly.

'She's not here.' Meadows re-folded his arms.

'Mr Meadows,' Adam dragged a hand over his neck, frustrated, 'I *have* to see her.'

Meadows looked him over, unmoved. 'Why?' he said flatly.

'Because …' Adam searched frantically for a way to make the man see the urgency of why.

'I want to know what your intentions are, Mr Shaw, before I—'

'*Oh, for fu—* I don't have time for any more psychoanalysis crap!' Adam grated impatiently. 'I need to see her! Now!'

Meadows pulled in a breath, his flared nostrils a good indicator of how close he was to carrying out his threats. 'She's out,' he said tightly, and stepped back into the hall.

Adam took a step forward, blocking him from closing the door. 'Where?' he asked, mustering up as much civility as he could and making sure to hold the man's gaze. 'I just need to talk to her, Mr Meadows,' he went on, hearing in his head the ominous tick of a clock as he did. Emily desperately urging him to '*Hurry*'. If he was insane, one thing Adam knew for certain was that he'd rather be mad, than that anything had happened to Sienna.

David Meadows regarded him through narrowed eyes. 'At her former boyfriend's house, I believe.'

'Her former …' *Oh God, no*. Adam felt a distinct shift in

the ground this time.

'He's rung her incessantly,' Meadows went on making his point, and clearly clueless, 'which I suppose at least means he's interested in her welfare.'

'Her *ex*? Interested in her welfare?' Adam raked a hand furiously through his hair. '*Dammit*, David, he tried to ...' Adam hesitated, realising the shock factor of what he was about to say might hit this man harder than any news he'd had himself today.

David paled, visibly. 'Tried to what, Adam?' he asked, his expression telling Adam he was getting the gist anyway.

'It's not her welfare he's interested in, David, trust me.' Adam made sure he did get the gist. 'I have to go to her,' he reiterated. 'I have to go *now*.'

David stared at him for a brief second, and then nodded decisively, plucked up his keys from the hall cupboard and strode through the door. 'I'll show you the way,' he said, slamming the door behind him and heading for Nathaniel's car.

Chapter Twenty-Three

Adam fumbled his phone from his pocket as it pinged an incoming text. Reading it, his heart plummeted. No, was all it said. One word. 'We have to get there, Nate,' he said quietly, his jaw clenching, every muscle in his body tensing.

'Next on the left,' David said, leaning forward in the back seat. 'Number thirty-four, about fifty yards up on the ... *Christ Almighty!*' David's eyes shot to the windscreen. 'What the hell is he doing?'

'The bastard's dead.' Adam reached for his door as Nathaniel slammed his foot on the brake, skidding his car up behind the Ford hatchback they'd just witnessed Sienna being forcibly pushed into the back seat of.

Adam was out of his door almost before Nathaniel had stopped, sprinting after the shit who'd twisted her wrists and manhandled her into the seat, too late. *Too fucking late!* Reaching the car as it pulled off at speed, Adam tried to catch hold of the backdoor handle, hoping against hope the guy hadn't dropped the locks. Hopeless, he knew it. Running alongside, he touched palms with Sienna through the glass, and then slowed as the car gathered speed.

She was terrified. Adam didn't stop to draw breath.

Turning around, he raced back, bypassing Meadows and Nathaniel, who were trying to have some sort of dialogue with the tearful woman on the doorstep. 'I don't know what's gotten into him,' the woman was saying. 'They had some sort of argument and ...'

Adam stopped listening, every instinct inside him screaming; Emily screaming loud in his head *Go!* He threw himself behind the wheel of Nathaniel's car, ramming the gearstick into first and pulling off.

'Adam! Wait!' Nathaniel shouted at him. 'You'll need eyes!' he said, diving around the front of the car and almost getting killed for his efforts. Adam slowed, but didn't stop as Nathaniel threw himself onto the passenger seat. He accelerated again, wrenching the gearstick through second and third into fourth.

'Left,' Nathaniel instructed him as he reached a T-junction.

Adam nodded and took the corner almost on two wheels. The car was way off, assuming it was the car. Tail lights were no indication this was the car they were looking for, but here at least the roads were relatively quiet. With luck, no other vehicle had passed after the bastard had taken the junction. *Luck? Jesus.* Adam pulled in a breath, used his wrist to wipe the sweat from his forehead – and prayed. 'Help me, Emily,' he said, out loud.

Nathaniel turned to look at him, briefly. He didn't comment. Adam was grateful. 'He's taking a right.' He nodded forward instead.

Adam saw the car ahead make the turn and cursed. He was heading for the dual carriageway, where, unless Adam was superglued to his tail, he'd be bound to lose him. And if he was, the piece of scum would be sure to try to shake him off.

'Fuck!' He banged his hand on the wheel and forced his foot down. Losing him wasn't an option. Losing Sienna ... *'I'm here,'* Emily whispered. She was. Adam knew she was. Why was she? *Help me*, he prayed again, silently.

The guy took a chance entering the dual carriageway. Adam tried to dodge after him, and got blasted by a car shaving past as he did. Not time for niceties, he nosed right out, yanking the wheel hard left as he did.

'Nice manoeuvre,' Nathaniel commented, gripping the dash with one hand and giving two fingers to the tooting horn-blower behind.

'Where is he?' Adam kept his eyes fixed forwards.

'Four ahead, outside lane,' Nathaniel supplied.

A cursory glance in the mirror, and Adam pulled out, getting another long blast from behind as he did. That *bastard*, who wouldn't be physically capable of arguing with another woman when he caught up with him, obviously knew he was being followed now. Adam's choices were two: keep after him, in which case the erratic driving might put Sienna's life at risk; or back off, allowing the guy to reach his destination, where Sienna would definitely be at risk. *No way*. Adam kept going, giving the Sunday driver in front several blasts of his own horn as he did.

'Dammit, he's moving over,' Adam cursed again, as the guy cut back into the inside lane, and then cursed furiously, as he deftly took a slip road off.

'Shit!' Adam hit the brakes, slowing from seventy to almost a stop, to a cacophony of car horns behind him. Heedless, he cut up the car on the inside without compunction, careering into the turn and only just making it.

'Oh, Jesus ... No!' Adam banged the steering wheel again, hard, seeing no car ahead of them at the roundabout. 'Where *is* the bastard?'

His heart thudding, panic twisting his gut, Adam barely gauged the gap in the traffic before heading onto the roundabout. Twice he went round it. 'Which way?' he asked Nathaniel desperately, uselessly, causing chaos as he drove and not caring.

'I don't know! Take the ...' Nathaniel started, and then stopped as Adam slammed both hands against the wheel, shouting, 'Emily, where are you? I need you!' Adam ran a hand over his eyes, heading back for the first exit off as Nathaniel stared hard at him.

'Show me, Emily,' Adam begged her. 'Please help.' Pulling onto the exit, he hit the brakes again and wrenched the gearstick into reverse. 'There,' he said, nodding to his right then craning his neck over his shoulder to steer the car fast backwards onto the roundabout.

'What? Where?' Nathaniel sounded as desperate and panic-struck as Adam felt.

'There,' Adam repeated. Hearing the wail of the sirens behind him, seeing the blue lights flashing, he kept going, towards the mini aurora borealis he could see swirling bright in the night sky. Emily, it had to be. 'That's where they are.'

He took the second road off, taking it at speed, the squad car close on his tail. That was good, if only he could keep ahead of them, by some miracle, he might just catch up. In which case, the police would be needed, if for nothing else, to stop Adam going up on a charge of manslaughter. He would kill him. For what he'd already done, the entire police force would be hard-pushed to keep him off him.

'Be careful, Adam.' Nathaniel twisted his neck to judge the distance of the squad car behind them. 'You'll be no good to her dead.'

Adam didn't answer, but kept his eyes on the road in front of him. His pulse racing, he took a bend, sucked in a sharp breath, and stepped hard on the brake, skidding to a screeching halt yards from the car in front. Wheels spinning, flames licking like hungry tongues at the fuel spilling from it, the car had turned over.

Adam's heart stopped beating. 'Jesus, *no*!' he shouted, banging his door open, galvanising himself into action, as the shrill wail of the siren died behind them.

'Adam, don't!' Nathaniel moved fast, out of his door on the passenger side. 'Adam! It's going to go up!' he yelled after him.

The front end was buckled, concertinaed into the middle. The tailgate ...

Adam squeezed his fingers into the inch gap. Gouging the skin from the back of his hand, ignoring the police behind him shouting, 'Get back!', he forced his hand in, leaned down on his arm, pushed his whole bodyweight down on it ... 'Move! You *fucking* ...'

Pushing with all his might, the tailgate finally gave. 'Sienna?' Her name came out a croak. Adam swallowed hard, dropped to his knees and crawled inside. She was there, blood on her cheek, trickling from her mouth, in her beautiful gold-flecked hair. Her eyes ... Adam groped through the twisted seats for her hand. 'Sienna?' He saw a flicker of life there.

She was alive! Choking back the fumes that seared the back of his throat, Adam wriggled further in. The gap was too small. Couldn't move the seats. *No time*. Squeezing further in, his arm outstretched as far is it would go, his fingertips brushed the door handle. He pushed harder, cursing his restricting clothing, he pushed further in, caught the handle and yanked it back, and then he was up, praying to God, to Emily, begging – *please don't let this happen. Take me, not her*, he scrambled back out, around to the back passenger door, and yanked it hard.

It wouldn't give. Adam tugged harder, slammed his hand on the chassis, glanced to the Heavens, and pulled with all his might. It creaked. It moved, barely six inches. Adam fed his arm in, then his shoulder. *No time*, he thought desperately, and then closed his eyes with relief as Nate and one of the policemen grabbed hold of the door, combining strength enough to drag it open.

Adam dropped down, crawled bodily into the space, checked as best he could no part of her body was trapped, and then, hands under her shoulders, he dragged her towards him.

'Adam!' He heard Nathaniel urgently behind him. 'Move!'

Adam tugged. Something snagged. Her top: caught on jagged metal. With shaking hands Adam reached down, flailed about, sliced through his wrist, grabbed hold of the cloth and tore at it; tore desperately at it, a flame licking at the bare flesh of his forearm, driving him on. 'Give, you *bloody* …!' He heard it tear, shuffled backwards, eased his hand back under the woman he would die with, here now, rather than leave, and pulled her free.

Lifting her into his arms, his knees almost buckling as he stood, his feet stumbling, Adam heard the whoosh and roar behind him. Instinctively he dropped down, covering her body with his own. 'If you take her, you take us both,' he choked, his face a breath away from hers.

Not yet. He heard above the popping and cracking and squeal of the fire engines.

Sienna tasted his salty tears on her lips, felt his hand on hers, his thumb gently tracing the back of her hand. Adam. She knew he'd come. Knew when she finally managed to text him her short, *No*, that he'd come. She didn't know how he knew, how … anything, but she knew.

Easing her grainy eyelids open, she gulped against the acrid dryness in her throat and tried to speak. 'Adam.' She squeezed his hand, and Adam was on his feet in a flash.

'Sienna?' he said, brushing her hair gently from her face. His arm was bandaged, she noticed immediately, his voice was hoarse. He smelled of smoke. She'd felt him. Her angel had come, her mum, her presence soothing, not frightening, she'd come to take her this time, Sienna felt sure. And then she'd felt him, felt Adam's presence and then, nothing.

Adam searched her face, looked into her eyes, his dark

espresso eyes full of undiluted fear.

'I love you,' Sienna managed, a tear of her own trailing down her cheek to escape onto her pillow.

Adam closed his eyes, and swallowed, and then leant in to touch his forehead against hers. 'Don't ever do that to me again, Sienna,' he said, easing up to look sternly back into her eyes.

Sienna smiled. He didn't scare her. Even at his most obnoxious he hadn't been intimidating. At his moodiest, broodiest, she couldn't help but love him. Could he love her, still, once all her secrets were out?

Adam's mouth curved into a slow reciprocal smile. He brushed her lips with his, and then, 'I love you, Sienna,' he breathed. 'For the rest of my life, I will always love you.'

He pressed his lips back to hers, but Sienna couldn't supress a titter.

Adam pulled away, his look this time quizzical. 'Erm, did I say something amusing?'

Sienna pressed a hand to her mouth, a laugh bubbling up in her throat. 'I'm waiting for the theme music,' she said.

Adam's look was still puzzled.

'*The Bodyguard*,' she enlightened him. 'Are you going to guard me?'

'Ah.' He got the drift. 'You're taking the pee, aren't you?' he said, his oh-so-terrifying stern look back, a twinkle in his gorgeous eyes.

'A bit.' Sienna did her best to look sheepish.

'I guess I'm not quite as eloquent as you.' He furrowed his brow. 'Which I suppose means I'm just going to have to show you how much I love you.' His mouth twitched back into its lovely, warm smile. Good. It suited him much better than a scowl.

'Promise?' Sienna reached up to smooth his permanently unruly hair.

'Fervently. And, yes, I will guard your body; with my life,' he said, moving in to cover her mouth softly with his.

'Ahem.' A cough from across the room interrupted Sienna's tongue's pleasurable reintroduction to his.

'Sorry,' Nathaniel said, blushing beetroot. 'Can I have a quick word?'

Adam glanced at him, and then pressed a kiss to Sienna's nose. 'Back in two minutes,' he said. 'Don't go anywhere.'

Giving her a reassuring smile, Adam pulled the door open, and then walked with Nathaniel back to the nurses' station, where David was conversing with the consultant. David had a hand on his chin. He was nodding over it. Adam couldn't read his expression, though. Couldn't tell whether the news was good or bad.

Feeling sick to his soul, he glanced at Nathaniel, who tried to look reassuring, but who actually looked as worried as Adam felt. Stopping in front of David, Adam pulled in a breath and tried to still his gnawing trepidation.

David nodded him a greeting, his expression still the one of puzzlement he usually wore around Adam. 'Good news,' he said, at last. 'At least, I hope it is for you.'

Adam took a second to assimilate, and then closed his eyes. 'The best,' he assured him, dragging his hands over his face and shakily up through his hair. 'Thank you.' He swallowed, and offered the doctor his hand.

'My pleasure.' The doctor smiled. 'I gather you're a bit of a hero.' He shook Adam's hand and pressed his other hand to his shoulder. 'Well done, and congratulations.'

'Yesss!' Nathaniel punched his other shoulder, none too gently. 'Well done, me old mate. We'll crack open the bubbly.'

Adam smiled wryly. 'Cheers, Nate.'

'Er, lemonade,' Nathaniel corrected himself, glancing at David, whose expression was back to unimpressed.

'Coffee,' Adam suggested, pointedly. 'I think we could all use one.'

'Black, no sugar,' David supplied.

'Oh. Ah, yes, right. I'll just go and get them, um ... Leave you two to discuss whatever it is you need to discuss.' Nathaniel pointed a thumb over his shoulder and about-faced.

Adam shook his head, watching Nathaniel making his indiscreet exit.

'Well?' David folded his arms.

Adam took a breath. 'I don't think you're going to be majorly thrilled,' he said, looking nervously up at him.

David drummed his fingers against his forearms.

'But I'd like to ask if you'd do me the honour of allowing me your daughter's hand.'

David breathed in, his impressively toned chest swelling and his look somewhere between relief and apprehension.

'And the rest of her, obviously,' Adam tacked on.

'*Ye-es*.' The man's expression was now one of quiet despair. 'Diplomacy would have been to stop at hand, Adam.' He shook his head and turned in the direction of Sienna's room.

Adam smiled. He wasn't actually that intimidating, he supposed, as long as he kept on the right side of him. No wish to invade the man's space with his daughter, Adam took a seat and waited, and debated. His next step was to ask Sienna, hope with all his heart she would consider marrying someone so messed up, and then try somehow to explain how he felt about the big white wedding thing. If she had her heart set on it, he'd do it, God help him, somehow he'd get through it. Even then, though, he needed to be honest.

Five minutes later Nate was back with coffee. 'Thanks, Nate.' Adam took the cup his friend offered him gratefully.

The coffee was pretty disgusting, but at least it was wet and warm, which might wash the petrol fumes from the back of his throat.

'So, you going to do the deed then?' Nathaniel asked, parking David's coffee on the floor and plonking himself on the chair next to Adam.

'I am,' Adam assured him. 'I wish you wouldn't make it sound quite so formidable though.'

Nathaniel folded his arms and eyed Adam knowingly. 'Isn't it?'

'Very,' Adam conceded nervously, and finished his coffee. It was still disgusting.

'Not as formidable as that, though?' Nathaniel nodded towards Sienna's dad coming back towards them.

Adam's mouth twitched into a smile. 'Maybe not.' Depositing his cup in the bin, he got to his feet as David approached.

So did Nathaniel. 'Phone call,' he said diplomatically, waving his mobile. 'I'll be outside, Adam, if you need any assistance. A lift anywhere, I mean,' he added quickly as David eyed him bemusedly. 'Or, you know, anything. Ahem, Mr Meadows.'

Nodding courteously at the man, Nathaniel headed swiftly off towards the exit.

David turned back to Adam, regarding him in that thoughtful way he had, and then he surprised him and offered him his hand. 'I didn't thank you,' he said. 'You saved my daughter's life, twice. Be careful with it, Adam.'

Adam nodded, swallowing back a different kind of lump in his throat. 'I will be,' he promised.

'Congratulations.' David Meadows managed a whole genuine smile, to Adam's amazement, and then nodded him on to go back to his daughter.

'Oh, Adam,' he said, turning back as Adam headed

off. 'In case you were wondering. Sienna went to see Joe's mother to ask her to have a word with him about stalking her. Just so you know.'

'Right.' Adam nodded his appreciation. He wouldn't be doing much stalking now, he supposed, from the burns unit. Sienna had yet to learn about his injuries, but that could wait until she was stronger, he decided. One step at a time, starting with this one.

Walking towards Sienna's room, he pulled out his phone, keyed in a text and pressed send, hoping she'd understand. He thought she would. He couldn't see Sienna getting in a strop if he didn't do it by the book. Mentally apologising to Emily, he loitered outside Sienna's room and waited.

Seeing it was Adam, Sienna immediately read the message: Marry me? One word. I can take it.

YessSSS! Sienna clutched the phone to her chest. Please, she texted excitedly back.

How do you feel about a small ceremony? Was Adam's reply.

She knew it! She knew he'd been scared. She didn't know how scared or what of. God, he really was hopeless, bottling things up in case he looked less than macho. Why hadn't he just opened his mouth and trusted her? Dad, Nate, Lauren, Nicole, Phil, Lily-Grace, you & me? Sienna pinged back.

And the baby? Adam suggested.

Oh God! He knew! How? Who? Ooh, flip. Sienna almost slid down the bed as Adam poked his head around the door. 'I'm sorry,' she blurted as he came in. 'Really I am. I wasn't sure. I … didn't know what to do.'

Adam was now definitely wearing his stern expression. 'First of all,' he said, walking across to her, 'don't be. If you're with a man you have to apologise to about something like this, then you shouldn't be with him. And secondly, why on earth didn't you tell me?' He searched her eyes, in his, honest bewilderment.

'How, when you ...' Sienna faltered, feeling her cheeks flush. 'You know, took all the right, um ...'

'Precautions?' Adam finished, obviously sensing her embarrassment. 'I'm obviously not as competent a lover as I like to think I am.' It was his turn to look embarrassed now. 'Faulty goods, I suspect.' He smiled apologetically. 'I would never have doubted you, Sienna, you must know that. You should have said something.'

'I tried,' Sienna said quickly, 'but there was so much going on. And then, when you said ...' Again, she hesitated, not wanting to appear to be apportioning blame when she knew her own insecurities had driven her to push him away.

'What did I say, Sienna?' Adam asked gently, now looking genuinely confused.

Sienna glanced down and then back. 'That you didn't want to have a baby.'

Adam stared at her, astonished. '*What?*'

'You said you wanted to wait,' Sienna reminded him. 'That you didn't want to go that route yet.'

'Not when we'd already *made* one.' Adam's look was now a mixture of incredulity and despair. 'I wish you'd told me, Sienna. I was worried sick. I thought ...' He stopped, sighing heavily. 'I wish you'd felt able to trust me.'

'I do!' Sienna blinked at him, startled. Surely he couldn't think that *she* didn't *trust* him? After all they'd ... 'You know I do.' But he didn't, did he? How could he when she'd run away? Run from him, rather than talk to him. 'Is this our first argument?' she asked, tremulously.

'Erm, nope.' Adam thought about it. 'Second, I think, or possibly third, can't quite recall.'

Sienna dropped her gaze. She should have spoken to him.

'Good job I love you really, isn't it?'

Sienna's heart bobbed back up from where it had flopped

somewhere near little foetus level. 'Still?' she asked, a smile curving her mouth as she looked back into his deliciously decadent chocolate-brown eyes.

'Forever and always. Fervently. Every beautiful inch of you, including your imminent bump, you twit.' Adam smiled his bone-melting smile, pressed the screen on his mobile, then placed it on her bedside table and proceeded to kiss her most pleasurably and thoroughly, as Whitney Houston began belting out, *I Will Always Love You.*

Epilogue

Adam managed a smile as Nicole walked towards where he waited nervously with Nathaniel on the quayside. 'Phil's just parking the car,' she said, leaning in to give Adam a kiss, and then wiping the lipstick from his cheek. 'I thought I'd come and give you a bit of moral support.'

'Thanks, I could use it.' Adam managed to say, though he wasn't entirely sure he'd manage to get whole sentences out for much longer.

'Scrubs up nicely, doesn't he?' Nathaniel grinned and indicated Adam's attire.

Nicole followed his gaze to look Adam up and down, who, freshly shaven and hair almost tamed, was as immaculately turned out as he could ever hope to be. 'He wears it well,' she conceded, taking in the three-piece grey suit, white shirt and blue silk tie. 'If only he could stop fidgeting in it.' She shook her head and attempted to pull his hand away as Adam checked his watch and then tugged at his shirt collar.

'I just can't get him to calm down.' Nathaniel sighed and reached to straighten Adam's now skew-whiff tie, again.

'What time is it?' Adam asked, croakily.

Nathaniel eyed the skies. 'About the same time as when you just looked. Stop worrying, Adam. She'll be here.'

'Right.' Adam nodded resolutely, drew in a breath, checked his watch, and loosened his tie. 'You don't think she's changed her mind, do you?'

'Adam, she'll be here.' Nicole sighed good-naturedly.

Adam wasn't convinced. 'You don't think anything's gone wrong then?'

'For God's sake, man, get a grip.' Nathaniel wrapped an

arm around him and gave his shoulders a firm squeeze. 'She loves you. You look so irresistible, *I'd* marry you. Nothing's gone wrong. She'll be here, trust me. She's probably titivating and whatnot.'

'Bound to be.' Nicole nodded knowingly. 'It's what women do.' Swapping amused glances with Nathaniel, she eyed Adam pseudo-despairingly – and reached to straighten his tie.

Adam nodded, pulled in another long breath and resisted checking his watch.

'If you don't stop doing that, you'll hyperventilate.' Nathaniel checked his, then coughed, then laced his hands behind his back and tapped a toe.

Adam nodded again, sure his restricting collar was way too tight to get the crucial words past the lump in his throat. She would be here. She did love him. He breathed more slowly and tried to reassure himself, but couldn't quite quell the sick panic rising inside him.

'The venue's ... different,' Nicole observed, glancing around at the balloon and flower festooned boats. Adam's, where the couple would be making their vows, most flower festooned of all.

'No expense spared,' Nathaniel assured her, also taking in the ambience. 'Did you see the band?' He nodded towards a narrowboat, on top of which was a five-piece band, complete with saxophonist and drum kit, while Adam considered whether to go and sit down, before his legs failed him and he dropped down.

Trying to think calming thoughts and failing, he glanced at Nicole, who offered him a warm, supportive smile. Adam was grateful. It must have been hard for her, coming here, doing this, given she was supposed to be maid of honour at his last wedding.

'Ah, here's Phil,' Nicole glanced towards the car park,

'and your gorgeous little flower girl. What do you think?'

Adam followed her gaze to where Phil was guiding Lily-Grace carefully towards him. Concentrating on her footwork and the ivory rose and butterfly wand she was clutching to her chest, she didn't notice Adam at first. When she did, she beamed him a smile which just about knocked his brand new black socks off. Adam's chest swelled with pride as he looked her over. Wearing a dove coloured satin dress, a pink ribbon around her waist and a little pink butterfly adorning her hair, she looked totally adorable. 'She's perfect.' He swallowed, wishing Emily could see her, suspecting she probably could.

Giving Lily a wide smile back, he caught Nicole's eye. 'Thanks,' he said, certain that Nicole would know he was thanking her, not just for this, but for everything. One day little Lily would want explanations, information to fill in the gaps about her natural mother. Nicole, Phil and he had agreed she would have that information when she was ready, making sure she had all of the good stuff. For now, though, Lily was content with Nicole as Mummy, Sienna as Auntie, and two Daddies in her life.

'She's yours,' Nicole said simply, reaching to squeeze his hand.

Adam nodded. There was no doubt about that in his mind, not anymore.

'She's here!' Squeezing his hand hard enough now to stop his circulation, Nicole pulled his attention away from Lily to the carriage coming resplendently through the marina gates, led by two white horses, complete with plumes. *Thank God*. Adam allowed himself to breathe out.

'Told you I'd do you proud, didn't I?' Nathaniel gave him a nudge, obviously as pleased as punch with the bridal transport, which had been his wedding gift.

'You did, and some,' Adam assured him, his heartbeat

ratcheting up to a whole new level. His mouth dry, his legs now distinctly shaky, he tried to compose himself as he waited for the carriage to draw to a stop.

Also grey-suited, David appeared first, glancing towards Adam, his relief on finding him there, where he should be, apparent. Adam really couldn't blame the man for that. Acknowledging him with a small nod, David turned back to the carriage, extending a hand for Sienna's – and when his bride finally stepped down, Adam's heart stopped beating.

'Wow!' Nathaniel whistled, also appreciating the view, then, 'Breathe,' he whispered sideways as David led Sienna towards them, Lauren close behind her, fussing and tweaking.

Pausing in front of them, David glanced proudly from his daughter to Adam. 'Worth waiting for?' he asked him.

Now definitely incapable of speaking, Adam nodded, his gaze fixed firmly on Sienna.

'Sorry we're so late,' Lauren said, flapping at her side. 'I couldn't do a *thing* with her hair.'

Adam took in Sienna's hair, magnificent, mesmerising red hair flecked gold, tumbling carelessly over her shoulders, her shy smile, her luminescent forest green eyes, her pretty freckles – he wanted to kiss every one of them, right there, right then. His eyes travelling downwards, sweeping the strapless dove satin dress, the pink ribbon positioned over her beautiful bump and under her far too tempting breasts, he swallowed hard. His woman, his friend, his lover, the mother of his soon-to-be-born child, she looked radiant, beautiful, utterly...

'Stunning.' He gulped back the tight lump in his throat – and promptly straightened his own tie.

Adam wasn't surprised to see the white Chinchilla cat perched atop his boat when he turned after promising to give Sienna all of himself completely. He wasn't surprised when it mewed and turned to pad silently off, casting him one last look with its all-seeing eyes as it went. Somehow he hoped he would, but Adam had a definite feeling he wouldn't see Emily again.

She hadn't been his guardian angel. She'd been Sienna's. She'd kept her safe. She'd refused to go away until he knew that life without love in it was no life at all. Pretty mean feat for a ghost. *Bye, Emily.* He smiled inwardly. Part of him would always love her, too. He had a hunch she knew that.

He was surprised, and pleased, particularly for Sienna's sake, to note their various neighbours gathered around, giving them a round of applause as they stepped down, the father of the rather better behaved teenagers applauding loudest of all, then giving Adam a wink and a thumbs up.

He was definitely surprised to see the woman he'd thought he might never see again there. His mother? Here? How? Adam watched, stunned, as she turned, obviously intending to slip quietly away unnoticed.

Seeing his shock, Sienna caught his hand. 'She did keep in touch,' she said, her wide green eyes looking apprehensively into his. 'We did a little digging and ...' She looked to Nathaniel, who ferreted quickly in his pocket and produced a wad of envelopes.

'Letters,' he explained. 'All returned unopened. There are more.'

Bewildered, Adam shook his head. He didn't need to guess who'd returned them. Glancing after her, he felt something shift inside him, years of pent up bereavement, almost, that she hadn't contacted him, hadn't wanted anything to do with him, emotions he'd barely allowed himself to acknowledge. Uncertainly, he looked back towards Sienna, not sure what to do, how he went about reintroducing himself to his own mother at his wedding.

'Go,' Sienna urged him, stretching to plant a kiss on his cheek.

Glancing after her again, and then back to Sienna, Adam hesitated for a split second and then ran, not wanting her to reach the car park and disappear from his life once more, possibly forever.

'Mum!' he called, slowing as she reached the gates. 'Mum?' he said quietly again as she faltered and glanced down.

Adam still couldn't quite believe she was here, that it was her, until she turned. And then he knew. She hadn't left him by choice. She'd left because her alternative was to stay in an abusive relationship. He didn't know what those letters contained, but he knew then that she hadn't abandoned him.

'Adam,' she said tentatively, searching his face, a sadness in her eyes that went way beyond anything he'd ever seen as a child.

Too choked to say anything, Adam simply nodded.

'You look ...' she paused, clearly trying not to cry '... all grown-up.'

Adam smiled reflectively. 'Getting there,' he said, hesitated, and then took a step towards her. 'You look ... exactly the same.'

'Flatterer.' She laughed, and dabbed at her cheek.

'It's one of my better qualities.' Adam took a breath, took another step, and then welcomed his mother into his arms.

'You have more. Many more, Adam Hamilton-Shaw,' she assured him, glancing over his shoulder as she squeezed him tight. 'Thank you,' she mouthed at Sienna, who'd chosen her moment and was now coming towards them, Lily-Grace's hand firmly in hers.

Sienna smiled, noting again how striking the woman's espresso-coloured eyes were, warmth and obvious love shining therein. Adam was definitely his mother's son. She hung back, giving them a moment, then, once the most important introduction was over and Adam turned, she stepped forward. 'I think a certain little lady might be anxious to meet someone,' she said, glancing down at their wide-eyed flower girl.

Adam's delighted smile was priceless. 'Mum,' he said, bending to sweep Lily up into his arms, 'this beautiful princess is my daughter, Lily-Grace. Lily, this is my mother.'

Lily regarded her shyly over her thumb, then, 'Adum's mum.' She nodded, turning back to Adam. She studied him for a moment and then reached out her free hand to tentatively track a tear down his cheek. 'Adum's sad,' she said, blinking curiously back at him.

'No, sweetie. Adam's happy,' he assured her, causing her little brow to furrow. 'Come on, we'd better join our guests before they eat all the cake.'

'Everything all right, mate?' Nathaniel asked as they strolled quietly back towards them, words somehow seeming superfluous.

'Excellent,' Adam replied, working to keep his emotions under control as he handed Lily to Nicole.

'About time, too.' Nathaniel gave Adam's mum a conspiratorial wink. 'Good luck, Adam,' he said, reaching out to shake his friend's hand heartily and then standing back to allow the father of the bride to do the same.

'From me, too. Be happy,' David said, over an emotional intake of breath. 'And make sure my daughter is. Or you'll have me to answer to.'

Adam laughed. He didn't doubt it. 'I will,' he replied and reiterated firmly what he'd told the man once before. 'For the rest of my life.'

Thank you

Thank you for reading *The Rest of My Life*. I really hope you enjoyed Adam and Sienna's journey as much as I enjoyed writing it. There's nothing quite like that feeling you get knowing that a reader has connected with your characters, laughed with them, cried with them, screamed at them, or even totally despaired of them. I think all authors would agree, that's why we write, to connect emotionally with people, hopefully leaving them with that all-important feel good factor. All authors, too, really value reader feedback. The road to publication can sometimes be a little bit bumpy and seeing your book finally 'out there' is truly amazing. Knowing people are reading it, though, and taking the trouble to leave a review on Amazon, a book review site such as Goodreads, or the retail outlet site, is equally amazing. Reviews can do so much to up a book's profile, along with that of the author, but they do sometimes truly inspire the author to keep writing and improving.

If you have time therefore, a one line review, or two, or more if you'd like to, would be hugely appreciated.

Please do feel free to contact me anytime. You can find my details under my author profile. And if you like the book enough to go in search of any of my other books, well, there's that amazing feeling again. Meanwhile, I'll keep being inspired and I'll keep writing!

Happy reading all!

Lots of love,
Sheryl

About the Author

Sheryl Browne is a member of the Romantic Novelists'
Association and was shortlisted for Innovation in
Romantic Fiction. She has several books published
and two short stories in Birmingham City University
Anthologies. A further short, written to script, was
performed live at the Birmingham Repertory Theatre.
When she's not writing, Sheryl can be found doing strange
things like skydiving from 20,000 feet or abseiling down
buildings, which possibly makes her a little bit mad.

The Rest of My Life is Sheryl's first
book published with Choc Lit.

Follow Sheryl:
www.twitter.com/SherylBrowne
www.sherylbrowne.com

More from Choc Lit

If you enjoyed Sheryl's story, you'll enjoy the
rest of our selection. Here's a sample:

Please don't stop the music
Jane Lovering

Book 1 in the Yorkshire Romances

*Winner of the 2012 Best Romantic
Comedy Novel of the Year*

*Winner of the 2012 Romantic
Novel of the Year*

How much can you hide?

Jemima Hutton is determined
to build a successful new
life and keep her past a dark
secret. Trouble is, her jewellery business looks set to fail –
until enigmatic Ben Davies offers to stock her handmade belt
buckles in his guitar shop and things start looking up, on all
fronts.

But Ben has secrets too. When Jemima finds out he used
to be the front man of hugely successful Indie rock band
Willow Down, she wants to know more. Why did he desert
the band on their US tour? Why is he now a semi-recluse?

And the curiosity is mutual – which means that her own
secret is no longer safe ...

Visit www.choc-lit.com for more
details, or simply scan barcode using
your mobile phone QR reader.

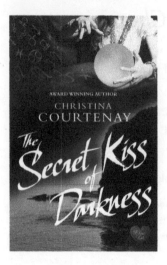

The Secret Kiss of Darkness

Christina Courtenay

Book 2 in the Shadows from the Past Series

Must forbidden love end in heartbreak?

Kayla Sinclair knows she's in big trouble when she almost bankrupts herself to buy a life-size portrait of a mysterious eighteenth century man at an auction.

Jago Kerswell, inn-keeper and smuggler, knows there is danger in those stolen moments with Lady Eliza Marcombe, but he'll take any risk to be with her.

Over two centuries separate Kayla and Jago, but, when Kayla's jealous fiancé presents her with an ultimatum, and Jago and Eliza's affair is tragically discovered, their lives become inextricably linked thanks to a gypsy's spell.

Kayla finds herself on a quest that could heal the past, but what she cannot foresee is the danger in her own future.

Will Kayla find heartache or happiness?

Visit www.choc-lit.com for more details, or simply scan barcode using your mobile phone QR reader.

Do Opposites Attract?
Kathryn Freeman

There's no such thing as a class divide – until you're on separate sides

Brianna Worthington has beauty, privilege and a very healthy trust fund. The only hardship she's ever witnessed has been on the television. Yet when she's invited to see how her mother's charity, Medic SOS, is dealing with the aftermath of a tornado in South America, even Brianna is surprised when she accepts.

Mitch McBride, Chief Medical Officer, doesn't need the patron's daughter disrupting his work. He's from the wrong side of the tracks and has led life on the edge, but he's not about to risk losing his job for a pretty face.

Poles apart, dynamite together, but can Brianna and Mitch ever bridge the gap separating them?

Take a Chance on Me
Debbie Flint

You know what they say about mixing business with pleasure ...

When the breakdown of her marriage leaves Sadie Turner a single mum, she vows that she will make it on her own. After all, why would a smart businesswoman with a PhD and the prospect of a life-changing deal on the horizon need a man?

But Sadie's man-ban is tested to the limit when she travels to Monaco to meet her potential investor. There she encounters Mac, a rough and ready playboy billionaire who lives life in the fast lane – and that's when the real adventure starts!

But Sadie's heart isn't the only thing on the line. There's also the business she's worked so hard to make a success; the business that could so easily slip out of her grasp if she doesn't seal the deal within thirty days ...

Visit www.choc-lit.com for more details, or simply scan barcode using your mobile phone QR reader.

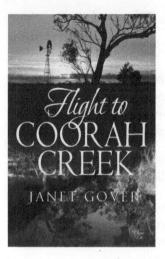

Flight to Coorah Creek

Janet Gover

Book 1 in the Coorah Creek series

Winner of 2015 Aspen Gold Award

What happens when you can fly, but you just can't hide?

Only Jessica Pearson knows the truth when the press portray her as the woman who betrayed her lover to escape prosecution. But will her new job flying an outback air ambulance help her sleep at night or atone for a lost life?

Doctor Adam Gilmore touches the lives of his patients, but his own scars mean he can never let a woman touch his heart.

Runaway Ellen Parkes wants to build a safe future for her two children. Without a man – not even one as gentle as Jack North.

In Coorah Creek, a town on the edge of nowhere, you're judged by what you do, not what people say about you. But when the harshest judge is the one you see in the mirror, there's nowhere left to hide.

Visit www.choc-lit.com for more details, or simply scan barcode using your mobile phone QR reader.

Introducing Choc Lit

We're an independent publisher creating
a delicious selection of fiction.
Where heroes are like chocolate – irresistible!
Quality stories with a romance at the heart.

See our selection here:
www.choc-lit.com

We'd love to hear how you enjoyed *The Rest of My Life*.
Please leave a review where you purchased the novel
or visit: **www.choc-lit.com** and give your feedback.

Choc Lit novels are selected by genuine readers like yourself.
We only publish stories our Choc Lit Tasting Panel want to
see in print. Our reviews and awards speak for themselves.

Could you be a Star Selector and join our Tasting Panel?
Would you like to play a role in choosing which novels we
decide to publish? Do you enjoy reading romance novels?
Then you could be perfect for our Choc Lit Tasting Panel.

Visit here for more details …
www.choc-lit.com/join-the-choc-lit-tasting-panel

Keep in touch:
Sign up for our monthly newsletter Choc Lit Spread for
all the latest news and offers: www.spread.choc-lit.com.
Follow us on Twitter: @ChocLituk and Facebook: Choc Lit.

Or simply scan barcode using your mobile phone QR reader:

Choc Lit   *Twitter*   *Facebook*
Spread